DRAGONFIRE

THE STARCHASER SAGA
BOOK VI

R. DUGAN

WAVE WALKER
press

For information contact:
R. Dugan
PO Box 1265
Martinsville, IN 46151
reneeduganwriting.com

Cover design by Maja Kopunovic
Map by Jessica Khoury
ISBN: 978-1-7339255-9-4

First Edition: June 2022

10 9 8 7 6 5 4 3 2 1

DEDICATION

To Katie and Meaghan,
who embody all that Sillakove Court is.
Never stop chasing your stars.

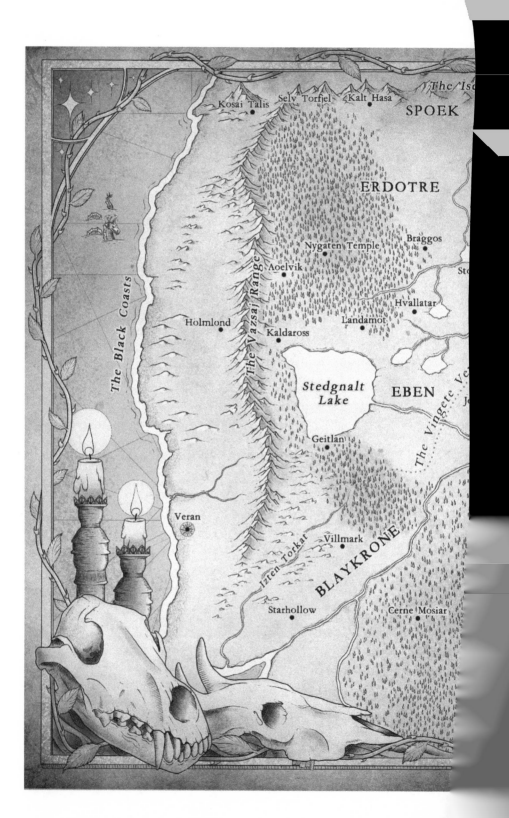

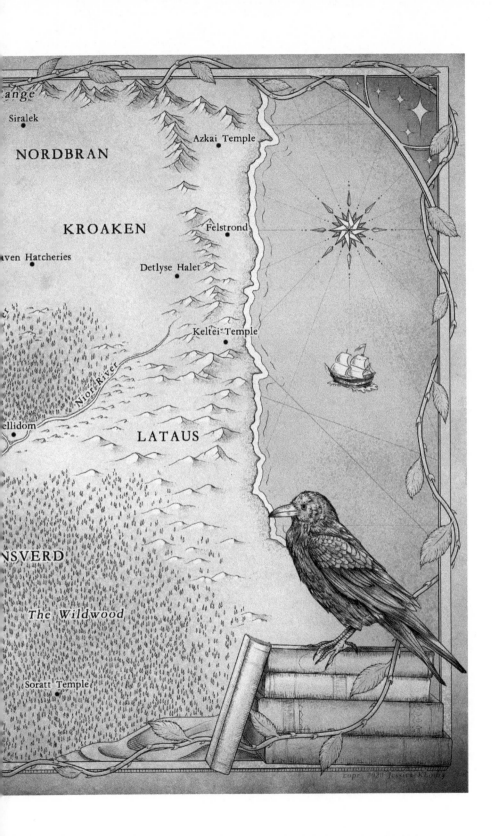

THE
MAIDEN

OF

FIRE AND
FURY

CHAPTER ONE

WITH EYES TIGHTLY shut and dawn's cold light painting her face, Princess Cistine Novacek chased the thread of a fallen star through the chasms of her mind.

She'd followed it for two days now, a beckoning power pinioning along the distant horizon, carrying with it the faintest trace of cedar and charcoal, dust and weapon polish, warmth and home and family. Or at least, she imagined it held those things; it was difficult to tell when this ability to sense that storm of power was so new to her, as unfamiliar and cumbersome to her mind as blades and fists once were to her hands. And the one she was trying to track had never tasted of this power before; he'd been a scarred and quiet but ordinary man as long as she'd known him.

Maleck Darkwind, her mentor and protector, her friend, the survivor of the former *visnprest* Order, had walked away from a life of augment-wielding and worshiping the power of the gods to become a warrior, a formidable blade, and a teacher to anyone who needed his wisdom, like Cistine.

And then the war camp. Then Kosai Talis. Then the marks around his *valenar's* neck.

Cistine had promised she would bring Maleck home. So here she stood, awake before dawn on yet another crag in the lower Vaszaj Range, unspooling the fingertips of her strange and unwieldy might to sense the current of augments forever moving across Maleck's body—to give them some direction to travel today.

If it was even him she sensed. The other Bloodwights must've rallied from their defeat at Kosai Talis by now. They were likely hunting her.

Her hand drifted down to the augment pouch lashed at her side, tracing the dark, churning current of power they'd stolen from Kosai Talis: one of the seven *Stor Sedam*, unique and terrible in its might, harvestable only once from a single well long since run dry...and coveted desperately by the Bloodwights. Just as they coveted Cistine's blood to open one of the Doors to the Gods and unleash augmentation's full might back into the world.

Then they would take Valgard in the north; then Cistine's beloved Middle Kingdom, Talheim; and even Mahasar in the south, where old enemies dwelled. Then the Bloodwights would take the rest of the kingdoms of the world, crowning themselves new gods, aided by their power-forged Balmond and *mirothadt* followers, augurs, criminals, and kidnapped children.

All they needed was to capture Cistine and spill her blood on a Door; yet she was searching, fighting her way toward them anyway, and toward the chance to do that very thing on her own terms. To bleed, and then come back fighting.

A rogue shiver swept across her armored body with the wind, nudging the tangles in her hickory hair and ghosting panic along her frayed nerves. Shifting her focus, she followed the dips and arches of the Sotefold Forest below the crags, and the faraway spine of the Isetfell Mountains capping the north; she searched for a thin strand of reason, the Key's sense of where augmentation pooled—where Maleck might be. But panic hummed and flurried louder than any power, its cruel song playing relentlessly in her exhausted mind, and with a curse she gave up, rubbing the chills from her arms. "Where are you going, Mal?"

The only reply was the wind in the pines, struggling to feel like early spring even while the darkness of *Nazvaldolya* still held the north in a furious grip; and then the even tread of footfalls from behind, careful to be known and heard.

She was no longer alone.

Strong arms wrapped around Cistine's waist, the scent of sandalwood and leather chasing out the chill from the air. "Good morning, Wildheart."

The sound of her Name soothed some of the shivers, and her *selvenar's* heat dealt with the rest. Lips curving of their own volition, she leaned back into Thorne's chest, curling her arm behind his head and burrowing her numb fingers in the sleep-mussed strands of his silver hair. "Hello, you. Sleep well?"

"Until I heard you leave." His chin hooked over her shoulder, nose brushing her neck, pebbling her flesh with a different chill altogether. "Had enough of being alone, or should I come back later?"

"Your timing is perfect, actually. I was just about to turn from thinking to panicking."

His arms cinched tighter around her waist. "What is it?"

She blew out her breath in a frustrated puff. "What *isn't* it? Being hunted by the Bloodwights, being hunted by the Chancellors, Ashe and Aden and Kristoff and Bres going to Oadmark, and us tracking Maleck...I've never been the best at tracking anyway, he only gave me a few lessons—"

Thorne squeezed her waist, halting the rambling tide. "You are more than capable, *Logandir*. You're the only one who can track him in this state. I trust you to find him."

A seam of pain cracked his steady voice—pain for a friend closer than a brother, lost to the chaos of addiction and his own worst fears. Maleck had fought desperately not to become like his elder brothers, twisted and insatiable to wield augments, to grasp more and more power; yet when they'd seen him last, when Ashe *fought* him near Kosai Talis, his only concern was to take the power she wielded.

Already, he was so far from their reach; the man who'd taught Cistine how to wield weapons and track and drink mead seemed lost. All that remained of him was that trace of cedar and charcoal and the strip of dark cloth tied around her upper arm, twin to the one around Thorne's—a banner of hope against these fears.

When she didn't speak, throat swollen with emotion, he pressed a kiss below her ear. "Tell me how I can help."

She nestled her head back into the scoop of his shoulder, fingers combing absentmindedly through his hair. "Just this, for now."

"You know you have me, however you need me."

She did know that; the betrothal ring on her finger was proof of it. But unspoken between them hung the choice they had yet to fully confront, had not even spoken of in the two days since she first broached it: whether Thorne would marry her if she went to bleed on the Door beneath the City of a Thousand Stars. Whether he would help protect her kingdom by the binding oath of matrimony, a wholly Talheimic tradition that would grant him the title of prince-consort—that would allow him to protect her kingdom if she died.

But the peace of this moment was too fragile to raise that subject again. So they stayed silent, wrapped up in each other, watching dawn chase out darkness from east to west: an outlaw Chancellor and a princess who'd set aside her crown for war, blended hearts sleepless together, watching another day break across a weary, war-torn kingdom.

Thorne broke the silence again after a time, his tone careful. "If you'd like, while the others are busy, we could train."

The hair on Cistine's arms and nape prickled. She twisted in his arms, looking up at him. "Already?"

"Time is short, and when we close in on Maleck, it may become dangerous to wield. Better we do it now, while there's still some distance between us."

So he wouldn't sense the augments she trained with and decide that her life, like Ashe's, was worth less than the power streaming over the reinforced threads of her armor and the Atrasat inkings below.

Oh, Maleck. His name ached within her.

Thorne unwound his arms from her waist and beckoned with a tilt of his head. Feet and heart heavy, Cistine followed him away from the open air and into the denser pack of evergreens. They moved south by the sun's light, away from the small camp they'd pitched the previous sunset. Thorne spoke over his shoulder while they went: "Ari and Tati went to Aoelvik this morning for supplies and to see if they have any augments to spare."

Cistine's stomach twisted at the notion. With augments in such short supply already and the cabal hunted by the Chancellors, they could not simply be asked for; Ariadne and Tatiana would have to discern if the nearby village could do without them, and if so, steal them.

She had never felt like a filthier thief, but they'd wasted too many augments breaking in and out of Kosai Talis. There were so few left for her to train with, and the promise of that training was all that had kept her from falling into the Courts' desperate hands and losing her life already.

Wartime necessity, she chanted to herself. Aloud, she said, "Is Quill on watch?"

"Unfortunately." Thorne held aside a snapped branch for her to pass below. "I don't know if he's slept since Kosai Talis. Pippet's fate still haunts him, and now that we've stolen personally from the Bloodwights..."

Cistine winced. She hadn't considered at the time how the Bloodwights might abuse Pippet in retaliation for Kosai Talis. There was much she hadn't prepared for in recent weeks, driven by desperation to end this war and save her Valgardan family.

Now was the time for deep breaths and measured steps. Now, despite the urgency pricking her fingertips and jostling her feet, was the time for training.

They reached a break in the trees, a flat span of rock against the backbone of the mountains dotted with smaller pinnacles descended from a long-ago landslide. It created a thick, natural barrier, the perfect sparring arena which Thorne stepped fearlessly into, shedding his armored shirt and tying his hair back. His Atrasat inkings glowed in the early-morning light when he turned back to face her, putting out his hand. "Augment."

Cistine chose a flagon of ravaging darkness and tossed it to him; rather than breaking it, he uncorked it, allowing a thin ribbon of shadows to snake along his fingertips and up his arm, settling into the star maps inked across his torso. "All right. Show me what you can do, *Logandir*. First, try to take the augment from me."

A memory of bleeding eyes and weakness and deep unconsciousness spun through her head, curling her fingers into iron fists. "I thought we were going to train to wield two augments at once."

"If that's where you want to begin." His gaze bored into her. "But you've been training for that since before you came back to us."

As was often the case, he knew her unspoken mind: the Chancellors might be convinced to spare her by a flashy show of wielding two augments at once, or three, or more; but it was the power to wrest an augment from another person's grasp, even from a Bloodwight's, that stood the best chance of saving Maleck. And more than that, training with two augments at once was an even greater waste until Ariadne and Tatiana returned from Aoelvik.

Cistine shook out her fists. "If this goes like it did with Vandred, back at the war camp—"

"You're in command here. If you start to feel overwhelmed, walk away. I won't stop you."

Of course he wouldn't. He was the shore, and she the sea—he adapted to her tides without trying to change them. If this training proved too much, she *could* give herself distance; but for now, she walked toward him, toward the call she'd been following for so much of her life without even realizing.

Come, it purred. *Come and see.*

Thorne offered his hand, and Cistine took it. Like a tether snapping taut between them, the bite of the augment reached out to her, too, lovingly caressing her knuckles, licking up her wrist. A smile tugged her lips when she met Thorne's eyes, sparking against the shadows—wild, just like hers.

Then she felt the shift. He'd taken hold of the augment, drawing it back, keeping it from her; allowing her to feel the difference between sharing and stealing. She scrabbled for that current of power again and latched hold of it, and the battle of wills began.

It was the strangest training session she'd ever known. With Quill, training was mostly physical, a barrage of blunted jabs knocking the wind from each other's bodies. With Maleck, the clash of steel was constant. But here in this forest glade, there was only the mountain wind stroking the treetops and playing the spires of rock all around them in low, moaning music. Nothing else. Not even their breaths created noise, muffled by the vastness of the world around them.

She felt strange. Internal. As if she was moving, but not—traveling the long paths into the dark recesses of augmentation, following the thread of that shadowy cord into Thorne's own being, his quiet might. When she'd grappled for this power against Vandred in the Isetfells, her actions were desperate and undirected, like wild hacking with a sword. Now that she was concentrating, she felt the terrible weight that had dragged the blood from her nose and eyes that first time. The pressure mounted while she maneuvered around Thorne's brutal grip on the augment, trying to pry his fingers loose.

He fought her silently but viciously. Sweat broke across his brow, and his mouth crooked to one side the way it did whenever he concentrated. His arm tensed, fingers locking around hers, and the cords of muscle rattled, dipping and rising like bucking waves. His boots scraped against the stone when he braced, and Cistine reached deeper and farther, heeding the call but also making a call of her own, tempting and coaxing the augment toward her fingertips, her own inkings.

He was so gods-forsaken strong, it took her breath away. And while she struggled to pluck the augment from his control, a strange, second focus took hold, gleaming at the edges of her mind, beckoning and prodding her to look, to pay attention, to take note of it.

Thorne broke away suddenly, dropping backward with his hands braced on his knees, and in a flash the augment was in Cistine's grasp instead of his. Trembling, she sent it skimming down into the threads of her armor and stepped toward him. "Are you all right?"

"Holy stars," he gasped. "Cistine, stars *above*, do you even know how powerful you are?"

"No?" The startled lilt in her voice framed a question. "I felt like my head was going to burst!"

"So was mine, and I was pouring every ounce of energy into holding onto that augment. Were you?"

She'd been straining, certainly, her temples still throbbing from the effort. But behind that initial pull and the surge of pain and adrenaline, she had felt something more. If she'd reached a bit farther, felt her way along that rope of white-hot energy, and seen it through to its end...she might have realized it *had* no end.

"There was more power in me," she admitted. "I felt it, but I was scared to reach for it."

Thorne came to her, unsteady yet unafraid, and took her shoulders. "You have to learn to reach for it, to make it yours. No one else can. Your family has been given an incredible gift by the keying to the Doors. This power *will* save Maleck and Pippet. I believe it will save all of us." He cupped her cheek with one hand, the other still holding her shoulder. "But none of what I want, none of what any of us wants, will matter if you don't find a way to reach for that power yourself."

She inhaled his encouragement and breathed out her nerves. "Well, that's why we train, isn't it? Are you ready to go again?"

"One more. You may find this difficult to believe, but when it comes to augmentation, you have me beaten already."

She offered the shadows back to him. The strand was already slimmer and less corporeal than before; to stretch their scant flagons between training sessions long enough for her to become capable of saving Maleck and Pippet, nevermind the times they would train with wielding two augments or more...

A gulf of misery opened in Cistine's stomach. "I remember how I felt when I first started training with Quill...like I would never be strong enough to face the Chancellors. It feels that way again."

"Look around you. Look where we are. No matter how many mountains you cross, there will always be more. That's the beauty and frustration of life. If you live a worthwhile one, you'll never stop climbing." He offered both hands to her, palms out. "First step."

She wiped her nose on her sleeve, mustered her determination, and stepped forward to lock hands with him. Palm-to-palm, she looked into his eyes and heeded the shadow's call.

It was midmorning when they made their way back to the camp at last, drenched in sweat and panting. Cistine's head throbbed and Thorne's feet snared on root and rock all along the mile-and-a-half journey; even with their filament of shadow spent, the weight of the power still coursed over Cistine's bones. She'd managed to wrestle the augment from Thorne once more before they'd switched to wielding two at once; but then her nose had broken open bleeding, and they'd paused, then tried, then stopped again.

It was like training the weakest muscle in her body, tedious and painful. But it had to be done.

The gentle cut of dark wings on the air greeted them before they entered the campsite, and Cistine jolted when sharp talons dug into her shoulder and a sleek head bumped against hers. "*Hello, Cistine.*"

"Hello, Faer." The familiar greeting tumbled from lips half-numb with exhaustion, and she stroked a finger against the raven's puffed-up chest while, across the small clearing where they'd settled in the night before, her gaze met Quill's.

He looked as tired as she felt, dark rings stamped around his eyes, dirt and sweat mussed into the augment-shocked silver of his hair. The bristles along the scarred underside were growing long, and neither Quill nor Tatiana seemed motivated to care for them—too caught up in their shared and separate hurts, secrets that danced like lightning along the back of Cistine's tongue. None of them hers to tell.

Quill was sharpening his dagger, but at the sight of her face, he frowned and lurched to his feet, whetstone case disappearing into his pocket. He crossed the small camp and took her chin, tilting her head up. "Nosebleed?"

She smiled sheepishly. "Training."

Quill's eyes jumped to Thorne. "And you think *I* push her too hard?"

Irritation sputtered along Cistine's nerves, and she swiped his hand aside. "It was my choice to keep going."

He rocked back on his heels, dragging a hand through his hair. "I know, I know, Stranger. Just...tell me how it went."

She studied him a moment, his glassy eyes and stooped posture, the slump of his neck and shoulders. Not angry with her, not overbearing like her suitor Julian Bartos once was when it came to training...but afraid. Helpless and terrified to lose another friend the way he'd lost his sister, and Maleck, and nearly Tatiana.

The way he'd lost his first child, and he didn't even know it yet.

Compassion shattered through the vestiges of annoyance, and she squeezed Quill's hand. "It made me miss the rock top."

A flicker of a smile traced his mouth, a memory of the cocky grin he wore perpetually when she first knew him. "Any time you want to spar, you know where to find me."

"I don't think you want that, *Allet*." Thorne clapped Quill's shoulder on his way to the husk of last night's fire. "She could knock you on your ass in a heartbeat with the power she's wielding."

Pride blossomed in Cistine's chest, and Quill swung a wide-eyed glance toward her. "What did you *do* to him?"

"I stole his augment. *Twice.*"

He whistled lowly, hooking his thumbs in his belt. "That's a stars-damned *lot* of power, Cistine."

"I know!" She grinned. "It might even be enough to save Maleck and Pip after all."

Thorne scooped up a water flask, took two deep pulls, then tossed it to her. "Today was one augment. It's impossible to know how many Maleck carries already. We need to be patient and practice often."

She raised the flask in a rueful toast. "Where would I be without you?"

"Living comfortably in Talheim, betrothed to Julian Bartos and shopping for wedding dresses," Quill snorted, and dodged when Cistine aimed a kick at his haunch.

Faer flared up all at once, but not at Quill's sharp pivot. "*Danger.*"

The word had hardly settled in Cistine's weary mind when the undergrowth parted to the south and Ariadne and Tatiana barreled into view; two women as different as day and night, one pale and one dark, one stocky and one slender. But the fury and despair in their faces made them like sisters.

Thorne reached them first. "What happened?"

Quill was beside him in two strides, gripping Tatiana's shoulder. "Are you all right?"

"Aoelvik has *nothing* to spare us." Ariadne's eyes sparked like struck flint. "They were attacked the same night we fled Kosai Talis."

"Their entire supply of flagons was taken," Tatiana added, voice brittle with rage. "Everything, even the ones they use to grow crops, all gone. They have nothing left to tide them over for the winter."

Cistine took in a shivering breath. "Bloodwights."

"Not just any Bloodwight." Ariadne yanked a crumbled wad of paper from her pocket and dropped it in Thorne's hand. "A man wearing a wolf skull. A man with braids."

Thorne yanked the paper open flat; Quill rubbed a hand over his mouth, cursing under his breath. Cistine didn't want to see the paper, that nightmare unfolding before her eyes. But it was impossible to look away when Thorne held it up to the light; impossible to ignore the way his voice broke when he murmured, "Stars damn it, Mal."

The crude sketch, a warning to the townspeople, matched Ashe's description of her *valenar* so perfectly, it was undeniably him—their friend who'd let augments corrupt his mind to save Aden and Kristoff from death.

"They're offering every mynt in their coffers for someone who finds a way to kill a Bloodwight," Tatiana said as Quill lifted the drawing from Thorne's hands. "Starting with him."

"Listen to me," Thorne growled, and Quill's gaze jumped up with frenzied, furious energy. "*No one* engages Maleck in combat except Cistine. He has an entire village's worth of augments at his disposal now."

Her throat swelled with fear. Could she even reach him, if he was power-drunk enough to steal from helpless towns? If he was that far gone?

"Kick out the fire and gather your things," Thorne added when none of them protested. "It seems Cistine's sense of him is true—it led us this far. Can you track him again, *Logandir*?"

She sawed her chapped lower lip between her teeth. "I'll do what I can."

She moved to the edge of the small clearing while the others dissolved into a storm of motion, snatching up satchels and weapons, stamping down any traces they were ever here—traces ordinary men and women like the Chancellors could track.

So many out for vengeance, so many different hunts. And *they* were searching now, not for the means to end the war, but for a friend who might be far beyond saving.

But they couldn't stop. *She* would not stop.

I'm not letting you go, either, Darkwind.

That promise pulsed in her chest with every beat of her heart, a vow she would keep at any cost. So with her eyes shut, she turned her senses to the web of power crisscrossing the northern kingdom and chased fallen stars.

CHAPTER
TWO

SHADOWS PAVED THE mountain faces, the endless, glistening ribbon of snow broken up by rock bathed in darkness. After two days of fruitless searching, Asheila Kovar was beginning to think something—a snowstorm, a Bloodwight, their own gods-forsaken bad fortune—had blown Kristoff's so-called Oadmarkaic village off the face of the mountain.

She didn't voice that thought while they scoured the terrain by dragonback, Bresnyar's powerful nostrils drinking in the cold, bitter wind; it would serve no one, and she wasn't eager for another lecture from Aden or Kristoff about how she ought to keep faith. Not when every day was a step closer to facing the Wing Legions, a step deeper into an uncertain future, and a step further away from her augment-addicted *valenar* left behind in Valgard.

Her vision flickered, trimmed in gold, and for an instant she saw miles and mountains spread out around them—not her sight, but Bresnyar's. Cursing, she shook away the filigree of her dragon's gaze and laid a hand on his shoulder, steadying them both. The random spurts of cleaving came more frequently ever since he'd saved her from the Balmond near Kosai Talis; in the past two days, she'd hardly slept for seeing his vision rather than hers, and there was no controlling it. Like the dragon himself, the cleaving collided with her life at random and sent it spinning off-course.

She ought to be used to such things by now. Being caught with her guard down, like the last breathless second before a blade plunged in, was becoming a way of life for her.

She flinched at a tap to the ribs from behind. "*What?*"

Aden dragged down the mouth guard of his armor to shout above the whistling wind, "*Athar* says we must be close. He recognizes the copses below."

Ashe squinted at the spruce ridge winding along in Bresnyar's broad shadow, all the same blue-green monotony as the last several miles; but they had little to lose except time, and time was wasting anyway. "Down there, Bres."

"Hold tight." The dragon's growl accompanied his tucking wings, and in a tight spiral they plummeted from among the clouds down to the snowbank. Ashe clung to Bresnyar's neck and shut her eyes, imagining they were back in the Calaluns of Talheim, dragon and future Wingmaiden learning to trust one another. When she wasn't carrying the weight of the need for a drakonian Legion. When the fate of all the kingdoms hadn't rested on her back.

If this was how Cistine had felt when they'd first traveled north to Valgard seeking a treaty with its people, she wasn't certain how her princess had survived the weight for so long. It caught up to Ashe the moment Bresnyar's talons dug into the seams of the rock, heaviness barreling over her chest and back and forcing her eyes open again.

More rime ice. More stone. More emptiness. It all reminded her of a war-torn tundra and a blade in her hand and an augur boy standing before her—dead eyes with life trickling back into them.

She swiveled and looked past Aden to his father. "You're sure about this?"

"Not enough that I'd stake my life on it." Tall and kind-eyed, his beard and hair crusted in snow, Kristoff Lionsbane slid from Bresnyar's back and hitched his weapons higher up on his shoulders. "But it looks more familiar than the last few miles of snow, anyway."

Snorting, Ashe dismounted on one side of Bresnyar, Aden on the other. While the former Hive Lord stalked through the drifts to help his father search the terrain, Ashe circled to her dragon's head and laid her hand on his snout, a faint stab of power slithering through the Wingmaiden's rune emblazoned on her palm. Against it, the *valenar* mark of blended blood felt so weak and quiet.

Bresnyar's nostrils flared. "Would that I could ease your burdens, *Ilyanak*. You carry so many different scents of pain."

"I'll be all right." The easy lie, safe and impulsive, scraped from her wind-battered throat. The arch-browed look from her dragon suggested he wasn't fooled, but he said nothing when she flicked his nose. "We just need to find Kristoff's tribe and land ourselves an Oadmarkaic translator. Simple."

After that, she only had to convince an entire kingdom to spare its warriors for a battle against enemies undefeatable and the twisted spawn of augmentation and *Gammalkraft*. Only had to entreat them with her stilted Talheimic tongue, her only claim to their land the rune on her palm—a woman unsworn to any one kingdom and a dragon exiled for the death of his last Wingmaiden.

Wild laughter bubbled in her throat, and Bresnyar's other knobbed brow bobbed to join the first. "Something amuses you?"

"The insanity of hope." She swatted him gently on the muzzle. "Go scout from above. I'll call if we need you."

In a burst of wings and snow, Bresnyar lurched back into the skies. Shaking the flurry off her hair and thickly-armored shoulders, Ashe strode to join Aden and Kristoff. She couldn't tell at a glance what they were searching for, prowling the spruces in a tight, familiar formation that could only be familial, known in the blood and bones. And Ashe, who had never truly been loved by either her father or the King's Cadre Commander who'd claimed to be like one, hovered at the fringes and watched, an aching emptiness in her gut.

Kristoff noticed her waiting, watching, and beckoned her to join him with a flicker of a smile. "I'm almost sure there's a game trail here," he said when she waded through the drifts to his side. "What do you see?"

"The same thing I've seen for the last two days: snow and rock."

"I think we both know you're more perceptive than that."

"Do we?"

"You would not love my sons if you were not a woman capable of seeing past the surface of things." He tilted his head. "You have a rare gift of insight, when you're bold enough to use it."

Memory rocked through Ashe, a trace of darkness and heat against the face of the mountains, a hand around hers, a whisper in the dark.

Fearless is my name.

Gold fringed her sight, then dappled away, leaving her heart cracked in two and Kristoff's face before her, full of compassion, as if he knew exactly what she was thinking.

"The fate-changers in this world are the ones who learn to see not what lies before them, but what lies beneath," he added gently. "The ones with the bravery to look twice."

Ashe pocketed her hands and hunched her shoulders. "Depending on who you ask, that's either bravery or charlatan nonsense."

"It's you I'm asking." Kristoff spanned an arm to the spruces. "What do *you* see?"

Fighting the urge to roll her eyes like a petulant Warden dragged off on morning patrol, she stalked deeper among the trees. Quiet as a shadow, Kristoff followed, giving her some distance.

Aden offered no such thing; he fell into step with her, thumb hitched into his satchel strap, eyes fixed ahead. "What did my father say to you?"

She shrugged. "Charlatan nonsense."

"And that's why you're helping now instead of scowling off to the side?"

"I'm helping because I have a duty to fulfill, even if I think this place looks the same as every other scraped-over inch of—"

Another spasm of gold bloomed across her vision, but this time it snared her in place, rooting her feet in the snow. She cast out an arm and caught Aden across the chest, towing him back. Through Bresnyar's vision, twice as perceptive as her own and measuring the trees from above, she saw a pale, serpentine path winding through the spruces.

"There *is* a game trail here," she breathed. "Someone's been kicking snow over it."

The moment the words left her mouth, a blade snickered from its sheath. Ashe and Aden whirled, hands to their weapons, a snarl booming from Aden's chest when he laid eyes on his father: stock-still behind them, a sword pressed to his throat. The man who wielded it could barely be Cistine's age, his eyes flinty and his barely-stubbled jaw locked when he faced them.

"Who are you," he growled, "and why are you here?"

Ashe fingered the hilts of her sabers, Starfall and Stormfury, measuring the distance from her to the man and judging whether she could make it before he spilled Kristoff's throat.

Then Kristoff sighed. "Stars, Dain, lower your weapon. It's *me*."

The boy's eyes blew wide, and the sword tumbled from his hand so swiftly it vanished into the snow. Heedless that he was now unarmed with Ashe and Aden ready to draw against him, he jerked Kristoff around by the shoulders and peered into his face. "*Nadrian?*" Before Kristoff could muster a reply, the boy's arms were around him, and laughter, not the battle cries Ashe had braced herself for, split the air. "I don't believe it! I saw, up above— was that *Bresnyar*? You found him again? Where? *How?*"

Dain. Ashe remembered that name now from Kristoff's story of Kalt Hasa and Oadmark, how he'd survived in the mountains for so many months: the man who'd dragged him to safety and stayed with the tribes to begin a new life.

Northern life seemed to suit him; fit, plump, and smiling, he peeled back to peer at Kristoff, then at Aden and Ashe. "Who are they? What are all of you doing on the game trail?"

"Looking for the tribe," Kristoff said. "Valgard needs aid only Oadmark can give."

All at once solemn and grim-jawed again, Dain scooped up his sword, spun it once, and clicked it back into its sheath. "If you say so, *Nadrian*, then it must be serious. Come with me...I'll take you to the Village of the Moon."

The tribe that had taken Dain and Kristoff from the Undertaker's doorstep and given them food and shelter while they recovered from years of imprisonment was a figment of another story Quill and Tatiana had told of northern tribes and vicious elements. A story of the *Aeoprast*, leader of the Bloodwights; a tale Ashe had not taken seriously enough until it was far too late.

Wariness pricked her chest when Dain led them from the spruce copse and into a small camp at the curved edge of a pond fed by a gushing waterfall. Children played among the drifts and tumbled on the shore; young men, most half Dain's age if that, sparred in the rays of sunlight glinting on snow or hurled snowballs at one another. Mothers and a few fathers skinned meat and watched the children, their dark eyes ever vigilant. There were very few men close to Aden's age, and none at all close to Kristoff's.

Heads turned at Dain's arrival, a few shouts of greeting floating on the frigid air in a language Ashe recognized but didn't understand—Oadmarkaic, the clipped, short syllables with which Bresnyar cursed or muttered at his most frustrated. Curious eyes followed them past tents erected of wood and hide toward what seemed to be the very center of the village, where a great fire burned. The youngest children were gathered there, weaving baskets under the supervision of the women—one of whom leaped up, beaming, and hurtled to greet Dain with an embrace that nearly barreled him off his feet. Her giddy laughter sliced Ashe's heart like a blade, and her marked hand curved into a fist of its own volition.

Joyful reunions were little more than a dream, and there was work to be done in the meantime.

"Dain," Kristoff said when the pair pulled apart. "Where is Nunajik?"

"Here." The voice, and the woman, emerged from one of the tents, sturdy and stern-faced, carrying an armload of freshly-hewn wooden pikes in her arms. A small girl trailed after her, chewing on her mitten, carrying a child-sized spear of her own. "I did not expect we would see you again, Kristoff."

"I wish it were under better circumstances." Earnest regret laced

Kristoff's voice, and he fell back a step, spanning an arm. "Nunajik, this is Aden, my son, and Asheila Kovar. Aden, Ashe, this is Nunajik—matriarch of the Village of the Moon."

"Nuna," she corrected, setting the pikes across the fire from where the children gathered. "We keep no formalities with those who are friends of Kristoff and Dain."

Beaming, Dain wrapped an arm around the woman at his side. "And this is Nanak. My *nuliask*." Ashe didn't need to ask what that word meant with the way they were gazing at each other like lovesick adolescents.

"Why have you returned?" Nuna asked with a daggered focus Ashe was grateful for.

Kristoff grimaced, rolling his shoulders. "Perhaps it's best if we sat down. This will be a long tale."

CHAPTER THREE

"SO. THE *AEOPRAST* makes war on your kingdom."

Nunajik's words rang hollow in the warm confines of her tent, and Aden Bloodsinger shifted his seat, adjusting the loose link of his arms around his bent knees. The fire burning in the low pit between them could have lulled him to sleep if not for the jabbing unease of his father's account and the somberness it brought to the tent.

Across from Aden, legs bowed below her body and hands fisted on her thighs, Ashe stared into the fire. Her blue-and-green eyes were distant, cold, seeing things in the dance of flames no one else beheld...a battle she alone had suffered and still fought within herself. Aden wished he could lift that burden from her, but a Tribune and the former Lord of the Blood Hive did not have the power to cure pain, only to walk beside those who felt it.

And here, he saw pain in plenty.

Arm snaked around Nanak's waist, Dain too stared into the flames. "You were right, *Nadrian*. They really did have designs on the North."

"We tried, but we could not stop him." Voice brittle, Nuna dragged her knife along the fresh spear balanced in her lap. "We could not stop our people joining his cause."

"I didn't return to shift blame," Kristoff said gently. "I've come to ask your aid."

Nuna's dark eyes flicked to him. "You know what our tribe has suffered. We do not have warriors to spare."

"Not warriors," Ashe said. "Someone who speaks Oadmarkaic and the common tongue of the Three Kingdoms."

Brow furrowing, Nuna glanced between them. "I do not understand."

"We've come for the northern Wing Legions," Aden said, and Dain's jaw parted in soundless shock, "to acquire their aid in our war. But we don't speak the language of this kingdom."

"We need someone who does," Kristoff added. "And who better to help argue our cause than the woman who has stood most passionately for it—who has delivered village after village from the *Aeoprast's* thrall?"

"But Bresnyar speaks both tongues, doesn't he?" Dain asked.

"Yes, but we're not sure anyone will listen to him," Ashe muttered. "He's an outcast in the Legions because of what happened to his former Wingmaiden."

Nuna set aside her whittling knife, gaze fixed on Kristoff. "You ask me, a woman of the tribes, to travel to the Hunting Grounds. To stand before the Grand Council in the shadow of the mountain, with my uncultured tongue and common ways."

Nanak spat something in Oadmarkaic, and Dain's lips tilted sheepishly. "She knows some of the common tongue, but she can't speak it."

"I think I caught the gist of that," Ashe said dryly. "She seems to disagree on your qualities, Nuna."

"Be that as it may." Nuna folded her hands in her lap and stared down at them. "No woman or man of the tribes has set foot before the Grand Council in my lifetime. It is forbidden...only the Legions speak with them face-to-face."

"We will protect you," Kristoff said with the same certainty that had made Aden brave in the face of Talheimic invasion as a boy, convincing him without a shadow of doubt that his father would bring Maleck home from that long-ago war. "More than that, Nuna, this is precisely what you hoped to do when our paths first crossed: to thwart this false god and open the eyes of his misguided followers."

"Those are your people," Aden added. "Oadmarkaics among enemy ranks. If nothing else, the Grand Council ought to know of *that*."

Nanak spoke rapidly to Dain, and he bobbed his head, eyes trailing to Nuna. "The Grand Council doesn't like to share. I'm sure it would turn a few heads if they knew their own tribes were off serving other powers."

Nuna's lips trembled around a slow, unsteady inhale. "What of *my* tribe? What of *Chena*?"

"We'll look after them." Dain squeezed an arm around Nanak, tucking her closer to his side. "You've taught Nanak well how to lead, and I spent plenty of time chasing my younger sisters before...well, you know. I won't let Chena out of my sight."

"If they do not accept my presence, I perish. We *all* perish."

Kristoff bent forward, earnest and fierce in the firelight. "If we don't try, we all die anyway. These Balmond cannot be stopped without dragonfire. For that, we *must* deliver Ashe to the Hunting Grounds."

A shudder passed through Ashe's body, so subtle Aden might've missed it had his sight not grown so attuned to her in Siralek, to every faint twitch that might precede an attack. But she did not lunge or strike now, merely shifted on her knees and stared more deeply into the flames.

"What claim does she have to their aid?" Nuna asked.

"She's a Wingmaiden," Aden said. "The first marked beyond Oadmark's borders."

Wide-eyed, Nuna swiveled toward Ashe. "Show me."

Ashe stripped off her glove, a small, vicious smile playing at her lips, and bared her palm to Nuna: the Wingmaiden's rune at the heel, and the *valenar's* mark across the center. She'd shown it to Aden the first night after Kosai Talis and told him everything, the story of desperate devotion beyond the Battle of Braggos pouring out of her like she'd been waiting weeks to tell him.

There was no point in admitting he'd already suspected. The wound Maleck had left behind with his absence was too deep, too painful still to remind her that the way they danced around each other left little to the imagination, especially to Aden, who knew them both so well. It would be cruelty to broach the subject while Ashe danced alone.

Nuna examined Ashe's palm, turning it this way and that toward the light. "How?"

"That's the easy question," Ashe said. "What I've been asking myself for months is *why*. Why did the gods choose me? But I'm starting to wonder if it's not for this." Her eyes gleamed with new fervor. "A dying woman gave me a starstone and warned me war was coming, something we couldn't face alone. Maybe it was always about this."

"You believe the gods brought you and the dragon together to battle the Bloodwights?"

Ashe shrugged. "You give me a better explanation for why an outcast Warden wears the mark of a Wingmaiden."

Silence gripped the tent for a time, broken only by the crackle of flames and steady breathing. Then Nuna at last looked at Kristoff. "If it is the will of the gods, then I will finish what my father began and end the *Aeoprast's* schemes. And if we perish, we perish."

A specter's smile flitted across Kristoff's face. "We cannot thank you enough, Nuna."

"Gratitude is empty unless we return victorious." She rose and dipped her head. "I will prepare. We leave at dawn. Dain, show them to a tent."

The guard was more than eager, chatting with Kristoff about matters of steel and the heart, his hand wrapped tight around Nanak's the whole way. Aden fell back into stride with Ashe, trailing them. "That went better than I expected."

"Begging aid from a tribe already sympathetic to our cabal is nothing," she said. "It's this Grand Council I'm concerned about. They must be the ones who cast Bresnyar out after Ileria died—the ones who damned him to a slow death in madness without a new Wingmaiden." Rage brimmed in her voice on behalf of her dragon.

Aden thrust his hands deep into his pockets. "Be patient. You won't win their aid with anger."

"What do you want from me? Docile curtsies and pretty words?" Ashe snapped. "I'm not Cistine, I don't play the diplomat. The Legions helped create this war by not handling the Bloodwights when they fled into Oadmark twenty years ago. If you think I'm going to let that go unaddressed—"

"All right, you make a fair point. And no, I don't expect curtsies and wordplay from you. You'd fall off-balance and embarrass us all." He dodged her swift blow aimed at his ribs. "Just be sure what you bring them is righteous rage for what they have and haven't done...not anger for Bresnyar. Or for Maleck."

She slowed to a halt, staring at him. The look in her eyes was impossible to decipher; he only knew he'd never seen it before. "I need you to believe I can do this, Aden."

The reckless, defensive faith of a Tribune toward his people surged within Aden, putting him before her in half a stride, his hands on her shoulders. "I do not doubt your strength. I have *never* doubted that. But belief is not blind...I see your pain as well as your power, and I know this world will do everything it can to make that a weapon against you. This is caution, not unbelief."

Ashe sucked in a sharp, shallow breath, lashes fluttering in quick blinks. With a dip of her head, she shrugged off his hands. "I'm going to train with Bresnyar."

He let his hands fall away. "I'll wait up for you." It was the only comfort he could offer, knowing how the nightmares plagued her since Kosai Talis.

Ashe's parting smile was crooked but genuine, a gleam of hope brighter than sun against snow. Then she was gone, back the way they came, toward the spruces and the hidden game trail.

Aden watched her go until she was a memory held in the shadows between the trunks—until a hand descended on his shoulder, a brawny arm looped around his back, and his father said, "Sometimes all you can do is wait for them."

Grimacing, Aden flexed his fingers over the cord that wrapped his upper arm, the armored threads the same as the knot Ashe wore on her bicep. "These days, it feels like waiting is *all* I do."

"It can be difficult to accept when a mission from the gods falls on shoulders other than yours, particularly when you're used to carrying the weight." Kristoff clapped him on the chest and steered him around toward Dain and Nanak, waiting in the distance. "You can't bear the burden, *Afiyam*. But you can help carry her."

As far as she goes, for as long as it takes. Quill's oath, spoken before Salvotor's trial, before the war, before Valgard went to Nimmus in a knapsack, returned to Aden as a dim echo on frigid mountain winds.

That vow was what it meant to be cabal. That was why Aden was here, and not tracking Maleck himself—laying to rest as best he could the memory of that mountain cleft and those anguished eyes, the godlike power careening out of control along his brother's body, turning to covetousness and insatiable thirst.

Maleck was no longer in his hands; only the Key had any hope of saving him. And the moment Aden set foot across the border of Valgard again, he would step back into the arena of sand and blood against Nimea, his former friend, his avowed nemesis. And when he did...

Gods help him. Gods help everyone he cared for when that day finally came.

So for now he was resigned, if not content, to be in this self-inflicted exile, putting his hands to use where he could.

Because that was what it meant to be Tribune. And that was Aden's duty from now until his dying day.

CHAPTER
FOUR

IT COULDN'T FEEL, but it could hear the rain. Gentle, constant, dripping in the leaves, dripping on its left only its left from the place where the fire and the lightning struck and slammed and burrowed, and the flagons the power they hadn't been enough to stop it

Mistake. Mistake. Mistake.

The man with the silver hair the blue eyes the man like a lion the woman with the dark hair and face of coming death they would tell him what a mistake it was, what he did, what he was, what he'd become—

What it had always been. What it had run from.

It shouldn't be raining. It remembered that, remembered silver hair and a gnarled leg, remembered blue eyes and an old woman's face, two voices in its head, two sets of hands guiding its fingers over wound muscle blood bone, *it shouldn't be raining it should have stopped hours days ago too much rain too much blood too much*

Blood.

Its hand tumbled to its side. Felt the power the current the energy *pulsing crackling begging take me use me use me USE ME let go let it all go let me go*

In the next, we learn to let you go.

Its fingers stilled.

I'm not letting go of you, either.

No.

Not its prize. Not for it to use.

But...

Mine. Mine. Mine.

Hers. Hers. HERS.

It should be two but it only had one and one more, it had the power and the thing sleeping in the brush ahead of it, the thing it had been watching and listening to for days with the thrashing, the threats, the screaming. It had the power and the creature it had one chance and one purpose and then, and then—

You'll pay for this you sealed her fate everything that happens now is because of you because of you because of YOU you traitorous thieving waste of air we should've smothered you instead of taking you should've seen what you were how useless how unteachable how much shame you brought and now you brought this on her—

Its head fell back against the tree and it listened to the rain.

Drip. Drip. Drip.

One. Last. Task.

Then it would be done.

But first.

Find her.

CHAPTER
FIVE

THE SMASH OF fists on ribs, as usual, bolted clarity back into Thorne Starchaser's world, bringing him out of the dark, close pocket of forest that night after Kosai Talis, out of his fear and disbelief, and back into the sunsplashed grove where he and Quill sparred with all their might.

Sweat rolled down the planes of Thorne's face and dripped from Quill's temples, where threads of his augment-shocked hair escaped their tie. Gaze and smile feral, cold steel in his grin, Quill danced on the balls of his feet and curled his fingers twice, beckoning. "Are you going to hit me or just keep admiring my face, *Allet?*"

Thorne plowed in, and with a laugh devoid of warmth Quill caught his punches one after the other, spun around him, and hammered an elbow into his ribs. Thorne twisted back, snagged his arm at the hinge and flipped him, but Quill landed lithe and graceful on his feet and swiveled under Thorne's reach, pinning his arm behind his back. "Had enough?"

Thorne bucked free, and their grappling dissolved into a furious set of blows, feet snapping across the leaf mold and fresh growth of spring's desperate gasps through the grip of *Nazvaldolya*. Exertion honed Thorne's focus like a blade until everything else fell away: the fury, the doubt, the wild hope and wicked despair. There was only him and Quill lunging through every breath of empty air between them, landing and taking blows, pouring out their frustrations as they had since before sunup when specters had driven them from camp at the same time—leaving Ariadne on watch and Tatiana and Cistine snoring where they'd fallen asleep the night before, map spread across their laps, leaning on each other's shoulders.

If only Thorne could give them that and nothing more: maps and tea and quiet days like they'd had in the Den when Cistine first came to them. Instead they were chasing Maleck, separated from Aden, Ashe, and Kristoff, and barreling toward two inevitable fates: Cistine bleeding on a Door or Valgard succumbing to utter Bloodwight dominion.

His steps quickened with his pulse, feet flying faster, blows landing harder, and Quill shifted from giving to taking, taking, taking. Concentration furrowed his brow and lined his mouth with every drill of a punch into his palms, his three-fingered hand taking as many hits as the whole, until the binding around his knuckles came undone and great hanks of hair swung loose, framing his strained features.

"What are you hitting?" he barked above the snap of fists against hands. "What's out there, Thorne?"

"You know *damned well* what!"

With a dull *crack*, Thorne's blow landed on a stiff hand, an outstretched arm. Quill stood his ground, no longer yielding to Thorne's rage but holding it captive, his fingers banded loose around Thorne's fist. Panting, they stared at one another.

"Tell me," Quill urged. "I can take it."

Thorne didn't want to add to the burden his friend already carried, the frantic need to find and save his sister and Maleck, yet desperation bubbled in him like miasma. "She wants me to *marry* her, Quill. So I can save her kingdom if she *dies* on the Doors."

Smiling wryly, Quill released Thorne's fist. "I doubt that's the only reason."

"But it's the one I can't stop thinking about." He swept both hands down his face, stubble pricking his palms, then back again to flatten his hair against his scalp. "I've never stood this near to losing her for this long."

"Not even in Kalt Hasa?"

"She was fighting my father then. This...she's walking toward it. This fate is *her* choice."

"And you want to save her from it. But not against her will."

Thorne bobbed his shoulders in a helpless shrug.

Quill deflated with a long breath, dropping backward onto the edge of a fallen tree and hanging his wrists between his knees. "Safety or freedom...that's always been this cabal's problem, hasn't it? We could've had peace in Stornhaz if we'd lived by the laws. Could've avoided all the pain in the last ten years if we were willing to accept how this kingdom treats its women and disabled, how the territories suffer during every season, all the deals made in the dark."

Hurt splintering in dull splotches everywhere Quill had struck him, Thorne slowly lowered himself onto the log beside his friend. "It's easier to make the hard choices when you're the one bearing the consequences. When it's someone you love..."

"You wonder why the easier path ever lost its appeal." A quiet chuckle unwound from Quill along with the last of his fist wrappings, and he flexed his bruised knuckles gently in the sun's light. "Listen. I know Cistine. The one thing that makes her different from all of us is that she isn't quick to look the Undertaker in the eye. She'll do everything in her power to make sure if she steps on that Door, she's stepping back off it. You becoming King is just the contingency, not the goal."

"But it could happen."

"And we could all have our throats ripped out by the Balmond tomorrow, but I don't see you acting like that's going to happen." Quill bent forward, rubbing his palms together. "She needs you *here*, Thorne. Not living in a future where she dies on the Door. Remember what Baba Kallah always told us? *Every day has enough problems of its own.*"

"*Stop trying to solve tomorrow before its time.*" A heavy smile trimmed the corners of Thorne's mouth at the memory of his grandmother's winking eye, her grinning face when she reminded him of that, over and over again. "Then you think I should tell her I'll do it?"

"I assumed you already did."

Thorne grimaced. "Agreeing to this—"

"It feels like saying you're all right with it. You're ready to watch her bleed."

He nodded. "Words fail."

"Well, I hate to be the one to tell you, but this is going to happen, Thorne. With or without your words. She's doing this whether she has your say or not." Quill clapped him on the knee. "But knowing her, she'll do it wiser and better with your support than on her own."

"Who will do what better?" The sound of Cistine's voice raised Thorne's spirits like little else ever could. But with the sight of her yawning and stretching in the sunlight as she joined them, there also came a feeling he was rapidly becoming too familiar with: a deep, aching melancholy, like he was gathering these moments to remember her by when she was gone.

Quill rescued him from his pained silence with all the usual swagger, climbing to his feet with a stretch of his own. "Just discussing your culinary habits, Stranger."

She pressed a hand to her chest in mock-offense. "*Excuse* me? I have improved my cooking skills beyond compare!"

"I'm looking forward to never experiencing that for myself." Quill mussed her hair in passing and aimed a whistle at the treetops, summoning Faer from his roost. "Tati awake?"

"Mmhmm. And Ariadne's asleep."

Quill saluted with two fingers and sauntered back toward the camp; Cistine's eyes trailed after him, budding with fathomless sorrow that drew Thorne up to his feet and to her side. "What's wrong?"

Her lips parted, her breath hitched, and she slowly shook her head. "It's not my story to tell."

Thorne nodded. "Training?"

"We might as well. It's not as if we can do any tracking."

The wretchedness of her tone gave Thorne pause again. "You don't sense him today, either."

It had happened the previous sundown, bringing them abruptly to make camp here near the outskirts of the mountain town Kaldaross: the sense of augmentation and power had winked out of Cistine's perception as suddenly as a star gone dark. She'd waded through the forest, fighting to recapture the sense of Maleck until night made the effort too perilous. Judging by the deep groove between her brows, this morning was no better.

"Maybe I never sensed him at all." Scowling, she unbanded the lightning augment from her pouch and passed it to him. "Maybe I've been chasing nothing all this time."

"I don't believe that. I trust your senses."

"That makes one of us."

Thorne gave up trying to cheer her and instead uncorked the flagon, withdrawing a skein of lightning from its lavender shell. Cistine beheld the power playing between his fingers, eyes shadowed with memory, thumb grazing the betrothal band around her finger.

Then, all at once, she centered herself. Her eyes flicked to his, and with a stab of primitive heat, Thorne spread his stance as well. "Come and take it from me."

She attacked, latching onto his arm and twisting it behind his back. He didn't fight her hold; his full concentration was on keeping the augment from her grasp. It was different from the tension of her hands around his elbow and wrist, immobilizing his dominant arm; the Key's power exerted pressure against his core like a hot blade pressed to his spirit, as foreign as the feeling of the augment gliding over his armor.

Yet it was becoming repetitive, this method of hers; the last two days while they'd trained, she'd fallen into a habit, the same ebb-and-flow in how she gripped and pulled at the power. In seconds, Thorne found a way to push around it.

A change in tactic was in order.

Cistine was better at hold breaks than maintaining her own grip on an opponent, so Thorne switched his bearing, snapping forward against her grasp. Her wild breath stirred his hair—a gasp of surprise and a curse.

Then it struck him like she'd taken the blade back from his spirit and rammed it into his chest instead. He *felt* her nudge open the door to her power as he, and the augment branching through his armor, slipped from her hold. And like a noose, she caught him fast at the end of that tether.

He couldn't move. He could barely breathe. It was spooling out of him like she was dragging his intestines up through his mouth, the pull stronger, the sensation deeper—the lash of a whip against his back, a knife to his chest, to his scarred abdomen.

Thorne let go of the augment, and the lightning flared out of him, turning the world to a searing dome of lavender-white as his knees struck the leaf mold. He retched, clinging to the rocks while the world spun tipsily and darkness climbed the edges of his vision.

Cistine's clammy palms met his cheeks, yanking his head up. Her face swam before his eyes, her mouth moving, asking him over and over, "What did I do? *What did I do?*"

Lightning crackled around her. She was the wild heart of both storm and fire, and for a moment Thorne knew what it would be like if she consumed him.

Her hands snapped away from his face. "I'm going to get the others."

"No." Thorne dredged his voice up from the grottos of his chest, where his breath came and went in an unsteady tide. "It was just...a surprise. What you could do."

"*I don't know what I did!*" Her voice shattered with panic. "I felt you trying to slip away, and I grabbed *something...*"

"You reached for that thread of deeper power. You pulled against it. I felt that. I felt..."

The power had *whipped* him, the shock worse than the pain, a memory of his boyhood, of the plains outside Eben; of the Battle of Braggos where something had torn deep, deep within.

Cistine slowly lowered herself back to her knees. "Maybe we shouldn't do this. Adeima won't know if I stop training. We can find another way."

Thorne craned his head back painfully, every nerve raw, and grimaced at the thin trickle of blood dripping from Cistine's nostril. He wiped it away, her breaths shaking against the pad of his thumb. "There is no other way."

"There has to be. Hurting you can't be my only choice."

"I swore an oath to the Chancelloress. And to you." He pushed himself shakily upright on his knees, coming aware only at the lick of wind on his soaked back that he was sweating like a man with a fever. "I swore I would help make you strong enough to save Maleck. And I will."

"But the cost—"

"You widened the door. It will be easier to do it next time. And the time after that."

"For me, maybe. But for you?"

Thorne could muster no reassurance with the brand of her power still throbbing inside him.

A chilly wind slithered between the trees, and Cistine shivered, climbing to her feet. She dispatched the lightning and offered her hand to him. "I don't think I want to train anymore today."

CHAPTER SIX

OVER AND OVER in her mind, Cistine saw Thorne fall to his knees in that clearing, gasping and heaving, pain lining every contour of his face. Her flexing fingers remembered the powerful surge of muscle when he'd broken away from her, and her spirit still sang with the craving, the brief but overpowering *bellow* of the augment when it slipped from her grasp and instinct made her reach out for it, seize and *take*, even from her *selvenar*.

She'd been so careful before, but in that moment, when he'd snapped free of her grasp and taken the augment with him—

"Cistine, are you listening to us?"

She startled at the rap of Tatiana's knuckles atop her head, jolting back from the sunlit clearing to the overcast campsite and the others gathered around her: Quill basking against a tree, arms crossed and Faer perched on his shoulder; Thorne on one knee across from her, studying the map spread between their bodies; Ariadne cross-legged at Cistine's left, still rubbing sleep from her eyes; and Tatiana, with that same cold ferocity in her stare as every day since they'd left the sanctuary of Holmlond for Kosai Talis.

"Welcome back," Tatiana said dryly. "I assume you're gathering the wittiest retorts about where we should go next?"

Cistine shook off the vestiges of the morning's training disaster. "Where are we now?"

"Here." Ariadne stabbed a finger at a plot just between the Sotefold's southern tip and the northern banks of Stedgnalt Lake. "Kaldaross is two miles southwest."

Thorne nodded to Tatiana. "Report."

Her eyes flashed up at Quill. "We had to move in and out quickly so no one would see us, but there was no unrest beyond what you'd expect in a kingdom at war."

"No bounties with Mal's mask on them, either," Quill grunted. "Which means no augment store raids."

"Yet," Ariadne said. "Kaldaross is the only city worth mention between the Sotefold and Stedgnalt. He came this way for a reason."

"If he's even still here," Tatiana muttered. "Do you sense anything yet, *Yani?*"

Cistine fidgeted with the starstone necklace Ashe had left to her, chafing the heavy gem along its chain. "Still nothing today."

Thorne's back rose and fell in a silent, weighty breath. "We risk drawing attention from the Chancellors if we linger in one place too long. With or without a sense of Maleck, we'll have to move again soon."

"We could circle Stedgnalt." Ariadne traced the shoreline with her fingertip. "Geitlan still lies in ruin. We can shelter there until Cistine regains her sense of his bearings."

"Better for training, too," Quill added. "Less people, less attention."

Tatiana rested her chin on her fist, gaze silently tracing the angles of Blaykrone territory where Geitlan lay. When no one argued, Thorne nodded, and Ariadne rolled the map. "We'll give it two more days. Tell us if you sense anything, Cistine."

He and Ariadne moved off to join Quill, speaking quietly of strategy; in their absence Tatiana stretched, laying a hand lightly to her abdomen. A faint grimace turned her features, then annealed into determination. "I've been thinking about Ashe's dragons."

"Praying, too, I hope," Cistine sighed, kneading her temples.

"I leave that mostly to Ariadne. But think about this...for your plan to retake Stornhaz to have even a small chance, we need a contingency just in case Oadmark kicks dirt on us and tells us to go to Nimmus."

"What did you have in mind?"

"I think we need to find Rakel. Devitrius, too, if that slippery *bandayo* doesn't catch wind and run first."

Cistine stared at her. "You want to *capture* Thorne's mother?"

"Those two managed to break into the City of a Thousand Stars, spring Salvotor from his confines, kidnap Pippet, and nearly kill Thorne, all in one blow." Tatiana's teeth gritted around those last words until she was practically spitting, the fire pulsing hotter and brighter in her eyes. "They might be the *only* ones who can tell us a way in and out without raising a single alarm."

Cistine pondered it, nibbling on her thumbnail already bitten to the quick through long, anxious nights. "Maybe. But I don't like our odds moving the army through the sewers."

"Better that strategy than none. Maybe it's not the whole army, maybe it's just us—getting you to the Door underneath the courthouse."

Cistine shot her innocent-eyed friend a dry look; trust Tatiana to cleverly play with Cistine's own desires, a subtle show of support to the strategy the entire cabal despised. "And how do you suggest we find her?"

Tatiana shifted her seat, curling her arms loosely around her ankles. "While you were in Talheim, there were a few times Devitrius reared his hideous head in the *mirothadt* ranks. As usual, even with Salvotor gone, those two are gaming for the stronger side. But I think we both know a certain High Tribune acting as Chancellor who could be convinced to capture, not kill them."

A smile dragged across Cistine's mouth. "I'm sure Sander will love the challenge of the hunt."

"Knowing him, he's bored out of his mind without us around." Tatiana got to her feet. "I'll tell the others and see who wants to write to him. Maybe Thorne will play me *koh, kendar, kest* for the honor."

Laughter bubbled in Cistine's chest, but it was short-lived; as with most things of late, this decision moved swift as a flooding river, with little time to pause and consider the outcomes. Her mind churned relentlessly through scenarios while Tatiana swaggered off to join the others: notions of the army or the cabal crushed in the sewers, drowned in the Ismalete Channel, or captured by the Bloodwights. Visions that they would be tortured, torn limb from limb—or reach the Door and find themselves fighting the *Aeoprast* for the right to spill her blood first.

Darkness drenched her nerves, the world tumbling closed like a frostbitten cloak pressed tight around her shoulders. A cold, skittering shiver capered down her neck and sides, and the first tingles of panic darted into her flushed cheeks and the tips of her nose, her bowels clenching tighter than her fists.

She bolted to her feet, bringing all their eyes to her—deepening that well of unease yawning in the pit of her belly.

"I'm going to gather herbs," she blurted. "For poultices. In case one of us gets hurt while we travel."

Quill arched a brow and Tatiana's lips thinned, but no one protested when she hurried off into the trees—and that was some relief. Rarely did they ever let her go off alone anymore, especially after the vow Quill swore to defend her. But she didn't need protecting today. She needed solitude.

Peace came almost too quickly when she left the cabal and forded alone through the trees. A smell of spring rain hung on the air from clouds boiling down across the mountains, choking out the sunlight that had paved her way to the grove where she and Thorne trained that morning; all was quiet and muffled, and she welcomed it, even if it made foraging difficult. The silence emptied her head, bringing clarity to the separate weights she carried.

Not just the burden of being the Key, or needing to train, or searching for Maleck; but Tatiana's secret pain hidden in her heart, and the deep, low thrum of the special augment in Cistine's pouch, and the unspoken fear of the Chancellors catching up to her before she was strong enough to face them. Worry for Quill, so eager to find his sister; and Ariadne, the spine holding all their broken ribs together, keeping them from crumbling.

How long could they keep fighting these battles? How long before they were dealt a wound no poultice or rousing speech could mend?

She wished she didn't have so many books on war theory rattling around in her skull, reminding her how many months, if not years, a war could rage on, and how few survivors might be left behind to celebrate its end—or become slaves to its victors.

She followed the sound of running water to a stream where Ariadne had gathered a breakfast of berries that morning and waded through the undergrowth by touch as well as sight, seeking glimpses and scents: lavender's distinct aroma, splashes of comfrey, white wisps of yarrow and hardy plantain fronds nudging up through the soil.

At least here, *Nazvaldolya* had not choked everything the way it fought to choke the hope from her. She filled her pockets with herbs until they bulged, then crouched in the waning light to bury her fingers in the dirt.

Gods, it felt miraculous to be in a place untouched by war. The smell of raw soil, the sound of running water, the whisper of the wind among the trees...they all reminded her of her garden in Hellidom, and of the Den where she'd first trained and begun to feel at home in this foreign kingdom. She wished she could excise this small pocket of peace from the rest of Valgard and linger in it until life made sense again; until she stopped feeling afraid, like she was living on borrowed time.

It was with her hands plunged into the dirt that she felt the sensation begin—not just in her gut, but within the ground itself.

Pestilence. Sickness.

The loam turned cold, gulping her body's warmth. The tiny roots of the weeds and hardy flowers shivered around her fingers like hairs standing at attention. Her own nape prickled, and she jerked to her feet and spun toward the stream.

And there he was. Not moving. Not attacking.

The wolf mask faced toward her. The hood was drawn up, hooked over the back of the jaw, hiding the braids that must be tucked into that dark robe. Through the empty sockets, he watched her.

For a long moment, Key and Bloodwight regarded one another warily, the span of water separating them. His body hummed with augments even across the distance; it *was* him she'd sensed these past several days, a taste over the miles between them. He carried so many separate powers, a web hemming his entire frame, when before he'd recoiled from the feel of them on *her* body.

But he was guttering. His presence, her sense of him flickered like a candle, strange and unsteady; one moment there, the next gone, like the previous night when she'd lost it completely.

Something was wrong.

Dampness plopped audibly onto the dry leaves of the opposite bank, a thick, heavy drip. Cistine's eyes tore downward to the sleeve of his black, armored cloak and the blood that ran from beneath it, speckling the foliage in dark scarlet dapples.

His arm was bleeding.

She drew her lip in sharply between her teeth, biting down, unsure if the tears came from that or from the sight and sound of his falling blood— or from the way he stepped toward her and broke down slightly, knees buckling. She reached into her pocket before she could question her own sanity and pulled out the yarrow with shaking fingers, scattering a handful of leaves and buds when she stepped forward as well. The momentum jarred her voice loose. "It's yarrow. We used it in salves in Hellidom. When...when I would come back from training after Ashe was gone, before we all left for Geitlan, you would make me sit at the table in the Den while you bandaged my knuckles. The ones I broke on Salvotor's face."

He didn't move away from or against her. He was another tree, another pillar of darkness within the darkness.

"I always seemed to tear something open back then, and you always knew exactly how to fix it. How to fix *me*."

She could feel his arms around her in Morten's house, welcoming her home from Kalt Hasa; could feel his head on her shoulder the night in Jovadalsa when he'd told her everything about his past, and when they'd said goodbye on the plains of Eben before she'd returned to Talheim.

How much of him was still left? How much of him was still *him*, and how much was the mindless, corrupted creature who'd strangled Ashe, who'd raided Aoelvik in his desperate search for flagons?

It didn't matter. Even if there was only a shard of him left, she would give him this gift and every other she could offer. She would give anything to bring him home.

She halted, offering the yarrow across the stream. "Let me help you."

Slowly, that masked head canted to one side. Blood ran freely when he raised his arm, revealing a slit in the sleeve, in the armor beneath, that went all the way up and back to the shoulder and down his side. Chunks of bone showed through the gash in his ribs.

Cistine's mouth flooded with bile. "Oh, gods."

He extended his arm toward her. The faintest current of a wind augment bathed his skin, and with a jolt of breathless daring, she considered taking hold of it. Now, before it was too late, before he sank any deeper, before this wound killed him...

She touched her fingers to his, the yarrow drifting on her palm.

Then he was gone, a flicker of black moving with the wind, bolting to the periphery of her vision. She sucked in her breath and spun toward him, fighting not to reach for her saber and dagger, not to react in fear. But still he did not attack; he lingered between the trees, masked face riveted toward her. Waiting.

Seized with reckless compulsion, Cistine stepped forward.

He vanished again, a dim thread of power parting the undergrowth where he passed. Molars gritted and a prayer offered up in a silent shout, Cistine darted after him.

Close as they were, he was still nearly impossible to track; that power was a waning, gasping thing, barely clutched to the tips of her fingers, his form hardly more substantial—a blur of black pinioning between the trees. After nearly a mile of running, she wondered if she was hallucinating. Then all at once she burst into a grove fringed with broken-down stone, red ivy and green lichen weaving on the sides of what was once a home, bathed in sunlight piercing through the clouds.

No trace of black. No shadows at all.

"No!" The frustrated sob tore from Cistine's chest, and she pivoted in place, gaze tracking the trees. "Where *are* you? Maleck? *Maleck!*"

But he did not come. No glint of light on white bone, no flirt of dark cloth—as if he was never there at all. Only a faint hum of power fading on the wind and the aberrant bend of the trees told her that he was anything more than a hopeful illusion conjured by her exhausted mind.

And there was a crust of blood, barely-dried, on her palm; Maleck's blood. That was real, he was real, and he was hurt. Maybe even dying.

She had to find him.

She fell to one knee, slamming her bloodstained hand into the ground, seeking the sensation of his darkness in the world and the augments webbed around him.

Come, the power whispered back to her. *Come and see.*

She teased that thread, as familiar as Maleck's hands guiding hers in a dance of blades. She tested the sensations of augments near and far like her very first lessons in the dim weapon room with him standing before her; she weighed every lick of power, searching for the difference.

It finally caught like a sizzling thread, springing her fingers away from the soil; the same current that had lived in the breathless space between them with his fingers hovering above her palm beside the stream. He was on the move away from her.

Cursing, she lurched back upright, spun in the direction she'd arrived...then hesitated. There was power in this grove still, a strange, smaller stamp—unfamiliar, and yet...

Slowly, she turned back toward that crumbled remnant of a home.

There was something there, tossed in the corner of the rock, stained bright red and black and brown.

Dagger drawn, she stalked carefully through the new spring grass. Eyes ahead and senses attuned on every side, wary of a trap, she tucked her back to the stone wall and sidled up to that soiled heap. A last glance to ensure no one was creeping up on her flanks, and she bent around the corner to examine it.

Then she started screaming.

CHAPTER SEVEN

SUBVERTING THE BLOODWIGHTS had become, with little contest, Tatiana Dawnstar's favorite pastime—better than any card game, better than the finest mead, better than the fiercest battle or the most pleasant night with Quill. Perhaps the only things that compared were finding the perfect gown after a shopping spree or coaxing a rare, genuine laugh out of her *valenar* these days.

Still. Little compared to well-plotted and exacted vengeance.

The specter's grip on her empty womb ached a little less when she sat against a tree at the edge of their camp, scratching out a letter to Sander. While a portion of her wished she could be the one to catch Thorne's treacherous mother, break her face with a well-aimed blow, and reel the secrets of besieging Stornhaz from her, this was enough. Setting the working parts in motion was plenty while they still hunted for the missing piece of their broken cabal.

Finding Maleck came before everything else.

A scrape of armor on bark, and Quill collapsed cross-legged beside her, bending his head to read over her shoulder. "Anything I should be worried about there, Saddlebags?"

She shielded the note with her arm. "Just penning a long-winded sonnet on Sander's finest qualities."

"So nothing to write, then."

She dug her elbow into his ribs. "Be nice. If Thorne ever succeeds in getting himself killed for one of us, you'll be serving under Sander."

"I'll defect to Talheim before I serve that preening peacock." Quill's gaze slid to her sideways. "How's your wound?"

Tatiana's fingers spasmed around the pen, a twinge passing through her middle—remembering the knife, the agony, the fear—and grazing the emptiness that lingered, the absence Quill knew nothing about. She couldn't bring herself to tell him, knowing just how deeply that blow would land...knowing it would shatter her *valenar*, a man of fire and steel with a core as gentle and welcoming as the brightest hearth.

He didn't deserve that pain on top of all the rest. Neither of them did. But part of being Quill's blended blood meant protecting him, even from the wounds she was forced to bear.

"I'm fine," she muttered. "Don't worry about me, Featherbrain...we have enough people to be concerned about as it is."

"You're not wrong about that." He dropped his head back against the tree, grimacing. "I was thinking this morning, I don't know what I'd do if I wasn't looking over my shoulder every day anymore. Adjusting to life after this war won't be easy for either of us."

"Assuming we both survive it."

He caught her chin in his three-fingered hand, the metal prosthetics a kiss of ice to her skin. He guided her face up toward his, intensity flickering in his eyes like summer lightning and augmented fire—two of Tatiana's favorite things. "There's no other outcome I'll accept."

His lips had barely grazed hers, opening up a fount of need in her chest, when a distant, high scream split the air.

"*Quill! Quill, I need you!*"

Tatiana's eyes snapped open, meeting Quill's an inch away, watching the storm and fire in his gaze turn to a raging inferno.

Cistine.

Quill released Tatiana and bolted to his feet, Thorne and Ariadne surging up across the camp, hands on their weapons, wide-eyed and swearing. With a whistle, Quill dispatched Faer, the raven shooting from his roost in the tree above toward that cry—the same direction Quill was already running, drawing his sabers as he went. "I'm coming, Cistine!"

Tatiana snatched up her own sabers, heart clashing into her throat, and raced after her *valenar* with Thorne and Ariadne toward Cistine's distant, half-hysterical screams. They surged over fallen trees and stream beds and crashed through the undergrowth more than a half-mile before they burst into an open glade.

No enemies, no *mirothadt*, no Vassoran guards awaited them. Cistine was alone, crouched in the shelter of a broken-down stone wall, and only now that terror slaked in the absence of combat did it occur to Tatiana to wonder why Cistine had screamed for Quill of all people.

He lunged to their princess's side, his gaze raking every shadow between the trees. "What happened, Stranger, what in Nimmus—?"

Then he looked in the shadow of the wall and broke down right beside her, sabers crashing at his hips and hands reaching forward, grasping desperately for something that lay before Cistine. Thorne and Ariadne panted up at Tatiana's flanks, weak daylight bouncing along their steel, and Thorne growled, "What is it?"

Cistine's face turned toward them, tear-tracked. "*Pippet.*"

The world cratered under Tatiana's feet. She didn't realize she'd staggered until Ariadne caught her elbow and steadied her, concern in the flex of her fingers. Pippet's name sobbed within her spirit: disbelief and relief and *rage*, loudest and most violent of all, a maelstrom beyond reckoning.

Her sabers plunked into the soil, hand gripping her side where Pippet's knife had torn into her in Selv Torfjel, ending their mission and the small life growing inside her. She did not move even when Quill touched his sister's cold face and breathed her name, even when he called, voice cracking, "Tati...Tati, *help me*..."

He tried to sit Pippet up, to gather her into his arms, but Tatiana couldn't bring herself a step closer. Ariadne squeezed her arm and brushed past, crouching at Quill's side, nudging Cistine gently out of the way. She bolted to her feet and backed up until she struck Thorne's chest, his blades back in their sheaths already, his hands gripping her shoulders and pulling her around to face him. "How did you find her?"

Eyes vacant, tone shocky, she whispered, "Maleck."

Clarity blazed through Tatiana. She swung away from Pippet and toward Cistine instead. "He was *here?*"

"He led me to her, and then he...he left, he disappeared—" Cistine's gaze lunged from shadow to shadow, then snapped back to Thorne's face, her mouth wobbling with anguish. "He was hurt, *badly*. I don't know how he's even still alive."

Alarm jounced over Tatiana's nerves, reflected in Thorne's flashing eyes and tight, feathering jaw. Then he shook his head. "We deal with the problem before us, then we go searching for the next. Quill?"

"She's unconscious." Voice brittle, he rocked his sister across his lap, Faer hopping along his thigh and crooning Pippet's name like a morbid lullaby. "I don't know why, I—Ari?"

Her gloved fingertips slid along Pippet's mouth, then peeled away, flaking a dark dust to the earth. "He drugged her."

Cistine banded her arms tight around her middle. "Do you think she tried to run? That she was afraid of him, with how he's...changed?"

"Not that I would blame her if she was," Tatiana muttered, "but I don't think it's that."

"We're about to find out," Ariadne said. "She's stirring."

And so she was; a crooking of limbs, a faint, fully-body spasm like an abrupted stretch. Tatiana's heart clenched along with Pippet's movements, her gaze marking how gaunt she was, just like in Selv Torfjel, but now with fresh bruises around her sunken eyes. Her caved-in cheeks, her twisted mouth...her face turned toward her brother's stomach, clenched with hidden pain.

Cistine turned in Thorne's embrace, keeping her back to his chest, her hope-torn stare on Pippet when the smallest, softest moan escaped her. Dark lashes fluttered open, revealing the eyes that had followed Tatiana for years, from dolls and picture books into fashionable threads and swordplay maneuvers and tracking, into *Heimli Nyfadengar* and the prospect of a life away from all this struggle, all this loss and grief.

The same eyes that had beheld her in Selv Torfjel. And tried to put a knife into her *valenar*.

"Good morning, Hatchling." Quill's voice broke around the familiar greeting. "Remember me?"

Pippet blinked drowsily up at him.

Then her hand shot out, jagged nails slicing across Quill's face, and before Tatiana even fully registered the slap of his blood on the grass, Pippet launched herself backward at Ariadne, bowled her over, and broke into a run straight for Cistine with a warbling scream.

Thorne wrenched her back, and Tatiana lunged—either pure instinct or a burst of the hatred still lingering in her from Selv Torfjel. The bar of her arm slammed against Pippet's throat, taking her feet clean from beneath her and sending her sprawling in the grass. The breath gusted from her in a violent rush and turned to gagging when Tatiana landed on top of her, smothering her mouth and jabbing a thumb hard into the bundle of nerves at the hinge of her neck.

The seconds it took Pippet to fall unconscious were the longest of Tatiana's life; when the girl was limp again, she rocked back on her knees. Ariadne had already pushed Quill up, and Thorne and Cistine put distance between them, hands to their weapons.

"She's still addicted," Thorne said. "Still craving."

"Not just that." Cistine took a step forward, eyes sliding slightly out of focus. "There are still augments in her body, in her armor. She hasn't even begun to suffer from withdrawal yet."

"Stars *damn* it!" Quill spat blood that trickled down from his top lip into his teeth. "The withdrawal is what *kills* them!"

"We know." Thorne stared down at Pippet's limp body, still pinned under Tatiana's knee; she couldn't bring herself to let the girl up in case this was all a ruse, biding her time until she could attack Cistine again. "The question is whether Maleck brought her to us to save her, or to use her to reach Cistine."

Cistine's hand curled into a slow fist against her thigh. "He's still himself. He's still *there*."

Four heads swiveled toward her, four narrow pairs of eyes trained on her face. Desperate hope clashed with cruel resignation—the feeling that both Maleck and Pippet were lost to them forever.

Cistine paced away from them, folding her shaking hands over her clavicles, gazing into the trees. "His wounds must've come from his brothers. From fighting them to rescue Pippet and bring her back to us."

A beat of silence, in which none of them dared dissuade her hopes. Then Quill asked, "Can you sense him now?"

Cistine shut her eyes and curled her hands into anchoring fists. For a time she was silent, as they all were. Awe and unease braided up in Tatiana's chest while her friend's power flexed around them. She was still growing used to all the things Cistine could do that no common augur could; all the ways *Gammalkraft* and the forging in her blood made her so strong, so unique—and so precious to all the kingdoms, in so many different and dangerous ways.

"East." Cistine's eyes darted open. "He's moving east."

Quill's gaze shifted to Thorne. "What's out there, do you think?"

Tatiana scowled. "More cities. More people carrying augments."

"And the battle lines, if they've fallen back far enough," Ariadne added grimly.

Cistine shook her head so hard her hair whipped her eyes. "I don't know what he's doing, but he's *not* joining the lines."

"I don't think he is, either," Thorne said. "I doubt even a lust for augments would convince Maleck to fight in his brothers' war. But if he's searching for power, we have to stop him before this goes any farther."

"What about Pippet?" Tatiana demanded. "We can't just drag her with us when she's like this."

"You say that like it's a choice," Quill growled. "That's my *sister*, Tati."

"I know exactly what she *is*. I've had her knife in me, remember?"

"So, what are you suggesting? We toss her into Kaldaross and hope some unfortunate *bandayo* has the decency to take her in?" Quill lurched to his feet, scrubbing blood from the scratches marring his face. "The safest thing for everyone is if she's with *us*, you know that."

Tatiana glared at him, frustration grinding against the secret held between her teeth; she couldn't tell him why even looking at Pippet filled her with such rage unless she told him the whole truth. But she would have to break him to spare herself.

"Quill is right," Ariadne intervened before she could make that reckless, damning choice. "There is no one in the kingdoms better suited to help her while she cleanses of augments."

"Are *we* even suited for it, really?" Cistine asked.

"Kristoff was able to help Maleck through this," Thorne said. "But I don't know how. Maleck was older, stronger, and his body had developed a cadence of addiction and weaning from his visits to Stornhaz. This is different. They haven't taken their time with these children like they did back then."

Quill stepped forward, palms spread in helpless appeal. "She's still my *sister*."

For a long moment, Thorne was silent, staring down at Pippet's unconscious form; and Tatiana wondered what Quill would do if it came to choosing his sister, or following Thorne.

But Thorne spared him the conflict with a small shake of his head. "We need reinforced rope like the Chancellors used with Vandred. Tatiana, Ariadne, will you risk Kaldaross to find some?"

Ariadne nodded vigorously; Tatiana didn't bother to argue. Thorne saw how badly she was trembling, how much she needed to be away from Pippet. From Quill. From all of this. So she didn't fight when Ariadne took her elbow, guided her up, and pushed her toward the southern edge of the glade—the general direction of Kaldaross.

"Are you all right?" she murmured when they'd ducked across the treeline, out of earshot of the others.

"Not even close." Tatiana rolled the stiffness from her shoulders and fixed her gaze ahead. "Let's just find that rope before Pippet decides to rip someone else's face off."

CHAPTER EIGHT

THE NIGHT BEFORE they reached the Hunting Grounds, after days of flying across Oadmark's snowy mountain ranges, Ashe could not sleep. From the moment Bresnyar announced a change in the wind currents during their descent to yet another hoarfrosted cleft to rest, she was wide awake, aching with the weight of responsibility bearing down across her shoulders.

She tried to tell herself this was no different from helping broker the peace between Talheim and Valgard or convincing King Jad of Mahasar of that alliance before its time, but her heart refused to believe it. She hardly picked at her rations, listening to Nuna, Kristoff, and Aden speak in low tones about the war, and the northern army, and the *Aeoprast*. Whenever Ashe thought of him, her memory trailed down a different path—to a wall of ice, a cold trail, a hand around her throat—and the emptiness in her chest slashed wider.

Kosai Talis felt like a waking nightmare, a vision of blood and terror, a glimpse back into Talheim's war against Valgard...a door she'd kept tightly shut for two decades. Her throat still throbbed when she moved at the wrong angles now, skin stamped with the undeniable proof of Maleck's hatred, but heart tugged with the memory of his breath on her cheek.

Mereszar.

Fearless, in the Old Valgardan tongue, because of what she'd said to him the night before they raided Selv Torfjel: *fearless is my name.* But he hadn't cared enough to protect her from the Balmond, and those memories as much as the impending meeting with the Grand Council kept her awake long after the others snored.

Giving up on the notion of rest when the moon and stars reeled high in the sky, she crawled to Bresnyar's head, draping her arm over his brow. His sigh steamed against her armored leg. "You too, *Ilyanak?*"

"Mmhmm. What does a dragon think about when he can't sleep?"

"His Legion." Bresnyar paused, thoughtfulness in his silence. "I've told you very little about my time in Oadmark, haven't I?"

She stroked her knuckles along the divot between his brows. "I've tried not to ask. I didn't want to bring you to that place if you didn't want to go there yet."

Bresnyar's eye cracked open, fiery pupil tracking her face. "I'm grateful for your discretion. Few who are not raised around dragons would see our hearts as...tender. Capable of being wounded."

"I don't know that I'd call you *tenderhearted,*" she said, and Bresnyar's snort rolled like a chuckle this time. "But I heard you back in the Calaluns, the first time you told me about Ileria...everything you didn't want to say. So, if you're ready to tell me now, I'll listen. Or we can just watch the stars."

For a time, they were quiet, and Ashe was content to lean into Bresnyar's warmth, feeling the steady lift and fall of his ribs against her spine—a comfort on troubled nights like these.

"Did I ever mention that the wound on my tail did not come from Chancellor Salvotor?" Bresnyar asked suddenly, and Ashe shook her head. "My scales were chipped as punishment for my failure to defend Ileria. Salvotor simply continued the work where he found the weakness."

Anger trembled in Ashe's gut. "The Wingmaidens did that to you? The women we're going to ask for *help?*"

"Aeosotu did that to me," Bresnyar corrected. "Each Legion has its Head—the head drives the body. The Head Dragon directs the other dragons, the Head Wingmaiden is responsible for the lives of the

Wingmaidens under her command. Aeosotu was Head over me, so my punishment came from him."

"Who ordered it?" Another name she'd eagerly add to the list of people she needed to personally fight after this war.

"One of the Grand Council. He and Ileria were...as you and Maleck are." He quieted while the pain rocked through her, her fingers digging into the mark across her palm. "But that was forbidden, and kept secret. I alone knew the depth of it...and perhaps one other, I was never fully certain. But her lover did not hesitate to order the punishment and watch it carried down after her death."

Ashe ticked her fingers against his scaled brow. "If I wasn't going to appeal to them for the preservation of all the kingdoms—"

"You would punch a dragon in the face, yes, I know."

"Are you mocking me?"

"Hardly. I admire your tenacity." He craned his head back, forcing Ashe to drop her arm. Concern tightened the lines of his beastly face. "It worries me to think of how I will face him after all this time, but face him I must."

"Be honest with me," Ashe teased, hoping to coax a smile from him. "Is it really that, or are you just nervous about introducing them to the likes of me? Outcast, Warden, Talheimic, and not the best with making friends. Embarrassed by your left wing, Scales?"

"By you, no. But that ridiculous moniker..."

"It could be worse. Maybe when we see them tomorrow, I'll go around calling you a soft-bellied lizard."

"Oh?"

"A gold-crusted chameleon filet. Or a salmon snake."

"How lovely." Bresnyar dropped his head, half-burying her lap under his snout, and she pushed at him, chuckling.

"Whatever I decide to call you, they're going to know you're mine. They don't cross you without going through me."

Bresnyar sighed. "They may very well make you prove that vow."

"And to cross either of you, they must go through *us*."

Ashe squinted against the eye-watering darkness of a land without ghostlight or candles until Kristoff's silhouette annealed into shape beside her. "You again? Why aren't you asleep?"

"I've been wondering that myself. It was either the weeks of patrols alone near Selv Torfjel, two decades being peacekeeper and prison guard in Kalt Hasa, or the fifteen years before that listening for Aden to creep out of bed and sneak sweets at unsightly hours of the night."

Ashe snorted. "He doesn't strike me as a sweets person."

"That may be because I was terrible at stopping him before he gorged himself sick." Kristoff gestured to her and Bresnyar. "Is this a private council, or may I?"

Ashe shrugged. "It's not much of a council, more a commiseration."

"All the better." Rubbing his hands together, Kristoff lowered himself onto the rock and eased back against Bresnyar's side. "So, what are we commiserating about?"

Banding her arms loosely around her knees, Ashe shrugged. "Whether tomorrow will be a disaster or not."

"I can all but promise it will be."

"Quite the help, this one," Bresnyar snorted.

"We all know it's the truth. We are an outcast dragon, an unlikely Wingmaiden, two Valgardan warriors, and a tribeswoman appealing for the aid of the Legions. I doubt if anyone has attempted such a bold request in the history of Oadmark."

Ashe grimaced. "If that's the sort of encouragement you're bringing, I think we're better off commiserating alone."

"I wasn't finished." Kristoff flashed a smile. "What matters most isn't how bold the request—it's how bold the one making it can be. Many times, I have seen men and women with courage beyond reckoning win their way in the world by making others believe the impossible could come true."

Ashe's pulse kicked in her wrists, her fingers flexing of their own accord. "Meaning?"

"You don't have to win them over to the soundness of your request. You do not have to make them believe in your cause. You must make them believe in *you*, and then they will follow you to *any* cause."

"Oh, is that all?"

Kristoff's hand cupped her shoulder, heavy but gentle—the same as his smile. "I have faith in you. The woman who won the trust and affection of both my sons can convince a kingdom to walk at her back."

Ashe's neck heated. "I'm not like that. I'm not Cistine."

"Nor do you need to be. Cistine danced with Chancellors and won." Kristoff's eyes glinted like the stars encaging them on every side. "What we need now is the rain-dancer and beast-slayer. A woman who can dance with dragons."

The world changed rapidly when Bresnyar flew them out of the mountains just after dawn; by the first rays of light spreading from the east, curves of dark stone and rock tumbled down into black shale hills and gave way to fertile grass—a healthier land than any Ashe had seen since *Nazvaldolya* had begun to strangle Valgard.

They skimmed for hours over green meadows surrounded by dark umber hills, the landscape dotted with full and healthy trees budding in springtime life. The wind turned warmer, and Ashe rolled her shoulders into it, shutting her eyes and leaning with the motions when Bresnyar swooped and glided along familiar air currents. His joy was unspoken and girdled with the unease of what was to come, but infectious nonetheless, weaving with the confidence rising in Ashe ever since her conversation with Kristoff the night before.

She was ready for this dance, ready to bring aid to the Three Kingdoms even if she won it with saber tip and dragon's claw. Starfall and Stormfury were familiar, friendly weights between her shoulders, and Bresnyar's bond pulsed like a second heart in the center of her rune.

For her people, for Maleck's people, even for Mahasar, she could do this. And she would.

Bresnyar tucked his wings suddenly, banked swiftly upward, and carried them through a frigid cloudbank for some time; then he dropped into a spiral through the filaments of misty cover and leveled out over what could only be the Hunting Grounds.

It was clear at once why the Legions had chosen it: naturally fortified and well-watered, the steep-sided valley broke open down the middle in a broad scoop, pennant-tipped tents erected on either side of a river spilling from the tallest mountain for miles. At sunrise, the valley would hang in its shadow; but even then, it would never be fully dark. Endless color bloomed in the bodies of dragons on ledges jutting out from both sides of the valley, their hides gleaming like gems embedded in the rock—scarlet, emerald, lapis-lazuli, beryl, opal, onyx. Most were drakons like Bresnyar, four-legged and two-winged, but Ashe spotted a pair of wyverns lounging on their backs, their two feet gently kneading the air, and others with four wings like a dragonfly's. Nuna hissed a vaguely reverent Oadmarkaic word at the sight of them, and Kristoff whistled under his breath.

"Stars above," Aden marveled. "Look at them."

"I'm going to set us down now." A shudder rippled Bresnyar's scales when he swooped west, following the river's course and landing more than a mile away from the last cluster of tents.

Ashe barely had time to dismount before they had company. The shadows reached them first, then the blare of a blown horn overhead. A pattern of hair-raising roars set Ashe, Aden, and Kristoff's hands to their weapons as they looked up at the knot of scaled bodies clustering high overhead in practiced formation.

"Welcome brigade?" Ashe muttered.

"Ileria's Legion." Bresnyar's raspy tone hung heavy with resignation. "And mine."

Mottles of crimson and pearl flashed across the grass, and with ground-shaking force dragons dropped one after another around them. Bronze harnesses, bits and bridles like horses, and single-seat saddles of the softest-looking leather gleamed with polish in the daylight. It was such a tame sight, Ashe nearly laughed; but there was nothing tame about the beasts' snarls, lips peeled back, fangs bared, eyes half-mad with rage reflected in the faces of their dismounting riders.

These were the Wingmaidens of Bresnyar's tales, clad in leather armor that exposed the skin across their clavicles and inner arms and their strong calves and thighs, most with their hair short or tamed into eye-wateringly tight braids and each armed with deadly sickles, wicked daggers, and swords half the height of the women themselves.

Aden, Ashe, and Kristoff moved in unspoken tandem, swiveling and trapping Nuna between them with their backs toward one another. Ashe's heart kicked wildly against her ribs when Bresnyar curved around them, tail lashing, bellowing back at his kin. One of the women flashed up her fist, and the others froze in place.

"Meriwa," Bresnyar rumbled.

The bronze-skinned, black-haired Wingmaiden replied in rapid Oadmarkaic. Nuna translated quietly for them, "She asks him who you are and why you were sitting on his back."

Bresnyar spat something in those same quick syllables, earning a head-shaking scoff from Meriwa.

"He says this is Asheila Kovar," Nuna went on. "She is mine. The males are her kin-friends, so they are also mine. And the other woman is of the tribes."

It was to Nuna who Meriwa looked now, vicious eyes narrowing at the syllables of the common tongue on her lips. She stepped closer, and Ashe rested a hand on Starfall, elbowing Nuna back against Aden's shoulders.

"I would not suggest drawing your steel now, *Ilyanak*," Bresnyar warned. "Meriwa is the Legion Head. If you threaten her, it's any guess which will reach you first—Wingmaiden steel or dragonfire."

Ashe kept her hand on the saber, but didn't draw. "Tell her we seek an audience with the Grand Council."

Nuna translated rapidly, and Meriwa's eyes flicked to Ashe with distrust and spite so palpable it soured the air. She grated out a single harsh syllable, and Ashe needed no translation to know the woman was asking *why*.

"Tell her it has to do with the *Aeoprast*," Aden growled. "The Bloodwights."

Meriwa's head snapped toward him, brow sketched low, mouth carving down at one side. Abruptly, she fell back several steps and shouted toward the Legion. The dragons all folded off to the sides like separate wings on the same beast, and the Head Dragon stalked forward; there was no mistaking his position or his right to it. His deep scarlet hide flashed like new blood, riddled with white ropes of scar tissue and spurs of bone-sharp scale jutting from his elbows, shoulders, sides, and flanks; horns arced away from the back of his skull in symmetrical curves, one hacked shorter than the other. His talons gleamed, digging into the soil as he loomed above Bresnyar. Considering her dragon could carry the entire cabal on his back at once, Ashe found that height difference utterly terrifying.

"I told you never to return here," Aeosotu hissed in the common tongue, and Ashe's stomach coiled up with fury. "Did you really believe bringing a tribeswoman to speak our tongue would help your case?"

"I thought perhaps you would listen to one of those you're sworn to protect, if you would not listen to me."

Aeosotu's lip curled. "You disgrace the Legion by your presence and by bringing a stranger on your back."

"She is no stranger to me. And I would not have returned if the need wasn't dire."

Fire sparked in Aeosotu's nostrils when he snorted. "Why does this man make mention of the *Aeoprast*?"

"You would know if you allowed them to make their appeal."

Aeosotu cast a scornful eye over Ashe, and she let go of Starfall to fold her arms. She was here on behalf of all the kingdoms; she wouldn't shake like a weak-kneed Cadre recruit standing before her new Commander. This was her mission. She was in control.

Fearless was her name.

Aeosotu cast his attention to Meriwa next. They exchanged words in Oadmarkaic, and Nuna hissed under her breath. Ashe glanced sharply at her. "What are they saying?"

"We are saying that it is not the Legion's choice whether we hear your words," Aeosotu growled. "Your report belongs to the ears of the Grand Council." He barked toward the Wingmaidens, and they advanced. Bresnyar's tail snaked away, leaving Ashe, Aden, Kristoff, and Nuna exposed.

"Bres!" Ashe snarled.

"It's best to let this happen, *Ilyanak*. They will take us to Ujurak." He cast his fiery gaze toward the spired peak from which the river flowed. "Into the mountain."

Ashe twisted and bared her teeth when the Wingmaidens laid hands on her and Kristoff and Aden, when they took Nuna's elbows and escorted her several meters away. Then Aeosotu surged forward, his clawed hand catching Bresnyar by the neck and slamming him to the ground in a bellowing heap, and Ashe's composure shattered. Starfall and Stormfury were already in her hands, sailing toward Meriwa's neck while she screamed at the woman to call off her dragon.

Something hard connected with Ashe's temple, knocking her off her feet. Aden roared her name. Fire painted the sky.

Ashe's world went dark.

CHAPTER NINE

IT SHOULD HAVE died.

Should have, but there was life, new, bright fresh real *powerful* surging in its veins, with the wind, and the lightning and the fire and the

Blood. On its hands.

Not its own.

A quiet man wandering the trees a guard with music humming on his hips it had just meant to take one just to mend just to feel just to *live*. Now there were three and there was blood but not its own. It should have died but here it was with empty hands and power and the flagon screaming in its pocket its chest its empty heart but

Not yet.

Not yet.

It could hear them whispering could hear the threats curdling the air, had followed them south and now here it was crouched in the vee of the trees watching. Watching everything below while every scent every sight every sound was danger and screaming and *please don't do this* and *let go of my children* and blood and fire ripping through its ribs.

It shouldn't be here.

And yet.

There were people below, men and women and *children* so many

59

children just like it like *her* like the bird it had left in the shadow of the wall with the woman, the woman with the power, the healing, that—

Yarrow.

Broken knuckles a bleeding ear damp eyes fixed on his face asking a silent, desperate question it did not know the answer to after the sewers after the grate with her sword lashed to his back, *is she alive is she alive is she*—

Mereszar.

It pressed a hand to its temple and shook its head and sound flooded back in, the screams from below, the men and women fighting and grasping for their children while they were dragged away by men, by augurs, by *mirothadt*—

No one had fought for it. No one had grasped for it. Except, maybe...

I love you, Allet. *Look at me—look at me, Mal! Don't go back to them. This is your home, we're your family*—

Family.

Family.

Down below tall columns of smoke came together and smoke, fire, darkness and air, and its brothers its family but not its true family stepped from the places between places and surrounded these people these Valgardans these *victims.*

"Which of you wants to be our messenger?"

It recoiled at its brother's voice, the leader, the young god, *Aeoprast,* pain flaring against its ribs in specter slashes, but one of the men sobbed and raised both arms in supplication and the *mirothadt* freed him and forced him forward. The *Aeoprast* caught him and it could taste that stinking, savage breath like being chest-to-chest again, like fighting for its life, her life, all their lives—

"Run all the way to the lines and tell everyone you meet along the way that this is what will happen to each and every village we find with man, woman, or child left in it," the *Aeoprast* hissed, "every last one, until the Key surrenders herself to us."

"The Key," the man gasped, "the Key is only a legend—"

His body burst into rain into mist into blood and its brother looked at the weeping survivors spattered in gore and praying to the gods the real gods the true and good ones. "I asked for a messenger."

A woman went this time and she did not weep, her face like flint her eyes like stone and it could feel her strength and remembered

Eyes blue and green and a set jaw and a storm in her face—

I am not afraid of you.

"Tell them what will happen to every village in every territory until she gives herself up at the gates of Stornhaz, beginning with this one," the *Aeoprast* seethed. "Beginning with every settlement in Blaykrone."

Forests and rivers and valleys, the Throat of God, the lake, the collapsing roofs and screams and the silver-haired man reaching always to the Blood Crown to shelter it with his bare hands his broken heart his blades—

Blaykrone. His territory.

Its territory.

The woman was gone like smoke like vapor and the *Aeoprast* nodded to its acolytes its followers and then all at once they were gone, the Bloodwights were gone and the pain in its side dimmed.

One *mirothadt* laughed, *laughed* when she drew her blades and spun them. "Just like the Hive."

That voice, that face—

Dinners and dreams around the supper table and the dancer with a wide smile and starlit eyes. Flame and blood and swords flashing as she took one head, two heads, three—

Blaykrone heads.

Its people.

It burst down from the trees and landed so hard it cracked the cold ground like glass, and the people screamed, villagers and acolytes and someone started to pray in loud sobs *not another one not another one oh stars please oh gods helps us please, please—*

"You." The dancer gaped at it, no stars in her eyes now, only hate. "*You should be dead.*"

Should be. But it wasn't.

And maybe this was why.

Power roiled in its palms in its chest in its heart and it looked at the people and breathed, maybe only thought it, *You are not afraid of me.*

A child stopped crying and stared at it.

And with these villagers these people with all of Blaykrone watching, it set its brothers' ranks on fire.

CHAPTER TEN

"ASHEILA. COME BACK."

She didn't want to. Her head pulsed, a looming center of agony on her left temple pushing out malignant fingers across her jaw, down into her ear canal, and across her forehead. But she'd been asleep for too long, dreaming of fire and skulls and screaming people, and that voice came with a gentle hand on her brow, reeling her back to wakefulness.

She squinted her eyes open and found it was mercifully dark, wherever she was. Kristoff's crossed legs shifted under her head resting in his lap.

"Do me a favor, will you?" Ashe groaned. "The next time someone knocks me unconscious and throws me in a prison, just let me die. Put me out of my misery."

He chuckled quietly. "I take it this is a habit of yours."

"Not by choice. It seems I have a very capturable essence."

"That makes us quite the pair, doesn't it?" When she groaned and pressed a hand over her eyes, Kristoff snatched her wrist, steering her fingers away from the wound on her temple. "Don't touch that."

"Cudgel?"

"Yes."

"How long have I been—?"

"A little more than a day."

"Gods, those Wingmaidens hit hard," Ashe muttered. "Aden?"

"Searching for a way out, though I've told him a hundred times already there isn't one. We're inside Ujurak, the Council's dwelling place, home of the dragons. These cells are impenetrable from within."

"Aren't we lucky," Ashe muttered. "What about Nuna?"

"Not with us. She may be pleading our case before the Grand Council."

Ashe twisted her head to take stock of their surroundings: plain, dark rock, cold against her back and thighs, and iron poles fitted into the maw of the stone—too close together for an arm to slip through. The only door latched from the outside, striped in light too warm for ghostplants.

A tall, dark shape cut across the glow, and Aden crouched, his hand on her shoulder. "You're all right?"

"Not really." She let her eyes tumble shut again. "This feels too much like the catacombs."

"I agree." His hand smoothed her brow, and when she moaned in relief at the clamminess of his palm, he left it there. "All of our best times: captured, imprisoned, locked away together."

Ashe winced. "I'm assuming they took Starfall and Stormfury."

"Yes." A vein of rage crept into Aden's voice.

"Bresnyar?"

"Alive, though I don't know where he is. He took a blow to the face trying to reach you. So we match, I suppose."

At this angle, she couldn't see any injuries on his face, but maybe he'd positioned himself in the shadows just to keep that from her. "How bad?"

"Not terrible enough to keep me from repaying them when the time comes."

"Both of you, enough," Kristoff interrupted. "Your pride will be the death of our cause. Is this treatment cruel? Yes. But we show ourselves worthy allies if we take the path of peace, not retribution. We won't let them provoke us."

Aden cursed under his breath. "I'm not used to turning my back on someone who's already proven they'll shove a knife into it."

"We landed in their Hunting Grounds on the back of an exile and entreated their highest rank without invitation. They're likely to feel the knife was in *our* hand."

"I hate to admit you have a point," Ashe muttered, "but if I was standing where Meriwa was, I would've knocked me unconscious, too."

Aden was quiet for a moment. "This hunt is yours."

As if summoned to the challenge in that, the tread of boots echoed from the walls. Ashe had lived and fought with enough warriors to know the sound of one approaching, a stride full of singular purpose. She pushed herself up from Kristoff's hold, and he took her shoulder. "Careful."

"This isn't the time for that."

Aden muttered something about stubborn Talheimics, but he hooked his broad hands under her biceps and towed her to her feet. She was grateful for the merciful darkness shielding her head from spinning when she shuffled to the iron bars. Meriwa met her there, a shadow slinking out of shadows, dressed in a filigreed black cloak with tassels strung from the neck that might denote rank in this place. She halted before the cage, laying back her hood, revealing her dark hair cropped to the strong line of her jaw and those amber eyes flashing in the strange firelight. There was a shallow cut on the side of her neck, angry red. The sight pricked Ashe with pride.

Meriwa folded her hands in the small of her back and regarded Ashe with the same kind of scornful scrutiny she'd endured from her parents' friends and the other Wardens when she'd returned from the war against Valgard. And perhaps it was the blow to the head dulling the edge of her wits, but she really didn't care.

"How's your neck?" she drawled.

Meriwa's eyes narrowed. "You are not Oadmarkaic. Why did Bresnyar choose you?"

Ashe arched a brow. "You speak the common tongue? Interesting. Nunajik made that sound rare, especially this far north. Who taught you?"

"Answer the rutting question: why did Bresnyar choose you?"

"He's the eloquent one. Why don't you ask him?"

"I can't. He's currently reuniting with his old Legion."

Ashe gripped the iron bars so hard, her knuckles throbbed. "If any of those gods-damned lizards lays a claw on him, I'll slice their throats open."

Kristoff sighed heavily.

"He is not yours to defend," Meriwa said. "He was Ileria's."

"And Ileria died. Bresnyar was held captive for years in a mountain prison just like this one until my friends set him free. And where was his *Legion*? You were content to let him rot in the darkness and go mad. You didn't give a *damn* who chose him or who he chose back then, so you don't have any claim to him now."

"And you believe you do?"

"You're damned right I do." Ashe leaned into the bars. "I'm a former Talheimic Warden who's going to chop off your head if anything happens to my right wing. Do you understand me?"

"*Asheila*," Kristoff murmured.

She forced herself to breathe deeply, to loosen her fingers from around the bars. "Will you at least tell him I'm all right?"

Meriwa raised a brow. "Tell him yourself. Do you not have a starstone?"

"I left it with my cabal."

"How very convenient. A Wingmaiden cannot communicate with her dragon if she has no starstone. It is the true mark of their bond. And you just happened to leave yours in your land?"

"You want a mark of our bond?" Ashe ripped off her glove, baring her palm in the light.

Meriwa studied the rune, face unmoved. "You could have easily branded yourself with that mark."

Ashe dropped her hand, studying the woman's cold countenance. "You like to have an answer for everything, don't you? Then why don't you try to explain the cleaving, if we're not really bonded?"

"Cleaving? I know no such word."

"Seeing through my dragon's eyes."

Meriwa scoffed. "Impossible. That takes decades to perfect."

"And yet, he and I can do it after a few months together." Ashe folded her arms and slouched her shoulder to the stone wall. "I suppose our bond is *just* that strong."

Meriwa's glare deepened, but behind it the first chink appeared in her furious armor—a flicker of doubt. "I will tell you the state of him if you tell me why he chose you."

"Why does it matter? You really think no one but you Oadmarkaics are worthy of dragon-riding?"

"Ileria was part of my Legion," Meriwa spat. "For her dragon to have chosen a foreigner is not only unheard of, it reflects shamefully on me."

"You're the ones who drove him out knowing he'd go mad without the Wingmaiden bond. You might say I saved his life."

"That is impossible. Bresnyar was doomed after Ileria's death. He was too old to bond with another Wingmaiden. They must be raised side by side, as he and Ileria were. Otherwise they will kill one another."

Ashe tipped her head. "That's why you don't like me: because if Bresnyar and I *are* bonded, then that means you were wrong. You left him to die without even trying to save him. How would Ileria feel about that?"

Meriwa's glare darkened so suddenly that Aden stepped forward and laid a hand on Ashe's shoulder. "You are a charlatan," Meriwa snarled. "Aeosotu will learn the truth of how you encharmed Bresnyar. And then you will lose your hands for having laid them on a dragon."

"Let's see what song Bres sings before you start passing judgement," Ashe gloated. "The gods brought us together because they don't care about your traditions and rituals—we were meant to fly together. That's why they chose us. And why we chose each other."

Meriwa's hands fell from their stern latch. Her shoulders bristled and her fingers strangled the bars. "Ileria was unforgettable. That he could discard her memory for a Talheimic slattern..."

Aden slammed his flat palm into the bars so abruptly, Meriwa jerked her head back. "Be very careful how you speak of my friend. These bars won't hold us forever."

Ashe propped her elbow on Aden's shoulder. "Why don't we take a more civilized approach? I'm not here to upset your way of life. I don't want anything to do with your Legion, except I think your dragons may be the only hope the kingdoms have."

Meriwa's eyes narrowed. "Why?"

"I suppose you'll have to convince your Grand Council to let us out of here if you want to know the answer to that." Ashe turned and stalked back to the recesses of the cell, not because she lacked things to say, but because dizziness was beginning to take its toll. She planted her hands against the wall and waited to hear Meriwa's retreat before she let her knees buckle; Kristoff's hand looped around her elbow at once, and with Aden beside him, they all settled on the floor.

"I'm surprised you didn't divulge everything to her," Aden remarked blandly, "just to see her hackles rise."

"She already despises me on principle," Ashe grunted. "Better to present my case to the entire Council rather than giving one person the power to twist my words and pit all the Legions against us."

Kristoff chuckled. "You're as skilled a negotiator as you are a warrior."

"Was that a compliment or an insult?"

He rested his hand on the back of her head. "If I thought you were doing a poor job, I would have intervened. But it's clear Meriwa cared for Ileria, so you have far more to prove than just your bond with Bresnyar. There's a measure of worthiness in Meriwa's eyes that you will have to meet."

"Wonderful news," Ashe muttered.

Kristoff's thumb circled the back of her head with light, steady pressure. "Today you showed that you aren't content to be measured against Ileria. You gave her something to think about. And *that* was negotiation."

Aden snorted quietly. "A true liaison."

Ashe smirked, eyes tumbling shut. Their quiet faith eased the panic of knowing that their waiting had barely begun.

And all the while, war ravaged the northern kingdom.

CHAPTER ELEVEN

THE DISBELIEF AND despair of Pippet's return haunted the cabal for days. They left off their hunt for Maleck, pulling back into the mountains, finding a defensible cave where they could shelter and regroup—and *think*.

Cistine's thoughts were a calamity between Maleck and Pippet. Sleepless nights brought her back to the streamside again and again, to the stir of a wind augment in her palm and the sight of Maleck's blood freckling the leaves.

How badly was he hurt? Would he die without help? Had she chosen to save Pippet, furious and cruel, over Maleck, who came to her for aid? Was saving Pippet his final penance?

Day after day, she reached out desperately for the sense of him, but it never flickered again. The third day, it drove her from the cave before dawn, Pippet's restless mutterings the quiet backdrop while she pulled on her boots and padded to the cave mouth where Ariadne sat, legs bent beneath her, head bowed in prayer.

Cistine squeezed her shoulder in passing. "I'm going for a walk."

"Searching for a trace of Maleck, you mean?"

Her fingers fell, and her friend's face twisted up toward her, gaze full of sorrow.

"I can't even find the words to pray anymore," Ariadne murmured. "It's all just his name and pleading. I don't even know what to hope for."

"Neither do I," Cistine admitted. "But I can't give up. I promised him."

Ariadne squeezed her hand gently. "Whatever of Maleck remains in him, he will be thankful you honored that promise."

The wind froze the tears on Cistine's cheeks when she started away from the cave. Breathing came easier once she was free from Pippet's malicious presence and the weight of worry and grief shrouding the others. Nature didn't seem quite as out of balance here, a thin layer of snow curbing the rock and dotting the hardy pines. The path looped lazily for more than a mile around the mountain's face, and she took every stride gladly, even the treacherous, slippery pockets.

This bit of the world made sense to her. Nature, gardens, things untouched by *Nazvaldolya*. Just like patrols and berry bushes and the music of the world, the Throat of God and the names of swords...

She slammed to a halt, legs tingling from the miles of walking, heart thudding in her ears. She faced a steep incline, the mountain to her right and another knot of trees thick on her left, the path dropping steeply before her toes. The Vaszaj Range spread out below, the Izten Torkat out there somewhere, the Muunvat River, and all the memories they contained.

Desperate, she cupped her hands to her mouth and leaned into the scream: "*Maleck, where are you?*"

Where are you? Where are you? The echo rippled back to her, but the mountains swallowed his name—a man the world already forgot.

Tears tracked down her cheeks, her arms swinging limp at her sides. "Where *are* you?"

"You shouldn't scream in the mountains, you know. Avalanches are a very real danger here."

The familiar, smooth voice made Cistine's heart leap with surprise—then crash with dread. It shouldn't be here. *He* shouldn't be here.

She whirled toward the treeline where two cloaked men parted from the shadows, knocking down their hoods. One, bearded and scowling and pale, the other brown-skinned and curly-haired, the most solemn she'd ever seen him.

Chancellor Bravis and Sander.

Cistine gathered her limbs close, backing away from them. "How...how did you know where to find me?"

"A certain note, carried by a familiar raven. It came to our camp and we followed it back to its perch." A note of sympathy touched Bravis's voice. "It's truly a wonder Thorne managed to evade his father for ten years with practices like that."

Cistine's teeth snapped together. "At least his father was the enemy he could see coming. He wasn't anticipating a *betrayal.*"

Sander's stride hitched, eyes flashing wide for an instant. Then his lazy grin returned. "Come, Princess. Surely you know by now we want the same thing. What's *best* for our kingdoms."

His gaze narrowed, tone silky. He'd only spoken to her like that once before, a day of blood and steel, horseflesh and lightning.

Cistine held his stare while she kept retreating, Chancellor and High Tribune closing in on her, her mind racing. The mountain behind her, the trees on every side, and the precious augments humming on her hips, begging to be broken and used.

Not just on *her* hips, either.

Her focus dropped to Sander's augment pouch, thoughts stumbling in their haste.

Was it possible—could even he be so gods-forsaken *brash*—

"I know you believe that fleeing is the right answer." Bravis flashed both palms, his grandfatherly face a betrayal, a lie in itself with the next words that fell from his lips. "But no one life is worth the thousands we would save if we opened a Door with your blood."

Fury twisted Cistine's lips in a mocking smirk. "You have it all figured out, don't you? Well, you thought it through faster than *Salvotor*, at least."

Bravis ignored that remark. "I watched you treat for Talheim's salvation, Princess. You are not a selfish woman."

Hysterical laughter bubbled in her throat. "You're right, I'm not! But I'm not your sacrifice, either."

"Try to understand, Cistine," Sander said. "Coming with us would be preferable to all this running, hm? Don't you want to save the kingdoms?"

Her back struck rock, and she faltered, staring at him.

What if he was right? She could stop training, stop fighting to be strong. No more of Pippet's cruelty, no more chasing the wind on Maleck's heels. It would be so much easier to let them take her; to lie down and be done with it.

No! Her mind roared so fiercely her spine lifted up from the mountainside. *No, no, no!*

She was the Wild Heart of Fire, Talheim's sole heir. She'd chosen this path for herself; no one, not even the Chancellors, would keep her from meeting her destiny on the battlefield of *her* choosing.

"I *am* saving the kingdoms."

Her hands fell to her augment pouch. Bravis tensed. From the treeline, the familiar creak of tautened bowstrings stroked against Cistine's ears.

Sander flashed out an arm, warning the Chancellor back. "Perhaps you ought to leave this to me, hm?"

Bravis looked between them, then fell back several paces, hands turned awkwardly back toward the trees—a silent signal waiting to fall. Cistine rolled the lightning augment in the curve of her palm, regarding Sander warily as he approached. His usual swagger was fixed in place, masking his true intentions. Was he coming close enough to snatch her up, or was there some other secret lurking in those mischievous, tawny eyes?

"If you come quietly," he murmured, "I'll ensure no one in the cabal faces a hint of trouble for aiding your escape. The Judgement Seat will be Thorne's again. Everything can go back precisely how it was. Isn't that what you want for them?"

"You know *nothing* of what I want," she hissed, holding her ground—reeling him in closer. Playing his game.

"Don't take me for a fool. You and Thorne haven't exactly been subtle, you know." He was close enough she could smell the spice on his clothes, obnoxiously present despite the hard life he led now as Chancellor in Thorne's stead, fighting on the front lines. "It's up to you to save them."

He entered her breathing space, and when she swung a punch at his cheek, he caught it deftly, pinning her arm against the stone above her head. His body wedged hers in place, heavy with muscle, quivering for battle.

"Twenty archers in the trees," he breathed. "Fire, water, and wind in my satchel. Just make it look like I tried to stop you."

She locked eyes with his, light dancing playfully in their amber depths. "Let's give them a show, Princess."

A wild grin yanked across Cistine's face. She crushed the lightning flagon in one hand, and with the other, ripped Sander's pouch from his side.

The clasp popped. His hand dipped inside, withdrawing the fire augment and shattering it, and with a shrieking flare their powers screamed across the rock, blowing them away from each other. Cistine slid the other flagons deftly into her pouch as she twisted away from Sander's onslaught and sent another burst of lightning to counter.

Bravis howled, diving for cover, and Cistine divided her focus this time; a cut of lightning from one hand toward the trees, blinding the archers, another shrieking toward the armored High Tribune.

His fire roared into place, blocking her blow. Whips of flame twisted with the tines of lightning, pushing against each other like furious wind currents, the pressure bearing Cistine back down the rock, heels skidding. She slammed a hand down to slow her descent, lightning cracking across the ground and blasting Bravis and Sander off their feet back toward the verge of pines.

Bowstrings twanged. An arrow shredded a strip of Cistine's armor— meant to cripple, not to kill. Of course. They'd never bleed her out anywhere but on a Door.

Gritting her teeth against the white-hot strip of pain, Cistine straightened. Blood leaked down her arm and lightning sizzled in her fingertips. Rage smoldered in her chest.

"If you would just *trust* me!" she shouted. "I'm not running—I'm trying to help!"

"You know nothing of war, and you are not Valgardan! You've proven where your concerns lie when you abandoned us to save your own kingdom!" Bravis punctuated the words with a sharp whistle, and the next volley of arrows screamed toward her.

Lightning broke wood. Cistine whirled on Sander when he swept up at her back, dissolving into a barrage of blows almost too quick to track. His masquerade of lovers had taught him well; as deadly with an augment as with a blade, he backed her closer to the mountainside, his fire burning up the cold air quicker than she could draw it in.

He slammed her against the rock again, a hand fisted in her collar. "You're meant to be better than this, you know. Now what?"

She caught his wrist in both hands. "Now *this*."

Reaching back into that chaotic place that was slowly beginning to feel natural and true, as much a part of her as the crown or her hard-won strength, she seized the augment from Sander—and *yanked*.

The breath came out of him along with the fire; unlike Thorne and Vandred, he didn't resist her at all. The augment snapped from his body into hers, and he crumbled at her feet. Behind him, Bravis recoiled; the archers at the treeline hesitated, coiled and primed but frozen.

Trembling with exertion, the inside of her nostrils searing, Cistine fumbled in Sander's pouch and withdrew the wind augment. "If you want to save Valgard," she panted, "*stop hunting me*. Let me do this. It's the only way we all survive."

Sander clutched his chest, gazing up at her with true shock in his eyes. But Bravis's jaw was already set, his hand rising to signal the archers.

Cistine shattered the wind augment, wrapped it around herself with the fire, and then she was gone—soaring back up and around the mountain toward their hidden camp, arrows catching fire and burning in her wake.

The journey was over in a heartbeat, though to her trembling limbs it felt longer. She landed gracelessly, spilling onto the path above the cave and rolling wildly down it. At the last instant, she remembered to dispatch the fire and wind, keeping them from Pippet.

Emptied, overtaxed, she curled on her side, clutching her bleeding arm. With the augments gone, it hurt worse, a mounting anguish with every throb of her heart.

Shouts. Footsteps. Knees struck the path, and Thorne's hands took her arm gently, above and below the gash.

"Ari, water and bandages!" he barked.

Cistine pulled her head up when a shadow fell across her face; Quill crouched before her, supporting her cheek with his three-fingered hand, the icy prosthetic mercifully gone for once. "What *happened*, Stranger?"

"Where did that wind augment come from?" Tatiana demanded behind him. "Who were you fighting? We could hear it all the way across the mountain!"

"Sander," Cistine panted.

"Sand—" Quill cut himself off, lurching to his feet. "No, that's it. That's it, I'm killing him this time."

"Slow down, Featherbrain!" Tatiana backed up in his path, gripping his biceps. "Breathe! Cistine?"

"They tracked us, the note we sent with Faer..."

Quill's back stiffened. He swung around to face her again. "Sander's with them now?"

"No," Thorne said. "He wouldn't be." He took Cistine's chin, turning her face toward him, his other hand tight around her bleeding arm. "He helped you escape?"

She nodded. "We staged a fight. It was the only way Bravis wouldn't blame him for this."

Quill shook his head, sinking back down on the path. "I'm so stars-damned tired of this."

Ariadne returned, water flask and bandages in hand, and Thorne peeled his fingers from Cistine's sleeve to let her work. She moved with quick efficiency, her gaze never leaving Cistine's arm, but a crease seamed her brows. "They're far too close. We can't stay here."

"But moving is hard." Quill's gaze darted back toward the cave. "If we just give it the night..."

Thorne shook his head. "We move back down into the trees tonight and hope no one tracks us. We'll do Pippet no favors being caught in this state by the Chancellors either, Quill."

His jaw shifted furiously, but he nodded after a moment and stepped into the cave to gather his sister.

Cistine leaned her head back against the dip of Thorne's shoulder while Ariadne knotted the bandage. His hand covered her brow, and he kissed her ear. "How do you feel?"

"Sore. Tired." A smile wobbled across her face. "I pulled out Sander's fire augment."

A chuckle rippled through his chest. "I wish I could've seen his face."

"He looked like you did, when…" The words died in her throat, the memory of that sunny grove and their fight over the lightning augment cutting across her mind.

What if she'd truly hurt Sander? What if he wasn't just surprised, but wounded? What did he see when he looked at her—what did *Bravis* see?

She swallowed, turning her cheek over Thorne's beating heart.

Her work finished, Ariadne squeezed Cistine's knee and got to her feet. Silently, she and Tatiana followed Quill to retrieve their belongings. After a moment, Thorne pulled Cistine up as well. "We should go. I'll get your things. You rest."

She flashed him a grateful smile and stood gazing back over the trailside while the others conversed in low voices at the cave mouth. A moment later, Quill approached, Pippet in tow. She didn't struggle for once, eyes fixed hungrily on the bandage wrapping Cistine's arm.

"All that blood," she breathed. "What a waste. You should be bleeding on a Door."

"If I ever am," Cistine said, "it's going to be on my terms."

Pippet's lip curled. "I hope you get it over with soon. Then I can have all the augments I'll ever need."

"That's enough," Quill said tiredly. His eyes found Cistine's, bright with apology. "I'm hoping she gets better once we're moving."

Cistine swallowed the knot in her throat. "I hope so, too."

CHAPTER TWELVE

Pippet DID NOT improve as they traveled. Perhaps it was cruel of her, but when Tatiana woke to the sound of Quill's sister sobbing in rage, writhing against her bonds while they made camp among the trees, begging and crying and threatening their lives for the augments they carried, she did not go to her. She lay awake, listening to the same voice whose sobs she'd quieted and fears she'd rocked back to sleep for eleven years shrieking like a fisher-cat in the dark, and did not move a finger to comfort her.

Not the first night, when she gnashed and flopped in the undergrowth like a fish; not the second, when she seemed determined to keep them all awake with formless shrieks and pained groans. Not the third or the fourth, when she spewed the same horrible insults and threats all night as during the day, then changed tactics to theatrical sobbing, claiming her bonds were too tight, *begging* them to stop hurting her.

Tatiana was awake for every second of it, and did not move an inch.

"I don't care if this makes me a horrible person," she muttered to Cistine while they built a fire and gathered sticks to skewer meat the fifth day after the attack from Bravis and Sander. Ariadne and Thorne had vanished to hunt, and Quill was some distance away with his sister, keeping watch over her, Faer their constant guard in the trees above. "I just can't face her yet."

"You don't have to," Cistine said. "But sooner or later the others are going to wonder why. You've always treated Pippet like your own sister, now you can barely look at her."

"She stabbed me." Tatiana snapped a stick over her knee for smaller skewers. "That ought to be enough."

"And it is." Cistine squeezed her shoulder. "But Quill especially knows better, he knows exactly how you hold a grudge. Eventually..."

Undergrowth crunched, and Tatiana silenced the princess with a hand over her mouth when Thorne and Ariadne materialized between the trees, holding a brace of hares each.

"Quill and Pippet?" Ariadne asked by way of greeting.

Tatiana gave a chin nod over her shoulder. "She needed to do her business. Quill was afraid she'd run."

"So am I." Thorne dropped his catch and kissed Cistine's head in passing. "I tried to talk to her this morning before we broke camp. She threatened to finish what my father began with me back in Stornhaz if I didn't leave her alone."

Guilt bladed Tatiana's chest. Her reasons for not wanting to help with Pippet were sound, she had no qualms about that. But while she avoided her, the rest of their cabal shouldered longer watches and more abuse than they ought to. And what greater vengeance could there be against the Bloodwights than to turn back the blade they'd made of Pippet and angle it against them instead?

Determination, frail and tired, sizzled in her spirit when the second set of footfalls announced Quill and Pippet's return. She forced herself to turn away from the fire and *watch* the girl who'd stabbed her march into their camp, bound and scowling, her mottled brown-and-black hair a filthy bird's nest, limbs coiled as if to flee at any moment. Judging by her skinned knees and dirt-pocked skin and the frown carving between her brother's eyes, perhaps she'd already attempted it.

Try, Tatiana chastened herself. *Just try.*

"You know, my offer still stands, Pip." The cheery drawl rang false in her ears and tasted bitter between her teeth. "I have some spare clothes whenever you want to get out of those filthy rags."

Quill's narrow gaze leaped to her, and she held his stare unflinchingly. Changing out of those armored threads would require Pippet to release the last of the augments she held, thin filaments so weak Cistine could hardly sense them anymore. She didn't have the strength and training to hold onto them forever—but the power nesting within her was another matter entirely. They hadn't sorted out yet how to address that without the shock of withdrawal slowly killing her. But if they could just do something about the augments that forced them to keep her bound, maybe it would move them all toward reconciliation.

But there was still only hate in Pippet's eyes. "The only thing I want from *any* of you is to watch you *bleed*. Then I want you to let me *go*!"

"Well, that's not happening." Quill gripped her by the shoulder and shoved her to her seat in the foliage. "So get used to rags, Hatchling."

"Don't call me that. Why do we always keep walking? What's in the south that's *so* important?" A beat of blessed silence. Then, "You're chasing *him*, aren't you? The one who stole me?"

Cistine and Thorne exchanged a weighted glance. They'd all hoped Pippet wouldn't notice how they'd changed tack two days ago, following a subtle but pointed shift in Maleck's bearing.

"He didn't steal you," Quill growled. "He brought you home."

"I'm not home, I'm a stars-damned prisoner." Pippet flexed against her bonds. "Just like I was in Starhollow, just like you all *want* me. You never loved me, I'm just a *pet*."

"That's not true, Pip," Cistine said.

The girl's feral gaze speared into her. "You can't help him, you know. You can't help *anyone*. You're not a threat, you're just a nuisance. That's why they're not here, that's why they haven't stopped you already...because you're a flea on their backs, they could crush you any time they want."

"All right, that's enough." Quill gave his sister's bonds a hard yank. "If you're going to champion the Bloodwights, you can do it with a gag in your mouth."

Pippet twisted to sneer up at him. "That's how you always wanted me, perfect and pretty and *silent*, so you didn't have to think about me while you were having adventures. At least *they* let me be free. I was more at home with them than I ever was with *you*."

The look on Quill's face, torment drilling straight to the heart, pushed Tatiana to her feet before she'd considered what she was doing. Her fingers, flexing wildly, wanted to form a fist and punch Pippet across the face. She tempered that violence with two deep breaths and whistled Faer down from the trees to her shoulder.

"It wasn't all bad, Pip. What about this one, hm?" Hope dashed through her when Pippet's gaze revolved slowly from her brother to Tatiana and the raven perched on her arm. "You remember sending him to us when he was hurt in Stornhaz? That was one of the bravest things you've ever done." The words were saccharine, the cadence all wrong, but stars help her, she was trying to buy a moment for Quill to wipe his expression clean, to not show his sister how deeply she'd pierced his armor with that last remark.

Pippet regarded Tatiana and Faer warily as they approached, her gaze lingering longest on the glossy black raven, drinking him in with a tilted head like a figment of some long-forgotten dream. Then she said, slow and raspy, "Bring that thing over here and I'll snap its little neck."

Tatiana froze. Cistine sucked in a harsh breath.

"Don't treat me like that girl from the hollow," she added in that same vicious tone. "She only cared about birds and dresses and playtime. She was weak, and I killed her. *We* killed her together, and I'm *glad* we did."

Tatiana trembled, sorrow and rage slapping against her insides like storm-churned surf. Quill's hand covered his mouth—stars only knew what he was keeping in.

"That girl is gone, I'm here now, and I remember *everything*," Pippet snarled. "I remember sending the bird out and I remember *him* bleeding in the hall and I remember every second after. You never looked for me and you never should've found me. I wasn't *happy* with you, I was happy with *them*! I want to go back, I want to go home to Selv Torfjel with my friends!"

"You aren't going back." Thorne's tone was a Chancellor's now, steady and frank—a wall for Pippet's cruelty to break against. "They will never lay a hand on you again."

She studied him with predatory stillness, a creature sizing up a rival. "We'll see about that. You weren't so sure after Selv Torfjel, were you?"

Fury rattled Tatiana's limbs, and she turned away from the girl, stalked back toward the fire, toward busywork, toward something she could bury her hands in.

"Did it die, *Tati?*"

She halted, the breath punched out of her.

"I could hear it, you know," Pippet went on, her voice cruel and low. "That heartbeat *racing*, like a little bird trapped inside you. Did it die when I stabbed—"

The crack of bone on bone echoed through the clearing when Tatiana lunged back and slapped Pippet straight across the mouth.

Ariadne shouted her name—in warning, not in outrage—and Quill hurled an arm around her waist and swung her away when Pippet's head snapped back around, teeth closing over the strap of Tatiana's augment pouch. The seam ripped and separated, but Quill caught the beaded leather with his free hand, tore it from her grasp, and pushed his sister over with one foot. Ariadne landed on her, pinning her with an arm across her throat. The impact knocked a yelp from between Pippet's teeth, and Tatiana didn't care for once; she hoped it *hurt*, she hoped Pippet was feeling a shard of the pain that dug into her own heart.

Quill yanked her around to face him. "What in Nimmus was that?"

Hot rage slashed her composure to ribbons, and she shoved him back a step. "Don't you *dare* yell at me, that *thing* is not Pippet, it's not our sister!"

"*No!*" Quill roared. "The heartbeat! What did she mean about a *heartbeat?*"

Everyone fell silent but Pippet, who managed, even with Ariadne's arm blocking her windpipe, a demented giggle.

Tatiana stared at Quill, chest heaving but no words escaping.

The arm holding her augment pouch sagged. Shock, then horror, lit through his eyes. "No."

A prickle of sorrow pierced her hate. "Quill, I'm sorry."

"*No*," he repeated, as if by one word he could erase the loss as quickly and finally as Pippet had ended that small life growing in Tatiana's womb. "There wasn't—Tati? Tell me you weren't—"

He couldn't bring himself to say it any more than she could.

His face blurred before her eyes. "Nightwing."

He took a step back when she reached out to him, the color, the shock, even the horror draining from his face, and in their place...devastation. He'd looked further from death when he'd fought for every breath on an Oadmarkaic lakeshore.

He slung the pouch into her hands and was gone, a blur racing away into the trees. Thorne and Ariadne stared after him, then looked to Tatiana, the weight of their heartbroken faces utterly choking her.

"Tati," Ariadne breathed, "oh, *Dawnstar*..."

Thorne said nothing, but came to her, his hand enfolding the back of her head and drawing her into his chest. She could've wept there—knew he was allowing for it—but she'd already shed so many tears for this loss, for the child she would never hold or rock or raise. This grief was not new to her. But to Quill...

Cistine's hand landed on her shoulder, drawing her from Thorne's grip and taking the pouch. "Go after him."

Tatiana dragged her gaze to the princess; then to Thorne, hands now flattening his hair from his brow, shock and sorrow ripping through his eyes. And Ariadne...she could not bear to look at her *Malatanda*, or at the creature pinned beneath her, who'd wielded her greatest weapon with all the precision of a seasoned warrior straight into Tatiana's heart. And into Quill's.

Biting back a curse, she bolted from the campsite.

Quill was not difficult to follow; for her, he never was. From lectures he'd crept out of, from the window of his Tribune father's apartment, all the way to Detlyse Halet and halfway to the Sable Gates. That throbbing bond brought her straight to him on one of the higher points of the Vaszaj foothills, rolling between stern, dark peaks and the expanse of Stedgnalt

Lake. He paced, twirling a cinnamon stick over his knuckles, gaze casting erratically between the distant horizon and the rock beneath his feet. The view would've been breathtaking, the world at their feet, the lake gobbling the horizon, and him painted against it, glorious and powerful and beloved, if not for the circumstances. If not for her heart trying with all its might to shatter no matter how fiercely she held it together.

Quill halted at her arrival, cinnamon stick jutting between one knuckle and the next. Wind-stirred and silent, they stared at one another. His mouth jerked, a pitiful attempt at a smile. "I was going to be a father."

She stepped onto the ledge. "You *are* a father. That hasn't changed."

"Right. But there's not going to be a baby. Because of..."

The smile wobbled, his eyes fluttering shut. He shook his head and turned away to look across a world stricken by war, this small slice a mere reflection that their own world, everything they held dear, was as broken as the rest of it.

Tatiana came to stand at Quill's side, not daring to touch him or break the dam of silence, not daring to release the unspoken understanding built up so deep and dark behind it, it could drown them both.

"How far?" Quill murmured at last.

"Six weeks, maybe a bit less. After Braggos..."

"I remember." That night of desperate passion tangled up in one another's arms when the panic of death's nearness had chased out any concern for safety, for herbs, for an unpromised tomorrow. "That's why you couldn't sleep, isn't it? Why the battlefields were harder for you after."

She slid her shaking hands into her pockets. "Papa always told me my mother's symptoms came early with me—nightmares first, and sickness. I suppose I'm just like her."

"And how sick you were, after Selv Torfjel..."

She shut her eyes against the memory of bleeding and pain, and how deep the emptiness reached when it was over.

"Why didn't you *tell* me?" His quiet voice broke, and her heart with it.

She forced her damp eyes open and squinted across the harsh light of the setting sun into the valley below. "I didn't want to worry you at first. I knew you'd just be more reckless, take more risks trying to protect us. And after...Quill, I couldn't. I didn't want to tell you I failed."

He turned to her, jaw hard, cinnamon stick cracking in his fist. "What in Nimmus is that supposed to mean?"

"I knew I was with child, and I still went to Selv Torfjel. I still jumped in front of that knife. I didn't protect her, I didn't..."

Quill's arms engulfed her, and he crushed her to his chest, the smell of cinnamon and sweat filling her head. "Don't you ever, *ever* say that to me, Tati. You did everything. You *fought* for that life. I'm the one who let you both get hurt. I'm the *bandayo* who put you in that place, because I didn't want to face the truth." Tatiana tried to squirm free, to look up at him, but he held her fast. "You're right. You're right about Pippet, that thing's not my sister. And I don't...I'm afraid Maleck brought her back just to break us. Or to steal our augments"

She had no comfort to offer when she feared the same; when the girl she'd helped raise and loved like her own blood had wielded the death of Tatiana's unborn child as a weapon; when her *valenar* held her to him and wept the same tears she'd shed in the medico's tent at the war camp, those first violent surges of insatiable grief in facing a life ended before it ever truly began.

It was just her and Quill against the world again. But now that they'd known something more, had *been* something more, with Pippet and with the life growing inside Tatiana—

It was not enough. And it would never be the same again.

CHAPTER
THIRTEEN

WITH THE PAIN in her head clearing, Ashe paced the cell, discussing with Aden and Kristoff how best to address the Grand Council when the time came. Their whispers barely stirred the shadows, but Ashe found solace in clandestine conversation; she made her case to them as if they were Oadmarkaic, and father and son counterargued so effectively she hit them both several times, eliciting chuckles that chased the lonely shadows back into the crevices of stone.

But whenever it came time to sleep again, Ashe lay awake for hours, trying uselessly to cleave, and when it failed to bring anything more than fragments of gold across her vision—proof that Bresnyar lived, enough to sate her fear—her thoughts turned to Maleck. She grazed her thumb over the *valenar* mark on her palm and tried in vain to strum the bond between them, to gather some sort of sense of what state he was in—whether Cistine had saved him yet.

If she even could.

Ashe wasn't certain how many days truly passed in the dark prison before the sound of a creaking iron door finally greeted her from sleep. Wide awake at once, she pummeled Aden's chest and rolled upright as Meriwa stepped into the cell. She carried Oadmark's own form of light: a jar of living flame. Ashe stared at it, hypnotized by its guttering contents. "Bottled dragonfire? Do you coat the inside of the jar with the liquid from their veins?"

Meriwa frowned. "You know of this?"

A flash of dancing blue eyes and a crooked grin she never thought she'd *miss*. Ashe shrugged. "I have a friend who's a bit of a dragon enthusiast."

Meriwa grunted, tucking the jar away. "Come. You've been summoned."

Ashe decided not to antagonize the woman who stood between her and the open door. She waited for Aden and Kristoff to join her, but when she stepped through Meriwa slammed that door again, locking them inside.

Ashe spun back. "*No.* They go where I go."

"The Council has no interest in your guards."

Aden's eyes flashed to Ashe, full of silent, simmering questions; if she protested, he'd fight—and likely earn himself a blow to the face or worse for it. Ashe clenched her jaw and gritted every tooth against the venom bubbling at the back of her tongue, against the urge to test Meriwa's mettle just as Meriwa was testing hers. Then she dragged in a full breath and offered Meriwa a scathing smile. "We don't want to keep the Council waiting, do we?"

With a last, fleeting glance into the cell, catching the dip of Aden's head, she followed Meriwa into the web of twisting passages that all seemed to lead to prison cells, heart racing with every stride. This was the closest thing to Siralek she'd seen since the night Maleck and Sander had freed them from the catacombs, her skin buzzing at the dark familiarity of it. An eternity seemed to pass before they emerged from that prison hive onto a balcony jutting over the center of the mountain, where breathing came easier. The walls were hard and slick, peppered with doorways large and small, and held the faint waft of sulfur; the middle was like a chimney, hollow and spreading up to a broad opening where a disc of blue sky peered down. Dragons drifted lazily through the mouth to settle on the chimney floor far below, curling against the warmth embedded beneath the stone. Ashe searched for a flicker of gold among the flock, but saw none.

"Where are you keeping him?" Diplomacy deserted her tone, her fingers curling around the stone railing so fiercely gravel scraped across the Wingmaiden's rune. A flicker of gold dazzled along her eyes, but nothing more, like filigree painted over darkness.

"He was banished from Ujurak," Meriwa said. "Aeosotu and the others escorted him elsewhere."

Perhaps that was cruelty to keep Ashe and Bresnyar apart; but it might've been mercy, too, to spare him paying some other penalty for setting claw within the sacred mountain from which he was driven.

She studied Meriwa from the corners of her eyes. "Tell me he's safe, and you'll have a civil prisoner to contend with. Taunt me about him, and I'm going to fight you every step from here to wherever we're going. And I'm going to do my best to embarrass you in front of your Council."

Meriwa's eyes narrowed. "That would harm your cause."

"That's a risk I'm willing to take."

After a long, tense moment, Meriwa said, "He is safe. For now."

She led Ashe up many flights of steps, closer to the opening above. Even with the warm stone floor shrinking beneath them, Ashe was sweating profusely by the time they entered another maw in the stone, this one easily tall enough for even a dragon Aeosotu's size to slip through. The span of the chamber at its end was almost dizzying, stacked with row upon row of ledges leading up to another opening in the ceiling, every level full of Wingmaidens and dragons. She couldn't fathom how many Legions were represented here; anywhere from several to dozens, perhaps even hundreds.

Ashe dropped her gaze and peered around the dark dish of the floor's center, and her stomach dropped with relief when she spotted Nunajik elbowing toward her, eyes glittering. The tribeswoman brushed past Meriwa without a glance and gripped Ashe's hand, drawing her into a sharp, unexpected embrace. "They are not convinced to hear your appeal yet. They want to know more about the woman you are. I will translate for you."

Disappointment crashed through Ashe like a stone dropped into her stomach. She was about to be scrutinized yet again by disbelievers, like she had been her whole life.

Defiance rippled in the wake of defeat, banding her spine with steel and setting her jaw like a bowstring. Swiveling out of Nuna's grip, she faced the lowest ledge in the room, a stone crescent jutting out across the floor like a beckoning hand, though its occupants looked far less inviting. The younger two were close to Ashe's age, the other pair far older—clearly family, all with the same brown skin and black hair, all postured in the same bored sprawl, all watching the proceedings with narrowed eyes.

The elderly man raised his fist, and a Wingmaiden hovering just outside the crescent loosed a horn from her waist strap and blew it. The sound roared through the chamber, bringing the level of conversation from loud chatter to dull murmurs. While the last of those whispers died, Meriwa strutted to the Council's box and leaned against it, arms folded, watching Ashe with hawkish intensity.

If this somehow devolved into a fight, Ashe would kill Meriwa first.

"You face Killik, Tapeesa, Novuam, and Asiaq." Nuna pointed to each of the family in turn: the older man and woman, the younger woman and man. "These are Allfather and Allmother, Allsister and Allbrother—the Grand Council. They have given wisdom and direction to the Legions of the Mountain for many, many years."

Asiaq spoke something under his breath, flicking a glance at his sister, and Nuna translated sheepishly, "But you are the first *kokma* to ever claim bonding to a dragon, and the first to set foot in Ujurak."

Ashe didn't need a translation to that word. She fought not to scowl. "Whatever questions they want to ask, I'll answer. I have nothing to hide."

Nuna translated, and the Grand Council looked among themselves in silent conversation. Ashe hooked her thumbs into her belt and rocked back on her heels, letting a streak of casual defiance brace her stance—telling them with her posture as well as her gaze that she did not fear them.

Fearless is my name. She clung to that oath while Killik spoke back to Nuna in tones as dry and cracked as his skin.

"Allfather asks how you came by a dragon."

"The gods sent a messenger to bring me a starstone." Ashe directed her focus straight to Killik, holding his shrewd, ancient gaze. "When I was in danger, I spoke into it, and Bresnyar heard. He came for me."

Even now, her bowels clenched at that blurred memory of rain and battle on the Talheimic cliffs, of Bresnyar's earth-shattering might and violent fire lighting up the night; how he'd swept into her life like a golden avalanche and helped her find the will to live again; helped her find *herself*.

Tapeesa spoke this time, and Nuna translated to Ashe, "Allmother asks how you are able to fly with no saddle."

"I'm not afraid of falling. Bres has never let me go."

A faint murmur swept the chamber at her irreverent address of her dragon's name. Meriwa's eyes narrowed even further.

Asiaq spoke in a slow, lilted drawl, his hooded gaze fixed on Ashe, and she stared right back at him. He reminded her of Sander, another bored and preening royal with a thirst for power and title moving beneath the surface of his cunning eyes.

"Allbrother asks if there is any reason we shouldn't throw you to the Legions to be torn apart and solve all our dilemmas at once." A faint note of apology flavored Nuna's translation this time.

"Because flames spread," Ashe growled, and Asiaq's head tipped at her tone. "If there's one of me, chosen by the gods, there could be more. Maybe next time you exile your dragons as punishment, they *all* come back with Wingmaidens from other lands. The gods aren't playing favorites with Oadmarkaics for dragon riders anymore. Throwing their chosen Wingmaiden to your Legions might just seal your fate."

The translation and rebuttal came quicker this time, a strange dance of an argument. "Allbrother says the Ancestors will not remove their favor from the chosen. They will not allow this honor to be taken from us."

"Tell Valgard that. They've seen it happen with their wells."

Hushed murmurs fanned over the walls at Nuna's translation, and Asiaq reclined in his seat, fingers drumming the stone, eyes boring into her like dagger-tips. Ashe ignored him and looked to his sister instead; plain-faced and small in stature, but there was something to the slant of her brows and mouth that made her cunning more visible than her brother's, sending a warning chill down Ashe's spine.

Novuam did not ask a question. Instead, she spoke a single word:

"*Apiriak.*"

A gasp journeyed around the room. Asiaq slid upright again, pinning his sister with a wide-eyed look, but the Allfather and Allmother nodded. Meriwa straightened in disbelief, arms falling from their cross.

"What?" Ashe hissed. "What does that mean?"

Beneath her tan complexion, Nuna paled. "*Apiriak* is the Test of all Wingmaidens before they earn their brand. Allsister is demanding you face it to prove your right to be Bresnyar's wing."

The chatter crescendoed in an ear-splitting roar, dragons and Wingmaidens alike adding their voices to the flurry, and this time it was Meriwa herself who took her horn and blew, bringing querulous silence back to the chamber. Allfather stroked his full, braided beard, regarding Ashe with the same scrutiny as countless men who'd falsely believed she owed them any explanation of who she was or where she stood.

He was Rion Bartos, Cadre Commander. He was Mad King Jad of Mahasar. He was Tribune Noaam over Siralek.

She wished she could pound her fist into his face until he bled.

After a moment's regard, he dipped his head, and the Allmother spoke rapidly to Nuna.

"You and your dragon will face *Apiriak*," Nuna raised her voice to be heard above the growing clamor. "If you survive, they will consider your honesty and hear your appeal. If not—"

"*Apiriak* takes you." Meriwa's hiss brushed the shell of Ashe's ear at her arrival, her hand already circling her arm and towing her toward the tunnel mouth. "We leave *now*."

This time, Ashe was content to go with her; the din in the chamber suggested more danger waited here than outside. But she held Novuam's stare while she backed away, and in those glittering eyes she found more cleverness than in all the room's other occupants combined.

Ashe's death in this Test would not be cold-blooded murder to separate them from their so-called Ancestors; success or failure rested on Ashe's bond with Bresnyar. And the Grand Council expected failure.

Scowling, Ashe snapped her arm free of Meriwa's hold and stalked back into the heart of Ujurak.

"Your disrespect for the Grand Council disgusts me," Meriwa growled when they moved out of earshot of the chamber. "No Wingmaiden would ever dare—"

"According to all of you, I'm a charlatan, not a Wingmaiden. So your reputation is safe."

Meriwa slid her hands into her pockets and quickened her stride; curiosity stoked by that uneasy posture, Ashe fell into step with her, weaving back across the balconies toward the prison.

"You're not so certain I'm going to fail," she said after a time. "You think there's a chance I could pass the Test, and that terrifies you."

Meriwa scoffed under her breath. "Only because I know Bresnyar. He nearly burst his hearts bringing Ileria to the *Innuin*. However you've enthralled him, he claims the same loyalty to you now, and you seem the sort to use his strength to your advantage."

"We share strength. I don't use anything he doesn't give freely."

A derisive snort was the only answer, and Ashe gave up that argument; it would lead nowhere with Meriwa still convinced Bresnyar had bonded with her against his will.

She studied her escort from the corner of her eyes, that face full of quiet violence. Meriwa wanted her gone, wanted her dead; yet she'd kept quiet, lingered by the Grand Council, and never spoken an ill word against her in the hearing.

"I'm surprised you didn't kill Nunajik and offer to translate in her stead," Ashe said carefully. "You could've twisted everything and given them a reason to kill me. Why waste your chance to have me thrown out of this mountain?"

Meriwa was quiet for so long, Ashe thought they might make the rest of the journey in silence and she would never have her answer. They slipped back into the prison hive before the Legion Head finally spoke, voice pitched low. "It is...beneath a Wingmaiden to learn the common tongue of your kingdoms. That is how bored tribesmen waste their time."

"And yet, here you are, wasting your time with me." Ashe regarded her more closely by dragonfire's light. "So, they don't know. Who taught you? Aeosotu?"

"Dragons know many tongues. They are forbidden to teach them to their Wingmaidens."

"Then—"

"I did not need to share my knowledge to see you dead, you are already going to die. Allsister did not offer you mercy, she outwitted her brother by offering a solution to a problem he could not solve." The look she shot Ashe spoke of a deep, personal rage, as if Asiaq's failure was somehow Ashe's fault. "And now you will perish for it."

"We'll see about that."

Meriwa shook her head. "Why risk so much? I'm certain the tribeswoman told you it was as good as death to come here, posturing with one of our dragons."

"Even if it was posturing, I'd still come." Ashe pocketed her hands and looked ahead, a trace of Cistine's face flickering through her mind. "Someone I love like a sister needed me to come here and appeal to your Council. I'd do it even if it cost me everything."

Meriwa's breath caught audibly, but she said nothing more when they reached the cell, merely unlatched it and shoved Ashe inside; the lock had barely clattered back into place before Aden and Kristoff were up, striding to greet her.

"How did it go?" Kristoff demanded.

"Did they harm you?" Aden added sharply.

"No injuries...not yet." Ashe tugged her hair back from her temples with both hands, knotted it, and met Aden's eyes. "Train with me."

"Why?"

"For the Test. If we're going to bring the Legions against the Balmond, I have to prove to these people I'm really a Wingmaiden."

CHAPTER
FOURTEEN

Maleck was running from the cabal.

Thorne could think of no other cause for his friend's erratic travels, spearing back and forth across Blaykrone territory like a specter. Cistine felt him traveling south one day, and the cabal pushed near to breaking on his heels, only to wake after a few fitful hours of sleep and realize the sense of him tacked sharply north instead. Then east. Then west.

"He's running from us," Cistine agreed bleakly one dawn, marking another course change on the map—north to west this time. "From *me*."

Thorne met Ariadne's eyes over Cistine's head and saw what he always feared most in his strategist's eyes: resignation and despair.

She believed it, too.

Hopeless frustration slithered through his chest, banding his lungs so tight it was difficult to breathe. Here they were, weeks deep into fleeing, with little to show for it. He and Cistine had taken to shorter training sessions at greater distances now that Pippet was with them, and they were no closer to finding Maleck or returning to the front lines. Every goal they held seemed to slip further and further from their grasp with each passing day. Maleck, the war, Stornhaz, even Cistine's plan with the Door...

Some plans he preferred over others; yet each one was thwarted, and he liked that even less.

A hoarse cry split the air, tearing Thorne from his reflections. His hand sailed to his dagger as he spun up off his knees too late. A lithe shape barreled from the trees, slamming into Ariadne so hard they both went rolling across the cold ground, and before Thorne fully registered the familiar mottled hair and wicked, grasping hands, blood flowed, leather snapped, and Ariadne cried out in shock and pain. Then Pippet was up, Ariadne's augment pouch in hand, sprinting into the trees.

Cistine snapped to her feet with a yelp, and Thorne pushed her toward Ariadne. "Stay here—I'll catch her!"

Swift as Pippet was, she lacked his endurance. She broke like mad through the undergrowth, and Thorne paced himself at a steady run after her, vaulting fallen trees and crashing through the foliage with his forearms braced, snapping branches. He kept his stride smooth and held that dark, bounding form in sight. In some ways, ever since he'd lost her in that corridor in the courthouse, it had been this: him always chasing her shadow.

With a last burst of speed fed by the memory of that night, Thorne launched himself over a log, palms skimming the arch, and slammed his booted feet into Pippet's back. She tumbled head-over-heels with a cry and fetched up hard against a stump, clutching her arm to her chest, sobbing. "*You broke my arm,* you *broke* it, oh stars, it hurts, it *hurts*—"

Thorne crashed down beside her, snaring her by her other elbow and spinning her toward him. Steel flashed from the nest of her body in a backhanded arc; Thorne seized her wrist and shoved it, and her, against a sapling, the impact rattling through both of them. "Aden taught me that trick, too."

She glared up at him, both arms unhurt, one holding a dagger—Quill's dagger—and the other Ariadne's satchel. "When I'm finally free, I'm going to kill you first. I'm going to make the Key *watch.*"

In one deft blow, Thorne knocked the dagger from her hand, spun her from the sapling and pushed her to her knees in the leaf litter and dead plants. "How did you come by that blade?"

"Quill let down his guard." Her tone was casual, a smug smile sprinkling the words. "*Oh, Quill, I can't feel my hands, please loosen my bonds just a bit, I'll behave, I promise…I know you're just trying to keep me from hurting myself, but you're hurting me…*" A nasty laugh spiraled from her. "He's so *easy*."

Thorne yanked her around to face him, wrists pinned in one hand, taking her chin in the other. She glared up at him without fear or love. Just hate and hunger and vindictive pleasure in eyes that never should have seen war. Eyes he remembered full of tears, that voice untouched by cruelty, screaming at him to get up when his father sent him to his knees in that apartment corridor.

"I'm sorry," he said, and she blinked—the only sign that perhaps he'd cut past that vicious guard for once. "I didn't save you that night in the courthouse."

"*Save me.*" Her lips curled. "I don't need saving."

She hurled her weight forward and broke his hold, jaw agape, mouth going for his throat so sharply he didn't have time to block.

A hand snared the back of Pippet's collar, ripping her from Thorne's hold and smashing her backward into a brawny grip: Quill, chest bleeding from a slash dealt by his own stolen *Svarkyst* dagger, falling back on his haunches and scooting away from Thorne, dragging Pippet with him. She bucked wildly, gnashing her teeth and screaming for the augment pouch dangling limp in Thorne's grip. "*Give those to me*, they're mine, I *need* them! You're just wasting them with all this training that doesn't *matter*, you can't keep her from dying on the Door and when she does I'm going to take *every last drop of augmentation* and I'll use it to tear all of you apart! Starting with *you!*" She slammed her elbow backward into Quill's abdomen, and he groaned but kept his grip. "I hate you, you're just like a slaver and the only reason I ever behaved was to make you love me so you'd let me *leave!* You're not my brother, you're not my *father*, I wish I'd put my knife in *you* instead—"

Thorne set the pouch aside, stripped the armored thread of Maleck's scarf from around his bicep, and went to them. Kneeling across Pippet's thrashing ankles, he gagged her and tied the cloth in the ratty tangles of her hair. She went on cursing, screaming, struggling, and over her head Quill met Thorne's gaze with such anguish in his face, it cracked Thorne's heart in half. Any reprimand for Quill's lax guard today died on his lips.

His friend was grieving the death of his sister, and grief was irrational—Thorne knew that better than anyone. Julian and Cistine had paid the greatest cost imaginable when he'd lost Baba Kallah.

He straightened and took Pippet under the arm, yanking her up beside him, speaking over her enraged squeals to Quill. "That wound needs attention."

Quill pressed a hand to his chest, blood spilling across his fingers. "It's just a scratch."

"*Nightwing.*" Defiant eyes slashed to Thorne's face. "I have her. Let Tati help you."

The fight went out of Quill's posture so abruptly, it sent Thorne's stomach into a plunge. With one hand, Quill freed Pippet's bonds from his belt and tossed them to Thorne; with the other, he kept pressure to his wound. Pausing just long enough to snatch up his dagger and Ariadne's pouch, he vanished back toward the camp.

Thorne held Pippet by the throat and banded her arms behind her back, ignoring her spitting rage and the half-muffled threats slipping around the gag. Despair churned in his middle, and fear for Quill, who counted wounds from his own sister as nothing. Three stark cleavings down his cheek from her unpared nails; a gash across his chest from her blade. How many more wounds would he take before she succeeded in what she claimed she wanted—killing the brother who'd given everything to keep her alive?

The uncertain future lurked beyond Thorne's sight on the short, fraught march back to the camp, where he shoved Pippet down beside the dying fire and went straight to Quill, seated on an overturned stump, head bent while Tatiana cleaned and bandaged his chest. He laid a hand on his shoulder, and Quill reached back and gripped it, his hold tight like a dying man clinging to the last thread of strength inside him.

Without letting go, Thorne looked at Cistine and Ariadne's faces, his strategist banding a cloth to the shallow cut above her hip where the *Svarkyst* steel had bitten through, severing her pouch. "We need a new plan."

"For Maleck?" Cistine asked.

"For her." Thorne jerked his chin at Pippet. "She's desperate because she's weaning from the augments."

Quill's head jerked up, grip flexing on Thorne's hand, eyes fixed on his sister who'd slumped on her side, panting and looking away from all of them.

"This will get much worse, much quicker from here," Thorne went on. "We have to stop hunting Maleck for now and focus on her."

"But we're so *close!*" Cistine protested.

"Today we are. But he'll shift his course again, *Logandir*. While he evades us, we have someone in our midst who needs our help *now*. I can't sacrifice her wellbeing for his."

It drove into him like a blade to let *Maleck* go, of all people, who never once let go of *him*; but this was the cost to lead.

Cistine relented by the bud of tears in her eyes, face turning west—the direction Maleck had gone. She was the Key and he was the call, and she could not pursue him now.

"Where will we go?" Ariadne asked.

Thorne glanced at the map, still spread out where Ariadne had fallen with Pippet on top of her. "The town of Landamot isn't far."

"You want to go into a *town*?" Tatiana scoffed. "In case you'd forgotten, the Bloodwights aren't the only ones who want to rip out Cistine's throat! Holmlond was supposed to be the last place we stayed that wasn't out in the wilds, remember?"

"I'm aware," Thorne said. "But I'm willing to risk that, because of the treaty, the Chancellors won't be quick to publicly declare the Talheimic Princess a fugitive in case word makes it past the Dreadline. They'll seize her by subterfuge, not mobbing her in the streets."

Pippet wheezed with vicious laughter, chilling Thorne to his core.

"You want to stay in a town until Pip dries out?" Quill said.

"I want her confined," Thorne said. "She's dangerous. We do what must be done—and we take the chance that word of Cistine's fugitive status hasn't spread to common inns and taverns."

"And if it has?"

Thorne held Cistine's gaze, waiting for the silent assent of her nod before he said, "Then we board in uncommon ones."

Landamot was a small but prosperous town of wood and stone, built on a broad span of land between two branches of the Ismalete River to the northwest and east, and Stedgnalt Lake to the south. Despite the early season and *Nazvaldolya's* chokehold on the north, the crops were fertile here, a plenteous and well-watered sanctuary on the verge of Erdotre and Eben territories.

Thorne and Cistine waited on its edge inside a verdant copse while the others scouted for danger in the dusty streets. Pippet lay unconscious at their feet, sweating and shivering violently, the first sign of the augments unspooling from within her body. Thorne fought not to panic at the thought that soon they might have to choose between feeding her a bit of their flagons or watching her body unravel itself.

Cistine fidgeted beside Thorne, playing with her augment pouch, her gaze remote. He didn't have to possess her power to know she was listening to the strange call of that augment they'd harvested from Kosai Talis, the bloodlocked treasure the Bloodwights sought so viciously.

It was strange and unsettling that they had not pursued her more fiercely since she'd stolen it, making ultimatums or drawing her to them. He tried to be grateful for the reprieve, but it stirred his spirit wrong, just like that look in her eyes.

"Is your silence anger, or are you thinking?" he asked.

Cistine's fingers peeled sharply away from her pouch. He held her gaze, waiting for whatever came from that pained and frightened look.

"I was thinking of the Dreadline, actually. I hadn't thought about it in weeks before you mentioned it. But it's still out there, pummeling the border between our kingdoms." She nibbled at the side of her thumb, peering into Landamot's streets. "We'll have to do something about that. Vandred hinted at how."

"Scheming, *Logandir?*"

She flashed him a half-hearted smile. "Always."

Her gaze dipped briefly to Pippet, a silent signal that she would not speak of her plans near the girl so desperate to betray them and return to her captors. Thorne hardly had time to nod before three figures materialized at the town's edge, moving swiftly toward them.

"All quiet," Tatiana declared, knocking back her hood. "No whispers about us at any tavern or inn."

"Even the ones of poor repute," Ariadne added. "We sold a blade for just enough mynts to pay for two nights. After that, we'll have to labor for room and board."

"Stars willing, we're here no longer than that." Thorne clapped Quill on the arm on his way past him toward the town. His friend hardly flinched at the gesture, troubled gaze fixed on Pippet.

They slipped into Landamot with her cradled in Quill's arms, ungagged and wrapped up in Thorne's cloak to hide her bound hands. Tatiana, Ariadne, and Cistine broke away at the central square to find food, and Quill led Thorne past a well flocking with gossips, down two serpentine avenues, and up a short stoop into a ramshackle inn.

They weren't preferable accommodations, dingy and dark and smelling of burned fish, but the keeper at the desk tucked into one corner did not even raise his head at their passing or remark on the limp, sweating child they carried. Indifferent hovels like these were breeding grounds for slave traders and flesh markets, and Thorne made note of the faded sign above the mantel and the lay of the corners before he and Quill mounted the rickety, unstable staircase. If he ever reclaimed the Judgement Seat, he'd have to do something about this place...and all the places like it.

Quill strode straight to the room they'd purchased, small and shadowy at the very end of the hall. A single bed and a roll of sleeping mats took up one wall, a washing bowl on a stand at the other side. The only window, to Thorne's relief, was barred and boarded, likely to keep illicit activity from notice or true captives from escaping.

Quill halted over the threshold, staring at the bed. Silent aggression played in his eyes, a wish that they wouldn't have to do this. When he didn't speak, Thorne forced himself to. "If we don't tie her down, she *will* escape."

"I know."

"I can do it," he offered quietly.

"No." Quill's voice cracked, and he cleared his throat. "No, I'm her brother. She's my responsibility. It has to be me."

The moment he laid her on the bed, Pippet began to stir. Her eyes fluttered open to the stained walls, the low, leaky roof, and a hiss rolled over her chapped lips. "*Where are we?*"

"Inn." Quill loosened her bonds just enough to wind the ends through the iron headboard. "It's for your own good."

She began to squirm. "Don't you tie me up again, you *bandayo*, I swear by all the stars I'll make everyone in this place hear me, they're all going to believe you stole me and you're doing *awful* things to me!"

Quill swiveled abruptly on his knees, catching Pippet by the chin. "Do you know who frequents places like this one, *Malatkas*? *Real* slavers. Real flesh-market traders. I know about stars-damned dens like these because I turned over a thousand of them looking for you for two months after I escaped Detlyse Halet. So believe me, they don't *care* if you scream, they don't care what threats you make, they *do not care* if you claim we stole you and we're hurting you. You can cry and howl and beg until you're hoarse, no one is coming to save you from us."

Pippet's whole body tensed, and Thorne stiffened in turn, hand falling to his knife, bracing for the retribution. "I hope you die here. I hope some drunkard catches you in a back alley and lays you open, I hope they pull out all your entrails one by one and make you *choke* on them while Tatiana watches. And if they don't, *I'm* going to do it, I'm going to get out of these chains and sink my teeth into your throat while you're sleeping! You're nothing, you're worthless, you couldn't even protect Tatiana from my knife or the *baby* inside her—"

"Thorne," Quill spoke over her. "Wait outside, will you?"

"Not a chance."

"I know what Cistine is!" Pippet shouted. "I know she's the Key, I'm going to take her with me when I escape and we'll go to the nearest Door and I'm going to rip out her *beating heart* with my *bare* hands and—"

"Thorne!" Quill snapped. "Wait for me out in the hall!"

Thorne didn't realize he'd taken a step toward the bed until that cry speared his feet to the floorboards and he understood how desperate he was to silence her. Pippet was reeling him in, nearer and nearer with his weapons in hand...weapons Quill did not carry.

When had he surrendered them? When had he resigned himself to these atrocities and threats from his sister's mouth?

Swearing, Thorne retreated out into the hall, banging the door shut and laying his fist into the opposite wall; the slam of bone on wood rattled through his whole body, jolting clarity back into him. The windowless hall, framed in ghostlamps strung from sconces, flickered before his eyes.

He could still hear every abuse Pippet hurled at Quill. The names she called him, the horrible things she threatened to do to all of them, bounded off the walls and rang in Thorne's ears. Yet Quill endured them to ensure she was safely bound.

Thorne slumped to his seat against the wall and leaned his head back on the stained wood, staring up at the ceiling.

In word and spirit, he'd fled so hard from the things Cistine asked of him...the pain of agreeing to marry her knowing what it would mean if she died on the Doors. He was not as strong as Quill; he'd left that room. He'd turned away from his duty as Cistine's betrothed, her *selvenar*, her friend.

He was a coward and a fool leading heroes, but he could not afford to give any less than what they gave: the loss of Tatiana and Quill's child, the choices Cistine faced, the pain Ariadne endured, the risks Ashe and Aden took...even Maleck's sacrifice.

It was time to stop running, to stand as strong as his warriors did.

The door opened and Quill emerged at last, wan and trembling. "She's asleep." He shut the door softly behind him and settled on the floor next to Thorne, cradling his head. "She's already worse. Weaker."

Thorne said nothing. Quill wasn't seeking consolation; he simply needed to speak it.

After a long moment, he dropped his hands and looked at Thorne with quiet defiance burning in his haunted gaze. "I can't give her more, *Allet*. I can't feed this addiction, even if it's hurting her. I don't know what kind of brother that makes me, what kind of heartless, selfish—"

"It isn't selfish. It's not for your own sake," Thorne said. "If it was, you wouldn't have endured it this long. You won't give in because you know taking off the edge won't save her any more than it saved Tatiana from the things she was fleeing with mead."

Quill turned his eyes back to the door, shoulders slumping deeper. "I can't lose her. But I don't know if I can save her, either."

"All we can do now is be with her through it." Thorne slung an arm around Quill's sloped back. "And with one another."

Posture crumbling, Quill hung his head, and Thorne rested his brow against Quill's temple, sitting with him while ghostlamps dimmed and darkness dragged itself down the hall to consume them. They did not move until the tread of three familiar pairs of feet mounted the stairs and Cistine, Tatiana, and Ariadne appeared, hurrying toward them down the corridor.

One look at his *selvenar's* face, and Thorne's heart dropped. He lurched to his feet, pulling Quill up as well. "What's wrong?"

Cistine halted, wide-eyed and ashen. "There are reports pouring in at every tavern. *Mirothadt* forces are sacking Blaykrone."

Thorne's heart jolted to a stop, then kicked forward with such speed he choked. "*What?*"

"It's been happening for days now," Ariadne said. "We just spoke to a family who fled a settlement in the foothills near Stedgnalt. Their home was burned to cinders, their children nearly taken. They make from here to the mountains...it seems most of the refugees have gone that way."

"Why haven't we seen anything? Heard anything?" Quill demanded.

"Because the people are escaping, not dying like they're meant to."

Thorne rocked back on his heels. "Escaping *Bloodwights?*"

"How?" Quill gripped Tatiana's shoulders. "How are they doing it?"

"They have help." Cistine's eyes shone full of hope despite her weary face. "A shadow, the family said, shaped like a man and wearing a wolf skull just like the Bloodwights. Wherever they send the *mirothadt*, he knows.

And he fights for the people."

Thorne sank back against the wall and dragged his hand down his face to stop it tingling.

"Mal," Quill breathed. "Mal's out there helping them."

Tatiana took his wrists and squeezed them. "This means there's enough of him left to save. *They* can be saved."

Cistine's gaze flicked past Quill and Thorne to the door, and some of the elation fizzled out in her eyes. "That's true. But Maleck is still addicted, whether he's helping these people or not. Just like Pippet."

"At least this proves there's something left." Quill dragged his three-fingered hand back through his hair. "In *both* of them. As long as that's alive, I won't stop fighting. Neither can you, Stranger."

"I'm not giving up. I just don't want to make things worse while I'm trying to fix this. I'm still not sure I can save them."

"We will find a way, Cistine," Thorne said. "We always do."

She said nothing, staring thoughtfully at the door.

CHAPTER FIFTEEN

Cistine HAD NEVER slept anywhere as derelict as the inn at Landamot; she couldn't imagine Ashe, much less Julian, having ever entertained the notion of their princess lying on a bedroll in these squalid conditions, staring at the rat holes in the seam where crooked floor met moldering wall, wrapped in nothing but her armored coat and a blanket of questionable stains.

But she was grateful for the heat of the hearth in the foyer seeping up through the floor so she woke warm, not chilled for once. And she was grateful that when she finally did concede to be awake after hours of tossing and turning, it was to the smell of pastry and fruit, hot tea, and the strange sight of a Chancellor crouched beside her bedroll, shaking her awake.

A Chancellor with black hair.

She sucked in a breath, but Thorne held up a finger. He tilted his head toward Pippet, who'd finally screamed herself hoarse with threats and false sobs hours ago and lay in a heap, gathering her strength for another shouting match. Then he backed from the room, motioning her to follow him.

Once they were in the hall, Cistine still dashing sleep from her eyes to be sure she was seeing clearly, a yelp came out at last. "What did you *do*?"

"Sold more weapons and bought a brick of dye." He handed her an apple turnover, a meat pie, and the tea in a wooden cup. "Our faces may be distinct, but in my case it's my hair that sets me apart. Quill's as well. As long as we're in common company, I think it's best we blend in."

"I won't say it's a terrible idea." She set the cup on the windowsill so she could thread her fingers through the ends of his hair. "But *look* at you."

"I know." Thorne shifted his weight from foot to foot. "My natural state, were it not for my father."

Cistine rocked her weight back against the wall to study him: broad and powerful, filling up the hall in his dark armor, with his raven-black locks and piercing blue eyes. "I like the silver better. It's a statement, owning your story from start to finish. And now it's part of who you are."

Thorne captured her lips in a brief kiss that warmed her better than any tea before beckoning her across the hall and down into the foyer.

"Where's Quill?" Cistine asked around the last bites of the meat pie. "I haven't seen him in hours."

Not since the last time Pippet had hurled abuse at him about the child he and Tatiana had lost; then he'd left without a word, ignored Cistine's half-awake attempts to snag his ankle and ask him if he needed her, and slammed the door in his wake.

Thorne grimaced. "We collided on my way out to the market this morning. Apparently he spent half the night tossing slavers out of their rooms and beating them bloody."

Cistine winced. "He's going to raise enough trouble to have us rousted from the inn."

"I think that's a fight he's willing to have."

They reached the hearth, the foyer empty around them, and Cistine tucked herself against the warm stones. She bit back a groan of pleasure when heat flooded her muscles, cramped from sleeping with little between her body and the floor. "Would he talk to you?"

"Less talk, more grunting and shifting to hide the blood on his knuckles." Thorne leaned against the opposite arch, rubbing his face with both hands. "It's chipping away at him, all of this...Pippet and Maleck, his and Tatiana's loss."

Cistine fidgeted with the cup. "I'm sorry I couldn't tell you sooner.

Tatiana swore me to secrecy."

"I'd rather you kept her confidences than sated my curiosity." Thorne moved to brush back his newly-darkened hair, then seemed to think better of it. Gripping his hands around his neck instead, he craned his head against the mantel. "But I regret Quill finding out the way he did."

They were quiet while Cistine finished her breakfast. Then she set the teacup on the hearth and faced Thorne, cracking her knuckles. "Training?"

"Not so close to the city. We could trek out into the wilderness at sunhigh, put some distance between us and everyone else."

And Pippet. The unspoken implication raked at Cistine's heart, churning up a desperate thought from the night before—something she hurriedly stuffed away again. "Well, in that case, I'm going after Quill."

"Cistine." Thorne caught her hand when she lurched up from the hearth. "Before you go, there's something I..." He trailed off, his thumb brushing her knuckles, then the betrothal band, lingering there. "I know I never truly gave you my answer after Kosai Talis. I'm ashamed to admit that was intentional. I knew it would feed the flames of this plan that could very well take you away from me forever. And as cowardly as it is, some part of me believed if I withheld my agreement, it could stop all of this from happening. Stop *you* walking away from me."

Nerves jangled in her stomach. "I know how hard this is for you."

"But it isn't about me. Or, at least, it shouldn't be. My concern must be for you...what you're sworn to do, what you've dedicated your life to defend." He framed her cheeks with his hands now, his smile small and lopsided, but genuine. "I feel like I've been losing you since the day I met you. What's one more goodbye?"

"Thorne..."

"My answer is yes," he said, and disbelief stilled her tongue. "Before you go to the Door and bleed for my kingdom, I *will* marry you, Cistine Novacek. It will be my honor and privilege. My only request is that you allow me to make it the wedding you've always dreamed of. I don't care that we're in the middle of a war. You've already sacrificed enough of your future, and you still have more to give. I want this to be the one thing you *do not* go without."

Heat sparked in the corners of her vision and pricked the tip of her nose. "I'll wear white, you'll wear black?"

"Fetching." A chuckle rumbled in his chest, and he kissed her brow. "We'll do it in front of everyone we know and love, and a few we hate."

"Why don't we just invite Sander and call it done, then?"

The laughter burst from him this time, and he leaned back to meet her eyes. "A dress?"

"Just for you." She slid her arms around his neck and rose to murmur against his lips, "Anything for you, Starchaser."

"Anything for *you*, Wildheart."

She'd never been more certain of those words in her life.

When they drew apart, she dashed tears from her cheeks and grinned up at him. "Thank you. I know what this means to you...it's not an easy choice. If I could spare you from all this pain, I would."

He squeezed her hand three times. "I would only be spared if I didn't love you. And I wouldn't trade that love to be free of all the pain in the world." He spun her by the hand and released her toward the door. She cast him a parting smile and hurried out, shut the inn door gently, then leaped in place and punched the chilly air.

She was going to be *married*. To *Thorne Starchaser*. And then—

Hastily, she banished that thought. Everything was uncertain, but she wouldn't let herself dwell on the eventualities.

She was going to marry her *selvenar*. That was pure joy.

"*Yes!* Oh, yes, yes, yes..." She leaped down from the stoop and landed with fists raised in victory, dancing and shimmying a victory jig down the street. Then she put two fingers in her mouth and whistled.

Faer came to her at once. With another signal, she sent him to find Quill, following the inky blot of his body through twisting avenues linked together by the sinew of shady alleys and dark shops. Not Quill's usual haunts, but a fair place to pick a fight.

She found him at a side well near the outskirts, bent on its edge with head hung, washing more blood from his hands than one inn's worth of slavers and vagrants. Faer glided down and hopped along the well's broken edge, croaking and flaring until Quill stroked a finger over his head. Heart in her throat, Cistine mounted the well's foundation and leaned against it, elbows propped back on the mossy rim, facing Quill though he would not look at her.

"You've been out all night," she said, because no other greeting would suffice.

His shoulders arched and slumped. "Couldn't sleep."

"Neither could we." She reached for his injured hand, and he ripped it from her reach, angling his body away without straightening up from the rim. It stung, just like every time she'd felt them turning away from her since she returned from Talheim. Like she no longer belonged with them, *to* them, the way they all belonged to each other.

She pushed away from the well and put up her hands. "Spar with me."

A low scoff, and he shook his head. "Not today, Stranger."

Fine. She'd seen Tatiana initiate this dance with him, and she never asked—she taunted. "Why? Because it won't fix what's wrong...what's making you hurt badly enough to do *this*?" She snatched his wrist, jerking his knuckles up into the light. Fresh blood budded across the bone, in the seams between.

Quill yanked free. "Because you're not the one I want to hit. I can't take this much out on you."

"Why not? I did it with you, after Julian—"

"This isn't a lover's spat. This is watching my sister die in front of me. This is knowing Mal's out there going up against his brothers *alone* and he wouldn't take my help even if I offered." His teeth gnashed audibly together. "This is knowing I'm the father of a dead baby, *valenar* to a warrior who's been carrying that loss alone, and knowing it's my fault it happened. Because I let Pippet get too close."

The taunts slid from her teeth. "Quill, that's *not* true. None of this is your fault."

"Semantics matter a lot less when you're standing up to your knees in the blood of everyone you love."

Silent, they stared at one another.

"If I hit you," he added after a moment, "it will be hard enough to break. And I'm not going to do that."

Throat raw with grief, Cistine stepped nearer to him. "Then tell me how I *can* help. There has to be some way—"

"Not unless you can fix everything this stars-damned war's broken. Not unless you can bring back the dead or turn time back so I can save my sister." A small, deprecating smile turned the corners of Quill's mouth. "We both know even *your* power has limits, Stranger."

"But this is *killing you*."

He blinked, slow and heavy. "It's killing all of us. Why should I be the exception?"

He turned back to the well, bracing his forearms on it again, tilting the bucket to bathe his knuckles. Cistine watched him through blurry eyes, her pulse thumping painfully against her chest.

Then, abruptly, that ache turned to ferocity, surging in her gut and climbing her throat. The wild heart of fire roared from ember to inferno so quickly it dragged a gasp to the backs of her teeth, where she bit down fiercely against it. The spark in her mind ignited, fanning into flame that reckless notion she'd toyed with ever since she and Ariadne and Tatiana had returned from scouting at the taverns.

"Do you have that brick of dye with you?" she asked, and Quill tapped his pocket. "Good. Thorne said not to come back until you've done that— he's worried the innkeeper might be growing suspicious."

With a two-fingered salute, Quill returned to washing his hands.

Cistine turned on heel and sprinted all the way back to the inn. The journey was just long enough for her to cobble together a hasty plan; she darted up to the stairs to the room and entered to find the others awake, but Pippet still asleep. A feverish sheen of sweat coated her brow, tremors feathering her limbs. Tatiana watched her with a look crossed between worry and anger, as she always did these days. Ariadne and Thorne consulted the map, and Cistine did not have to look twice to know they were comparing the reports of the wolf-masked Bloodwight to Maleck's movements these past weeks. She'd measured them by ghostlight the night before; they fit perfectly.

"Quill needs you," she announced. "He found a slaver nest in one of the taverns and he needs help rooting it out."

Tatiana arched a brow. "What's he planning to do, cleanse this whole town before we go?"

Cistine bobbed her shoulders. "You know Quill. He wants a problem to solve, even if he can't fix the one in front of him."

But I can. Heady excitement trilled through her.

"It could draw attention," Ariadne warned.

"I think that's why he wants you. He thinks the four of you could do better than just one man pummeling his way through six."

Tatiana straightened, jaw squaring. "*Six?*"

"The four of us?" Thorne spoke at the same time.

"He said he doesn't want me mixed up in it." The lies rolled off her tongue so effortlessly, it was almost terrifying. "I offered to watch Pippet."

With a heavy sigh, Thorne rolled the map and stood. "Which tavern?"

She named one at random. "Just hurry. Quill was so anxious for a fight, even Faer looked nervous."

"You're sure you'll be all right here alone with her?" Ariadne asked.

"I'll be fine. I'll stay right by the door until you come back." Lies on top of lies.

Ariadne and Thorne hurried out, but Tatiana paused with her hand to the frame, looking Cistine up and down. "I don't like that look in your eye, *Yani.*"

"Quill and I argued." One truth, given frankly, to anchor all the lies together. "I never like fighting with him, but especially now, when he's hurting the most I've ever seen him..."

Tatiana grimaced. "That makes two of us."

She slipped out, shutting the door behind her. Cistine locked and chained it, then turned back to the bed.

Pippet did not move even though it was just her and Cistine now, and the augments humming in Cistine's pouch—which she unthreaded from her belt and tied around the washbasin's column, tossing the bedrolls over it for good measure. If this went awry and somehow Pippet slipped free, that might win her a few precious seconds to subdue her.

But there was no give in the rope binding Pippet's wrists to the headboard and no guile in her unconsciousness; when Cistine stretched out a hand, the heat burning in Pippet's skin was no lie, either.

Had Maleck been like this when Kristoff found him as a boy, the enthrallment of augmentation broken by his encounter with Ashe? Had he too sweated and shivered, begged for augments or for death, utterly inconsolable and full of vitriol? Had Kristoff weaned him, bit by bit, with augments that were not yet a commodity, or had Maleck struggled through by that powerful will she'd long admired in him, and paid the price in deep silence and fits of absentmindedness—an unwhole mind the cost of his freedom?

There was still so much she didn't know about him, and she would pay a king's ransom to have the chance to find out. She had this one chance to learn if it was possible. One gods-given opportunity to see just how far her power could go.

If she could sever the threads like she had with Vandred, if she could set Pippet free from the addiction without ending both their lives, then she could save them all.

A shock, the others said—the shock alone could kill her. But this would not be like anything the army had done to the children they'd rescued. This was like nothing anyone else could ever do. And Pippet was already dying; the only life Cistine gambled with now was her own.

She lowered herself onto the bed and laid her hand on Pippet's clammy brow. The girl's lashes flicked apart, breaths tightening at the sight of Cistine, top lip fluttering back from her teeth. "What—what are *you*—?"

"I'm saving my friend."

Cistine plunged her power straight into Pippet's core.

It was not the same as with Vandred. The web of power around Pippet had grown dim over the days, the different augments bleeding out of her, untrained hands too weak to hold tight to them. Cistine broke through those bonds like cobwebs, drawing the power into herself—lightning and ice and fire, mere gasps of godlike might. Then she went deeper, holding Pippet fast by her brow when she started to squirm.

More power brushed aside, tendrils and sheaves Cistine tucked into her own body, stowed away against her Atrasat inkings. Then all at once she was there, like breaking the surface of dark water into a cave at Pippet's center.

It was not empty.

She found the twisted knot of power fed to Pippet like it was fed to Maleck before her, a seething mass of the gentler augments that could twist and scar and corrupt from the inside without killing. Pippet's very essence cleaved to them with desperate longing, an inarticulate howl of need Cistine could *feel* within her own head, her spirit, her heart. Pippet would kill and maim and break the world for this maelstrom of power.

Cistine shrank against the furious might of such need. How could anything she did matter more than this burning conviction that without augmentation, Pippet would simply shrivel up and cease to be? How could one woman take this much craving and cut it away while still leaving behind enough essence to survive?

Then she felt it, like a hand to her back, like a familiar, bass murmur in her ear: *You know because you've already seen life beyond it. You have already weighed the cost.*

Maleck.

For a moment, he shone like a beacon in her mind—the man who'd paved this road for Pippet and Cistine long before they ever dreamed they'd walk it. He'd showed them through word and deed that there was a life on the other side of this addiction—there was hope. There was love and purpose, there was blended hearts and blended blood. There was strength, freedom, *family.*

This was the first step to making it whole.

Maleck's memory poured through her, and in a burst of power Cistine drove in like a blade and started cutting.

Distantly, pain burst through her. She heard screaming and couldn't be sure if it was her or Pippet, or both of them; there was thrashing and agony, blood and terror, and so much howling inside her, outside her, that the world seemed to drum and tilt and crash in on itself.

But she did not let go, did not stop. She severed in broad strokes, hacking away the hold this power had over Pippet, yanking it out of the girl and into herself until she tasted blood in her mouth and the cavern within Pippet began to dim.

It was not like Vandred; this knot was so much smaller, the venom so much harsher and quicker, like a young serpent's bite. Pippet's desperation struggled against her more fiercely with every tug, every yank, but she kept hacking down at that knot of power until it was just a flicker, a small thread tethering her to the darkness while Pippet's will battered hers, the very feeling of it a threat, a plea, a promise of death.

Slamming. Snarling. Screaming. Severing. It was Cistine's whole world, her whole life, all she was made of and meant for and able to do.

Then a burst of sound, breaking wood, shouts and swearing, and with a gasp Cistine flooded back into herself, back into the world. Pippet arched under her hand, jaws parted in a shrill bellow that lost all sound when she lost her breath, blood flecking her lips and staining her nostrils. Then she slammed back onto the bed, a limp heap.

Someone launched into Cistine, shoulder pounding shoulder so hard she toppled from the bed. The crack of her head on the floorboards made her dimly aware she was already bleeding. There was a muffled pound of footfalls, then a hand slid under her cheek and lifted her up from the floor.

Sandalwood and leather and sweat. *Thorne.* "What in the *stars* is wrong with you, Quill?"

"What's wrong with *me*?" Quill's cry was furious, brutal, bringing a second shock of clarity. "What in *Nimmus* is wrong with *her*?"

Panting, Cistine forced her eyes open. The world hung askew from the safety of Thorne's grip, but Ariadne and Tatiana were visible at the wall, gaping open-mouthed with weapons in hand. Quill knelt on the bed, holding Pippet's bloodied, ashen face in his hands.

"What did you do?" he roared. "What did you *do*, Cistine?"

"I had to know," she rasped. "If I could do it, if I could take the augments, save her...save *them*..."

He blanched. "You used my sister to test your *power?*"

"You said...if I could help you save her—"

"Save her! Not kill her! Stars *damn* it, we don't know what you can do, where the limits are, if this will *kill* the person you use it against!"

"Is she dead?"

"That's not the point! You're not a god, you don't have the right to play with our lives like this!"

"Quill," Thorne growled. "Enough."

"*Stop defending her*! Stop pretending we're trusting our lives to anything more than an untrained, coddled princess who thinks she's some sort of gods-sent savior!"

Every word struck like a blade. Tears, not blood, filled her eyes now. "Quill..."

"No. I'm done." He brandished his dagger, severing Pippet's bonds and lifting her limp body from the bed. "We're getting our own room, and if you cross that threshold, I *will* put you down."

Deafening silence gave that cruel oath all the time it needed to deal as much anguish as possible.

"Don't come near her ever again," Quill added. "The next time you want to gamble with a life, use your own. You're welcome to kill yourself flexing your power, but you're not taking my sister with you."

Like a dark and vicious storm, he and Pippet were gone.

CHAPTER
SIXTEEN

ITS BROTHERS WERE growing clever.

They knew they couldn't stop it, their warriors couldn't stop it so instead they brought the forged, the abominations, and unleashed them on the villages. Everything was smoke and char and flame, fang and claw, screaming, *screaming*—

So many to save and it was not enough. It was losing. They were going to reach her and she would come and lie down and bleed on the Door at their feet and the power would return and it could drink its fill and forget these people forget its people forget Blaykrone

Forget.

It was forgetting.

Forgetting why it hadn't used it yet and why any of this mattered and why it was sitting in a pool of its own blood again, looking up at the stars.

Athar, why do I bother getting up?

Snow and ice and fire and war, its hands empty, its head full of red hair and blades and screaming. The girl with two-colored eyes.

You know why.

It didn't. Getting up was too hard. Rising and fighting and being the only one here, the only one going to war for these people who hated it scorned it screamed at it sent it out to die again and again...

Too much. It did not want to get up anymore.

It shut its eyes and stopped following the world. It followed the light instead.

Tell me how we come back.

Distant, bright, pulsing. Stars and storms and hickory hair and green eyes, darkness and blood and a hive of power hidden somewhere deep, hidden far below like another well, like a Door, like a promise.

We come back because we know there's redemption, Afiyam.

It felt her reaching, felt the pulse, the ember of power lighting up the night it had lived in for so long, had run deeper into every day.

I don't believe that.

Yes, you do. You know there is.

Guttering and flickering and dying out, helpless, full of despair just like it, just like the pain that kept it down in its own blood this time—

You know because you've already seen life beyond it. You have already weighed the cost.

She *flared*, the power scythed out from her and jolted it up from the tree with a gasp, a bellow—

"*WILDHEART!*"

The forest stirred at its shout. Quieted. Settled.

Gasping, it staggered to its feet, turned northwest. Felt not only her but the darkness, but the focus, but the *rage*—

They would feel it, too. They would find her.

So it did the only thing it could think of. Took the flagon, took the power, and brought it into itself—stopped running, and stopped bleeding and stopped fighting.

It had found one once. It would find one again.

That was how it would turn them away from her this time.

It would breach the City of a Thousand Stars.

CHAPTER SEVENTEEN

THE GRAND COUNCIL and the Wingmaidens were taking their time preparing for this *Apiriak*—time that raced against Aden's will like a river around stone, eroding his patience. They should've been back in Valgard by now, back in the war with their cabal and their people. He should've been helping Thorne, searching for Pippet...for Maleck. Even here in Oadmark, he wouldn't have minded lending a diplomatic voice to Ashe's, or fighting at her side if that was what this mission demanded of him. It was all this stars-forsaken *waiting*, in the embrace of stone that reminded him far too much of all the dark places he'd visited both under and against his own will.

It was some comfort to have his father here, at least, who'd learned to take imprisonment in stride. But even Kristoff showed signs of restlessness after more than a week with nothing to do but stretch their legs and spar and talk, making up for twenty years apart.

"Does this place remind you of Kalt Hasa?" Aden asked one morning—or night. His sense of time had fogged after Ashe had returned from standing before the Council, and he no longer knew if he slept in day or dark. Not that it mattered in this dragonfire-lit corridor.

Kristoff sat beside him, their backs to the stone wall; Ashe drowsed, her head on her folded arm, and in thoughtful silence Kristoff removed his armored cloak and draped it over her. "Yes and no. The walls, the feel of this place...being caged." He rocked his head against the stone to look at Aden. "But I fear the dark less with you at my side...and I will kill my way from this mountain if it means keeping you safe."

Aden flashed his father a smile. "And here I believed I'd outgrown the need to have someone ready to tear apart the world on my behalf."

Kristoff winked. "Someday you'll understand this for yourself, Aden— a good father never loses the instinct to step between his children and danger. Even when you're ancient and gray, even if you have a sword in your hands and you're perfectly capable of facing all the foes of this world alone, I will be there. I made that vow when you were born, and I'll keep it to my dying day."

"Which will not be any day soon. That is *my* vow."

"Just the same." Kristoff rested one hand on Aden's shoulder, the other on Ashe's. "My purpose here is to keep you both alive so you can fulfill *your* calling. I will let nothing stand in the way of that."

Aden's retort cut short when Ashe roused, head lifting from her arm, gaze swiveling toward the prison hall. "Bres?"

Before either of them could speak, she launched to her feet, staggering to the cage bars and gripping them, first sagging, then stiffening to slam her open palms on the iron.

"Ashe!" Kristoff lurched upright. "What's the matter?"

Aden towed his father back by the arm. "She's cleaving." On the verge of sleep, with her defenses lowered, it seemed she'd achieved at last what she'd spent days fighting for: to see the world through her dragon's eyes.

All at once she was upright again, profaning brutally, swinging a wild punch into the cage bars—a strike that echoed in Aden's chest and rattled his heart itself. "*Ashe.*"

She didn't seem to hear them when they repeated her name in chorus; she broke into wild strides like a prowling creature before the bars. "Oh God's bones, oh, *damn* this, damn them, *damn them...*"

"Ashe." Kristoff's tone was quiet but fierce. "What did you see?"

She walked to the wall, jerked back and paced toward them, yanking her hands through her hair and folding them behind her head. She buried her face behind her arms, elbows pressed together, muffling her voice. "It's an arena. It's a *gods-damned* arena."

Horror iced Aden's veins. "*What?*"

"Bresnyar can see it, he's out there now...they're going to send us to fight something!" Ashe's voice cracked, and she spun to face him. "An *arena*, Aden!"

Her horror tasted like his own, like every nightmare Mira had helped him conquer of that place he'd finally walked out of and slammed the gate on, once and for all; that *Ashe* had crawled out of beside him, bad dream by bad dream, memory by memory.

They were sending her back.

Did they know? Had they reeled her reputation from Bresnyar, who first found her by seeking the legend of the rain-dancer and beast-slayer from the Blood Hive? Was this meant to be a test—or a breaking of her body and spirit so absolute, she could make no demands?

Cursing, Aden stepped into her path. "*Asheila.*"

"*What?*" she barked, sliding to a halt. "Get out of my way!"

"Not until you listen to me."

"I don't need a lecture, I need to *think!*" Ashe slammed the heels of her hands against her brow. "I need to cleave with him again, damn it!"

Aden rested his hand on her shoulder. "Stop."

"Don't tell me what to do!"

"And don't *you* forget who fought beside you in the Hive. I know what this means for you."

Ashe twisted suddenly, plucking his hand from her shoulder and jamming his arm back toward his chest. Aden trapped her fingers between his wrist and side, pinning her close to him.

"If you want a fight, I'll give you one," he said, "if that's what you need."

Slender hanks of hair trailed like blood across her brow, and she would not look at him. "I don't want to do this."

"I know."

"What do you need?" Kristoff asked.

"I need to *cleave* again so I can get a better look at what I'm up against."

Ashe yanked free of Aden and dragged her palms down her face. "But I can't. I can't control it because I can't let myself give up control long enough to be less than *useless* at this!"

Her self-loathing dragged across Aden's throat like a dagger, but his father's composure did not waver. "Control means everything to you."

Ashe dropped her hands and glared at him. "Control is how I *survive*."

"Then let's place the power back in your hands." Kristoff returned to the wall where they'd been sitting, smoothing his hands along its uneven edges until he found what he searched for: a blunt splinter of rock half the size of his palm. Crouching by the strongest trail of light along the bend in the tunnel, he gestured to Ashe. "Tell me precisely what you saw."

Frowning, Aden crouched beside him. "What are you doing, *Athar?*"

"Sketching a map. It's almost certain they won't give her the lay of this arena before she enters it, but she has an advantage they doubt: the strength of her bond with her dragon."

Slowly, Ashe bent to her knees on Kristoff's other side, hands braced on her thighs. "It was vague. It's not going to be enough."

Kristoff rested his hand on the back of her head. "I have faith in what you remember."

Ashe swallowed audibly, gaze fixed on the rock. Aden thought her chin trembled.

Kristoff put stone to stone. "Tell me."

And in the low, hoarse tones of a Blood Hive fighter, Ashe told them of the arena waiting on her horizon.

CHAPTER EIGHTEEN

TATIANA HAD NEVER seen Quill so furious.

She'd hoped during the first long hours in their separate room with only her enraged *valenar* and his unconscious sister for company that this would all amount to raw emotions and misunderstanding, and things would be made right when Quill saw that Pippet wasn't going to die. That even the feverish shakes and sweats had left her.

But then Pippet woke, and everything was worse.

The screaming didn't resume; neither did the threats, the insults, or words of any kind. Pippet lay on her side, eyes open but glassy, fixed on the door. She didn't answer when spoken to or rouse when Quill offered her food and drink; she just blinked at him, then curled tighter on herself.

The fury on Quill's face sent Tatiana out of the room at last, only to find Cistine sitting against the opposite side of the hall, legs folded, chin in her hands. She scrambled up when Tatiana emerged, eyes shining with despair.

Tatiana snatched her by the elbow. "Trust me, you don't want Quill to see you right now."

They stepped out onto Landamot's cold, gray streets, shoulders hunched against the wind. Chin tucked into her collar and eyes downcast, Cistine whispered, "How is she?"

"Awake. But not answering us."

Cistine's head sank even lower. "Gods, Quill was right...I shouldn't have done that. I shouldn't have gambled with her life, and I shouldn't have lied to all of you."

"That's true. You were reckless, wonder of wonders. But Quill overreacted, too. It's not like Pippet was getting better and you made things worse...things have just gone from terrible to a different kind of bad." She pocketed her hands and shrugged. "She's not hurling abuse anymore. That's something we should be thanking you for."

Cistine shot her a crestfallen look. "But I lost Quill's love to do it."

Tatiana wanted to argue, but after seeing the look in Quill's eyes when Pippet had refused food and drink yet again, she wasn't certain if it was a lie. "Well, you haven't lost mine." She wound her arm through Cistine's. "I'm willing to wait on passing judgement until we learn what's going on in Pippet's head. For now, I'm just glad she'd not threatening to break Faer's neck or reminding us about...you know."

"I do." Cistine bumped her temple against Tatiana's. "Now, where are you dragging me?"

"To find parchment, since I used the last of mine writing to Sander." Tatiana swallowed a spurt of nerves. "I think it's time I wrote to my father."

Cistine's steps slowed, nearly towing Tatiana to a halt on the main thoroughfare. "You mean about the—?"

"The baby, yes." Tatiana yanked her back into stride. "But also the part you wanted *Heimli Nyfadengar* to play in your little scheme."

"*What?* Really?"

"Stars, could you be any louder?"

"I'm just..." Cistine shook her head. "Tati, you said..."

"I know what I said." She looked left and right along the sleepy avenue, then pitched her voice lower. "Ashe is off chasing dragons. Iri and Saychelle are out there in the wilds risking their lives hunting for the rest of their Order. Now even *Sander* is putting his own skin to the flame looking for Devitrius and Rakel. I know the risks if the Guild joins rank with us, but I also know the outcome if they *don't*. Something this cabal taught me—"

"We're always stronger when we stand together."

Tatiana nodded. "I can't stop thinking about this siege on Blaykrone. What if one of those villages Maleck spared is the one where Kadlin and my papa and the others settled? Maybe while I've been trying to protect them, someone else dragged them into this fight." She broke her grip on Cistine to rub the chill from her arms. "I'm not the one who gets to decide if they're part of this war, but I can at least offer them a place with the winning side."

Distress tugged at the corners of Cistine's mouth. "Paper it is, then."

The city drowsed around them as they wound through its streets, stone-and-wood structures wrapped in a thin veil of early-morning fog. Another chill scampered along the back of Tatiana's neck, snaking tight like a scarf, and her hand drifted toward the knives belted under her armored cloak. "Cistine."

"I feel it, too," the princess muttered.

"*Nazvaldolya?*"

"No. Not Bloodwights. This is something else."

Cistine yanked her off the road and into a small, musty shop; the keeper looked up from her counter when their boots brushed the threshold, her expression crossed between surprise and unease. "I didn't expect anyone to be out at this hour."

Tatiana strolled across the room, mustering her most charming, disarming smile. "I'm looking for paper. And maybe a hint as to why it's like a pyre for the dead out there."

Cistine browsed innocuously by the storefront windows while the woman fetched a ream of parchment and laid it on the counter. Tatiana didn't miss how her hands rattled slightly when she set down the stack. "We haven't seen a Vassoran presence since the war began, but they swarmed the outskirts this morning. Ordered us all to remain in our shops."

Cistine glanced sharply over her shoulder. Tatiana ground her cheek between her molars. "Murderers in the streets? Bloodwights around?"

"Stars, I pray not. They didn't say why, only told us to take shelter."

"Well, they should've gone house to house," Cistine interjected sweetly, pulling away from the windows. "There were plenty of people out and about on our street. Maybe we could shelter here until they release us?"

"I don't see why not. The more sales, the better."

Tatiana didn't have the heart to tell her she'd just given the woman her last mynt, earned at a gambling table in the same tavern where they'd learned about the siege on Blaykrone. Stuffing the paper into her satchel, she joined Cistine just out of sight of the windows. "We should've brought Faer."

"I know." Cistine dragged her lower lip between her teeth. "Here, come over by the door."

They busied themselves at the shelves on either side of the slanted frame, pretending to browse notebooks full of pressed flowers while they watched Vassora materialize between the buildings. Five of them. Ten. A dozen, then more. Far too many to be in Landamot for a simple patrol.

A pair posted themselves at the corner outside the shop, passing a flask. They spoke in whispers, but with the tight shawl of fog hugging the city, the words were impossible to miss. "News from the front is the Bloodwights are drawing back into Stornhaz, regrouping inside the wall."

"As if they have any right to our home, stars damn them," the other scoffed. "What in Nimmus set them off this time?"

"If you believe the rumors, someone raided their augment stores."

"You're joking! What *bandayo* would be mad enough to try?"

"We're all going to be that desperate soon. Why do you think the Chancellors have us out here chasing rumors about the Key instead of at the front where we're needed most?"

Cistine's eyes blew wide, a small hiccup of shocked terror meeting the hand she pressed to her mouth. Her gaze latched onto Tatiana's, and the urge to run bounded up in her so quickly she nearly leaped through the doorway, brought down the guards, and took off with the Princess in tow. But the men were already capping the flask and scurrying off to meet their companions by the well; they exchanged a flurry of words, then turned toward Landamot's derelict edge. In seconds, they were gone.

Cistine dropped her hand. "We have to get the others *now*."

"It's too late." Tatiana stared after the vanishing guards. "They're heading toward the inn."

CHAPTER NINETEEN

THORNE WAITED DAYS to visit Quill—for both their tempers to cool and for Tatiana to leave the room at last before he slipped in to speak frankly with his friend. He found Quill posted on watch at Pippet's bedside while she slept, the storm in his gaze not abated in the least.

Thorne shut the door softly but sharply. "We need to talk."

Quill didn't look away from his sister. "I don't have much to say."

"I'm not surprised. You said quite a bit the day you threatened Cistine."

A twitch of the shoulders, and that was all.

Thorne forced himself to release the tatters of rage that had blinded him when Quill slammed Cistine to the floor, and when Cistine had lied to them and sent them out to meet Quill in the streets so she could steal a moment alone with Pippet to try to reel her back from the edge of Nimmus.

He'd already spoken to her about that; she'd apologized a hundred times. It was Quill he needed to see now...and Pippet.

It was the first time Thorne had laid eyes on her since the touch of Cistine's power, and his heart ached at the sight of her, small and feeble, lost in the filthy sheets. "How is she?"

Some of the tension loosened from Quill's shoulders. "I don't know. She sleeps longer and deeper than she did before, and I don't know if that's a good thing. I don't know what she *did* to her." He grazed a hand over his mouth and cursed. "I doubt *she* even knows what she did. You all like to call *me* reckless, but I don't play with people's lives this way."

"Think what you will of her, but if you ever speak to Cistine the way you did that day—"

"What are you going to do, Thorne? Ream me? Kick me out of your cabal?" Quill named the possibilities flatly. "Do I look like I give a damn?"

He didn't, and that disturbed Thorne most. Quill had been the first to choose Sillakove Court, even before Aden, throwing in his lot with the son of a cruel Chancellor for the sake of a better world. He'd fought for Thorne and Baba Kallah the day they were dragged before the tribunal, had been restrained by no less than ten Vassora to keep him from Thorne's side on his way to the whipping post. Yet in the face before him, there was only the burning, haggard desperation of a man so far past the end of his tether— and pain lurked in his clenched jaw and wet eyes.

"I would never turn my back on you, *Allet*." Thorne sat himself against the wall to wait for Pippet to wake—to see for himself the consequences of Cistine's actions.

He didn't know how long he slumbered, but he woke to screaming.

"Quill! *Quill, help me!*"

Thorne surged up from a dreamless slumber, eyes shooting to Pippet on the bed, cowering with the wall behind her, still shrieking her brother's name. A man in dark armor loomed above her, sword angled toward her throat to silence her scream.

Thorne lunged to his feet, but Quill reached them first, exploding from his own exhausted doze on the floor and slamming the Vassoran guard against the wall so hard, bone snapped and he crumbled dead to the floor.

A second man was already inside, and Thorne was on him in an instant, cutting his legs out and jabbing a blow under his chin, knocking him in a heap in the doorway. Pippet screamed again when a pair of guards leaped over the body of their fallen friend, blades hunting for Thorne's flesh. Quill seized him by the collar and yanked him out of harm's way, and in a well-learned pirouette they snapped apart and attacked as one.

Thumps and grunts resonated from the room down the hall,

simultaneous to the ruckus in theirs; Ariadne, fighting for her life. No sound or sign of Tatiana or Cistine, and Thorne prayed it would stay that way. These Vassora aimed their blows not to kill, but to dismantle. To capture.

They were here for the Key.

Thorne and Quill brought them down and dispatched them, leaving all but the one who'd threatened Pippet unconscious but alive, and Quill spun back toward the bed. "Are you hurt?"

Pippet cringed against the headboard, hands clapped over her ears, and shook her head with a wild look that gave Thorne pause. He couldn't be certain if it was some elaborate trick, or perhaps the nearness of mortality had startled her too badly to reach for her vitriol. But for the first time since that night with her hands in his jacket in that abandoned corridor when she'd screamed at him to get up, he saw something more than an acolyte when her gaze flashed to him, full of fear.

Quill looked at his shaking sister with no warmth or trust, no hope in how she'd screamed for him. He snatched her bound hands and hauled her down the hall where Ariadne was already dispatching the last guard. She spun at their arrival, blade dipping. "You as well?"

Quill nodded grimly. "We need to go. *Now.*"

Boots thundered up the stairs, and Pippet recoiled, flattening herself against the wall. Thorne snatched his sword harness from behind the door and whirled, letting out his breath only when Tatiana and Cistine crashed up the landing and skidded to a halt.

"Vassora," Tatiana panted. "They're here for Cistine."

"Already dealt with," Ariadne said.

"More are coming. They have most of the city on alert."

Thorne cursed under his breath. "Get your things."

Tatiana darted down the hall to her and Quill's room, but Cistine froze, her gaze trained on Pippet, who stared right back at her. It reminded Thorne of the tension snapping between Cistine and the *Aeoprast* outside Kosai Talis, but for once, Pippet didn't spit threats at the Key.

Quill slid an arm in front of his sister, angling himself between her and Cistine. "Whatever you're thinking, *stop.* Before you cause more trouble."

"Quill," Thorne growled.

With a swift blink, Cistine broke eye contact, barging through the doorway into their room. Quill maneuvered himself and Pippet out of her way—out of reach. The entire silent exchange set Thorne's blood aflame with bitter anger, but he would wait to address his warriors and his princess until they were safe from Vassoran hands.

In the end, there was no easy escape from the city, its edges already patrolled by Vassora who might've tracked them ever since Cistine's skirmish with Bravis and Sander in the mountains.

They had no choice but to fight to freedom.

"This is for your own protection," Ariadne said while she bound Pippet's hands to a hitching rail near the town's eastern edge. "You're better off far from this fight."

"I'll be back for you." Quill didn't spare his sister a glance, focus trained around the stable's shadow where they sheltered, watching the guards prowl at the nearby treeline. "And if you try to run, Faer will hunt you down."

Pippet didn't so much as nod, her unfocused gaze trained on her hands while Ariadne tied off the knot and stepped back. Cistine, pressed against the moldering stable wall beside Thorne, frowned. "If they try to come for her, she can't fight back."

"And now she cares," Quill muttered under his breath.

Tatiana jammed an elbow into his kidney. "Not helpful."

"Let's focus our anger where it belongs," Thorne snapped. "I don't need to be nannying all of you."

"Just the Key." Quill's head dipped below the line of his shoulders. "What are we waiting for, then?"

He shot from cover, taking aim at the nearest guard and bringing him down with a hard shoulder check. The others were after him in a synchronized lunge, meeting the Vassora blade-for-blade before they could wave for aid. The blur of steel and bodies was nearly welcome after all the heartache and confusion of Pippet's condition, Cistine's power, and chasing Maleck. Thorne didn't realize how badly he'd craved normalcy until battle offered a sliver of it. Every fight was the same stretch and grind of muscle, the same rhythm and beat like the dances Baba Kallah had taught him as a boy, twirling with his feet on hers through the apartment on those rare occasions when both his parents were gone.

Now he whirled through the guards, a different dance but just as familiar, bringing them down with hard blows and grazing slices; these were his people, after all, men he'd fought with on battlefields like Braggos; and he was their Chancellor. He prayed they might remember this mercy if the gods saw fit to return him to power.

If he didn't have to become King instead.

The thought roared through him, tipping his balance, and a blade sailed straight for his arm—a deadening blow. But Faer's shriek heralded the raven's arrival, slamming into the guard's face and knocking him reeling, talons tearing skin. Thorne dispatched the guard with a hard punch to the nose and whirled, seeking Quill in the fray. He was already on his feet, bleeding from the mouth, eyes wide.

With Faer here, there was no one to pursue Pippet if she struggled free.

Quill speared back toward the city's edge, and Thorne followed, leaving the women to clear the path to their escape. His throbbing heart already told him what they would find: the bonds unraveled, Pippet gone.

Nothing prepared him to duck around the stable's edge and find her still there, eyes fixed in the distance, breathing ragged. She flinched when Quill loosened the knot and did not resist as he slung her over his shoulder like a grainsack.

"Lead on," he panted to Thorne.

The way back was clear, a thin path opening into the forest behind Landamot; but from behind them came raised voices and pounding footsteps. So they ran with all their might, breaking into the trees and fleeing, Pippet a silent weight over her brother's shoulder while he took the lead; the others fell in beside them, quiet as death.

They journeyed for countless miles while the sun crossed the sky, even when the hard pace on the uneven terrain made them all limp. They ate and drank once they slowed from a run to a walk, picking through stream beds more than once and spreading out over mile-long stretches, then coming back together to confuse the trail. It was all trained into them, maneuvers they'd perfected during a decade living in the wilds, Cistine silently following their lead. Thorne was not too tired to be proud of them all when they finally stopped at nightfall to make a fireless camp among the trees.

Quill settled Pippet against one where she slid down, knees pulled to her chest, bound arms looped around her ankles, rocking in place. Quill vanished into the undergrowth, rolling kinks from his shoulders, and Tatiana settled to watch the girl from a distance. Cistine posted herself even farther away—silent respect for Quill's wishes—and Thorne sat beside her while Ariadne pulled dry rations from their bags.

"Am I just being hopeful," Cistine said the moment Thorne settled down, "or is there something different about her?"

He watched Pippet across the camp, who shook her head when Ariadne offered her food and water. "No. You're right, something is different. But it's too soon to say what it is."

"Do you think I made things worse?"

It was the first time she'd dared ask it, though he'd been waiting for days. He considered it, leaning his head against the tree at their backs. "Quill is right that we aren't certain what your power can do. Vandred didn't live long enough to for us to find out. But that you both live, without using a blood augment...that gives me hope. Maybe your power *is* the answer we've prayed for. To save Maleck and Pippet. To stop the Bloodwights."

A thin, encouraged smile tugged at Cistine's lips. "I hope you're right. Because after what we heard in the taverns in Landamot...I have to find him, Thorne. I *have* to."

Silence reigned for a few moments. Then Thorne said, "What happened in the town today?"

Cistine sighed. "We went for paper so Tatiana could write letters. We overheard the guards talking...something's changed on the front. The

Bloodwights pulled back into Stornhaz. It sounds like someone was foolish enough to raid the City's augment stores."

A bewildered curse escaped Thorne. "*Who?*"

"I don't know. Maybe the Chancellors found Rakel already and had the same thought about using the sewers for a siege."

"Bravis would never risk it. He was too shaken that the City fell to begin with." Thorne pressed his palms together and rested them against his lips. "If the army is planning to move on the City and this was a first strike to see if they could, we may not be able to wait for Ashe before we confront them."

"Confront them with what? I still don't have the augments I need to open the Door under the courthouse."

"No, but you have a bit more training in wielding and stealing augments, and we can lie our way through the rest. Maybe this is why they sent so many guards here to chase a mere rumor."

Cistine was quiet for a moment. "They want to capture me before they storm Stornhaz."

"That's my assumption. But we can't risk open confrontation with the Chancellors unless we know for certain they're desperate enough to try and retake the City."

"What did you have in mind for finding reports?"

"The same way we found them here: inns, taverns, and shops where gossip flows freely."

"That's a risk with the Vassora on the hunt. If they catch up to us again..."

"We'll go carefully," Thorne assured her. "But we'll hear no reports at all in the wild, and I think we've been far from news of this war for too long. Your gossip's ears must be itching."

He held her gaze when she turned to him, let her see the truth behind the snag in his words, the catch in his breath. It gnawed at him every day knowing his kingdom fought against the *mirothadt* forces and the Balmond while he ran, trained her, and tried to save Maleck. All of it necessary, but it was still a free-bleeding wound.

Cistine's hand crawled across the leaf mold to take his. "What city did you have in mind?"

"A remote one east of here, a barge port between two river branches. My father used to say news flows more freely down the Ismalete's banks, and I think he might've been right for once." He squeezed Cistine's hand and turned his gaze to the blackness crawling across the eastern horizon—a way paved in shadow. "We go to Hvallatar."

CHAPTER TWENTY

THE DARKNESS PARALYZED Ashe. She couldn't move; not her limbs, not her eyes, not her dry tongue bonded to the roof of her mouth. She could only stare in petrified horror while the Bloodwight slid its body above hers, blade upraised, wolf mask leering in the darkness.

"Maleck, don't," she wheezed. "*Mal*! Stop!"

He didn't hesitate at his name, didn't speak hers this time when he reared back and drove his blade into her chest.

Ashe gasped awake to the sound of her bones breaking under the knife, realizing only once she'd shot to her feet that the sound wasn't her sternum shattering but the cell door clanging open.

"*What do you want?*" she roared, still blinded by panic.

Meriwa stood in the doorframe, brows arched. Aden hovered at the cell bars nearby, shoulder leaned against them, deceptively calm, his father at his side. But the Legion Head paid them no attention, her pitying gaze fixed on Ashe. "The time has come. *Apiriak* commences."

Cold dread crawled from Ashe's hairline down her spine, but she parried it with a vicious thrust. This was her proving ground, and it was precisely how these people expected her to fall—just like Rion and the Wardens had once expected her to fall without them.

But there would be no fall. She'd readied for this, turned her focus from the arena to what was waiting for her within it: Bresnyar. Her dragon would be with her, their reunion so close it throbbed in her heart.

I'm coming, Scales.

She sent the thought into the void with the mad hope they might cleave; she'd tried to practice while they were imprisoned, but apart from that moment on the edge of waking when he'd showed her the arena, she'd never managed more than a dull flicker of gold in the darkness behind her eyelids.

Today, none of that mattered. She and Bresnyar would fight their way through this trial, make full proof of their bond, and present their case before the Grand Council.

Shaking off the last threads of her nightmare, Ashe strode to the cell door. "I'm ready."

Meriwa's smile suggested disbelief at best, and more likely scorn. At her short whistle, a pair of Wingmaidens materialized from the dark hall, weapon-strapped and grim-faced, dragging Aden and Kristoff from the prison behind Ashe.

"Wait," she snarled, heels catching on the stone, "this is *my* test! They're not part of it!"

"I'm aware." Meriwa's brawny strength bucked against Ashe's resistance. "They're going to watch."

Watch you perish. The words were inferred only by the slant of her brows and the cruel tilt of her mouth. Teeth gnashing, Ashe looked back at Kristoff and Aden; the latter seethed visibly, but the former watched her with nothing but that quiet belief she'd already come to associate with him, as if she'd already won this Test and was merely here to mop up the mess left behind.

For now, Ashe chose faith over fury; it was all that kept her from kicking Meriwa in the kidneys on the long trek down the spiral of staircases toward Ujurak's floor, and through a long tunnel growing colder and darker as they went. If not for the bottled dragonfire on the hips of the Wingmaidens before and behind them, the shadows would've choked Ashe. On impulse, she touched the braided cord on her upper arm, bringing a shred of Maleck's memory into the darkness with her. *What are you, Asheila? I am not afraid.*

But her knees still threatened to shake when the nightmare at last appeared down the tunnel ahead, beckoning like a beast's gaping jaws: the flurry of chattering voices caught on elliptical walls, the smell of sunbaked sand and sweat colliding with the reek of old metal and leather and *blood*. So much blood, and fire, the animal stink of Viperwolves and Dahadts and serpents and wildcats lunging across the melee-stricken arena—

A shoulder checked hers sharply from behind; Aden barged forward, ignoring his captor's shout, dipping his head to breathe against her ear, "You are the rain-dancer and beast-slayer. Lady of this Hive. You do not break."

She looked up at him, those gray eyes blazing with the same memories, the same hate, the same rage as hers; but beyond them there was belief even stronger than his father's, so absolute it crushed her first blooms of self-doubt like he'd crushed her under his boot so many times in Siralek—until hate had become understanding, and friendship, a bond no one else in the cabal would ever understand.

"You do not break," he repeated.

His guard caught him, hustling him and Kristoff past Ashe toward the end of the tunnel that opened up into the arena. Ashe jolted after them, and Kristoff turned back just enough to press a kiss to her brow, fleeting and unprovoked and so tender it halted her in shock. Then they were both gone, turned through a seam in the wall.

Meriwa took Ashe's shoulder, her touch surprisingly light. "This is cruel and unfair. They should not do this to you."

"Well, maybe if someone had said as much to them," Ashe grunted.

"It is not a Wingmaiden's place to speak to the Grand Council unless spoken to first." Meriwa gazed ahead, eyes distant with memory. "But this is wrong. *Apiriak* is what a Wingmaiden spends her whole life training for. It is the test of the bond, the proving of dragon and Wingmaiden." Her ruthless eyes slid to Ashe. "You will never survive it. They should not give a Wingmaiden's trial to a lost girl from another kingdom."

Ashe's hands curled into fists at the tilt of Meriwa's mouth, the silent dare for her to sling a blow—to give Meriwa a reason to send her out into that arena with bruised ribs, a limp, *something* to cripple her. But fletches of gold danced across her vision, and her anger stilled swifter than a hound catching a familiar scent.

She took a step back toward the tunnel mouth. "If my bond with Bresnyar is so impossible, why are you trying this hard to provoke me?"

Meriwa's eyes narrowed, and she gave no retort.

"I thought so." Smirking, Ashe backed away again, arms spread. "I hope you're ready for a show, *Legion Head*. Bres and I are ready to give you one."

"You're going to die in that arena!" Meriwa snapped. "You will not see tomorrow's sunrise!"

"I wouldn't be too sure. Where I'm standing, it seems like the gods are betting on *me*."

Ashe's heels contacted sand, and with a low, harsh clatter, a grate tumbled into place between her and Meriwa, blocking Ashe's escape back into the tunnel. And blocking Meriwa from reaching her.

The exultant roar of Oadmarkaic voices brought Ashe spinning on heel, half-blinded by the sun bouncing off the sand—and too deafened by their cries to hear the deeper snarling until slavering animal jaws clicked shut an inch from her throat.

Instinct sent her diving left, rolling through the hot sand, grains catching and scraping her filthy Valgardan battle armor. She rocked upright and feinted left, then back again, shaking the sun-seared scorches of hot blue from across her vision, trying to gather the full measure of what she was facing.

Weight pounded her flank from the right, spinning her into a jutting shear of stone gouging up from the sand, and with a curse Ashe grabbed the hot rock and scrambled on top of it, flipping into a crouch on its pinnacle and sweeping her surroundings.

Not quite as large or as high as the Blood Hive, this arena was clearly forged of imported sand splashed among the natural stones in the shadow of Ujurak. The mountain loomed up to her left, the wide-open expanse of sky to her right, and on every other side there was uneven stone and wooden seats three levels high, slick walls, and that gods-forsaken sand. Just how she remembered it from that brief glimpse through Bresnyar's eyes, despite all her reservations about her memory—almost exactly how Kristoff had sketched it. Days of recreating this place in her mind, reinforcing its shape and boundary in conversation while she sparred with Aden, made this feel less like Siralek.

She was ready.

Below, Oadmarkaic creatures prowled in loops: jagged-haired, horse-sized wolves, mouths dripping saliva, scarlet eyes aglow between sunlight and mountain shade. There were more than the two who'd attacked her already, dark blots circling other clots of stone, closing in. What she didn't see was the most important thing of all.

She did not see Bresnyar.

Her gaze shot to the stands, finding Aden and Kristoff on the lowest level at the top of the wall, held in place by the Wingmaidens, unseated and braced forward with mirrored intensity as if they'd leap to her aid in a heartbeat. Her gaze met Aden's, and his barely-perceptible shrug was the answer to a question she feared.

He didn't see Bresnyar, either.

Ashe's focus found the Grand Council next: Allfather, Allmother, Allbrother and Allsister seated together in a viewing box like Noaam's in Siralek. Mother and son looked utterly bored, but Killik and Novuam watched with feral intensity, angled forward in their seats the same way, regarding her with the same taunting venom.

Where is your dragon, Asheila Kovar? Those stares all but screamed. *Why can't you find your mount, Wingmaiden?*

The scrabble of wicked talons on stone jerked Ashe from her thoughts. Bresnyar was not dead; she could feel him like she felt Maleck, like the dragon's two hearts beat with her own wild pulse in the Wingmaiden rune on her palm. He was here, but out of sight. So, until he decided to show his glorious golden face, she would deal with these wolves herself.

She hunted the arena for what Siralek taught her would always be there: a weapon kept handy for the sake of spectacle. Judging by the loops and patterns, this sand had been raked over recently and thoroughly.

"Just how many prisoners are you sending to their deaths here, Council?" The sound of her own voice, unshaken and furious, gave her strength and sharpened her focus; in seconds, she spotted the distant glint of a blade partway across the arena, its half-buried blade winking in the angled sunlight.

She cracked her knuckles, pressed against the scars on her palm, and coiled her muscles to leap.

Fearless is my name.

With a mighty lunge, she flipped over the wolves, landed in a crouch on the sand, and broke into a run.

Aden's voice led the riot of sound from the stands, a cheer of her name blending into a hundred inarticulate cries and throaty howls when the wolves gave chase. Despite the pliant footing, their steps had weight, drumming into Ashe's soles, the backs of her knees, her head.

She shut the sound out. This was just Hive training, the sand familiar under her feet, her toes gripping and flexing in her boots the way they had during hard runs around the arena. She had done this before, survived it before, and she would do it again.

Hot breath licked the back of her armor, and with a curse and a kick, Ashe snapped her heel into the wolf's jaw, handsprang forward, and lifted the sword from the sand. Whirling in an upswing, she spilled the creature's throat, spraying blood across her armor, the rocks, and the sand.

And the fight was on.

There seemed to be no end to the wolves; no matter how much Ashe hacked and swung, their ranks replenished. They fell and fell and attacked again, barreling relentlessly toward her under the hot sun, and even when sweat stung her eyes and repetitive motion seared her muscles, their numbers did not falter.

More were being unleashed from somewhere, keeping the spectacle alive while the sun crawled across the sky. These furious Oadmarkaics were determined to wear her down, heedless of how many of their own fell. Like the *mirothadt*, like strikes from Salvotor and the Bloodwights against their cabal, against her, against *Maleck*...it didn't matter. The enemy had an endless well of energy, and Ashe...

Ashe had so much to lose, and more still being taken from her with every beat of her heart, every second skimming by. Boredom seethed from the stands at the monotony of falling creatures and swinging blade; whatever these people had expected to see, it was grander than this.

Unlike Blood Hive onlookers, they didn't come to watch a woman be shredded to ribbons by wolf claws. They wanted to see a Wingmaiden and a dragon tested, and they only had one of those things.

She was failing by no fault of her own.

Bres, where are you?

Gold splashed across her vision, and for an instant Ashe didn't just see, she *heard*: the roar of the arena, but muffled, the slam of blade on flesh distorted, the angle wrong, the depth askew—

Hot, hairy flesh crashed into her head and chest, bowling her over into the sand and pressing her down so hard she lost her air. Choking, gasping on the old-meat-and-blood stench of the wolf's hide, she thrashed and jabbed; but she was at the wrong angle, her blows weak and imprecise, and those cruel claws tore at her Valgardan battle armor, shredding down through the reinforced threads.

The spirited cries revived above her, and distantly she was aware of Aden shouting at her to get up, get up *right now*, but she was sinking deeper, the sand giving way below her body, those jaws cutting toward her throat—

You do not break.

The words jolted through her, a burst of lightning, brash rage tunneling through her chest.

Do not break.

Sucking in that rotten scent so deep it left her gagging, Ashe screamed in the wolf's face, screamed with all her might, and somehow the sound became words. "*I am not afraid of you!*"

The wolf recoiled at her atavistic howl, one predator snarling into another's face, and with a wild buck Ashe twisted her sword, found flesh, and dug in. Galled by the creature's pained yelp, she planted her feet into its stomach and flipped it, landing on top, drawing out the blade and shoving it in again.

But the second her knees hit the sand on either side of the wolf's ribs, the second her blade plunged in, a vicious crack tremored through the arena. It was a sound she hadn't heard since the winter she went skating with Viktor Pollack on the lake near Middleton, two young Wardens so full of carelessness and flirtation they thought meant something more...and he fell through the ice, forcing her to dive in and save him.

Ashe lunged backward, but it was too late. Whatever strange surface they'd hidden under the sand gave way at the shift in her weight, and Ashe and the wolf plunged down into darkness.

Up, Asheila. Get up.

Not Aden's voice this time. Not his anger propelling her from the thick, humming stillness inside her head.

Ashe, you must get up.

Could she? Was there enough of her left to piece together, to pull herself from these shadows?

Asheila, listen to me, if you do not rise, you will be devoured. Get up NOW!

Her eyes sprang open, a thin seam of gold dancing at the edges of her vision before vanishing, leaving her utterly in darkness again.

Holy gods, she was *blind*.

"*Ilyanak*, do you hear me?"

She sucked in a sand-choked breath and coughed, feeling desperately along what felt like rock beneath her. "Bres? Bresnyar, where *are* you?"

"To your right." His warm breath chased the chill from her body, but when she twisted that way, there was more darkness. "You do not see me."

"I can't see *anything*! Did that fall—?"

"You are not blind. You're beneath the arena with me." A distant rattle of thick chain scraped in the dark. "I cannot come to you, do you hear why?"

He was bound. They'd *bound* her dragon like a cavern in Kalt Hasa, sent him back to his own Nimmus and left him here to rot as punishment.

Shaking with rage as well as nerves, Ashe turned a full circle, seeking some sort of light, anything—but there was none. "This isn't a test, it's an execution! What is the *point* of this if they can't see us?"

"They can see. The arena floor is built of Ujurak's volcanic glass—dark on one side, clear on the other. The break cleared the sand, so they can see us. We cannot see them."

"Where's the gap? Why isn't there any light?"

"I heard a stone wedge into the hole when you fell. *Ilyanak*, listen to me. The darkness is the least of your problems. You did not fall alone."

Ashe spun toward the sound of his voice, the shadows so thick she couldn't see even a glint of his scales. But before she could tell him that the darkness was, in fact, at the very peak of her current worries, a strained growl sliced through the still air.

Ashe froze, empty hands curling into fists. "Wolves?"

"I can see them. They're circling you."

"I take it they can see *me*?"

"Their sight is as good as mine, if not better."

She had no weapon, no way to see where the first strike would come from, no light by which to find her way. "Can you burn them?"

"Not without catching you ablaze. Dragonfire does not discriminate."

Cold sweat dewed her neck and palms. Her cheeks and nose tingled, she couldn't force her lungs to expand to a full breath, and even in darkness, the world tipped and tilted.

This was panic. This was knowing death stalked her from feet away and being powerless to defend against it, to fight for herself or her dragon, chained in the shadows. This was being utterly out of control, brought lower than Siralek had ever managed.

Because if she died here, Bresnyar died with her, and Aden, Kristoff, and Nuna would be next. Then Valgard and the rest of the kingdoms would fall under a tide of Balmond—all because Asheila Kovar had failed. Because she lost control. Because she let them all down one last time.

Pain thrummed through her side, and a wolf's growl boomed in the dark, scenting injury. Scenting blood. Ashe clapped a hand to her arm, finding tackiness where claws had pierced through the armor—and once again she grazed the strip of Maleck's scarf. The scent of cedar and charcoal washed over her, and in a gut-rocking crash, she saw a way forward—a thin seam of hope, impossible and dim. But it might be the only way to save them all.

Memory plucked her out of the pit, took her back to a mountainside in the shadow of Selv Torfjel, to Maleck and Bresnyar walking with her in the gloom.

What frightens you about the cleaving?

Not being in control.

There was no control here. Not over her life, not over her death. And as easy as it was to claim fearlessness when she controlled the outcome, that bravery was a pretty mask for all the things that terrified her.

Losing Maleck. Losing the cabal. Being trapped in the darkness, in the sand. Facing the enemy without a sword in her hand. Spending one second longer without her dragon.

Fearlessness would never be her truth as long as she tried to control these outcomes. The control was, itself, fear under disguise.

Ashe's fingers swiftly worked at the knot, unspooling the cord from her upper arm.

"*Ilyanak.*" Bresnyar hardly breathed the word—all the sign she needed that the wolves were drawing nearer. "Your scent has changed. What are you—?"

"Trust me, Scales. I know what I have to do."

This test would not be her undoing if she embraced true fearlessness, true courage; if she gave up the need to possess the outcome and leaned on someone else's strength to shore up her own. Just like she'd learned to with Maleck.

Fearlessness was easy with him at her back. It was time to put that faith in someone else: in her dragon. And in *herself.*

Breaths rattling but hands steady as if the gods themselves guided her, Ashe bound the cloth around her eyes, plunging herself utterly and absolutely into the shadows. She breathed in her courage, breathed out her terror.

I am not afraid of this.

Fearless is my name.

She raised her head, and against the cloth's chafing threads, opened her eyes at last.

The pit opened wide around her, a world dazzling in gold filigree, stamps of heat pulsing where the wolves prowled. A cold scrawl of metal showed her sword just out of reach. And in the center of the small room, Ashe saw herself burning like a star. When she twitched her right hand, she saw it move. When her left foot skimmed the stone, she watched the faint puff of dust it raised.

She saw everything through Bresnyar's eyes.

ILYANAK. His reverence, disbelief, and exultation surged through her as clearly as if he'd roared them toward the sky.

In his perfect sight, Ashe watched herself brace forward, watched the wolves drop back and coil to spring.

They moved as one, beasts and Hive Lady—Ashe kicking the blade up into her hand, the wolves leaping. Steel and fang met in a screaming dervish, and by her dragon's vision Ashe guided herself, turned her blade left and right, cut and carved down the creatures.

She was there to meet them at every turn; her steel sang as loud and wild as her pulse, triumph surging in her veins, Bresnyar's twin hearts crashing in tandem with hers through every blow. They brought down wolf after wolf until they scouted the pit and found it empty but for the fallen creatures, their bodies growing dim as their living warmth faded; and Ashe and Bresnyar were left facing one another.

She watched herself approach him, saw herself through his eyes as she had the day the bond had forged between them. She laid her hand to his muzzle, feeling both the heat of her palm on his nose and the rub of his scales on her own skin. It should've disoriented her, being within his senses and hers as one, but few things had ever felt so right. So much a part of her.

"What do you say we get out of here, Scales?" she panted.

His breath warmed her bloodsoaked face. "What say." *NEVER HAVE I KNOWN A WOMAN SO MAGNIFICENT. NOT EVEN ILERIA…*

Ashe popped him on the muzzle. "Stop that. Ileria was magnificent in her own way, I'm sure."

The cold of stone and darkness consumed her in the absence of Bresnyar's breathing. The quick heave of his ribs stilled.

"Asheila," he choked after a moment, "you can hear me?"

"Weren't you just saying something about how magnificent I am?"

This pause was so heavy and absolute Ashe wondered what the spectators were thinking, if they *felt* the depth of this silence and the shock riding along it—an awe she didn't comprehend.

"*Ilyanak*, I did not say it. I *thought* it."

Ashe blinked, cloth dragging her lashes. "Is that…not normal?"

"Not in this age. A bond…a *cleaving* so strong has not been spoken of in our lore and history for more than a thousand years."

Ashe's knees buckled. "You're *joking*."

"You should know by now I do not jest about matters of this importance."

Ashe's breaths turned ragged. "What in God's name *are* we, Bres?"

His muzzle pressed her rune. "We are one, until the stars burn out."

Heat budded on her lashes, and Ashe sucked in a harsh breath. "Let's get you out of these chains."

Following the path of his sight, she brought her blade down on his tether, strike after strike to the same link until, with a timely blow and a wrench of his sinewy neck, the metal severed. Ashe skimmed her hand along his side, gripped his wing joint, and swung onto his back. "If anyone tries to leash you again while I'm still alive, we eat them. Old Legion or not."

He snorted. "I would very much like to see you try to eat a dragon."

"It can't be that hard. One bite at a time."

Bresnyar's laughter shook the walls, and with an arch of his neck he shot fire upward, shattering the roof in a thousand brilliant shards. Light pierced the cloth around Ashe's eyes, but she didn't remove it yet.

Bresnyar spread his wings and lunged, rising up from the arena's broken middle, surging half the height of Ujurak in a few mighty strokes. Through his eyes, Ashe saw the world open around them like one of Cistine's books, the horizon fizzing with colors she'd never seen before, palettes and hues undetectable to weak mortal eyes—the dish of the blue sky, the glitter of sunlight on faraway waters, the thin seam of the whitecapped mountains lining the horizon.

The cloth caught her tears when they escaped. "Gods, I never knew. This is what the world looks like through your eyes."

"Beautiful, is it not?"

Ashe laid her hand to his neck. "It's something worth fighting for."

She felt the smile tug his lipless mouth, then his wings folded close and they fell in a glorious spiral back to the arena, slamming into the stable stone at the edge of the glass, sand flurrying around them.

Dead silence greeted their descent; no cheers, no jeering. Ashe slid from Bresnyar's back and followed his sight up toward the Grand Council's viewing box, where the ruling family had all come to their feet.

As one, Ashe and Bresnyar sketched bows.

Killik spoke rapidly off to the side, and Bresnyar's voice echoed in Ashe's head: *HE DOES NOT BELIEVE WE'RE BONDED.*

What more does he want? For me to breathe fire?

THAT MIGHT BE A START. BUT FOR NOW...

"Sever your sight," Bresnyar said aloud, and Ashe removed the cloth, blinking her eyes open. Her dull human senses greeted her: an arena washed in drab tones of taupe and gray, the people indistinct shapes above.

"Cleave again."

With a deep breath and a prayer to the gods, Ashe shut her eyes and reached out to Bresnyar with mind and heart, curled fingers raking the rune, and she felt him reaching back to her. When she looked again, color seeped back into the world, fletched and dazzling—this time with no need for cloth.

This was utter control, and utter trust.

She and her dragon tilted their heads in synchrony, blinking in unison. They swiveled to gaze at the stunned, silent spectators, and Aden and Kristoff grinning, and the Grand Council and Meriwa, halfway down the stands to their viewing box, pale as turned milk, gaping shamelessly.

"Any more tests?" Ashe's shout carried thinly in the utter silence. "Because my dragon and I can do this all day."

Killik dropped back in his seat, muttering under his breath.

HE SAYS THIS IS NOT POSSIBLE.

"I promise you, it is," Ashe said, and when Bresnyar barked the words in the Oadmarkaic tongue, Tapeesa uttered something so sharp there was no doubt she'd cursed. "It's time you started wondering what's happening with the rest of the kingdoms. I think it's fairly obvious the gods are trying to get your attention."

Killik looked to Tapeesa, then Asiaq, who sat forward with hands cupped to his mouth, staring at Ashe in wonder; Novuam rose halfway from her seat, hands gripping the armrests and furious gaze locked on Ashe.

I think she wants to kill me, Scales.

SHE WILL HAVE TO FIND HER WAY PAST ME FIRST. AND I CAN ASSURE YOU, NOT EVEN THE ALLSISTER POSSESSES STRENGTH ENOUGH TO TAKE YOU AWAY FROM ME.

The silence dragged on, and Ashe wound Maleck's scarf around her scarred palm and held the fabric tight to her skin, pressing it to the very center where her pulse beat hardest.

I did it, Mal. I did it. Mereszar crawled out of the ashes in this place. Her mouth curled at the sly joke, imagining how he would've smiled to hear her say it. *Gods, I hope you're proud of me.*

At long last, Killik spoke a few short, chafing syllables. Ashe severed the bond, looking to her dragon for confirmation. The glint in his fiery eyes said it all, but still she was glad he uttered the words so all could hear:

"The Grand Council will hear Valgard's plight."

CHAPTER TWENTY-ONE

T HE ARENA HELD its breath while Meriwa summoned Nuna from among the stands; the tribeswoman appeared with a wide smile quickly schooled back into a somber face when she reached the Grand Council. Killik spoke sharply to her, and Nuna translated to Ashe, "Make your appeal quickly."

For the first time, Ashe was grateful for every moment they'd spent imprisoned here. She'd rehearsed this enough that her voice didn't even waver. "I'm sure Nunajik has told you Valgard is at war. The first encounter we had with this enemy was here, inside Oadmark's borders. Two Valgardan warriors faced a creature that called itself the *Aeoprast*."

A stir of whispers traveled through the stands. Meriwa's arms tightened in their cross, her eyes falling to half-lid.

"What the *Aeoprast* really is, we call a Bloodwight...a creature who aspires to eternal life by abusing gifts from the gods." Asiaq sat up sharply in his seat when Nuna translated this; Novuam sank back down into hers, fingers springing free of the rests. "We've tried to stop them, and so far, we've failed miserably. They have an army of criminals, and they've taken children and...corrupted them." A flash of Pippet's masked face ripped through her memory, bringing her voice low. "They're no better than slaves."

Tapeesa slammed her fist on her thigh when Nuna finished speaking. Killik tipped his head, eyes narrowing.

Now she had their attention. She forced away that dark memory of Pippet, focusing on the Grand Council above.

"The Bloodwights continue to advance across Valgard with the help of the Balmond—abominations knit together from children and animals. Because of their armored flesh and addiction to augments, they're almost unstoppable. And the Bloodwights will use them like a battering ram to smash down any resistance they face...not just in Valgard, but in Talheim and Mahasar. And then they'll come for you. They'll find a way to break into your mountain halls and use their lightning augments to tear your dragons from the sky."

The whispers were louder when Nuna translated this time.

"These Bloodwights are like nothing we've ever fought before. They have no qualms about who they use or hurt to reach their goal. And these Balmond...we've only seen one creature capable of killing them, and that's *him*." She laid her hand on Bresnyar's neck, and every eye followed the motion—all but Meriwa. She looked toward the distant frame of a scarlet dragon perched high above the arena in Ujurak's shadow: Aeosotu, a silent spectator to his former Wingmate's near-death.

This time, after Nuna translated, Killik responded, harsh and raw. Nuna turned to Ashe. "Allfather asks what you wish of us."

Ashe let her hand fall from Bresnyar's neck. "The Balmond don't stand a chance against dragonfire. If you send your Legions to help, Valgard might have hope of pushing back the enemy lines. There are too many for Bresnyar to bring down alone. If he fights them, he falls. Sooner or later."

Her voice shook around the unbearable truth she'd known ever since the Balmond had leaped on Bresnyar's injured tail while he'd defended her on the path near Kosai Talis. He was not indestructible; she was here to save him as much as Valgard, because no one should stand alone for the salvation of a kingdom. Not a dragon. Not a princess. Not the Key.

"Stand with us. Fight with us," she urged when no one offered a reply. "This is not just a threat to the Northern Kingdom...countless men in your southern villages died facing the *Aeoprast*. Countless Valgardans have died now. Even Talheim risks its future to end this war. Either you can face the Bloodwights alone when the rest of us have fallen, or you can stand with us now and we'll destroy them together."

Meriwa dropped her gaze from the upper ledge to search the stands. Asiaq reclined, resting his chin on his knuckles and muttering to Novuam. She rolled her eyes.

Frustration cracked through Ashe's composure, and she stepped forward. "To Nimmus with all these gods-damned borders! The kingdoms need each other. Without your dragons, we fall. But without our warriors, they'll kill your dragons. This isn't something you can hide from forever, even in your precious mountain. So on behalf of all the kingdoms and your own land...get off your asses and *fight!*"

Silence descended through the arena, and Ashe struggled to catch her breath; she'd shouted so loudly her head spun, but she felt like she could fight this whole place, fight the Balmond themselves. Punch the mask off a Bloodwight's face. Rip Maleck from his brothers' ranks and back into her arms with her bare hands. She wanted a sword. She wanted a war. She wanted to channel every ounce of this energy into battle, and she wanted these Legions to fly into it beside her.

Killik and Tapeesa consulted in swift, muted syllables. Then Killik rose and addressed Nuna, who smiled sadly at Ashe. "The Council will discuss this matter with the Legion Heads. They will send for you when the time comes. Until then, you return to the mountain."

Ashe let out her breath in a short surge. It wasn't the rousing agreement she'd hoped for; but when she met Meriwa's eyes, hope sparked in her chest. There was a look there she knew all too well from her own eyes caught in mirrors and still waters so many times.

The look of a woman shouldering the weight of responsibility—and trying to decide how best to carry it out.

CHAPTER
TWENTY-TWO

IT HAD DONE the impossible. Again. Had gone where they said it couldn't go, shouldn't go, had crept and craved and *taken...*

Too much. Too much, far too much. But with the song and light and power inside it, it didn't care what they said what it did what it crawled through and up and out of, how it went back to the sewers where it had promised *never again* after its failure after it fled after it left her behind—

Maleck. Stop.

It shook its head shook away traces of rage hate screaming that clung to it like shadows like an augment like *power* that set the whole world spinning, an axis of stars and lights and logs and grass and distant color, the roaring in its ears and around it and ahead...

It had taken an eternity to come here, to seek to find to follow the pulse, the falling star to the place where it crashed into the earth, not the meadow not the hollow not that star but *its* star, the one it followed to death and danger and beyond.

To this place.

It remembered this place this story this dark blot on a map where its leader its brother the man with the silver hair once told it *news flows more freely down the Ismalete's banks* it could hear any report on anything near barges and ports and water, it could find anything, anything, *anyone....*

She slept below, dark and silent and shaking with nerves and wonder and tension and anger and *power* and—

Its hand spasmed against its side touched the power the small storm cradled in its fist. *Mine mine mine mine it's mine why should I give why should I let go could use could keep could fight*

But the things it heard. The plans being made.

It had to choose, had to choose *now right now right this instant* where it would go and how it would do this and when, and why—

In the next one, we learn to let you go.

It did not want to let go did not want to go down there did not want to give and see and then flee.

So it stayed while the stars cycled, shadow against shadow, night against night, waiting. Fighting itself. Fighting everything.

Watching Hvallatar.

THE
BRIDE

OF

LOVE AND
SACRIFICE

CHAPTER TWENTY-THREE

TATIANA COULDN'T STAND the strange way the cabal carried itself to Hvallatar, like a body shielding broken bones—or how she, of all people, was the one keeping the peace.

It was nearly impossible, loving two people who refused to speak to each other. Loving Quill with his mute rage and his gaze perpetually fixed on his sister, waiting for the next outburst; and loving Cistine, miserably silent even when she and Thorne disappeared for hours every dawn to train.

It was no small relief to reach Hvallatar at last. Like Hellidom, it grew naturally from the landscape around it, an array of wooden homes half-buried among the trees at the southeastern edge of the Sotefold between two branches of the Ismalete Channel. Tatiana wished they could stay at its modest two-level inn, but she knew better than to broach the subject after the disaster in Landamot.

Still, she leaped at the opportunity to patrol with Ariadne, leaving the tension of their cabal to prowl the congested streets for some news from the war or a hint of what the Chancellors were planning.

The reports were not happy. The stink of augments hung perpetually across the whole kingdom. The lines had fallen back twice. The Bloodwights had pressed further south before retreating inside Stornhaz; a few travelers claimed to have seen them, which was why they were running east, where the wilderness was broader with more places to hide.

And then there were the attacks close by. A Bloodwight brasher than most, wearing a wolf mask, blazing through the dark with lightning and dimming the days with ravaging darkness. No one knew what to make of him or why he lingered in the west when the rest of the Bloodwights had withdrawn to Stornhaz.

Tatiana hated the look on Quill's face when she and Ariadne told them everything they'd heard around the campfire that night, the way his brow scrunched and his bleak stare shifted so cold.

"He isn't going to stop, Thorne," Quill rasped. "We need to find him before these reports turn to massacres."

"I know," Thorne said, steady despite his haggard appearance, tired and unshaven. "But first, the Chancellors. I need to know what they're planning with the City, how desperate they are. If they truly plan to raid Stornhaz, that will endanger more lives than a stroke of Maleck's hand ever could."

Quill shook his head and shoved aside his bowl of thin stew, and Tatiana halted with her spoon halfway to her mouth. She couldn't remember the last time she'd seen him eat. She knew it couldn't have been that long ago, because he was still standing; but his wrists and cheeks were adopting a harsh thinness.

"Aren't you going to finish that?" she asked.

"Not hungry." He popped a cinnamon stick between his teeth. "How long do we plan to stay here, exactly?"

"Today and tomorrow," Thorne said. "Patrols at sunset and dawn. Cistine and I will take the night, you three take the morning. Once we've slept, she and I will see what we can find in Hvallatar. Perhaps more talkative bargemen come in with the morning tide."

Ariadne's lips quirked, but Quill scowled. "Let me handle it. I can wrestle reports about Stornhaz from a few drunk sailors, that's nothing."

Thorne held his gaze calmly. "Once I see you eat more than a few bites and look at something without glaring, I'll consider it. Until then, none of us needs the consequences of your fists flying in temper rather than temperance."

Tatiana stifled a wince on her *valenar's* behalf and set aside her own bowl, braced to step into Quill's path if he decided to do something more than stare Thorne down with half-hooded eyes, jaw ticking.

But he relented after a moment, rising sharply to check on Pippet bound around a sapling nearby, sleeping with her head against its soft, smooth bark.

Tatiana couldn't rest that night, not even after the fire fully died and Thorne and Cistine disappeared on patrol. If it wasn't her own racing thoughts, Quill's restlessness brought her back to consciousness again and again, his hand stroking her back, jittering unevenly from shoulders to waist and back again.

She flipped over to face him, slinging an arm across his middle. "Pippet or Maleck?"

"Both." She might've mistaken his husky voice for sleepiness if his eyes weren't fixed on the dark gaps between the budding trees above.

"We'll find him. Losing sleep isn't going to help."

"I know that."

"So go to sleep."

His abdomen flickered like a laugh was trying to crawl out, but it didn't escape his downturned mouth. He craned his head, chin to his chest, peering down at her. "You know, back when we were in Hellidom...and in Veran, after the drinking, you kept calling me the strong one. The steel in your spine. But the way you've held this cabal together during this war, even after you lost the baby...you've been *our* backbone, you know that?"

Tatiana scoffed. "Right."

"I mean it. You are. You're *my* backbone." Quill took her hand in his and drew it across his body, resting over a scar that laced his bare hip, nearly a twin to the one that had ended the dream of their first child. "I think if anyone could survive this war, it's you. You're the sunrise after the storm. The first star at dawn."

Icy fear trembled in Tatiana's guts, and she propped herself up on her elbow, peering down at him. "What's wrong?"

"Nothing that hasn't been wrong for the past few months."

"Nightwing."

His eyes dashed to her face, stamped with wetness, truth trembling on the tip of his tongue—but somehow he choked it back. "I'm just reminding myself I don't have be afraid about what happens to you. No matter how bright the fire burns, you're the one who's going to walk away from it."

She slid her hand from his and cradled his bearded jaw in her hand. "But not without you. Right?"

Quill twisted his head and kissed the inside of her palm.

Uneasiness coiled in her chest, and she couldn't sleep even after Quill dozed off. She was still awake when Cistine and Thorne slipped back from patrol, and the Princess crouched at Tatiana's side to touch her shoulder. "Your turn."

She nodded, rolling over and flicking Quill's cheek. His eyes opened too swiftly for him to have been asleep after all.

The world was silent while Tatiana dragged on her armor and bound her curls. Cistine sat next to Thorne's bedroll, her back pressed to his while he slept with his head on his arm, and she scribbled feverishly on a piece of paper lifted from Tatiana's pack. She didn't glance up even when Quill stumbled over her things and knelt to shove them together again without a word of apology.

That tension between them chafed at Tatiana. She'd never realized how much Quill's love for Cistine meant to her as their friend until it grew cold as an untended hearth.

With slow fingers and a heavy heart, she strapped on her sabers and followed her *valenar* into the trees. Ariadne greeted them not far from the edge of the western river branch, the patrol boundary they'd established by map the night before, with cups of hot, spiced milk from a vendor in town.

"I think I love you," Tatiana moaned, wrapping her hands around the warm mug.

"I thought that was obvious," Ariadne said wryly, and Tatiana hip-checked her, taking the lead from the river's edge toward the sleepy town. Mist and shadows curled between the log homes, a banner unraveling out to a thin median of trees, then opening along the field of stumps where

Hvallatar harvested its lumber to send along the barges.

Tatiana was grateful for the chance to patrol. It felt natural, little different from Hellidom, and she could almost imagine there wasn't a war or missing friends or Cistine's desperate plan hanging above them. It was just Tatiana and her two favorite people, sipping drinks and keeping the world safe.

They passed more than an hour in silence, leaving the lumbering grove for the forest again and listening to it slumber around them. There was nothing but the sound of their footsteps crunching old, dry leaf skeletons underfoot; no nightbirds trilled, no wildlife rustled on the ground or in the trees. Tatiana became more keenly aware of that silence as the world drifted from darkness to the pale bruise-blue of an overcast dawn, anxiety ticking up her spine.

Something should have awoken by now. They weren't making enough noise to scare away every creature.

She flicked Quill's elbow, then grazed hands with Ariadne, and they both nodded. They'd sensed it, too.

Tatiana tapped Quill again. Down low at their sides, they flashed a quick round of *koh, kendar, kest*. When Quill's knife cut her cloth, Tatiana mouthed a curse; then she passed him her cup, linked her fingers, and looped her arms above her head, pirouetting in place in one long, exaggerated stretch and yawn.

When she faced forward again, walking was more difficult, ice climbing the cracks of her joints. "Bloodwight. Wolf mask. Following us."

"*Maleck*," Quill growled.

Ariadne cast a sharp glance at him, following the brush of his hand to his hip, and with a spark of dread Tatiana realized exactly why Maleck was following them. "Are you wearing an *augment*?"

Quill's face was expressionless.

"When did you even realize he was *here*?" she hissed.

"Last night. Saw him watching on the hills while I was hunting."

"What did you do, bring your flagon so you could lure him out? You know only Cistine is supposed to carry them on patrol!" Quill's eyes flashed, but he didn't reply. Tatiana's teeth snapped together. "Ari, go back to camp. Find her."

Ariadne broke swiftly away, arcing into the trees. As one, hands to their weapons, Tatiana and Quill spun to face the empty gaps between the broad trunks behind them.

"Where in Nimmus did he go?" Quill snarled.

A flicker of movement shuddered through the foliage, swooping after Ariadne. Tatiana hit Quill in the side, and they gave chase.

Maleck traveled with half the speed of most Bloodwights, a familiar hitch in his stride adjusting for wounds, and right now Tatiana was grateful he was hurt. They had to keep him from catching Ariadne—and then keep him from leaving before Cistine reached them.

They broke the edge of the lumber grove, Ariadne already a faint shadow in the distance, sprinting toward their camp. Maleck's stride lengthened to an unnatural lope, either drawn after his fleeing prey or strengthened by the sense of their augments nearby.

"*Maleck!*" Quill roared, and he halted like he'd slammed into a wall. Tatiana stopped too, wary of that sudden predatory stillness, but Quill advanced like there was no danger at all. "Don't move."

Maleck stepped after Ariadne.

"Don't you *dare!*" Again, Maleck halted. "After everything we've been through, you don't get to walk away from me." Quill raised his voice to a shout when Maleck twitched forward. "*Don't you walk away from me, Darkwind!*"

He turned this time, and Tatiana grimaced. That mask made his movements feral when he tilted his head, focus spearing toward Quill, who halted at last and jerked out the augment from his pouch, holding it up between two fingers.

"Is this the only reason you're here?" he snapped. "Just this, and nothing else? Not your cabal? You're just going to stroll into Hvallatar and take our flagons and go back to your blood family. Well what about Sillakove, you stars-forsaken *bandayo*? *What about me?*"

Even from a distance, Tatiana felt the hot power curling from Maleck's body. How many augments were fleshed out across his armor? What were they doing to him? Was he even sane enough to recognize them?

Quill advanced, and when Maleck stiffened, Tatiana's toes curled in her boots. She'd sparred with him enough to know what was coming. "Quill, come back!"

He ignored her, rattling the flagon. "This is all you care about, Mal?" A vicious smirk hung in his voice, and he tucked the flagon away in his fist, shifting it behind his back and beckoning with his free hand. "Then come and take it from me, *Storfir*."

And just like every other time Quill used that name, Maleck lunged at him.

Unnatural cold blew through the grove, sucking up Tatiana's scream and hurling her backward. A shell of ice broke up through the ground, enclosing Quill and Maleck in an augmented dome unleashed from her *valenar's* hand—a second augment he wasn't supposed to be carrying, stolen from Cistine's satchel.

Inside those frozen confines, he and Maleck brawled, sabers against augments.

Howling, Tatiana threw herself at the ice, slamming her palms into it. It was inches thick, as sturdy as the shell over the lake in the Isetfell Mountains where she'd watched Quill plunge almost to his death. And this was like watching him die again. Just as helpless. Just as infuriating. Just as *terrifying*.

Wind and darkness slashed through the dome, forcing Quill back again and again. He sprang up as many times as Maleck sent him down to his knees, but each recovery met with a fresh assault, battering him against the slick walls. There was nothing in those blows but mindless rage, bordering on hatred—as if nothing really mattered except that augment in Quill's back pocket, its presence erasing the wolf-masked savior of Blaykrone and turning him wild again, a creature of senseless need and hunger, like Pippet in Selv Torfjel.

If Tatiana just had an augment of her own, a way to reach Quill, then even if Maleck killed them both, they would die together. But she'd left her own pouch back at camp like Thorne had ordered them. And with her gloves pressed flat to the achingly-cold ice, she realized Quill had planned this *precisely*. He'd drawn Maleck out with the augments and attracted his full fury, leaving none of it to spare for her. He'd pushed her out and protected her, and now Maleck's rage was directed only at him.

The same moment Quill's deadly cleverness sank in, Maleck's wind augment hit him across the chest, blowing his sabers out of his hands. In pure desperation, Tatiana yanked out her saber and hacked wildly at the dome. Screams tore the breath from her lungs while she chipped at the wall—not fast enough.

She couldn't get through. She couldn't reach him.

Quill's lips peeled back, not in a grimace, but with laughter. His words were muffled through the ice, but she could still hear him. "Losing your edge, *Allet*."

The second flagon shattered; lightning speared straight down into the ground, turning the grass black in a crescent and fizzling out as quickly as it came. The burst of energy boomed within the ice, sending cracks spiraling through it, but not deep enough to destroy it. Quill had sent it down, not out; the dome was intact and the augment gone, far from Maleck's grasp.

Snarling with fury, Maleck grabbed Quill by the throat and slammed him against the ice, and Tatiana swung at the wall with all her might. It didn't give way, but something else did—bones, flesh, when Maleck drove blow after blow into Quill's face.

Blood freckled the scorched grass. Quill twisted against the hand around his throat, but those fingers could close like iron bands, could stop any hold break, could make someone feel safe or trapped depending on which side of Maleck they faced.

Today, it was killing rage that directed his fists into Quill's vulnerable guts and heaving sides, breaking things, rearranging them, perhaps even permanently. Tears coursed down Tatiana's cheeks, her voice torn from screaming Quill's name while she chiseled at the ice without enough strength to break through. She was losing him blow-by-blow like she'd lost their child, that feeling back within her, the horrific separating, tear by tear, something she loved being ripped from this world a piece at a time.

Quill raised his head weakly between strikes, his gaze fixed on Maleck's face. "Hit me all you want. I'm not finished with you."

Crack. Maleck's fist broke Quill's eye socket.

Tatiana choked on a sob, but her *valenar* didn't even look at her. "I'm not leaving this town without you."

This time Maleck's punch shattered his nose.

Quill spat blood and coughed. "You're just going to have to kill me, Darkwind! I'm not leaving you behind!"

The barrage of blows ceased. Fist drawn back, Maleck stared at the man dangling from his hand.

Then he flung Quill to his knees and took his head in both hands at an angle, and Tatiana dropped her saber and slammed her palms into the ice, sobbing, screaming in rage—

The dome turned to steam under her gloves.

"Maleck, *stop!*"

Cistine's cry jolted Tatiana, the cords of the Princess's augmented fire shivering into focus through the dancing green dapples across her vision. She'd screamed so loud the blood vessels in her eyes burst, and now she staggered, fighting to regain her sight while Maleck released Quill and spun to face Cistine.

Quill crumbled into the grass and stayed there. Tatiana flung herself over him, shielding his body with hers while Cistine faced Maleck; Thorne and Ariadne flanked her, weapons drawn.

"Maleck, what did you do?" Cistine's voice broke, her gaze cutting to Quill and Tatiana.

Maleck's head swiveled. Tatiana glared up at him, sheltering Quill's head and shoulders with her arms, daring him to strike at them again. Daring him to make one wrong move.

With a clap of howling wind like thunder, Maleck was gone.

Tatiana yanked away when the others slid to their knees on the charred grass. Ariadne pulled Quill onto his back, and he convulsed, eyes squeezing shut. His chest jerked in rapid, agonized pants. Blood flecked his lips.

Cistine pushed the black-dyed hair from his brow. "Quill, look at me..."

"You let him get *away*." His eyes flickered back open, dim slits full of accusation bordering on hate. "After I just...you let him *leave*..."

She fell back on her heels, tears cutting down her cheeks. "I didn't...I didn't mean to..."

He opened his mouth, but only blood came out this time, and he crumbled back, shaking and spitting, into Ariadne's grip.

"Is he dying?" Tatiana's voice broke, her hands struggling to hold up his head.

"I don't know. But there is a medico in Hvallatar," Ariadne said tensely. "Do we risk it?"

"Of course we do." Thorne's voice was level, but terror burned in his bright eyes. "Cistine, run ahead and tell her we're coming. Ariadne, go back for Pippet."

Cistine sprang up, squeezing Tatiana's shoulder and shedding a token of the augmented fire into her. The warmth hardly grazed the chill sliding across her body while her sisters took off at a run in opposite directions. Thorne bent over Quill, murmuring his Name, trying to soothe him and seeking the best way to move him, and Tatiana clung to his hand, weeping uncontrollably.

If he died from what Maleck had done...

She didn't know if she would ever forgive them.

CHAPTER TWENTY-FOUR

THANKS TO CISTINE, the medico was ready when Thorne and Tatiana bore Quill into her two-room home between them; only her wide eyes betrayed surprise at the state of him, sagging between their shoulders.

"Lay him on the table," she ordered, and the moment he was on his back she began to search him from head to foot, probing his sides and stomach while he vomited into a bucket Thorne held.

"My head," he groaned, "it's *killing* me..."

Pippet huddled against the wall where Ariadne had pushed her down, ordered her to stay, and then stepped out to keep watch. Eyes fixed on the table where her brother spasmed in agony, she chewed on her sleeve and whispered at a break in the flurry, "Quill?"

"He's going to be *fine*, Pip." Cistine's shaky reassurance was lost in the next round of vomiting. Tatiana gripped Quill's hand through the surges, her eyes trained so furiously on the medico that Thorne stepped between them.

"Tatiana," he murmured. "Out. Go with Ari."

"Like *Nimmus* I'm going *anywhere*," she spat.

The medico paid Tatiana no heed, her focus on examining Quill's skull for fractures, then on bracing and wrapping his ribs while Thorne gently pushed up his knees to arch his back; he was too weak to bow upward on his own.

"Is he going to die?" Cistine's voice was hardly more than a breath. She leaned into the wall, arms wrapped around herself, cheeks soaked with tears.

"Under the proper conditions, no." The medico retrieved another satchel of herbs from the wall and handed them to Tatiana. "Grind these and make a tea. It will put him to sleep and offer some relief. You," she pointed to Thorne, "come with me." He followed her into the second room, which housed her bed and a writing desk. She faced him in the narrow space, hands on her hips. "I don't know your face. Who are you?"

"A traveler," he lied quickly. "My companions and I were passing through the forest when we were attacked. We're grateful for your help..."

"Yrin," she supplied her name when he trailed off. "And you are—?"

"Julian." He blurted the first name that came to mind. "We've been fleeing east to Lataus."

Yrin folded her arms and glanced past him. "I've been the medico here for nearly a decade. I've seen young men crushed by trees, I've used healing augments to repair shattered limbs, I've removed arms that couldn't be saved and mended my share of split faces and gouged eyes from fights at the local taverns. But I have never seen *anything* like this. What happened to him?"

"As I said, he was attacked."

Yrin's piercing eyes held his. "By a wild creature, I would say. Is this something I should expect to see more of?"

"Stars willing, no."

"Stars willing. Should we gather a hunt for this creature?"

Thorne shook his head. "If this happens again, it will be to one of us, not anyone in Hvallatar. I give you my word."

"Then you can also give me one reason why I shouldn't have you chased out before you bring us more trouble."

Thorne narrowed his eyes. "Can he travel?"

She pressed her lips together. "Frankly, I'm stunned he isn't hemorrhaging internally. A shattered eye socket and cheekbone, a dislocated jaw, a broken nose, cracked ribs, a fractured sternum...shall I go on? If he moves from that table right now, I expect him to crumble into a heap with all his bones out of joint."

"Then we have to stay." Thorne fisted his hands, pocketing them to hide their shaking. "How long until he's fit to travel?"

Yrin rubbed her brow. "The herbs will help. But without a healing augment..." she trailed off. "I've used all mine, but a few of my contacts have more. I can send for one, but it will be at least three days before it arrives."

Thorne brushed aside a prickle of wariness. Each day they lingered tempted the Chancellors closer—not to mention the Bloodwights. But for Quill's sake, they needed that healing augment. "We would be in your debt."

"Oh, these services aren't without cost. You'll pay, and if you can't, you'll find work here such that you *can*."

Thorne dipped his head. "More than fair."

Yrin swept up her cloak from the bedpost. "Then I'll send that note. You're welcome to wait with your friend until I return."

They stepped back into the front room, and Tatiana and Cistine straightened. Cistine's eyes danced fearfully between Thorne and Yrin, and he made a smoothing motion with his hand. "We'll be here for several days." When Yrin stepped out, he added quietly, "She's sending for a healing augment."

Cistine frowned. "She knows where to find one?"

"For a cost. We work to pay off Quill's recovery."

Cistine's jaw tensed. "I'll clean every house in Hvallatar if I have to. Whatever he needs." She glanced out the door and added, "Do you think she could find a second one?"

Thorne's heart lurched like a downhill stumble. "You can ask her, if you think it's worth it."

She offered him a glance full of sympathy—but beneath it, sheer determination. Then she squeezed Tatiana's shoulder and ducked outside, calling for Yrin to wait.

Tatiana traced Quill's cheek with her knuckles, shuddering slightly with every intake of breath. Thorne stepped up behind her and cupped her shoulders, squeezing gently. "Take Pippet and find her food. Tell Ariadne what we're going to do."

"Why don't *you* tell her?"

"Tatiana." He let a note of steel slide into his voice. "I need a moment alone with him."

Tatiana grumbled, kissed Quill's motionless lips, then gripped Pippet by the elbow and stormed out, slamming the door. Thorne's last glimpse of them was Pippet's wet eyes fixed on her brother; then they were alone in the silent house.

He took a chair from the wall, pulled it over to the table, and sat. "Feigning unconsciousness won't spare you, Nightwing."

Quill's chest rose in a long, unsteady breath, then sank again.

"You had my orders not to engage Maleck, especially not in battle. What in *Nimmus* were you thinking?"

"That I couldn't let him go." Quill's voice slurred—from the tea and from his sore jaw. "That I'm tired of losing every damned fight. I just wanted to win for once. I promised him, promised Shei. Wanted to keep my word."

Thorne sat forward, folding his arms on the table. "I'm aware of the role you play in this cabal. You take the blows when others can't. But this is different, Maleck's strength is unmatched in this state. You knew better."

No answer. Thorne heaved a sigh.

"I let things go after Landamot," he said. "Cistine begged me not to ream you for threatening her. And I allowed it because I know deep down that's not the man you are. But if you keep behaving like this, hurting this cabal, harming *yourself,* I have no qualms about sending you back to Hellidom."

"Would *you* have let him walk away?"

Thorne rubbed his face. "I would've had no choice. This is Cistine's hunt, not ours."

"Then maybe I don't belong in this cabal, because I can't do that. I can't just give up on him."

"I am *not* giving up." Thorne bent forward, bracing one hand over Quill's heart. It raced and leaped against his palm. "You two are *equally* important. You're both my brothers. But *my* role is to keep *you* alive while Cistine saves Maleck. I take that task as seriously as she takes hers. And I expect you to take it seriously from now on, too."

Quill was quiet for a long time. The beats of his heart slowed into a steadier cadence. "I wasted two augments. I didn't even think...I just knew having them would draw him out, and I couldn't give them to him once they did. And when I dispatched it...Nimmus' teeth, Thorne. That rage..."

Thorne grimaced. Seeing the state of Maleck and Quill when they'd arrived was enough. He couldn't imagine the nightmares Tatiana would have of that fight.

"What if we can't pull him back from this?" Quill's eyes slid open and his hand closed around Thorne's wrist, those two false fingers cold over his Atrasat inkings. "What if I pushed him over the edge?"

"There's nothing we can do but trust Cistine," Thorne said, and Quill's eyes fell shut. "I have to believe that even if we can't save him, she can."

"She let him go today."

"He fled," Thorne corrected. "And that...that gives me more hope than anything."

"Why?"

"Because that's not what a Bloodwight does when it wounds its prey." He patted Quill's chest lightly. "But it's what Maleck always does when he hurts *you*."

CHAPTER TWENTY-FIVE

THE MEDICO'S HOME was quiet and dark when Tatiana finally slipped back inside. Ariadne had taken charge of Pippet again, and Thorne had gone to find work for them. Cistine was chasing after the medico, weaving her own dangerous plans. So Tatiana, at last, was alone with her *valenar*.

In silence, she slung straw mats off a shelf and lined them up beside the hearth. She stoked the fire to the height she knew Quill preferred— always a touch on the sweating side, ever since Oadmark. She gathered an armload of blankets and pillows from under Yrin's bed and lined them up as best she could, the world a tearstained blur.

"Is this cheating-you-at-cards angry," Quill's voice rasped from the table, "or fighting-with-torn-armor angry?"

She shook her head. "Can you move?"

A beat. "Think so. The tea helped. Everything's dull now."

"Good." She slipped under his arm and helped him down from the table, and though he grimaced and held his breath the short distance to the hearth and the mats, he went without protest. Once he sank to his knees and settled on his side, Tatiana let the tears flow, a bitter, silent torrent. She pulled the blankets around him and stretched out at his side, pillowing her chin on his chest. "You broke your promise."

His eyes fluttered shut. "I know."

She traced her fingers lightly over his bruised ribs, the contours of his injured face. "I could kill him for this. I could kill you *both*."

"Don't. Mal's not himself."

"Fine, then I'll just blame you."

"I didn't want to let him go, Tati." His voice hitched. "I just...wanted to save one thing. I couldn't save our baby, and Pip...I don't even know about her. I just wanted to save *someone* who was counting on me."

"If you're going to save anyone, I'd rather it be yourself."

"Point taken." His breath staggered out harshly. "I haven't been thinking clearly for a long time, but I'm trying, Saddlebags."

She bit her lips together, hating that she understood his devastation enough to hurt for him. She wanted to be angry; anger was easier than facing that she'd nearly lost him again.

"Pippet's worried about you," she offered, hoping to bring him some relief. "That's a good sign."

"For her, or for Maleck?"

"I don't want to talk about Maleck right now."

His eyes blinked open at half-mast, dimmed by pain. "I'm sorry I put you through this. You deserve better."

"Fortunately for us both, I've always known what we both deserve." She slid the hair from his sweat-soaked brow. "You can't trade your life for Maleck's. If he was here, in his right mind, he'd say the same thing. He'd never trade his life for yours."

"Debatable."

"No. He'd make the smarter choice, find a better way, whatever that looks like...you know he would. And he wouldn't scare half his *valenar's* life off trying to bring you back, either."

"All right, fair."

Sighing, she pushed herself under his arm. With some effort, he worked his hand over to grip her hip.

"I can't lose you, either," she said. "Not after everything."

His fingers traced the scar above her hip. "I hear you, Saddlebags. I do."

They lay together in silence, the crackling fire beside them, Quill's breaths whooshing unsteadily beneath her ear. On the verge of sleep, Tatiana dredged up her voice again. "Remember what you're made of, Featherbrain. Gods-forged from the stars."

"I remember." He sounded mostly asleep, too. "But we're all made like that. Even Mal. I just wanted to bring him home."

Tatiana swallowed and ventured a thought. "So does Cistine."

"Right."

"She saved your life today. You know that, you stubborn *bandayo*? The only reason she didn't throw Maleck in a headlock today was because she wanted to get to you first." She flicked her thumb over his knuckles. "She's the only person in all the kingdoms who *almost* loves you as much as I do."

Quill was silent for so long, she thought—nearly hoped—he'd fallen asleep. Then his voice dragged out husky under her cheek. "I look at her and sometimes I feel like I don't know her anymore. The things she can do, the things she *chooses* to do. That's not the stranger I saved in Veran."

"Did you ever think maybe she feels the same way? Maybe what she needs more than anything right now is the teacher who first showed her she *was* capable. The one who made her realize being strong wasn't something to be afraid of, as long as she mastered it and not the other way around."

This time, his silence did give way to snoring; but Tatiana didn't rouse him. She stared at the slip of window visible above the table's edge, tears finding their way from her eyes again.

She was afraid to close them. Afraid that in the silence while Quill drowsed beside her, she'd find nothing but wolf skulls and brutal blows waiting in her dreams.

CHAPTER
TWENTY-SIX

ASHE'S ELATION AND pride from the test soured all at once. One day she was grappling with Aden and reliving the *Apiriak* with him and Kristoff, relishing her newfound ability to cleave with Bresnyar at will; the next, she woke with a yawning pit in her chest and a fluttering pain in her palm. Once she assured herself these things had nothing to do with her dragon, she knew it was Maleck.

Then the fear engulfed her. Something had happened, some line crossed, plucking their bond and sending a dark resonance deep into her body. She carried around that weight in silence for most of the day, dry-tongued and lead-limbed, hovering at the edges of Aden and Kristoff's conversations and grateful they didn't force her to join in.

For once, it was a relief to hear footsteps in the prison tunnel. Excitement pushed through her unease at the sight of Meriwa's dark hair and expressionless face emerging from the shadows, peaking when she spotted Nuna at her heels.

"A verdict?" Ashe demanded.

"Yes. We are leaving," Nuna said. "Meriwa's Legion will escort us to the border of the Hunting Grounds."

It took Ashe a moment to fathom the words, pulse slowing, dread icing her throat. "An escort. That's all?" The silence sparked like damp summer heat mushrooming into a storm. "The Council isn't going to help us."

Pity hung Nuna's lips in a frown. "They don't believe Valgard's mistakes with the Bloodwights are Oadmark's to repair." Meriwa spoke to the tribeswoman on a quiet aside, keeping up the infuriating ruse of her own ignorance, and Nuna translated, "Unless you wish for someone to decide Bresnyar ought to stand accused of breaking his banishment, she suggests we take this small mercy and flee."

Rage colored Ashe's world. Weeks they'd spent here, her life put to the test in that arena, only to be told it was all for nothing. It had only been a taunt, a smug game for these northern bastards to entertain themselves with.

She stormed toward Meriwa, itching to wrap her fingers around the woman's throat, but Aden's grabbed her arm, swinging her to face him. "Don't tempt fate. It was their Council's choice to make. Valgard *will not* impose its desires on its neighbors at the tip of a blade."

He was right. She knew better. She was no longer the Talheimic who won tenuous truces by steel and threat.

She swiveled back to face Meriwa. "At least give us our weapons."

Nuna translated for her, then back again, "When we reach the border. Now come. Time wanes."

They left by a different path than the one to the Council chamber or the arena, descending to the base of the mountain and following a dark tunnel through the sweating stone and out onto a ledge behind the waterfall of the neighboring mountain. They skirted the base of Ujurak and emerged into the Hunting Grounds to find most of the Legions dormant; it was the dead of night, the sky ink-black and littered with stars, their cold light shedding on the path where Ashe stalked after Aden, Kristoff, and Nuna down the riverbank. Meriwa's Legion appeared along the way, more than a dozen women enclosing them on all sides. Far too many to fight even if Ashe wanted to.

But God's bones, having their help would've changed everything.

Their dragons waited at the end of the valley, saddled and bridled—even Bresnyar, who lurked some ways off from the others, rhythmically flexing his wings in preparation for his first long flight in weeks.

Ashe went to him, grabbed the bridle, and flicked his cheek. "Open your mouth." He obliged, and she removed the harness, tossing it aside. "Remind me whose brilliant idea it was to come here—mine, or yours?"

"It may have been a joint decision."

"Well, we both deserve a boot to our backsides."

"I think we will find that in plenty when we return to Valgard."

"What are you doing?" Meriwa asked when Ashe ducked around Bresnyar's side and loosened the saddle, letting it slither to the ground.

"I like to be as close to him as possible. It lets me react to every shift he makes. A saddle gets in the way." She curled her lip. "Or do you find that offensive, too?"

Meriwa turned without speaking, mounted Aeosotu, and clipped her heels into his sides. He surged upward with a grass-bending snap of his wings, driving grit into Ashe's face. She cursed him while she mounted, Aden behind her, Kristoff and Nuna after him.

Ashe fumed every mile they flew, the night peeling away before them like a ribbon. There should have been something exhilarating about this many dragons parading silently through the clouds, dapples of emerald, sapphire, ruby, bronze, gold, silver, and topaz banking in and out of sight. Any other time, she might've marveled at this impossible procession she was part of—a Wingmaiden unaccepted, but with her own dragon's heat burning beneath her.

But not today. Not when a gray haze swirled in the eastern sky, promising a dawn that could very well be one of her last. She didn't want to think of how many encounters with the Balmond Bresnyar would manage to scrape out of before one of them bowled him over and put their claws in his throat. She didn't want to think of how long *she* would survive after that; what it would be like to lose one of the greatest pieces of her heart, when she'd already lost so much.

She wasn't certain how much she had left to give.

Meriwa yipped suddenly, and Aeosotu tucked his wings and dove. The entire Legion toppled from the sky, alighting on a long shelf of snow and rock that demarcated the edge of the Hunting Grounds. The Isetfells spread before them, icy and bare and silent.

At Meriwa's shouted command, the Legion dismounted. Ashe and her companions followed suit, and Meriwa stepped to Ashe's side, slinging Maleck's sword harness from across her own shoulders. She didn't give it up right away, studying the sabers. "These are Valgardan weapons. Yet you are Talheimic."

"You don't miss anything, do you?" Ashe snatched the harness from her, scowling.

"You truly believe what you said—that this war belongs to all kingdoms, as we all belong to each other."

"I wouldn't have said it if I didn't believe it." Ashe lashed Starfall and Stormfury across her back, then hesitated. "I didn't always. I would have gladly left Valgard to its own problems even a year ago. But my time there with my princess made me see things differently. See *them* differently." She glanced at her friends lashing on their weapons, silhouetted in the coming dawn. "I don't care if Aden and Kristoff are Valgardan, they're family. And I don't care if Bresnyar is a dragon, he's mine, too. I'd lay down my life for them. Your tribe isn't the people you're born to, it's the ones you choose to be with. I protect my own kingdom, and I protect my tribe."

"Those are not the same to you."

"Not anymore."

They were silent for a moment. Then Meriwa murmured, "You asked me how I knew the common tongue of your kingdoms. Bresnyar taught it to Ileria, and Ileria taught it to all of us. Her Legion, her...tribe."

Ashe glanced sharply at her, caught by that wistful tone. Meriwa stared across the mountains, the wind tugging threads loose from her braid.

"She was my sister." Pain cracked behind every syllable. "She was not like us—not like you, not a warrior. If not for the bond that formed between her and Bresnyar when they first met, she would not have joined the Legion. She fought out of duty and love for him, but her heart was in books and learning. She dreamed of becoming one of the Council, if it were possible."

Ashe cast a wry glance toward her dragon. "He seems to attract that kind of woman. We have a friend like her."

"Good. The world needs that. We needed *her*, just as she needed us. Ileria gave something to the Legion that it never had before or since: perspective. She had no end of stories about the Three Kingdoms, and no end to her hopes for the future. And we loved her for it. She was more than my sister...she was *our* sister. As Bresnyar was our brother. As Aden is yours." Meriwa slipped her hands around her neck and craned her face up to the stars. "To see Ileria's dragon choose another has been pain beyond reckoning...as if Ileria could be forgotten. Replaced."

The edge of scorn loosened from Ashe's chest. A hint of guilt slipped in, making room for something she'd never thought possible to feel toward Meriwa: compassion. "That's not what this is. I'm not a replacement for your sister. Bresnyar still tells me about her to this day...she's part of everything he does, everything he *is*. But you can love more than one person in a lifetime. Sometimes that's the only way you survive."

"I see that now. I see the love between you, and your bond is true. And what I allowed to happen to him, what Aeosotu and I exiled him to when she died...it was cruelty. We did not fight for him. And in her name, I will not make that mistake again." Meriwa fingered the starstone around her neck; then she ripped it off and held it out to Ashe. "When your need is greatest, call into this. Aeosotu will hear you, and this Legion will come. So will any others we can convince."

Ashe blinked. "You're joking."

"I am not."

"Well, I doubt your Grand Council will approve."

"The Council does as it pleases," Meriwa said, "but our Legion is called to defend Oadmark, and defend it we will...with or without their consent. Asiaq would have argued to fight for the kingdoms if he was not fighting his sister to become Council Head when Allfather passes."

"You two schemed this up together?"

To her shock, Meriwa's cheeks pinked. "You are not wrong, that you can love more than once in one life."

Ashe raised a brow. "So this is what you and the Allbrother want?"

"Asiaq knows right from wrong. When it was our task to defeat these creatures, we failed. That is why the Council fears to try again," Meriwa said. "Many moons ago, we fought this *Aeoprast* and his kind on the Hunting Grounds when they came to steal our dragons. Ileria perished in that fight."

Ashe almost choked. "The *Bloodwights* killed her?"

"They were not then as you describe them now...tall and disfigured. But even then, against their powers, it was an unwinnable battle...as yours is unwinnable if you stand alone." She set her shoulders back. "These young gods roam Valgard now because the Legions failed to maintain order within Oadmark. To that end, we are duty-bound to wipe out this blight from the kingdoms. And...in Ileria's memory. We will not allow a sister's blood to be spilled without retribution."

Ashe deliberated, clutching the stone. She could see no trap in this; the worst that could happen was Aeosotu ignoring the summons, and then Valgard would be no worse off than it already was. "I won't say this doesn't surprise me. But I'm grateful."

Meriwa scoffed. "Do you have a sister?"

Ashe's memory filled with hickory hair and dancing green eyes. "You could say that."

"If you ever lost her, you would feel as I feel. You would know that to do as she would have done is an honor to her memory. And that to honor her memory is to keep her alive."

Ashe grimaced. Depending on how plans had progressed in her absence, she might find out exactly how Meriwa felt—and sooner rather than later.

"Go now," Meriwa added, "and go carefully, Dragonfire."

Ashe frowned. "What?"

Meriwa's brow arched. "That is what Bresnyar calls you, is it not? *Ilyanak*. Dragonfire."

A wry smile tugged Ashe's lips. "That he does."

She walked to join her dragon, Nuna, Kristoff, and Aden on the edge of the cleft, looking across the distance to their homes—their kingdom.

"Are you ready?" Aden asked.

Ashe tweaked the new starstone hanging against her chest. "More than

I thought I was."

He cast her a curious glance, but said nothing as he offered his hand to help Nuna mount. Kristoff brushed past Ashe with a touch to the back, and she paused in following him to rest her hand on Bresnyar's neck. "Dragonfire?"

He swiveled, hot breath pouring over her head. "Fitting, don't you think? It's what your spirit is forged of."

After what she'd accomplished here—if in clandestine orders and stolen alliance with the Allbrother and a Legion Head—and what she saw when she looked deeply into herself through her dragon's eyes, Ashe had no argument. Her soul *was* dragonfire, her heart steel, her face set to the south. And she would not fear what was to come...not with a Legion of Wingmaidens to summon and the purpose of the gods drumming in her veins.

Mereszar was not afraid.

CHAPTER
TWENTY-SEVEN

IT HAD CROSSED an unforgivable line.

Blood on its hands in the moonlight blood crusting its knuckles like sunlit days and rock tops and wrapped hands cinnamon sticks a grinning face *Is that the best you can do? Hit me,* Storfir!

It had done too much, broken ruined destroyed one of the best things that had ever happened to it.

Of course I forgive you, this scar is nothing, it just gives me charm!

There was no coming back from this.

It hadn't meant to hadn't *wanted* to but the power sang to it and then *screamed* at it and then it went away, went so quiet that everything inside it went quiet, too, and then it had broken open in rage like fire like power like an open well like *augments*

The augments did this to it to *him* to the man in the grove with black hair that should've been silver on one side and with the cinnamon and the wrapped fists and the wildfire eyes.

It cradled its head in its hands and dampness leaked from under its mask, dripped from its jaw.

It had just wanted to see them to meet them to be *free* and instead it had killed him murdered him broke him beyond repairing, it didn't know how it knew that but it knew the truth. It had killed one of its brothers, not the ones in the masks in the city in the villages but one it loved, one that had never hurt it.

Too far too far too far too far too far

It was too late to fix this but it had to do *something* had to make this right somehow *somehow*

It had to go back.

After days sitting and remembering and feeling blood on its hands and its heart stopping and starting over and over again, it had to go back. Had to make it right had to make the sacrifice matter, for the man with the cinnamon sticks and the feral smile, for the woman with two-colored eyes in the snow, for brother and father, for hearth and home, for family.

For...

Thorne. And Aden. And Ariadne. For Tatiana and Pippet and Kristoff and Cistine.

For Quill Nightwing. For Asheila Kovar.

And for itself.

For *himself.*

He struggled up from the ground where he'd fallen and not moved for three days. And he turned, for the last time, back toward Hvallatar.

CHAPTER TWENTY-EIGHT

THE GENTLE PLUNK of piano keys greeted Cistine when she descended from the upper level of the inn at dawn four days after Maleck's attack. She carried a letter in her fist and a weight in her bones that had nothing to do with the work she'd done cleaning shops and delivering parcels today, or the three days previous while they'd waited for Yrin's messenger to return with the healing augments.

The parlor was deserted except for a single lonely figure: Ariadne, seated at the communal piano, coaxing a quiet melody from its keys. Cistine recognized the tune Maleck and Ashe had played by violin and piano in Aden's old home on Darlaska. Ariadne played it without any left-handed accompaniment; somehow it was sadder that way.

Cistine lowered herself onto the bench, and Ariadne shifted to make room without breaking the tune. "How were your tasks around town this morning, *Logandir?*"

"Exhausting. But it gave me time to think about something. I wanted to show you this." She set the letter on the keys, and Ariadne stopped playing. "This is what Thorne will take to my parents, if...if the worst happens. It's written in cipher to prove I wrote it of my own volition, just like the note Ashe took to my parents when I decided to stay for negotiations."

Either Ariadne read very slowly, or she read it many times. Cistine fidgeted, drumming her fingers on the edge of the bench and peering anxiously toward the door. Thorne had sworn to meet them here after his morning in the lumber fields, and they would all go together to Yrin's house, where Tatiana and Pippet waited with Quill. Every minute was a step closer to having that healing augment in her hand, to having Quill strong. To chasing after Maleck again.

Guilt still hung heavy in her chest, and she hadn't been back to see Quill because of it. He was right; they had nothing to show for his broken body because she'd let Maleck escape, her focus on reaching Quill before catching him. Working for his cure was her penance, but she wasn't certain yet what to say to him.

"This is very good." Ariadne returned the note to its envelope, sliding it across the keys to her. "Well done, Cistine."

She blew out a swift breath, pocketing the letter in her armor. "Well, it did take me four drafts to write it."

"I admire that dedication, though the dark circles under your eyes are worrisome."

The inn door creaked open, and Thorne's head jutted inside. "The messenger is here. With both augments."

With a shared glance of relief, they snatched up their provisions and followed him out into the brightening, sparsely-filled streets, where Cistine practically skipped. Finally they could move on from this town, one step closer to taking the Door beneath Stornhaz now that she had her healing augment.

They entered Yrin's house in a single line—and hope perished on the threshold with the flick of a knife going straight to Thorne's throat. Cistine didn't even have time to scream before a hand closed over her own mouth, deadening a shout of rage.

Vassoran guards filled the room. They'd already pulled Quill, shirtless and doubled up, from beside the fire, already banded Tatiana's arms behind her back and wrestled Pippet to the floor. Now Thorne and Ariadne's necks reflected on the flat blades of the knives that restrained them, and Cistine couldn't catch a full breath past the thick leather covering her mouth. A tide of panic washed over her, spinning the room in a brutal spiral.

There *were* healing augments here, as promised—and more. Fire, water, darkness, and light on these guards' hips, the taste saturating her tongue. They'd come prepared.

Cistine's eyes shot to Yrin.

The medico stood off in a corner, one arm wrapped around her body, her other hand covering her mouth. She met Thorne's eyes first, then Cistine's. "I'm sorry for this, but I know who you are. The dye doesn't hide that striking silver hair well enough, Chancellor Thorne."

He cursed, jolting forward, but the knife at his throat restrained him.

"I couldn't risk you drawing attention to Hvallatar again," Yrin added. "This time, it was one of you hurt. Next, it could be one of ours. My duty is to these people. I will not bring this feud between you and the other Chancellors or the creatures that stalk you to *their* doorsteps."

Cistine wrenched her head, and the guard's hand slid down to cup her throat from behind. But at least she could speak. "I know exactly how you feel. Your people, your kingdom, before anyone else." She flicked a glance around the room at her struggling cabal, at her *selvenar* who turned his head to watch her. "We'll go quietly, but Quill won't make it far if you don't give him that augment."

"We don't have time." The guard behind Tatiana gave her an impatient jerk toward the door.

"Please!" Cistine bucked her own captor's hold. "I'll go wherever you take me, even to one of the Doors! I won't fight. I swear, I won't fight. Just *heal him.*"

Quill stared at her, mouth slanted at a strange angle, trembling. He looked so much like his sister right before she cried.

For a long moment, no one spoke. Then Yrin straightened. "Unless you wish to bring a corpse to the Chancellors, the girl is right. I will do my duty, but I won't have them in Hvallatar a moment longer when I'm finished."

Cistine sagged with relief when Yrin stepped forward and broke open the flagon with her armored gloves. Quill's Atrasat inkings glowed as the healing augment seeped across his body, stabilizing broken bones and glossing over contusions, strengthening him enough that he straightened, that familiar iron might banding his frame again. With the span of days since he'd received the injuries, many of them would still have to heal on their own, and there would be scars left behind; but there was a spark rekindled that had been lost before, numbed by analgesics and agony, burning in his eyes when he rolled his shoulders despite the guard drawing his arms behind his back.

"Well? What are we waiting for?" he muttered.

A flicker of a tense smile crossed Tatiana's face, vanishing again when the guards marched first her, then Pippet and Quill, then Ariadne from the house. They tried to drag Thorne next, but he planted his boots and gazed at Yrin for a long moment. Then he said, quietly, "I won't forget this."

Her eyes narrowed. "Threats won't help your case, Chancellor."

"It isn't a threat," Thorne said. "You healed Quill after he was already in Vassoran hands. If Hvallatar ever falls into need, you know which Court to reach out to. If not to me, then to Chancellor Sander."

Yrin blinked, but said nothing while the guards marched them from the house and on a humiliating journey through Hvallatar. All along the street, heads turned when they passed. Mouths that had complimented Cistine for her errand work now ran endlessly with conjecture, and she wished her itching gossip's ears would block out their words: wondering if she was a criminal, a thief, a murderer...if they were all deserters.

They were all those things to some extent. And now they were prisoners, after weeks of keeping one step ahead of the Courts' designs. She'd failed Adeima's mercy and Sander's provision, failed her oaths, failed herself.

When they left earshot of the people, traveling through the brief pocket of forest toward the lumbering grove, one of the guards finally spoke. "Here is how this will go. If one of you resists, another will take the blade. If the Key reaches for a flagon, we'll remove her hands and use a healing augment to cover the holes."

A snarl ripped through Thorne's chest. "If you lay a finger on her—"

"Threats," the guard spoke over him, "will not be tolerated. Bite your tongues or we'll strip those cords from your arms and gag you."

"Where are you taking us?" Ariadne demanded.

"To the war camp at Lake Erani. Chancellor Bravis eagerly awaits your arrival."

Cistine shot a bleak look at Tatiana. Lake Erani was south of Stornhaz, less than two days' ride from Hvallatar. The lines had crumbled south of the kingdom's middle.

An awful feeling of dread made wild, helical rounds in Cistine's stomach as they passed through the trees. The nausea didn't abate even when she forced herself to breathe deep and even the way Mira had taught her, and nervous energy pulsed in her fingertips every step from Hvallatar through the neck of the forest to the lumbering grove.

Which was not empty.

The workers had been hard at their task the last four days, Thorne among them, felling half a dozen trees that now lay in long hurdles, drying in the sunlight. The guards had left their horses here to graze, with one man at watch over them.

He was dead now, decapitated, his blood painting the stumps and grass.

The Vassora pulled them all to a halt, facing the black-clad figure waiting halfway through the field—the source of the sickness in Cistine's gut, the tremble in her hands.

He'd come back for them. For *her*.

Wolf mask glinting in the midday sun, he watched them. Faint currents of darkness eddied around him, whispering shadows borne on a wind of his own making. It looked as if his cloak dripped from his body and curled through the grass, beckoning them forward.

A pouch unsnapped. Someone reached for an augment—Thorne's captor. Thorne slammed shoulder-first into the man, knocking him aside and diving on top of him as a whip of darkness slashed a trench into the soil. Cistine twisted free of her guard's hold and leaped to Tatiana's aid, sweeping the man's legs so her friend could flip him over her head. In seconds, the entire cabal was free, Thorne breaking Pippet loose and shoving her behind him.

In those few seconds, Maleck took two of the guards and their augments and left them in twisted heaps on the grass, their power thrumming over his body.

The Vassora lunged for cover. Thorne grabbed Cistine's arm and they ran as well, the cabal all around them. Backs pressed to a stack of logs, they listened to the blasts of power as one of the Vassora dueled with Maleck—and lost. Pippet huddled tight against Quill's side, hands over her ears, eyes squeezed shut and mouth open in a soundless wail.

"The horses?" Ariadne's fingertips were pressed lightly into the soil, preparing to launch her body upward at the first word from Thorne.

"If we leave, the guards will die," Cistine protested.

Tatiana winced at a snap of bone, a scream. "They're dying already."

Cistine swiveled to look over the logs. Four Vassora remained, huddled behind the next stack of wood. A fifth had made it halfway to the stump where the horses were tethered; Maleck crouched over him now, divesting him of his augments. He tucked two away and shattered a third on his hip. The ground quaked, rattling the logs as he slowly advanced on the others.

In a single blink, Cistine saw how this would go.

He would not stop; whether because they'd taken the cabal captive or because of the augments they wore, he would carve his way through these Vassoran guards. And with enough power humming in his body, by the time they were cut down it would no longer matter why he came.

He would kill them all. The obsession would take hold.

And she couldn't let him do it. Not only for the people he would cut down in his mindless hunger and the ones he would kill after this, accidentally or purposely, but for *him*...the true him. The man he would be when he came back. Even if she was unprepared, undertrained, unsteady, even if it cost her everything, she could not let him do this.

Cistine stood, shedding Thorne's grip from her arm. The rest of the cabal hissed her name in alarm, in warning, but she did not heed them.

The Wild Heart of Fire walked onto the battlefield, unafraid.

She knew the moment he sensed her. He struck out an arm, cutting the air like a sickle, and a blast of augmented fire shrieked toward her. Even before its heat consumed her body, he turned away from her, his attention spearing back to the guards huddled behind that wooden heap.

Cistine batted the flames aside, and they smashed into one of the stumps, setting it smoldering. He tossed another glance her way, and this time sent wind from his other hand. It wrapped around her body, and she seized it to her own will, sending it up and out harmlessly.

His focus fixed fully on her now, the guards forgotten. Hands cutting to the sides, he unleashed a cyclone of flames that ripped deep ruts into the ground, screaming like specters straight toward her. She deflected these, too. In the corner of her vision, the surviving Vassora broke cover and fled, deciding their lives meant more than the prize of delivering her to the Chancellors.

His head turned after them, and his body began to follow.

"Look at me," Cistine said sharply, "not at them. They don't matter. Look at *me*. I came for you. For *you*, Darkwind."

Halfway in a pivot, he froze.

Cistine kept walking, shifting herself into his path. "That's your *true* Name. Darkwind, look at me. I know you remember me."

He was as still as a man carved of stone. The razor features of his wolf mask did not shift, but his eyes bored into her through the holes in the skull when she came to a halt before him, closer than anyone dared come to a Bloodwight with any hope of surviving.

But he wasn't one of them. He was her teacher. Her *friend*.

"I'm the Key," Cistine whispered. "If anyone can help you, it's me. And I think you know that. That's why you came to the stream that day. You've been following me, looking for me. Fighting for me. Because I made you a promise, and you knew I would keep it."

His whole body trembled. Cistine wondered if it was the taste of power slithering over her bones that made him strain in muscle and sinew, towering above her.

The air was still. The wind held its breath, waiting to see what she would do. What she would dare.

He didn't move when she raised her hands, tracing the mask's muzzle with her fingertips, palming the sharp cheekbones, following the angles toward the far edge. When she reached the hinge of his jaw, he ducked his head like a dog being freed from its tether. Cistine fitted her fingers around the edges of the mask and slowly separated it from his head.

It didn't give all at once. There was a strange, sucking pull, as if the skull itself resisted her. But with the same steady pressure with which she first drew him into her trust, into her heart, she pried it loose, freeing a tumble of filthy braids below.

Cistine wanted to weep when he shuddered before her, but she held her composure until he unbent his head and she saw his face for the first time since Selv Torfjel. He was gaunt, haggard, newly-scarred by his brothers and their *mirothadt* while he'd fought for his people.

She finally sobbed, dry with heartbreak, when his eyes found hers— dead eyes, void and flat, belonging to the death-god from the Vingete Vey who'd struck such terror into her when they first met. He'd gone back to that place where there was no wind or light or music, where no one could reach him. Not even Quill. Not even Ashe.

The mask thudded to the ground between them.

"I'm so sorry." Her voice cracked with tears. "I'm sorry you had to make that choice and I wasn't there to help you fight them. But I'm here now. I'm here, Darkwind."

He felt more animal than human when she touched him, his skin shivering when she took his hand. The wind augment spooled from his arm to hers; he neither resisted nor gave it, it simply flowed. His Atrasat inkings flickered through his tattered armor, a trail like starlight igniting beneath her hand when she slid it up his arm.

He did not attack again. He did not pull away.

"I told you," she whispered, "on Darlaska. Do you remember? I told you I would never let you go, Maleck Darkwind. And I won't. I won't let them have you."

A great shudder went through him like a sigh through ancient trees. "*Logandir.*"

Cistine's heart leaped.

He knew her. *He knew her.*

Tossing caution to Nimmus, she brought his head low with both hands, pressing her brow to his. "Let me take it, Darkwind. Let me bring you home."

For a moment, aside from his twitching skin, stillness consumed them both. Then he gripped her wrists, anchoring them together, making them one; and Cistine reached into the vein of augmentation between them, the power in his body roaring and surging against hers, and began to unravel it from inside him just as she'd done with Pippet.

The instant she plunged in, she knew it was too much. Sweat broke across her brow and bile flooded her throat at the sheer depth and darkness of what lived in him. His fingers fastened hers to his hair, shaking so violently he ripped the backs of her knuckles to ribbons.

But she did not let go. And he did not let her release him.

On and on, Cistine dragged at that humming chain of power, ripping it off its spindle, tearing it out of his body and into hers. Her nose opened in a fount. Blood spewed from her lips. She coughed and gagged, but she held on to him, reeling with no end, too much catastrophic energy slamming into her body for any one person to hold. She kept drawing it out like an infection, but she would die before she struck the bottom.

Then there were hands on her body, wrenching her back from the edge of oblivion. Thorne's hands. Quill's. Tatiana's. Ariadne's. They siphoned the power away when she gave it up, scattering it between them—taking the vestiges so she could carry the brunt.

With their strength bolstering hers, she dug down to the end of that chain, the lid to the remnant of his obsession. She focused all her might and gave a desperate heave, and the knot of power resisted her—the part of him that did not want to give up the augments. That had truly become Bloodwight.

His hands shot from her knuckles to her throat and bore down, cutting off what remained of her breath.

Ariadne snarled. Tatiana cursed. Thorne roared, "*Darkwind! Enough!*"

His head snapped toward his Chancellor, wobbling with uncertainty.

Then he made the choice. For Thorne, he let go of the power—and of her.

Cistine slammed the door over her might wide open, latched onto the last of the augments, and yanked them out of his body. The force struck her like a kick to the sternum, and she barreled backward, spitting blood, while he crumbled before her.

Together, they fell.

The others closed around them, shouting their names, feeling their pulses and cradling their heads, but Cistine only cared for Maleck. Her fingers hunted desperately through the bloodsoaked grass, catching his. She squeezed his hand until hers ached.

Nothing. He was still as death, wrapped in those black funeral robes.

Cistine started to weep. She was too late. There was too much damage. She'd killed him to set him free.

And then, just when exhaustion tugged a black veil over her eyes, when the world was only a pinprick of reason in a vast sea of shadows...

Maleck's fingers flexed. He squeezed back.

CHAPTER TWENTY-NINE

J UST TO BE clear," Bresnyar's breath warmed Ashe's shoulders where she crouched on the ledge of the mountain overlooking Lake Erani, "your best idea for assessing the status of the fronts is to capture a High Tribune?"

Ashe rested her elbow on her bent knee, surveying the fog-wrapped valley below. "Secondhand reports from outer patrols and deserters aren't reliable enough."

"Fair." Bresnyar settled back into the mountain's shade. "However, I still think you and I could've captured our quarry much quicker than Aden and his father."

"Obviously. But one glimpse of a golden dragon and everyone would know what we were up to. Lend me your eyes, will you?"

Bresnyar grunted, and Ashe cleaved to his sight, shaking her head to orient her vision; far below, the tents crystallized into focus, illuminating tears in mud-spattered cloth and bodies huddled among the canvas folds. Trickles of blood and flecks of gore marred the lake's shoreline where men and women bathed the grime of their own bodies and their dead friends from their armor.

They'd been in battle recently. A fragrance of despair plumed the air, so thick Ashe had no need of Bresnyar's sense to smell it. It weighed against her body when she severed the bond to Bresnyar and kneaded her temples, grimacing. The headaches would still take some getting used to.

Her sight had barely readjusted when the plod of boots on stone and the clatter of falling pebbles reached her ears. She jerked upright, and Bresnyar said, "It's them."

Ashe turned toward the trailhead, a smirk crawling across her face when first Aden, then Kristoff appeared—then Sander, looking utterly put-out, winded from the climb. "I lead Kanslar Court, I make the sacrifice to play Chancellor, and *this* is how I'm treated. Dragged from my bed at dawn on the *first* day I'm allowed to sleep in for *stars-know* how long."

"And here I thought you'd be happy to see us," Ashe drawled.

"Do you really think I would've made the climb here if I wasn't?"

Laughter scraped from her throat, and they embraced, the smell of old embers and lingering spice wafting from Sander's armor like a welcoming all its own. "Still the same lazy, entitled Tribune."

"Hardly lazy!" he protested, shoving her out at arm's length. "Do you know what I've been doing this past week?"

"Not sleeping, apparently," Kristoff chuckled, reclining against Bresnyar's shoulder.

"No, because our Chancellor had me on the hunt." Pride and mischief hung at the corners of Sander's grin. "I've sniffed out Kanslar's former stewardess."

Kristoff snapped upright. "*Rakel?*"

Sander nodded. "It was a bloody battle, and I may have made enemies of Benedikt and Valdemar with my focus divided. But I did manage to find her."

"What does Thorne want with her?"

"The truth of how she and Devitrius slipped so easily into Stornhaz the night this stars-forsaken war broke loose." Sander folded his arms. "It's true they had a traitor among the Vassora, but even so. Their paths and means of entry were unknown to us."

"Were," Ashe echoed.

"I risked my lovely and valuable neck stealing into an enemy camp to find her, but I'd say it's a due well paid. With a sprinkle of Tyve truth-telling poison, she gave us everything."

"You know how to enter the city," Aden said.

"I do. Though I'm still curious as to what Thorne's plan is for that. The note dear Tatiana sent was infuriatingly vague, to say the least."

Kristoff and Aden exchanged a heavy glance, and Ashe clapped Sander on the shoulder. "Let's build a fire and eat. We'll tell you everything."

It took the better part of their hastily thrown-together meal of hare meat and mountain berries to explain where they'd been since the war camp fell, what they were doing, and why. By the end of it, the High Tribune had forsaken his meal, arms crossed on his knees, staring off into the valley where the new camp lay.

"Those Balmond are the stuff of nightmares," he muttered. "We lose more warriors to them than blades or bows or sickness put together. You and your dragon might've saved us all, Ashe."

She toyed with the new starstone around her neck. "I don't know how much grace the Council will give Meriwa and whatever Legions she brings, so it's best to wait and call on them when we need them most. We may only have one chance with them."

"For taking the City, you mean."

"Do you think it's possible?" Kristoff asked.

"And would the Courts stand with us to make it happen?" Aden added.

Sander tipped his head left and right. "I like to think. These are indeed desperate times, perhaps enough to consider retaking the City. But they hunt the Key night and day, their focus split between her and the lines, particularly after I...*failed* to capture her." He smirked at the story he'd told them—his sham duel with Cistine in the mountains. But it quickly dropped away to a frown again. "If they lay hands on her before she's ready for this fight..."

A hot flush consumed Ashe's head, so abrupt and dizzying her stomach somersaulted. She shoved aside her own sparse ration, following Sander's gaze toward the valley.

"As for taking the City itself, that does have merit," Sander went on. "But the Bloodwights withdrew inside the wall, and that will make a siege infinitely more complicated. Even with Rakel's report, I fear what would become of our ranks in the attempt."

"Hence the dragons," Aden said, "and Cistine's training."

"I pray that will be enough."

Ashe gritted her teeth against another flush overtaking her nerves. "Is there anything else we need to know about the...about the—God's *bones!*"

"What is it?" Aden demanded.

"I don't *know*." Ashe lunged to her feet as well, rubbing gooseflesh from her arms. "Something's wrong, it feels like—Bres?"

Then it slammed her all at once, a feeling like a blade slicing clean through her from head to groin, the agony so blinding and sudden she had no defense against it.

She screamed and broke down sideways, crashing into Aden and dragging them both to the ground. The grip of his hands on her arms and the cold brush of the icy rock beneath her was a thousand cuts slashing her body, but when she tried to tell him to let go, all that emerged was another scream.

"Ashe!" Aden bellowed. "*Asheila!*"

Pain seared through her in waves, locking her body into rigor, and a distant sensation slithered into her like something was wrapped around her heart, her spirit and then *ripped* out—

Bresnyar!

But this wasn't him and it wasn't her, but it *was,* it was something cruel and furious and full of terror and hate and—

Darkness.

Absolute darkness.

⌒〜〜⌒

Asheila Kovar walked shadowed paths through a world that was not hers to see. Flickers of memory came and went; lightning strokes and starlight framed horned, skulled creatures crowding her sides, tracing the contours of men born from deepest nightmares.

Not hers. *His.*

He was standing on the path before her, his twisted, filthy braids tied back from his eyes, his body warped.

Maleck.

He turned like he'd heard her. Grief and shame and *agony* danced in his dead eyes.

Let me go. Just let me go, Asheila. There's no coming back from this.

She was almost in reach of him for the first time since that mountain path outside Kosai Talis. Her body ached for him, to touch, to tether, to draw him back.

You're wrong, Darkwind. Come back, I need you to come back. I need you to stay. For me.

He looked away, into the shadows beyond. *Death is easier. You do not know what I've done.*

She slid her hand into his, a shock like lightning arcing over her skin, and he stiffened, too. *I don't care. You don't get to leave me. You don't get to die. This isn't how our story ends.*

He still looked away from her, into the shadows.

She squeezed his hand. *Mal. Please.*

A long, painful, empty moment of silence and terror.

Then he squeezed back.

Ashe gasped awake on the cleft, the agony finally releasing her head until she slumped and curled on her side in a heap, soaking in wild breaths. Aden was gone, shouting to Bresnyar; Sander and Kristoff crouched beside her, and Kristoff took her shoulder. "Are you all right?"

"What in *Nimmus* was *that?*" Sander's voice was level, but concern blazed in his eyes. "It looked like one of Mira's fits."

"It's not, it..." Ashe braced a hand over her racing heart. There was something beneath it she'd barely noticed the absence of, consumed with dread and determination for weeks in Oadmark. But now it was back, an ember pulsing into flame again.

She flexed her hand and looked at Aden as he spun toward them.

"Bresnyar just received word through the starstone. They have Maleck."

Kristoff fell back on his heels, swearing in relief. Ashe staggered upright, panting and dizzy. "What else did Cistine say? Anything?"

"Word didn't come from Cistine. It came from Thorne." Aden's gaze was troubled. "They've gone back to the Den."

CHAPTER
THIRTY

THE FLIGHT TO the Den was a heart-pounding blur, breath stolen by the wind and fear ticking down every notch of Aden's spine. They had Maleck—but in what state? After the war against Talheim, he'd come back shaken, quiet, plagued by nightmares. Would this be different? Better? Far worse with how far he'd fallen?

Before Bresnyar even landed on the clifftop above Hellidom beside the gushing Nior Falls, Aden was down and climbing. His feet and fingers flew on familiar handholds he'd forced the cabal to ascend and descend countless times during their first five years in the city; then he ran, full speed and reckless, lunging across the natural bridges hemming together the halves of land over the river.

Up the steps, onto the veranda, into the Den. None of the apprehension from his last visit here found its way into his chest as he slammed inside, kicking the door shut behind him. "Thorne, where are you?"

He waited, ears pulsing with the heartbeat of quiet. An answer finally came, a shrill, high crack of disbelief from the bedroom hall. "*Aden?*"

His legs nearly failed him. For a moment, his heart truly did. He spun in the direction of that voice, shock and shame warring in his chest—that in his haste and fear for Maleck, he didn't think of her first.

That she was *here* at all—shouting his name.

"Pippet." He shoved away from the doorpost and shot down the hall, past closed door after closed door, until one sailed open: Baba Kallah's old room. "*Pippet!*"

And there she was, looking like she hadn't slept or eaten in weeks, old sweat and grime caked in her hair, eyes silver with tears. He knocked his name from her chest when he slid to his knees before her, yanking her against him, burying his hand in her hair and pulling her into his shoulder. He shook like he never had before, not even in his first Blood Hive match, and she clung to him, sobbing and gasping in heaves.

"I'm so *s-s-sorry,*" she retched, "I hurt you on the mountain and I...and I hurt Tatiana and the *baby* and Ari and Quill, I didn't want to, I was just so h-*hungry* and I hated *everything—*"

Shock after shock. Her. Ari. Quill. Tatiana and a *baby.*

Later. He shoved it all aside. Pippet was dangerously close to hyperventilating, her sobs wild and endless. He freed his fingers from her hair and unlocked her arms from around his neck, taking her face in his hands. "Listen. Breathe with me."

For more than a full minute, he guided her from shallow, panting gasps to deeper, steadier drinks of air. The wobbling pallor faded from her complexion, and her slim, strong fingers took his wrists. "I'm the worst student," she whispered. "I'm the worst *sister.*"

"You," he thumbed fresh tears from the sides of her nose, "are neither of those things. You fell. Everyone in this cabal has fallen. But I'm here, and the falling stops *now*. Do you understand?"

"But I hurt them."

"So have I." He smoothed the hair from her temples and lifted her face again when it fell. "This is grace. We embrace it, we don't waste it. That's your next lesson."

Her face crumbled and she pushed forward into his arms again. This time she cried steadily, with exhaustion and grief but not hysteria. Aden scooped her up and carried her to Baba Kallah's old bed. He sat them both on the edge, rocking her gangly body in his arms, smoothing her hair, kissing her head.

"I love you," he told her over and over, "and that will never change."

"I love you, too," she whimpered against his neck. "So, so, *so much*."

It was nearly an hour before the weeping tapered and she crumbled into sleep, curled against his chest. Only then did Aden realize the door still hung open, and its frame was not empty anymore.

"That's the most I've heard her say since...everything," Quill said gruffly, rubbing an arm across his eyes. "Welcome back."

Aden didn't answer for a moment, too stunned by the bruised state of Quill's face and the awkward, achy way he held himself. At last, he managed, "How did you wean her?"

"We didn't." Wonder—and oddly, guilt—touched Quill's voice. "Cistine...pulled it out of her. Her *and* Mal. All the augments."

Aden swore softly. "How is Maleck?"

Quill rubbed a hand through his mismatched hair. "He's been asleep since it happened. Pip was the same way, after. We just have to wait it out."

"And the others?"

"Just got back from letting Cassaida and Oskar know we're here."

Aden's stomach interrupted his reply, a low, ravenous grumble that woke Pippet with a sleepy giggle. Eyes brightening, Quill gestured with a tilt of his body. "Ari's making scones. Sounds like you could use a few."

"Don't go," Pippet begged.

"Oh, I'm going." Aden stood, still cradling her in his arms. "And I'm taking you with me."

She nestled closer to him but cocked her head into Quill's touch when he smoothed her hair in passing. Aden paused in the corridor, studying Quill's drawn, wounded face, his heavy gaze.

"It's done," Aden reminded him. "We brought her home."

"No. Mal and Cistine did." The haunted look lingered in his eyes when he led them down the hall, toward the waft of voices from the entryway and the kitchen beyond. Aden glanced back at Maleck's closed door.

Cistine had taken the augments from him, but would that be enough?

Stars. He prayed it would.

CHAPTER
THIRTY-ONE

MALECK DARKWIND WOKE to the smell of home.

Unbelievable as it seemed at first, it knew these walls—knew the grain of the honey-colored wood from the moment it opened its eyes, knew the lay of ceiling boards and the shape and weight of the mattress under its back.

He knew it. He knew his home by the cedar aroma of his own bedframe, his armoire, the trees clustering outside the window and the way the light slanted through the glass. Knew by the distant murmur of voices from the hall, the rush of the Nior and the roar of the falls beyond.

Perhaps it had all been a nightmarish dream. Cistine's imprisonment in Kalt Hasa and Baba Kallah's death and the war and Talheim and—

Stars above, he hurt. One twitch to rub his gritty eyes, and his body burned like soaking in fire. He flopped back with a moan, gripping his ribs in one hand, covering his eyes with the other. The scrape of scar against scar from his palm across his left cheek told him all he needed to know.

This was real, every Nimmus-cursed and Cenowyn-blessed second from the time he'd left for Siralek to stop the Tumult until log-riddled fields and the scream of flagons and the mask falling from its head and her face, her brave and loving face right *before* it, and its hands around her throat and the life winking out in her eyes—

Cursing, Maleck surged to the door, breaking down against it with his hand gripping the knob. He froze there, terror ripping into his middle.

They might've brought him back, but their family was not whole. Not after what he'd done to Quill, to Cistine.

He yanked his hand back and staggered away until his haunches encountered the windowsill. Sinking down, he buried his head in his hands.

Stars above, what had he done, what had he *become*?

That was the nightmare, those spectral flashes of hunger and hate curdling the very blood in his veins. He'd felt the obsession flow out of him while Cistine cut away his mangled, vicious edges, forging a seam for the man he'd once been, the man he'd wanted to be, to crawl out of the beast's carcass that had yearned to take and take and take.

She'd died with his hands around her throat. That was the last thing he remembered.

Knuckles rapped on wood. "Maleck?"

His heart lurched at that voice. In the havoc of addiction and battle and need, he'd almost forgotten Kristoff was alive.

Yet he couldn't bring himself to lift his head when the knob turned and the door squeaked open. Quill had taunted him night and day about his noisy door, no matter how many times Maleck had reminded him he did it so he would know if anyone entered, the way he hadn't known when his brothers came to take him that first time.

Quill. Quill was gone.

"And here the others told me you were asleep." Kristoff's voice was gentle, measured, not a hint of the scorn Maleck deserved riding the even keel of his tone.

He shook his head. "Leave me. I can't face you."

"I think we both know that isn't going to happen." With a soft *thump*, Kristoff settled in. Maleck raised his eyes to find the man who loved him like a father, loved him more than he'd ever deserved, sitting against the bedframe. In the tightness of the room, their boots nearly touched. "It didn't work when you tried in the tundra. I won't leave you now."

"This is different. Whatever you hoped to find in me, it's gone." He turned his head to stare out the window. "Leave me."

"If that's what you want. At least let me thank you first."

His eyes jumped back. "*Thank* me."

"For saving my life that day in the forest when we faced the *Aeoprast*. If not for you, I would be dead now."

"That isn't—"

"Maleck. I was blood-bonded to a medico. I know what damage a man can survive and what he can't. What was broken in me during that fight was beyond repair until you gave me that healing flagon. I owe you my life."

"I have taken more life than I've given these last weeks."

"Haven't we all?"

Frustration bounded up in Maleck. "Not like this. Look at me, *Athar*." He spread his hands slightly. "I deserved that mask I wore. I deserve all of it. I *killed* for augments."

"You saved lives as well. Ariadne says you brought Pippet back. There was still a piece of you fighting to break through."

"Then that piece should've done what was necessary to stop the rest of me."

Kristoff watched him narrowly. "You mean *killed* yourself."

Maleck stared at his hands, covered in half-healed sores and scars from battles he dimly recalled against his brothers—and common men when he stole their flagons to feed himself.

"Is that what you think *Pippet* should have done?"

Maleck flinched. "She is not like me. And it would not have had to be a killing. Had Cistine taken the augments from me when I first found her, I would have bled to death and that would have been the end of it."

"Do you know what it would have done to Cistine if you'd died in her arms? She loves you, Maleck."

"Then she should have let me go. *You* should let me go."

"No. She saved you *because* of that love. She knew you were worth the risk, that you could come back from this."

"I do not believe that."

"But I *know* it." Kristoff leaned forward, earnest and full of conviction.

"I've seen you come back from it before. I've helped you crawl from this darkness. I'm your father, Maleck. I will not abandon you. Remember what I taught you last time?"

We come back because we know there's redemption, Afiyam. You know because you've already seen life beyond it. You have already weighed the cost.

Dampness crawled down Maleck's cheeks. "Quill and Cistine..."

"Alive and well."

Unbearable hope burst from Maleck's throat in a breathless heave. "They *live?*"

"Of course they do. You didn't strike as hard as you thought."

Maleck rubbed a hand over his mouth, but that did not stop the shaky, wonderous laughter falling from his lips. "May I see them?"

Kristoff hesitated. "Cistine sleeps. But the others are in the kitchen."

Nerves fluttered at the base of Maleck's stomach. "How long have we been here?"

"Two days. Don't worry, Cistine slept nearly this long after the war camp fell. This is not unusual."

Maleck's fingers sought a path through his braids, but the snarls were too numerous. He gave up. "Will you walk with me?"

Kristoff's smile softened. "Through this darkness and every other."

The short journey to the kitchen was the longest and most fraught of his entire life. Bile blocked his throat by the time they stepped into the ghostlit room and he laid eyes on the five gathered at the table in quiet conversation, sharing a plate of cherry scones.

Aden. Quill. Ariadne and Tatiana. Pippet.

They fell silent, looking up at his arrival. For one moment, the world held its breath, and Maleck with it.

Then Aden bolted to his feet and hurried to clap him in an embrace. "Welcome back, *Allet.*"

Vision a hopeless blur, Maleck pressed his brow to Aden's shoulder and did not raise his head until a small, warm hand slid into his and tugged. Such strength in those fingers, despite how they shook.

Aden released him, and Maleck turned toward Pippet's solemn face.

Pain radiated from her and boomed in the chasm of his chest, a perfect harmony to his agony. He knelt, cupping her sharp cheeks in his hands; she touched his in turn, wiping away tears. "Darkwind, why are you sad?"

"Because I have found something very precious to me," he murmured, "and I'm afraid to lose it again."

Her face crumbled, and she burrowed into his arms. He held her so tightly it made his body ache all the worse, wishing that by the might of his grip alone he could piece back together what his brothers had shattered in their spirits, in their lives.

He did not know how long he and Pippet clung to one another before he felt strong enough to let her go. The shadows in her face also crowded his, and perhaps they always would. But they had each other, so they did not walk alone.

With a last, fleeting kiss to Maleck's cheek, Pippet padded back to her chair between Quill and Tatiana and curled into it, hugging her knees. Maleck straightened and faced them, the weight of their attention pulling his gaze just short of their faces. "Forgive me."

"Forgiven," Ariadne said, her tone the warmest he'd ever heard, and she reached to squeeze his hand.

Tatiana folded her arms over her navel, body lifting and settling with a deep sigh. "I'm glad you're in control again."

"That makes two of us." Quill's hollow agreement brought Maleck's gaze tugging reluctantly up to him. Relief perished quickly under shame's stranglehold at the state of his face, its fresh wounds in the shape of fistmarks, his eyes sunken into swollen, graying sockets.

"Nightwing," Maleck rasped. "I thought I had...I know I nearly—"

"You remember it?"

Maleck winced. "Every blow. I couldn't bring myself to stop. Forgive me, please, *Allet*, if you can..."

Quill pushed himself to his feet with a harsh scrape, and Maleck forced himself to hold fast at his advance. His side twinged with a half-remembered dream of near-fatal pain, harsh blows from a different brother, but he ignored that as well. He deserved whatever strikes came from those fists, whatever judgement and retribution Quill deemed fit. He would take every strike until Quill was satisfied justice had been meted out, until their scars matched. He didn't recoil when Quill halted before him, hands forming fists at his sides—

Then his arms were around Maleck, pounding him on the back so hard it knocked a sound from Maleck somewhere between a breath of relief and a sob. Quill kissed his temple and let out a half-wild laugh. "Stars *damn* it, I missed you. You almost made me come all the way to the Sable Gates to find you, you stupid *bandayo*."

"I will never, never let it come that close again. I swear by my own life and all I hold dear."

"You'd better not. Tati might finish us both next time."

"That's for damned certain," she muttered, but even her eyes weren't wholly dry.

Maleck clapped hold of Quill by the nape of his neck and held on with all his might, and wept yet again. This was what he'd come back for, surrendered to Cistine for—this was the man whose love and courage and shed blood had drawn him back from the edge of oblivion, made him fight those last steps to be redeemed.

This was family. This was *home*.

There was only one piece of it missing. And when Quill finally released him and they drew apart, the dread in his heart spread and blackened.

He could sense she was close. Yet Asheila had not come for him.

CHAPTER
THIRTY-TWO

THIS WAS RIDICULOUS. It was just a threshold, just one more step into the Den.

But Ashe couldn't bring herself to walk through that door.

She'd dreamed of this moment since Holmlond, but now that it was here and she *knew* Maleck was on the other side of that door, she was stalling like a new Warden putting off the pain of her first sparring match. She'd spent far longer than needed on the clifftop above the falls, seeing Bresnyar off to hunt and scout for danger. Then she'd taken her time descending into Hellidom, drinking in the familiar clusters of wood-and-stone homes within the city the cabal once called home. Now she paced the veranda, growling under her breath to herself, "Just go *in*."

But she couldn't. *Mereszar*, Dragonfire, the warrior who'd stared down countless enemies and triumphed fearlessly, was afraid to face her *valenar*. Afraid that whatever she saw would only remind her of his hands around her throat. She was being cowardly, and she couldn't seem to find a way around it.

The door creaked open, and her heart twinged in a blend of disappointment and relief when Kristoff stepped out onto the veranda, rubbing his hands against the chill. "Ah. I was wondering if you'd gotten lost." His smile held no accusation as he reclined against the Den's railing.

"Good to see you found us. Bresnyar is off scouting, I take it?"

"He is." She thrust her shaking hands deep into her pockets. "How is...everyone?"

"Tired and famished, but glad to be together again."

"That's good." She paced another loop with him watching her. "Aren't you going to lecture me for hiding out here?"

Kristoff tapped his elbows with his thumbs, somber gaze taking in her scowl, the challenge leaking from her posture. "When Aden's mother died, I almost didn't attend her pyre burning."

Ashe halted, staring at him. "*You?* The perfect *valenar?*"

He chuckled hoarsely. "I'm sure that's how Aden tells it. His memories of those days are...clouded. By his own grief and by mine. I'm sure he wouldn't believe it if I told him that I considered neglecting the burning and going about my duties like she never died."

Ashe bent her shoulder slowly to one of the veranda's columns. "Why?"

"Because love is not a straight and even path between us and the ones we cherish. Because it is not easy, or enjoyable, or even *bearable* all the time. I was terrified to see Natalya on that pyre. I was terrified for my last memory of her to be that illness-ravaged face, her eyes closed, no more precious smiles on her lips. It haunted me long before I ever saw her lying there."

Ashe swallowed a fist-sized lump in her throat. "But you went."

"I went. Because as difficult as love is, it's never about us. I went to honor her memory and the bond we shared that I carry with me beyond death."

Ashe's gaze floated to the door. "You're saying Maleck needs me."

"I'm saying he hasn't stopped glancing over his shoulder since he first noticed you weren't at the table."

Reluctant laughter dragged from her chest. "Still the same Mal."

The moment the words left her lips, the ache of *missing* him seized her so brutally that she punched the door open, Kristoff silent on her heels down the short hall past her old room and straight into the kitchen where her cabal gathered.

Where her *valenar* sat among them.

She fought the urge to wince when his head snapped around at her arrival. His face was a patchwork of new wounds from battles she knew nothing about, and the lines around his eyes had deepened, the scar on the right turning to a blistered furrow.

But those eyes...dead eyes with life trickling back into them when he beheld her.

"*Asheila.*" Maleck jolted from his chair, then stood gripping the table, fingers flexing. "I...I am *so*—"

"Stop. If the next words out of your mouth aren't *I love you and will never leave you in such a ridiculous, dramatic way without saying goodbye ever again,* I don't want to hear it."

He blinked, then frowned. "You may have to repeat that if you wish me to recite it verbatim."

Broken laughter ripped from her throat. "You stupid, beautiful braided *bastard.*"

He stepped forward at the same time she did, pushing himself away from the table. Ashe lunged to meet him at the edge of the counter, pulling his head up with her hand to his cheek and looking into his eyes—sorrow and regret and relief and *love* guttering in their depths.

"I saw you," she said. "In between. Somewhere. I saw you in the dark."

"I heard you. You brought me back."

He reached for her, then hesitated, fingers flexing like he'd struck a wall he couldn't reach past. His gaze fell to the fading necklace of bruises around her throat. Shaking his head, he began to withdraw.

Not this time. She grabbed his hand and towed it around the back of her neck, and his eyes fell shut. He slammed a kiss to her brow, his jagged breath stirring her hair. That was the only apology she needed; that tenderness, that comfort, and the sobs hitching his chest. It was more than enough.

She craned her head back and possessed his mouth with hers, pouring a full month of missing him, of dread and grief and fear into the kiss and beckoning him to taste in return that she was no longer afraid. She kissed him until she felt the first edges of that gap between them knitting shut and it no longer seemed he would vanish when she opened her eyes again.

Then a quiet voice, familiar and unexpected as a blow to the gut, tugged her attention. "That's *so much* kissing. They're worse than you and Tatiana."

Ashe's eyes jerked open, and she yanked away from Maleck, looking to the table where the others sat—to the wiry figure tucked into the chair between Tatiana and Quill, gathered up so small against its back she all but vanished. Numb with shock, Ashe's hands dropped from Maleck's face. "*Pippet.*"

She fluttered her fingers in sheepish reply.

Shaking clarity back into her head, Ashe pointed to the floor. "Come *here.*" Pippet uncurled from the chair and padded to stand before her, shoulders bent, head slumped, gaze fixed on the ground. "Listen to me," Ashe said, and Pippet winced. "I'm sorry."

Her head snapped up, eyes wide with shock. "*You're* sorry? What *for?*"

Ashe gripped Pippet's shoulders. "Because I made you a promise that I would always be there to protect you, and when you needed me most, I was dancing and drinking instead. I wasn't there that night. I let Salvotor take you. I'm sorry...and I don't need you to tell me it's all right," she added when Pippet's mouth sprang open. "I need you to say you forgive me."

Pippet gnawed her lower lip. "But it wasn't all your fault."

"Not all of it. But that vow was mine to make and mine to keep, and I didn't." Tugging her sleeve down to cover her knuckles, Ashe brushed away a tear that slid over Pippet's lashes. "Do you forgive me?"

She nodded, short and jerky. "I really missed you, Shei."

Ashe groaned. "Are we really starting that now?"

A peek of a smile dawned on her face. "Quill said I could."

"Well, I'll allow it. Actually, you can call me *anything* you like." Ashe brushed her cheek again. "Because I missed you, too. More than you'll ever know."

Pippet lunged up, wrapping her legs around Ashe's waist and her arms around her neck so she had no choice but to carry her back to the table. But she didn't mind; the girl was lighter than before, well-trained muscle wasted in favor of using augments in battle. And no matter how heavy she was,

Ashe would've carried her to the ends of the kingdoms and beyond if that was what she needed.

Maleck pulled out the chair beside his, and Ashe dropped into it, adjusting Pippet in her lap. Kristoff settled between Aden and Ariadne, helping himself to a scone.

"So. We're back," Ashe said as Pippet nestled her head under her chin.

Quill cleared his throat. "You're back."

She reached across the table to bump knuckles with him. "And your face looks like a story waiting to be told."

"Oh, we have plenty of stories," Tatiana grunted. Maleck sank down, avoiding her eyes. "I'm sure you do, too."

"But those will have to wait until Cistine's awake," Ariadne added.

Ashe glanced past her, to the dark hall and the doorless room beyond. "Is she all right?"

"Sleeping," Ariadne said. "Thorne is watching over her."

Maleck's fists flexed on his knees, his gaze averting from the hall, and that told Ashe much about her princess's condition and what had caused it. But not quite enough. "What happened?"

Quill, Ariadne, and Tatiana looked around at one another with a sort of withdrawn, fathomless shared memory that made Ashe reach for Maleck's hand and cling to it with all her might.

She did not let go while the others told them what had transpired in Hvallatar.

CHAPTER
THIRTY-THREE

CISTINE WASN'T CERTAIN how much time had passed, or where she was, when she woke from her dreamless slumber. The first things that struck her were the smells of naked wood and weapon polish, and the grainy starch of disused linens.

She was lying face-down on a familiar bed.

She sucked in a breath lingering with flecks of cherry, sugar, and cinnamon, and tears welled in her eyes. Pain dug mercilessly into her temples, a dull, hollow throb that didn't ease when she sat up, straining to hear the chug of watermills and the rush of the Nior River.

It was like nothing had changed. There was the distant crackle of the oven and voices murmuring on the other side of the hall. Her books and clothes were precisely where she'd left them the day she and Julian ran to find Thorne on the plains outside Eben.

But now Thorne was sitting in the wooden chair at the bedside, slumped with chin to his chest, softly snoring.

Shoving back the blankets, she struggled up, took a step toward him, and broke down against the bedpost. Weakness throbbed down into the pits of her body like she'd trained with Quill for days and nights without stopping. Her abdomen and limbs ached as badly as her head; she felt dry, wizened, like overbaked clay. She barely managed to choke Thorne's name.

His eyes sprang open, and he cursed, surging to his feet and taking her elbows gently. "Steady, Wildheart."

"What happened?" she gasped. "Why are we in the Den? Did I—is Maleck—?"

"Awake. I heard him talking with the others." Thorne tucked her hair behind her ear. "You did it. You brought him back."

Joyful, exhausted heat branded her eyes. "I need to see him."

Thorne pressed his lips to her brow and pulled her up from the bedpost, looping his arm around her waist. They shuffled together down the dark hall, past the steps leading up to Thorne's old chamber, out into the kitchen where everyone was gathered except Ashe and Quill.

Silence fell when they entered the room. Cistine's eyes leaped straight to Maleck, sitting next to Ashe's old, empty chair. He came to his feet at once, then froze, staring at her, tensed as if to move away. A strange energy crackled between them; not the might of an augment, but a tether forged in that moment when he'd revealed his power to her, and she took it from him. She hardly knew how to look at him now. His face, so beaten, so tired, filled her with sadness; yet those braids, that firm, kind mouth, and those eyes were just the same as she knew and loved.

"Darkwind," she murmured.

"*Logandir*." He opened his arms, face heartbreakingly uncertain, as if she hadn't wanted to embrace him every day since they'd parted in Selv Torfjel.

Being in his arms was another piece of home fallen back into place. His heart thudded hard and quick against her cheek when she sank down against him. She could feel the augments were gone; his body was clean, only the faintest scar of an aftertaste slithering along his bones.

"I owe you so much more than my life," he murmured. "I owe my soul to you, and that is a debt no man can repay."

"I don't want you to repay it. I just want you to live. To stay with us. That's all I ask."

Maleck squeezed her tightly, then released her when Thorne approached, swift and all but silent. Cistine shifted out of his way so he could grip the sides of Maleck's neck and look him deeply in the eyes.

"Listen to me," Thorne said. "I am not interested in apologies. I've heard what you did for Blaykrone, for *our* people. No matter what's happened, you are still one of us. We will find a way to put everything right, and we'll do it together. Do you understand me?"

Maleck dipped his head. "I do."

"Good. Welcome home." Thorne pulled Maleck in close, then drew out his own chair and the one beside it at the head of the table.

Cistine sank down, tears of relief staining her vision. "I never thought we'd have a chance to come home."

"Well. After you gave us the wind augments you stole from Maleck, we couldn't think of anywhere else to go," Ariadne admitted. "To heal."

"We didn't know what state either of you would be in when you woke," Thorne added. "It was the best place to shelter until we knew."

"Does anyone else know we're here?"

"Cassaida," Tatiana said. "She's been in charge, so she had the right to know. Besides, we have a dragon on watch...we're as safe as we can be."

As if summoned by the mention of her dragon, Ashe entered through the doorway to the other hall, Quill on her heels, both with arms full of rations. Relief flashed across Ashe's face when her eyes fell on Cistine; Quill simply looked at her, a strange war in his tired eyes.

"Finally decided to join us, Princess?" Ignoring the unease between them, Ashe let all the food tumble from her arms and bent over Cistine's chair to wrap her shoulders in a hug from behind. "It sounds like you had quite the adventure while we were in Oadmark."

Cistine craned her head to look up at her Warden. "Don't mind us, what about the dragons?"

"We have at least one Legion on our side, maybe more. Enough to help even the scales against the Balmond a bit, anyway."

"And Sander is of the opinion the Chancellors may be desperate enough to risk taking the City," Aden added, "if everything were to fall into place for it."

"But it hasn't yet," Cistine said. "I still don't have the augments I need."

Maleck cleared his throat, a single, soft beat that deafened the room and brought every eye to him.

Cistine's heart began to pound.

Ashe frowned. "Maleck."

He leaned back in his seat. "I heard your plan, long ago. I don't remember how, but I knew what you needed. It had to be me who retrieved this....my penance and my purpose. The only thing that could turn the tide of this war." He pulled something from his pocket. "All of it for you, *Logandir*."

He turned his palm out to her, bearing two jars: one ice-white, one scarlet-black. Even without touching them, Cistine knew what they were: the source of that last trace of augments she'd felt on his body when she hugged him. Not *in* him—but on his person.

Two augments. One blood. One healing.

CHAPTER
THIRTY-FOUR

THE UNBEARABLE SILENCE broke under a staggered, open-mouthed breath, which Thorne only realized came from him when Cistine's hand tightened in his.

"A blood augment and a healing augment," she whispered. "Now we have one of each."

Thorne hadn't realized how deeply he'd wrestled against the vain, selfish hope that another plan would come to fruition in the absence of those augments until all hope cracked apart, and his heart with it. Suddenly Cistine was drifting away from him into dark waters, and though he clung to her hand with all his might, it was not enough to save her.

"How did you come by these?" Aden demanded.

"I stole them from my brothers when I took Pippet..." Maleck quieted, frowning. "No. That isn't right. This pair I stole from the City of a Thousand Stars. I used the first to save my own life."

They all gaped at him.

"You *broke into Stornhaz?*" Tatiana demanded.

"In a manner of speaking." He shrugged. "The *mirothadt* there do not resist the Bloodwights or those masked as them."

Ariadne sank back in her seat, hands folded behind her head. "That was why they withdrew. Because you broke in."

Cistine shifted eagerly in her chair. "Do you know their formations? Guard rotations? Could you teach them to Ariadne?"

Maleck blinked. "I could try. Why?"

Quill crossed his arms and slouched in his seat. "Because we're going to sack the City. And you may have just handed us the victory, *Storfir*."

Cistine's eyes flashed around the table. "Can our allies be ready to stand with us now, against the Chancellors and then the Bloodwights?"

Ashe nodded. "Whenever you're ready, we'll call on them."

"But are *you* ready to face the Courts?" Kristoff asked.

Cistine laid a hand over her stomach and took a deep, shuddering breath. "I've already showed them what a princess can do. I think it's time to show them what the Key is capable of."

Thorne had never felt prouder of her; nor had he ever been more terrified in his life. It was happening all at once now, a great surge toward the future he'd feared so much for so long. One that might destroy his dreams and dismantle his own plans.

One that might end his *selvenar's* life.

Tatiana spanned her hands on the table's edge. "Are you sure, *Yani*? Once we bring the Chancellors into this, there's no turning back."

"We'll have to face the consequences," Maleck added, "as individuals, and as a cabal, for what we've done. What we *are*."

Quill scoffed. "Nothing new."

"Sillakove is used to being punished for its choices." Ariadne shrugged. "What's one more confrontation, if it saves our kingdom?"

"Then we're all in agreement that this should be our strategy?" Thorne asked. "Stornhaz, the Door, the augments—all of it." The cabal looked around at one another; then they nodded, one by one. The last scrap of Thorne's hope at a diplomatic denial cracked into shards, and his heart began to bleed. "Tatiana, Ariadne, and Ashe, then. Ready yourselves to travel."

"Not quite yet." Cistine swallowed audibly. "There's still one thing we have to do to prepare."

She met his eyes, and his heart stumbled. It shocked him that the words came steadily from his own lips. "We have to plan a wedding."

All was quiet for a moment. Then Maleck said, "Pardon me?"

Ashe crossed her arms. "Contingency. If Cistine falls, Thorne upholds the Talheimic line of succession." The words were crisp, curt, revealing nothing of the pain that ravaged her eyes—a pain Thorne's heart echoed.

"We won't take long," Cistine vowed. "We still have to write to our allies and tell them to meet us at Lake Erani in one week. And while those letters go out, we'll take care of things here."

"And what does that look like, exactly?" Quill asked. "For *valenar*, it's usually done behind closed doors."

A blush crossed Cistine's cheeks. "Talheimic weddings require at least two witnesses, one on behalf of each person, to prove there's no coercion. But usually there are more. It's a festival, like after Salvotor's conviction."

Maleck and Quill exchanged a glance. Tatiana asked, "Do we have time for that?"

"We'll make time," Thorne said firmly.

"It's not as complicated as it seems," Cistine assured them. "We already have all the witnesses we need, and an officiant to make the vows legally binding—"

"Define officiant," Tatiana said.

Thorne and Cistine pointed to Aden. "Him."

He rubbed his furrowed brow. "I should never have taken that Tribune position."

Kristoff slapped the back of his head. "Don't be sour. It's an honor."

"And then we go to battle," Cistine said softly. "And we win."

There was no nodding this time, no smiling; only solemn looks and a quiet that went deep into the Den's very bones, turning its settling shudders to mournful sighs.

Cistine got to her feet. A sham smile turned her mouth, trying and failing for warmth. "Thorne, will you walk with me?"

He snapped to his feet. "Of course."

Nightbirds trilled in the bushes outside the Den. Ghostplants broke softly at the edges of the path under their feet, painting the trail with the shining imprint of their boots. They climbed high on the flat rocks, and it almost felt like any night in the last decade, when the Key was just a young legend and the Doors were sealed to them forever.

A harsh chuckle slipped free of him, and Cistine glanced wide-eyed over her shoulder. "What's funny?"

"Just...when I realized the straits I put my kingdom in to protect you, I begged the gods for a chance to prove myself worthy of my title again. A chance to put my kingdom's needs first." His gaze drifted to the augment pouch always lashed at her hip. "I got precisely what I asked for and nothing I wanted."

"I feel the same way." Her smile small and sad, Cistine halted. "Do you know where we are?"

His gaze roamed the familiar slab of rock, a dull ache pulling at his middle. "This is where I taught you the constellations."

"Mmhmm. It's where I first began to think of you as my friend." Her smile was wider and warmer now, the one he'd fallen in love with long before he'd known that love for what it was. "And now you're so much more than that. You're more precious than anything in my life, Thorne Starchaser."

His Name sang through him, stirring his core while he watched her walk the edge of the rock, toeing ghostplants in the cracks, shedding their luminescence against the contours of her armor and the silhouette of her face as she turned to face him; there were tears on her cheeks.

"I have to ask something from you," she croaked. "Well, two impossible things, actually."

Though he feared he'd regret it, he said, "Name them."

She blew her cheeks full of air. "I need you to do it. The knife, on the Door. You have to be the one."

Horror turned his bowels to water, and he took a step back from her, shaking his head. "Cistine. I can't."

"I *know*." Her voice cracked. "And I don't *want* you to, but there's no one else I trust. Especially not myself. I'm not a warrior like the rest of you. I'll lose my courage if it's just me and the Door. But I know you'll make it as painless as possible, and then you'll bring me back."

His clammy hands rattled, his upper lip and nose and cheeks turned numb, and all he could think of was his nightmare of her bleeding to death in his arms under Grimmaul's knife, his father's knife, but never, *never* his own. "You're asking me to take your life to the last inch and then bring you back. Even I lack that faith in myself."

"But I *don't.*" She took a step toward him, light fanning out beneath her feet. "I trust you with my plans, with my Name, with *everything.* That includes my life and my...my death. I know this is cruel and unfair, and you're perfectly within your right to hate me for it, but I *can't* ask anyone else, because I don't trust anyone else to save me. I trust *you.*"

Every word slammed into him with tidal force, dragging his heart further and further from shore. She *trusted* him. Despite all his flaws and falters, despite all the ways he'd failed his kingdom as a Chancellor...

But he would not fail this time. This test. He owed Valgard this, and he owed it to her. "If this is what you require of me, then you have it, Cistine. I'll guard your life with everything I am. I *will* bring you back."

Her cheeks fluttered, trying for another smile and failing. She shifted, linking her fingers together before her, stretching out her arms in an anxious bow, and her nervousness made Thorne even more nervous in turn. She'd stood firm and looked into his eyes when she asked him to make her bleed so their kingdoms could both survive, and *now* she struggled to meet his gaze? What in the stars could this second impossible question be?

"There's something I can't do myself while I'm busy convincing the Chancellors not to kill me before we retake the City," she said carefully, "but it will be a test to see if the marriage oaths will hold...if Talheim will respect them."

Thorne tipped his head. "Tell me what you need."

She let her arms swing loose at her sides. "I need you to cross the Dreadline and bring the Wardens at the northern barracks to fight with us."

Thorne stared at her. "You want me to go and flaunt my title as your...*husband.*" Stars, no word had ever tasted stranger in his mouth.

Cistine nodded, lips peeling back in a grimace. "I want them to know I sent you, to see you for what you are to me. And to *them.*"

He rubbed a hand over his mouth, rubbed some feeling back into his face. His tongue, unfortunately, was beyond help.

"I understand if you don't want to do this, either," Cistine added. "And if it has to be me, then I'll go. But I already feel pulled a hundred ways, and I *need* to stand before the Chancellors as soon as possible, but this—"

"Cistine," he choked at last, and her words stumbled to a halt. "I've already agreed to take a blade to you. I think I can manage to stand before your people first."

A relieved smile cracked the tension on her face, and she crossed the rock and flung her arms around him. He swept her off her feet and held her against him with all his might, as if that alone was enough to save her. To hold her into this world.

As if he had the power to do that, when every plan, every scheme, every hope they had and every vow he'd made to himself hinged utterly on learning to let her go.

CHAPTER THIRTY-FIVE

CISTINE CHANGED INTO her old, soft pajamas well after dark, when all the letters to their allies were written. She felt strangely brittle the longer she was awake, body aching and mind darting constantly back to the lumber grove and the anguish and *power* when she'd unspooled Maleck's augments. With every passing hour, her memory of those moments sharpened and the rest of it blurred, like she'd become more than human for an instant, something infinite and unbreakable.

It terrified her.

Dressed again, she rubbed her cheeks clean of grit and sweat and tears, belted on her augment pouch, and slipped out to find the kitchen deserted apart from Maleck, sitting at the table, spinning his cup on its axis.

Cistine hesitated in the doorway. She didn't just see him there; she *felt* him, a blazing white imprint on her mind like staring too long at the sun. He was a dapple in her vision that didn't go away when she blinked, burned into her like an inking.

The cup stopped twirling. "I feel you too, *Logandir.*"

She stiffened. "Can you read my thoughts?"

His diaphragm seized, stomach sucking in like he wanted to laugh. "No. But your stillness is easy to read after all this time."

"It's like you glow. I can feel you under my skin." Cistine padded to the table, taking the chair across from him. "It's not that way with Pippet."

"She carried far fewer augments than I. And from what Ariadne says, she didn't resist as brutally as I did."

Cistine accepted that, hugging her arms around her middle and watching the cup start spinning again. "Where's Ashe?"

"Helping Aden put Pippet to bed. She refused to rest without both of them there."

His tone was flat, giving no hint to what he was thinking or feeling. Cistine studied his face, but it gave few clues, either. "How...how do you really feel, Mal?"

The cup kept turning, then clattered down on its base. "I feel like I left my home for a moment, and while I was gone, something wicked took up residence inside. It's gone now, but its taint lingers on everything. I can feel it here." He tapped two knuckles over his heart. "Mostly I feel like myself, but there are moments I can taste those augments you wear, *Logandir*, and I don't know if I should flee from you or take them."

She caught her breath warily. "You still crave them?"

"It isn't a craving, it's simply the way I've been thinking for some time now. The day I brought Pippet to you, I found a man carrying a healing augment. I saved my own life with it, but at the cost of his. That was what the obsession told me: all augments are mine. I can take as I wish."

"So it's not the urge you struggle with, it's having the same thoughts as before, even without the hunger to make you act on them."

"Precisely. And how long before that fades?"

"I don't care if it ever does. You can't flee. You have to stay with us, Maleck."

He sent the cup tilting again. "And now I wonder if you hear *my* thoughts."

She reached over, stopping the spin with her hand over his. "I mean it. Don't go."

He raised his eyes from the cup to her face. "Why risk so much on my behalf, *Logandir*?"

She forced a wobbly smile. "Because in this life, we save you. And in the next, we learn to let you go."

Maleck flipped his hand beneath hers, squeezing her fingers. Then he frowned. "You're trembling."

"It's not you." She took back her hand and rubbed her face. "I'm just feeling overwhelmed."

"The wedding, or the siege?"

"Are those my only two choices?"

He rose, pilfered through the cabinets for a moment, and returned with a jug of mead and a second cup. Filling them both, he pushed one toward her, pointing to her around its edge. "Remember. Sip." When she nodded, he released it to her and took his own drink. "What concerns you about the wedding? That it will be too much for wartime celebration, or too little compared to what you've always envisioned?"

Cistine pondered his question while she sipped. All her life, she'd dreamed of her wedding day, an affair of importance for the entire kingdom. The lords and ladies gathered together, distant relatives to the tenth cousin flocking the Citadel's wide glass parlors. Towering cakes in seven flavors, fruit platters and flutes of champagne, sweet harp music and elegant dances beneath iron chandeliers dripping teardrop crystals. Her mother in gold, her father in white, and a husband whose face had changed as often as her suitors did, one kiss, one courtship after another. Often it was Julian, other times a faceless character while she waited for another interested man to fill the role.

When she imagined it was Thorne, suddenly the vision shrank. The crowd, the cakes, the music...none of it mattered as much as the man who would take her hand and bind his future to hers.

"No. The wedding isn't something to worry about, I know that," she admitted. "That's just one day, there's a lifetime after it for balls and celebrations. It's everything *else*." She drank this time to steady her nerves. "A few months ago, I didn't know you *could* steal augments from someone. Now I've weakened a Bloodwight and I've saved you and Pippet. My powers keep expanding, and that terrifies me because I don't know where it stops. Now I have to think about a wedding, all these battles, and this meeting with the Chancellors..."

Maleck held up a hand. "What did I teach you about balancing things?"

She squinted at him. "Weren't most of those lessons nonverbal?"

He snorted softly. "When did you start to notice the weight in the hilt of the weapons?"

"Once I let everything else fall into place."

"And when you shoot with your bow, do you concentrate on shaft, string, and target? Or do you set your eyes to one place and let your gaze guide your arm?"

A reluctant smile tugged her lips. "The latter."

"When we allow things to take their proper place, the rest falls into perspective. First, the wedding. Then the Chancellors. And then the battle." He refilled her cup halfway. "Your power is like a garden...it does not require constant tending. It will grow as you grow. Watch it, water it, weed it. But don't hover over it so intently you starve it of the sunlight it needs to flourish."

Cistine let out her breath in a slow sweep, sinking back in her chair. "What did I ever do without you?"

"I don't know, but it seemed to involve an awful lot of running."

She laughed, setting aside her cup and fingering her pouch. "Can I ask you something about augments?"

Maleck's brow furrowed. "I will do what I can to help."

She drew the dark flagon from her pouch and set it on the table between them. "Can you tell me what this is?"

He reached across the table, but only touched his fingertips to the sealed case. Even so, Cistine tensed. It was a test for them both—her willingness to trust him this close to the power she carried, and his ability to walk away from it despite the urgent memory to take, take, take.

Finally, Maleck withdrew his hand. "I have never felt its like before."

Cistine swallowed. "What does that mean to you?"

He watched her shrewdly. "It means this augment is uniquely powerful and extraordinarily dangerous. How did you come by it?"

"I stole it. That's why we were at that temple in Kosai Talis when you fought Ashe. Mira called this one of the *Stor Sedam*...seven augments with no equal. We think the Bloodwights are trying to find them all to enslave the kingdoms."

Maleck's frown deepened. "The lock around it?"

"I think it's a bloodlock. And I might be able to open it because *my* blood, like my father's, is bound in *Gammalkraft* and augmentation just like this."

"But you haven't tried yet."

Hands shaking, she stowed the flagon away again. "I'm afraid to. And I'm afraid if I have the chance, I'll use it, even though I don't know what it is. That I'll hurt someone I love." She took a shaky breath and another sip of mead. "But I don't think I'm enough, Mal. I don't think my power is enough. I'm afraid that to stop the *Aeoprast*, I may have to use it, no matter what the consequences are."

Maleck was quiet, hands gathered into his lap, the lines of his shoulders flexing as if each breath took effort. Cistine stayed with him, waiting for some reassurance, for a promise that as someone who knew augments intrinsically, who knew personally what the Bloodwights could do, he saw some solution that would spare her ever having to open that flagon.

But he didn't speak again.

CHAPTER
THIRTY-SIX

THE SOUND OF humming drifted from Baba Kallah's old room.

Strange as it was to be back in the Den at all, Tatiana's exhausted mind struggling to comprehend the chaos of the last several days, it was that sound that caught her on her way back to Quill's room from bathing in the river. With her hand on the knob, she turned down the hall to listen to that familiar tune, a pitchy, practiced lullaby—but not a Valgardan one. She'd heard Ashe sing it to Maleck on restless nights in war camps scattered across the northern front when his nightmares overwhelmed him.

Frowning, she bundled her filthy armor against her silk nightgown and padded quietly down the hall.

The humming stopped when she reached the door, interrupted by a quiet curse and the sound of ripping hair, and for an instant she considered walking away from it the way she'd been walking away from every curse, every insult, every scream since Maleck brought Pippet back to them.

But things were different. Their cabal was back together, even Maleck, whom she was also taking great pains to avoid. But after seeing Pippet with Ashe and Aden and Maleck today, she couldn't deny the change.

Tatiana swallowed deeply and nudged the door open with her hip.

Pippet sat at Baba Kallah's old dressing table, failing miserably to drag a brush through her wet hair. A glance at the washbasin confirmed an unceremonious dunking. Gray grime and flakes of skin muddied the water, and puddles soaked the floor all the way to the plush bench where Quill's sister sat cross-legged, brush yanking at her knots.

Setting her armor on the floor, Tatiana leaned against the doorpost and watched her.

She hadn't let herself believe it, even in Hvallatar, when dragging Pippet from Quill's side every night had proved an effort beyond her and Ariadne's combined strength. But seeing Maleck now, so much like his old self, the truth was arresting: whatever Cistine had done in Landamot, it had changed Pippet just like it changed Maleck, freeing her from the obsession that made her so cruel. And Quill must've seen it, too; because tonight, for the first time, there was no watch on his sister's door. Only Faer, roosting atop the wardrobe.

Pippet raised her eyes to the mirror just then, caught sight of the reflection, and stiffened. For a long moment, she and Tatiana stared at each other.

"Aren't you supposed to be asleep?" Tatiana asked.

"I woke up. Bad dreams." Slowly, Pippet released the brush. It hung from her tangles, jammed hopelessly in, knocking against the side of her face. "I'm sorry."

"For what you're doing to your hair? You should be." Tatiana shrugged up from the doorpost. "Let me help you with that."

Pippet flinched at her approach, and Tatiana hesitated, watching her gaze sink to her lap. Her shoulders rounded—anticipating a blow, just like when she'd faced Ashe in the kitchen. But the cabal had never struck her, never even raised a finger in anger except when she was trying to kill them.

Just how many times had the Bloodwights disciplined her with their fists?

"I know you hate me." Pippet spoke miserably toward her crossed legs. "And you *should*. I killed your—I took your—"

"*You*," Tatiana said fiercely, stepping up behind her and seizing the brush, "were very much not in control."

"But I hurt—Tati, stop!" Pippet snared her wrist, and Tatiana couldn't help how her muscles coiled to block a blow. But Pippet merely twisted to look up at her, eyes wet with anguish. "I hurt you and Quill. I took your baby and I made you *remember* it."

"You didn't make me remember. I never stop thinking about her." Tatiana's voice cracked. "Do you know who else I never stopped thinking about?" She tapped Pippet's nose, then pushed her around to face the mirror. Gently, she extracted the brush from her hair. "You know whose room this used to be?" Pippet shook her head. "Baba Kallah's. Now, there was a woman who had more reason than most to hate the world. Plenty of bad things happened to her...a *valenar* who didn't love her, a son who mistreated her, a life trapped in a courthouse while her three closest friends left. But out of everything she could've done, she chose love. For Helga and Iri and Sigrid. And she chose to love Thorne. She taught him the kind of love he taught all of us. Do you know what kind?"

When the girl shook her head again, the brush dislodged. Tatiana drew Pippet's mess of hair behind her head and tugged her face up gently until their eyes met.

"The love of never letting go."

Slowly, beginning at the ends, she worked the bristles through Pippet's hair; and while she worked, she told Pippet secrets she'd always kept from her. About the long months drowning in mead and ale, of running from enemies inside her, from fears that had seemed too big to conquer. Stories she'd tried to spare the girl who cartwheeled and played in Starhollow, her only escape into the world through the doorways of books and daydreams.

But now that girl was a young woman with wounds and scars, with sins and regrets heaped on her shoulders. Someone who could fathom the same darkness in Tatiana.

"What made you change your mind?" Pippet asked. "About the drinking, I mean."

"Oh, a lot of things. I was losing Ari and Mal, I'd already lost Cistine. My position in Thorne's cabal was in danger, too. But what changed me for good was realizing I wasn't just afraid...I was wounded. It was bleeding over everything in my life, and if I didn't heal that wound, I would always come back to the bottle."

Pippet laid a hand over her chest. "I want to *kill* them, Tati. I want to kill all of them like they almost killed me."

Compassion bloomed hot in Tatiana's heart, and tears slid down her cheeks. She set the brush aside and took Pippet's shoulders, turning her on the seat. "I know. And I'm going to help you heal *that* wound."

"*How?*" Her bottom lip quivered. "I don't want to go back, I don't want to drink or fight or *be* like that..."

"You won't." Tatiana brushed her damp hair from her eyes. "As soon as it's safe to travel, we'll take you to Holmlond. To Mira. You remember how she helped Cistine and Ari during the winter? She can help you, too."

Lips parting in surprise, Pippet studied her face. "You're going to do that for me, even though I—?"

"Listen, Hatchling. I know what an addiction is like...how it makes you feel like a different person, like you just can't stop. But I had a choice when I was drowning in the bottle. You didn't. Now I'm choosing again. I'm choosing to love my little sister."

Pippet buried her face in Tatiana's stomach. "*Thank you.*"

Tatiana pulled Pippet tight against her, holding her close and shielding her from the pain with her embrace. And in that moment, she had never felt more like a mother.

She thought Quill was asleep when she slipped into his room hours later, the bed, table, and armoire all splashed in moonlight. But the moment she crawled under the blankets and pressed her stockinged feet against his bare leg, he mumbled, "How's Pip?"

She frowned at the profile of his face. "How did you know?"

"Lucky guess." He turned his cheek against the pillow, bruised eyes searching hers. "Well?"

"She's...herself," Tatiana admitted. "Just like Maleck. Whatever Cistine did to them, it may not erase what they did, but it took away that madness. I wasn't sure after Landamot, but..."

"You're starting to believe, too."

Tatiana arched one shoulder, trailing her fingertips down Quill's bare chest. "I'm open to the possibility that, reckless as she was both times, maybe Cistine did the right thing." Quill grunted, and Tatiana rolled her eyes, nudging his ribs. "Don't be a Featherbrain. You believe in her, too. That's why you were the first one over that woodpile when you saw what Maleck's augments were doing to her."

"Right." Quill blew out a long breath and pinched the corners of his eyes with his three-fingered hand. "Which means I've been treating her like *baesj* for no stars-damned reason."

Tatiana levered herself up on one arm, peering down at his ashen face. "She did break your trust."

"Because she knows me too well. She figured I was so scared after everything we'd lost, I wouldn't let her take that risk with Pippet...not even if it would save her life, bring her back to us." Quill waved a vague hand toward the door. "If it was just me, I'd be building my sister's pyre now. Instead she's right here, humming her favorite songs and eating Ari's scones. Because of someone I've been treating like an *enemy* for giving us that chance."

Tatiana gripped his chin, looking deep into his agitated eyes. "You're not the first person in this cabal to let his emotions run away with him."

"But I'm the one wasting all this time. You know where she's going next. Where this ends."

It struck Tatiana like a kick to the spine, all the wind knocked out of her. Why Quill looked so heartbroken, so furious with himself; why it mattered enough to keep him awake this long into the night.

Because Cistine was going to the Door in Stornhaz to bleed. The whole cabal had wasted so much time being lost and furious with one another, and now time was picking up speed, barreling toward an inevitable end.

"I thought it had to be *me* who saved Pip," Quill rasped. "I let my pride get ahead of me. I got one sister back and I've spent every day since blaming the other one. And now it's..."

"It's *not* too late," Tatiana said. "It's not. You can make amends before we go to Stornhaz. If you don't, you'll spend the rest of your life regretting it, Quill. I know you."

He grimaced, swooping an arm around her back and bringing her to lay on his chest. Head tucked under his chin, Tatiana settled in, shutting her eyes to focus on the beat of his heart.

Stars, she was thankful for that sound. Thankful he was still *here*.

"So what are you going to do?" she asked at length.

He shifted her in his grip so she lay in the crook of his body, half on her side, looking up into his face. "Live," he said simply, and it was the most wonderful word she'd ever heard him speak. "I'm going to live and follow Thorne and Cistine through this and out to the other side of the war. And then I'm taking you and Pippet to Blaykrone and we're going to find Mort, and you and I, we're going to raise a family." His hand rested over her stomach, thumb brushing the scar above her hipbone. "We're meant to be parents, Tati. We're meant to have a life after this war. And I'm going to make sure it happens."

Grinning, Tatiana pressed a kiss to his jaw. "Being back in the Den is making you sentimental."

"What can I say? I've missed home." He nuzzled his face into her hair. "Missed *this*, too."

So had she—more than words could say.

CHAPTER THIRTY-SEVEN

IT WAS A relief to be out of the Den, the cabal's overwhelming attention and the flurry of letter-writing traded for the night's cool embrace. The familiar damp, clean scent of Hellidom, home and haven for a decade, washed Maleck's senses as he picked his way up to one of his favorite pools near the base of the falls.

He'd never told anyone about it. The rim of rock filled to its brim every few days with the Nior's spray, offset some distance from the full body of the falls and sheltered under a broad swath of high ghostplants; but with those shifted aside, one could see down the sweep of the valley, across the glittering ghostlit expanse of Hellidom, all the way to the forest beyond. He'd come here often to think over the years, to escape Tatiana and Quill's hectic energy, Ariadne's palpable concerns, the weight bearing visibly down on Thorne and Baba Kallah's shoulders. He'd retreated to its sanctuary more times than he could count when Aden had left for Siralek.

He sought its refuge now, bearing the unease of Cistine's plans and his own part in them across his shoulders...and the prickling aftertaste of that new augment she carried.

Its stain slathered across his skin though he'd hardly touched it, and that over an hour ago. He nearly welcomed the icy shock of the late-night air chasing it away when he disrobed and slid into the water; fighting to level his breathing at the penetrating chill, he crossed the pool in one stroke and laid aside the ghostplants, streaking soft pinkish-violet sap along his forearms. Folding them on the rim, he laid his chin on his elbow and watched the city spread out below, his thoughts churning.

He wished he'd offered Cistine some reassurance before she finally left him for bed. But that augment's power had muzzled him, the sheer depth of its darkness eye-watering and terrifying, tying his tongue. No wonder his brothers wanted it...and no wonder she feared having to use it. If she broke the seal and unleashed that might, he had no idea what would come.

But it did not feel right. It felt world-ending, whatever waited inside that flagon—the only one of its kind.

He tried to pray she would never have to use it, but the words wouldn't come to his darting mind.

A twitch of shadow rippled below, following the same winding, inarticulate path he'd taken to arrive here. He didn't need a glimpse of red hair or two-colored eyes to know who approached; the distant smell of rose and leather already told him.

He turned, spreading his arms on the stone, watching guardedly when Ashe emerged through the ghostplants, painting shimmering streaks of peach, lime, and lavender on her hair. "Well, this is nice. Why haven't we been up here before?"

His heart galloped at the thought of bringing her here in those early days when she was still utterly beyond his reach, a wary, furious Warden with a shrapnel wound and a mouth full of razored insults. Half of him feared the notion and the other half thrilled at it; she likely would've dared him to swim unclothed with her just to make him suffer.

As if he'd known anything of suffering back then.

The thought dragged his gaze away, though he still watched from the corner of his eyes while Ashe dusted off her arms and sat cross-legged on the shore. "It's been a day."

He sighed. "It's been a year."

"True." She pulled something from her pocket and tossed it from hand to hand. "Why did you come out here?"

"To think. To gain clarity."

"Fair. I know how hard it was for you, having all that attention today."

The catch in her tone brought his eyes back to her. He squinted, letting the moonlight bring the planes of her face into relief: drawn and haggard, carrying shadows in ways his fingers itched to draw. "And how is it for *you*?"

"Cistine getting married, you mean?" Her mouth jerked at one corner. "Where do I even start?"

He surged away from the wall and stroked toward her, leaning his arms on the edge of the rock nearest to her instead. "I've been the poorest excuse for a *valenar* these past weeks. But if I can offer you anything, even my ear and nothing more..."

Ashe wrinkled her nose. "You could let me wash your hair. Not to...actually, yes, to be fully offensive, your *smell* is offensive. I wasn't crying because I'm glad to see you earlier, I was crying at the stench."

Laughter clawed from his throat. "Flattering as always."

She stopped throwing the item in her hand and held it up instead. The scent of cedar soap filled his nostrils. "May I?"

"If you must." He dunked himself, emerging with teeth chattering, and turned to face the parted fronds and the city below while Ashe lathered the soap and undid his braids. It was slow, humiliating work; he could feel every snarl she wrestled and the oily grime slithering off his scalp when her nails dug in. Embarrassment flushed his whole body, wondering what she must think of his filthy, unkempt state.

But she made no remark. Her ministrations, while firm, were still gentle. And with every pass of her fingers freeing the knots from his hair, something tugged loose from the tangles inside him, too. The pressure in his chest eased slightly. He reclined back against the rock, and Ashe stretched out, finger-combing his hair down over his clavicles—brushing the scar above his heart in featherlight strokes.

Gooseflesh pebbled his shoulders when he craned his head back to peer up at her. "How do you forgive a wicked thing, Asheila?"

Her eyes gleamed brightly in the dark. "By loving it so hard you shed light on its darkest parts."

He wrapped his hand around the back of her neck and brought her mouth down to his; for the first time since the war camp fell, a corner of his spirit gone dead and dark reawakened in brilliant flame. She steadied his head with both hands and kissed him without regard for what he once was, like she had never and would never stop loving him.

Stars, he hadn't realized how much he needed it until the sweet sugar-and-cherry taste of her breath chased away the fear that in the hours since their reunion, she'd grown to resent him as much as he resented himself.

When they drew apart, Ashe rose to her knees and unclipped her armor. Maleck turned to face her, pulse crashing. "What are you doing?"

"Joining you." She dipped into the water with him, soap wielded like a weapon, but her touch was gentle when she took his arm in one hand and drew it out to the side. Slowly, she lathered away the blood crusted above one of his newest scars, the near-fatal wound dealt him when he rescued Pippet from his brothers; then the blood caked in the hair on his chest. Then his back. Then his navel. "How many battles did you fight?"

His eyes crashed shut at memories of fire of lightning of ice darkness hate want *need*— "I...cannot remember anymore."

The soap grazed across his shoulders and down the dip of his spine. "I heard you talk to Cistine. She really thinks you'll run?"

Heat covered his cheeks. He stared into the city, unspeaking.

Ashe's hand snagged under his arm, pulling him around to face her. "You're not serious."

"I won't deny it's crossed my mind a dozen times since I woke," he confessed. "The weight of what must be redeemed is...almost unbearable."

"Why? You didn't think that when it was me, after Siralek."

"Asheila. I tried to *kill* you. And when that failed, I left you to be fodder for the Balmond." The weight of that sin bore down on his shoulders, nearly enough to drag his head below the water. "I don't know how to come back from that."

"You say that like you never tried to be anything better, even when you were that far gone." Her eyes narrowed. "Tell me why you hesitated that day near Kosai Talis."

He kicked back from her, cold sweat joining the water trickling from his sopping hair. He saw ice, stone, and blood; saw her face swimming into focus, heard the word that had shattered through the incessant craving for augments, for power, for the Key, the word that gave him the power to walk away when ending her life would've been simpler. The same word that had struck him when he saw Quill lying on the ground, bloodied and half-alive, and knew why he refused to leave even when Maleck was killing him. The word that had brought him back to Hvallatar, to find Cistine after everything.

"Say it, Maleck." Ashe stroked closer, skin gleaming in the moonlight. "If you're going to leave us, say it one last time before you go."

"No."

"Why *not?*"

"Because I break everything I love!" The words tore out of him as he gripped her shoulders. "I broke this cabal, I broke Quill and Cistine, and now I've handed over the weapon to do it again! If she dies on that Door, do you think Thorne will ever forgive me? That *you* will?"

"I learned a long time ago not to hold anyone else responsible for Cistine's choices."

"Enough of her choices, then. What of the things she plans to do? Do you truly believe the Chancellors will take sides with someone who became a Bloodwight, healed or not?" He framed her face with both hands. "Whatever comes, I *can't* stay."

"And I can't let you go."

The words fell sharp and simple in the drop of the wind stirring the ghostplants. Maleck's hands fell from Ashe's face, splashing in the water.

She laughed harshly. "You know that, don't you? You're too deep. You're in my heart, in my blood. Having you beside me in battle or in the Den or on some Talheimic rooftop or lost in the forest feels more right than anything else in my life. I'm not letting you walk away from this."

Choked, Maleck stared at her. "I don't know how to be anything you deserve."

"I can tell you where you start." She came chest-to-chest with him, winding her arms around his neck. "You stay tonight. And you stay tomorrow, when you want to run again. You choose me every day, Maleck."

Though sense told him to pull away—that he didn't deserve this, that he might even hurt her—base need drove out common sense. He dropped his brow against hers. "You *are* my choice. You always have been, from that first day you walked toward me in the Den. Even when I thought there was no hope for us."

Her breath grazed his lips as she slid her hand into his hair, letting the soap drop into the water. "I chose you, too, you know. Before I even knew what the choice was."

Then her mouth was against his again, calming the screaming specters in his head, chasing the flighty energy in his hands and feet away. Farewells slid out of his mind and there was only this—only her. His anchor. His reason to stay.

"You don't have to be all right," she said against his mouth. "Not yet. You just have to walk toward us, not away."

"Just one step?" he asked wryly.

"Just one more step." Both her hands took his cheeks again, and when he opened his eyes, she was an inch away, challenge burning in her gaze. "Forget about the fight. Just be here right now, with me."

He slung an arm around her waist, towed her against him, and kissed her with all the promise of a man who would never flee from her again. And he lost himself in that love which never stopped burning, the beacon that guided him home—somehow bright enough, despite all his mistakes, to set his darkest parts on fire.

CHAPTER THIRTY-EIGHT

CISTINE COULD HARDLY believe this day was happening.

It was nothing like she'd ever imagined, the pageantry thrown hastily together over two days gathered around a sketchbook with Tatiana, Pippet, and Maleck, crafting ceremonial designs while the others dispatched letters and Ashe communed into Meriwa's starstone. Every scrap of joy felt like something she'd wake up from in the turn of a moment, finding herself back in the forests of Blaykrone still hunting for Maleck.

It all finally settled in when she looked at herself in Tatiana's full-length mirror at the alabaster dress spread across her bosom and upper arms, thin mesh and real diamonds glinting like stars against her collarbones and bare shoulders, crusting the bodice. When she met her own gaze in the glass, the reality of what she was doing and *why* plunged steep into her stomach and sent up a burst of fluttering nerves.

She rested her hand over her middle and swallowed a surge of lightheaded shock that she was doing this without her parents or her people around her. That the Princess of Talheim was being *wed* outside the borders of her own kingdom.

That she, Cistine Novacek, would be a wife by sundown.

"I think...I need a moment," she mumbled, gaze fixed on the slack face in the mirror—*her* face, painted in stunning and gentle ferocity.

"I'm not surprised." Tatiana gave the diamond-dotted skirt a wistful tug. "You know, when I stole this from a merch caravan all those years ago, I really hoped I'd get to dance over Salvotor's corpse in it. Well, fewer bloodstains this way. Coming, Pip?"

Pippet slid from the bed with a shy grin Cistine's way—still not as full of chatter as she used to be, but at least her smiles came more easily now. "You look so pretty, Cistine."

"Thank you, Pippet." She squeezed her hand and gave her a twirl to follow Tatiana from the room. Once they were gone, Cistine collapsed on the edge of Tatiana's bed, stroking her thumb along the empty base of her marriage finger where the ultramarine ring had sat until last night, and stared down at her silver-slippered feet; feet that would wear battle boots again tomorrow, marching to meet the Courts and then to retake the City of a Thousand Stars.

Feet that would stand on the Door and face the possibility of death to give the kingdoms a fighting chance.

"Gods, help me," she whispered into the thick silence. "I don't know how I'm going to do this."

A quiet knock stirred Cistine from her thoughts enough to look up at the doorway, blood fizzing with nerves; Quill found her gaze there, shoulder propped to the frame, studying her with overbright eyes.

"You look beautiful." His voice was gruff. "Like a queen."

Half-panicked laughter popped from her lips. "You should see me in a crown."

"I don't need to. It's not the clothes. It's just you." He slid his hands into his pockets and shrugged up from the doorpost, stepping into the room. "I never wanted what my father had as a Tribune, but that doesn't mean I don't know royalty when I see it. I've always seen it in you."

"Thank you." She could hardly coax volume to the words, her nerves singing with uncertainty. He'd barely spoken anything to her but criticism and scorn for weeks, and if he came for that today, she wasn't certain she could endure it. "Was there something you needed?"

Quill slumped onto the bed next to her, pulling his hands from his pockets to smooth down his legs. Cistine watched him, heart thundering with unease.

"I don't...do well," Quill said at last, "when my sister is in danger."

Cistine slumped, clasping her hands around the sides of her neck. "I know, Quill."

"That's not what I...let me finish." He grimaced, turning his hair across his head. "Pippet's always been my weak spot. That chink in my armor. But all this time, I was looking so hard at one sister, I lost sight of the other."

The breath hitched in Cistine's throat.

"You're doing this for us," Quill went on quietly. "All of this. The wedding, the augments, the risk. That's for *us*. And I let myself waste all this time being angry about something that already happened...I wasn't thinking about what's coming. And now it's too late."

"No, it isn't."

But they knew; as surely as they'd both known what was coming for her in Veran the night they met.

"I don't regret any of this," Quill said. "That tavern, the training, Oadmark, Hvallatar...any of it. The only thing I'm sorry for is that I pushed you away and I might not get another chance after this. And you deserved better. You were scared and struggling, and I should've been there, hands up, ready to take your blows the way you tried to take mine."

Silent, heavy tears spilled over Cistine's lashes. She did nothing to stop them even though they made the kohl run. "But you *were* there. You made me want to prove myself twice as hard. You gave me a reason to fight for what I knew I had to do. What I still have to do."

Quill's eyes turned to her, bright with anguish. "I'm not ready to say goodbye to you yet."

"Then *don't*. Just tell me we're all right."

He flipped his hand over on his leg. "We're all right, Stranger."

Cistine laced her fingers with his and leaned her head on his shoulder. "I want you with me when I face the Chancellors. You and Maleck."

Quill pressed a kiss to her head. "I'll be there. As far as you need me to go, for as long as you need me to stay. I'm not breaking that promise again."

And he did stay, the minutes beating by as her heart slowed and steadied. He freed his hand to wrap his arm around her shoulders instead, and just like that night in Veran, the shelter of his arm spoke safety and peace over her. The hot-blooded fears chilled. The way cleared again.

He shook her lightly after a moment. "So. You're getting married today."

They both burst into laughter at the wonderful absurdity of it, and even though it wasn't really funny, they kept cackling until Quill complained his ribs hurt and Cistine's cosmetics were half-ruined.

She shoved him. "Go make sure Thorne's not in the Den! It's bad luck for him to see me before the ceremony."

"You Talheimics and your stars-damned superstitions." With a dramatic eye-roll, Quill lurched up from the bed. "Sure you'll be all right in here by yourself until then?"

"Yes." She blew out a steady breath. "I think I might pray, actually."

"Good thinking. You're going to need it."

She aimed a kick at his haunch on the way out, then dragged herself up and back to the mirror, staring down her reflection. She tamed her flyaway tresses and thumbed the running kohl from her cheeks, listening to footsteps thump through the Den—then finally fall silent.

"You can do this." She gripped the sides of the mirror, staring herself down in the glass. "You *are* doing this. You're marrying Thorne Starchaser." Giddy excitement washed through her, and she clapped both hands to her cheeks. "You are *marrying* Thorne Starchaser! Today! Holy gods!"

The laughter bubbled up again, and she whirled and danced through the room, sliding on the waxed floorboards and doing a dozen victory jigs to let loose the nerves. She didn't care if it meant she'd arrive hot and sweaty and less than perfect at her own wedding.

Today, she was marrying her best friend. Nothing else mattered.

CHAPTER THIRTY-NINE

THE WEAPON ROOM was a place caught in time, its corners full of memories and shadows, the dust puffing under Thorne's boots as he slipped inside. When he closed his eyes he could almost imagine if he stepped back down into the hallway below, between the rooms Ashe and Julian once occupied, he would hear Tatiana and Quill bantering in the kitchen, debating when to visit Pippet again. Ariadne and Maleck would be discussing strategies over a map and cups of tea, Baba Kallah baking and giving advice whenever they asked.

Breathing deeply of the dust-freckled air, Thorne opened his eyes.

The Den was silent beneath him, in a world so different from the one in his memory. Everyone was preparing. It was time to retrieve his gift and join the festivities hastily cobbled together for his *selvenar*.

He smoothed his hands over polearms and daggers, axes and knives, making his way toward the sword racks so often untouched since the cabal kept their preferred sabers in their rooms. That was why Thorne had hidden this blade here in the first place—this gift that was also a curse.

He withdrew the scabbard from its niche behind the sword shelf, turning it over in his hands. The leather had maintained well, and without even unsheathing it he knew the sword was in flawless condition. Undullable steel, Salvotor had called it when he'd presented it to Thorne the day he became High Tribune of Kanslar Court; neither time nor blows could blunt its edge. It was the first and only gift his father had ever given him.

Thorne had fought his way from Stornhaz with this sword a decade ago and never drawn it since. Every time he clasped the weapon, he felt his father's fingers curling over his, guiding the strokes. And even now, grasping sheath and grip, he couldn't bring himself to unleash it. Memories bonded the steel in its scabbard.

Stornjor, Baba Kallah would've said if she saw him now, *what is it you fear?*

"That I'm going to lose her. All of them. That they'll never see the world they've fought so hard to create." His hold on the sheath became white-knuckled. "We're on the precipice, Baba. I don't know if I'm a powerful enough Chancellor to see us all through to the other side."

Thorne could almost feel his grandmother's gentle fingers on the hinge of his elbow. *You do what you can. The rest is in the gods' hands. But if they call on you, you will know where to go. Be still and listen. And trust, Stornjor. You are a good Chancellor and a great man. You can do this.*

Thorne bowed his head, staring at the faint lick of blue-black steel visible beyond the sword's crossguard. "*This.* Do you mean a Talheimic wedding, or a battle to reclaim Stornhaz?"

Oh, battle is nothing for you, mighty, muscular warrior. It's all the rest of it you're fretting over. But you are doing the right thing today, and with all you've promised to Cistine. This is how you find peace...step by step up the mountainside.

Thorne smirked at this one-sided conversation carried out in the dark. "Gods, I wish you were here today."

But of course, there was no reply.

Thorne breathed deeply and strapped the sword to his back. Retreating to the steps, he looked once more around the loft, then shut the door.

Hellidom was a festive hive of activity, as it had been since dawn when Thorne and Ashe went to meet with Bresnyar on the outskirts and she drilled him yet again on how this Talheimic ceremony would unfold. Meanwhile, she and her dragon would communicate throughout the day and alert of any threats approaching the city; but for now, there was no hint of danger except being trampled underfoot or buried by garlands and streamers.

From the Den's veranda, Thorne spotted Cassaida's daughters, Greta and Svetlana, twirling down the trail toward the heart of Hellidom while tossing knots of streamers to Pippet and Tatiana across wooden posts staked on either side of the path. They'd cleared a broad swath beside the Nior at the base of the rock top where Cistine and Quill so often trained—and Thorne often watched, disguised by shadows, marveling at the strength in the princess who'd found her way from physical weakness to power.

A surge of breathless, disembodied joy speared through him at the thought of her, and he slid down the railing and strolled under the streamers, ducking as the knots flew back and forth above his head. Pippet spun past him, and he ruffled her hair. "Keeping them all in line?"

"Just like you!" she laughed. "Look out!"

A hand latched onto Thorne's shoulder, an arm swooped around the back of his neck, and Quill slapped him on the chest, steering him down the path. "I've never seen this city so alive. Almost doesn't feel real, does it?"

Thorne smirked. "Tell me you aren't enjoying it."

Quill grinned, thumbing his nose. "Oh, it's the most fun I've had in months! No one's even tried to kill us yet today. Almost forgot how that felt."

Thorne couldn't remember the last time he'd seen his friend look so carefree, his smile still in place when they reached the end of the canopy and surveyed the people dashing across the Sanctuary City. At the rock top, musicians tuned their instruments; hewn wooden seats already lined the shore, facing a woven birch canopy where they would stand to take their vows—another Talheimic tradition.

Thorne swallowed a spurt of unease. He could do this...one step at a time.

"All right, well, if you're just going to stand there slack-jawed, I'd better get back to the preparations before Shei takes a sword to my neck." Quill hooked his thumbs in his belt and strolled away, whistling, and Faer alighted on his shoulder.

Thorne curled his arms behind his head and stretched away his tension. Then he followed his friend into Hellidom to offer his aid—letting the loudness of life and the happiness he'd fought for consume his cares, if only for one day.

⁓

The whirl of preparations reminded Thorne of a wind augment held in his fist, tamed but forever on the verge of bursting out of control. He dodged flocks of squealing children, passed through slices of glittering regalia on bodies he'd more often seen in working clothes, and smelled a hundred scents: spiced wine, perfume, pastries, and other things he couldn't distinguish.

War-weary faces transformed into smiles when parents saw their children steal leftover streamers from the arches and dash through the town, flaunting them on the breeze. Frequent patrons of Hellidom's only tavern emerged to see what all the laughing and chattering was about—and offered their opinion on where the casks of wine ought to go. Several wooden tables were pushed together down the center avenue, creating a long stretch of seating where the cooks and bakers would compile their offerings at sundown.

Long before Thorne felt ready, midday was upon them, and he followed Aden between the clustered seats to the arch at the riverside. Ariadne had woven it with wisteria and plumeria, shedding a gentle citrus smell over the stone, but he wasn't certain it was strong enough to hide the nervous stink from his underarms.

Aden watched him fidget, one brow vaulting. "Nervous, *mavbrat?*"

"What gave it away?" he muttered, tugging at his collar. "This feels...too formal. And too *public.*"

"Trust me, you'll have plenty of time for the informal, unpublic things tonight." Aden clapped him on the back. "I can't say I understand these Talheimic rituals, but I understand why you do this for her. It speaks to the leader you are...the *valenar* you'll be. And that's why we follow you, Thorne, even into the things none of us understands."

With a dip of his head, he indicated the cabal in the first row of seats—Ariadne and Kristoff beaming with satisfaction; Tatiana, hand joined with Quill's behind Pippet's back, and her palms splayed on their knees, fingers dancing with delight. Maleck and Ashe consulted one of his sketches and compared it to their completed work. In the shelter of their bodies, they bumped knuckles and swapped smiles, and Ashe winked at Thorne. He mustered a queasy smile in return.

On the rock top above their heads, the musicians struck a tune, and Thorne's stomach plunged to his knees. He resisted the impulse to cross his arms or rake back his hair as the audience rose to its feet, cued by the sweet melody as Ashe had instructed them that morning.

"It's going to be all right," Aden assured him. "This is the moment you've waited for."

A pale flash moved at the dip in the path, and then she was there.

Stroked by the fingers of sunlight, gleaming from head to foot in a gown of purest white studded with stars, Cistine stood at the end of the path, gathering herself—and Thorne had to do the same. He wasn't prepared for the heat to glaze his eyes, for breathing to suddenly become difficult. He'd seen her in dresses and armor and shirts and pants, but this...this was different.

What it symbolized. What it meant. And *why* she wore it, despite the Nimmus his father had put her through in gowns just like it.

For him. Just like she'd promised that day outside Stornhaz, when she'd walked away from him.

There would be no more walking away. Not after today.

Her eyes jumped across the narrow aisle to Thorne, and he offered his hand. The breath settled through Cistine, familiar as training, as battle, as his own face in the mirror; then she started down the rock, the music swelling with her steps.

Stars, he would never grow used to seeing her walk toward him this way. He would never forget how it felt, just like that day on Eben's plains when she'd returned to Talheim; and he would never stop hating the distance between them, however great or small, until it vanished.

Her fingers met his, and he drew her into the shelter of the wooden canopy beneath the arch of flowers, eyes skimming over her—appreciating the dress, the curves beneath it, and the dark belt around her hips.

He chuckled. "You brought Nail to our wedding?"

Cistine pulled a face. "You can never be too careful."

Aden snorted under his breath, and Cistine stomped his foot. Then she was solemn all at once like it had never happened, hands folded before her, nodding him to go on.

With a lionlike smirk, he did.

"We all know the importance of what we're here to witness. For the first time in remembered history, our kingdoms join in a union of flesh and blood. Chancellor Thorne and Princess Cistine have chosen to become *valenar*, husband and wife—a union of power to reflect the union of kingdoms in trust and endurance until both are no more."

Someone took in a sharp breath, but Thorne didn't look. His eyes were fixed on Cistine, watching the faint stain of a blush spread across her cheekbones.

"In honor of Talheimic traditions, they've elected to give gifts to one another," Aden said. "I'm beginning to see a pattern with Talheim and gifts, but I digress."

Cistine stuck her tongue out at him while Ashe crossed to the arch and pressed something into her hands: a careworn book smelling strongly of ancient places and musty paper.

"This is a book of truncated Valgardan epics." Cistine offered it up to Thorne. "I know you've learned most of them by heart because Baba Kallah used to read them to you every night. But I think it's worth rereading, to remember why you fight your battles. *What* you're fighting for."

Sillakove. The Starchaser's story contained within this book, no copy of which Thorne had seen, much less touched, since he'd fled Stornhaz with his cabal. It felt like clasping arms with an old friend when Cistine handed it to him.

"Never forget where you came from," she whispered, "or who you *are*."

Thorne had to clear his throat several times before he could even bend to set the book at his feet. He unstrapped the sheath around his back and smiled when Cistine's eyes widened.

"This blade was one of the last forged from the heart of the star that gave Starhollow its name." This time he recognized Quill's voice cursing in quiet awe. "It doesn't have a happy origin, so it never saw use with this cabal. But as your weapon, I hope it has a happy future." He didn't let go when Cistine grasped the scabbard, holding her gaze across it. "This is a blade that cannot be dulled or broken, just as your strength and spirit have never been and never will be."

Tears slipped over Cistine's lashes when she took the sword, weighed it in her hands, then lashed it on over her back. There were a few chuckles at that, Thorne's among them; but he'd expected nothing else from her.

"I was told there were also rings involved," Aden said blandly. "Gods only know why."

Ashe gestured rudely at him, and as the cabal broke into laughter, Cistine fished a studded black band from a cord under the collar of her dress, broke the clasp, and took Thorne's hand in hers. "In Talheim, the ring represents eternity. An endless loop and a lifetime of love and devotion, no matter how you feel about each other in the worst times. It's a promise to always redeem the marriage, to never forsake it. And I'll never forsake *you*."

He was acutely conscious of how unsteady his grip was when he took her hand in turn and fished out the ring she'd given back to him the night before, sliding the black-banded ultramarine stone onto her finger. "In Old Valgardan, we have no word for severing the *valenar* bond. It's a life's commitment to protect and endure. I will protect and endure with you always, Cistine, no matter what comes for us."

Her grin nearly crinkled her eyes shut when Aden drew a red sash from the pocket of his armor and wrapped it around both their arms, over their joined hands. "In Talheimic tradition, there is a cord that can never be cut, a bond only the True God himself can sever. They call it the greatest oath, the essence of unity and the vision of eternity. And by this cloth, I declare you bound by it, if you wish."

"I wish it," Cistine said.

"I wish it," Thorne echoed.

"Then in the eyes of the people and all the gods, you're bound." Aden stepped back, smirking. "You are one."

With the sash still joining them, Thorne brought Cistine's arm behind her head, gripping her hair and waist. He swung her low, his mouth seeking hers and feeling the tremble of her happy breaths on his tongue while he kissed her breathless, kissed himself into oblivion—another thing he'd never grow tired of, as long as he lived.

And behind them the people of Hellidom surged to their feet, cheering and whooping and whistling, filling the Sanctuary City with sounds of happiness untouched by war.

CHAPTER FORTY

THERE WERE FIVE things Cistine would always remember about her wedding day.

The first was when the people gathered at the long tables down Hellidom's central thoroughfare after she and Thorne signed the marriage contract Ashe had written the night before. With pens to paper, they were truly one by the law of the Middle Kingdom, and they celebrated that union around platters of roasted boar, spiced sprouts, peppery potatoes, and cake. Quill, sitting across from her, recounted the story of Cistine's first disastrous attempt at cooking, and she flung a spoonful of potatoes at his face. Thorne flicked her ear, and she snapped her teeth at his fingers, eliciting booming laughter from him—and she realized this was family, and home, even though it wasn't Talheim.

The second was when they all streamed back to the rock top after sunset, and the musicians played their lutes and fiddles and drums while the people danced. When Ashe climbed onto the rock top and took up a violin and added her melody to theirs, and Quill swept Pippet off into a jig, and Greta and Svetlana, giggling, grabbed Aden's hands, and Ariadne and Tatiana bet their dancing skills against each other.

The third was when Quill and Tatiana taught her a Valgardan line dance, a wild and whimsical array of pounding feet, clapping hands and endless spinning, changing partners in dizzying twirls that turned the city to amber-and-green streaks like summertime. Cistine's cares floated away, and she forgot about the world outside Hellidom; she forgot everything but the sweaty confection of people around her, friends and strangers coming together to celebrate life and unity and the future.

The fourth was during that dance, when she traded partners from Tatiana to Ariadne, locking eyes with Thorne across the rock top. He lounged in a chair with Aleida perched on his knees, bouncing to the rhythm of the music while he and Cassaida chatted. When his gaze found hers, Cistine's feet almost lost the tempo. Her heart slammed down into her soles and her stomach swung into her throat, forcing tears to her eyes.

There was no name for that emotion. She didn't even try to search for one. But when Thorne's smile softened, she knew he felt it, too.

The fifth was after that dance, when she collapsed into one of the chairs and watched the cabal celebrate. There seemed to be no slow Valgardan dances; Quill and Ariadne shimmied back to back, shoulders to shoulders. Tatiana, Thorne, and Kristoff danced side-by-side, Aleida on Kristoff's hip now, her arms hugged shyly around his neck. Aden and Hugo yipped and howled in a stomping circle, and Ashe came down from the rock top and danced with Maleck's hands on her hips and her back to his chest.

For the first time since the war began, they truly looked happy.

And she was so gods-damned close to losing all of this.

Her hand flew to her mouth, breaths halting, tears stabbing her eyes. One battle, one plan, one dangerous grasp for the redemption of all the kingdoms, and this might be the last time she saw them all laugh and dance together. The last time she heard this music, held these people, lived and loved with them. The last time she was *alive* to feel any of it.

Panic shoved her up despite her exhaustion. Suddenly, this moment felt like the last of everything: the last dance, the last drink, the last celebration. The last moment the cabal was whole. The last time she would have her warriors with her.

Her cabal. Her Valgardan family.

Gasping for breath, she elbowed through the crowd to the edge of the path, spinning back from the slight elevation to look down at all of them, washed in the lowering sunlight and ghostplant sap that stained the rock while they danced unafraid beneath the stars.

But this might be the end of Sillakove. Of Valgard. Of *her*.

Fierce, raging love and endless terror stole what remained of her breath. Tears dripped from her chin and stained her dress, and she clapped both hands to her mouth when the first sobs escaped. Then she snatched up her skirts, turned, and fled from the celebration of her marriage—from everything she stood to lose.

In the garden, among the plants and weeds, with the distant sounds of life painting Hellidom's air, Cistine found peace in hard work.

So much overgrowth climbed these trees and plants she'd once loved. This garden, which had allowed her to pour so much frustration and confusion and energy into it, had gone rote while matters in Stornhaz and elsewhere consumed her. The last time she'd set foot here, Julian was alive. Baba Kallah had just died. She barely remembered the person she was back then, the princess of books and beauty who was buried over time in the weeds of politics, panic, and pain, tangled in vines of loss and nightmares and grief and war.

But she'd come to find that princess today, to pull her from her fertile grave and dust her off. That princess who'd crossed borders to save what was precious to her, who'd risked everything for the people that were hers to defend...Cistine needed her for the coming fight, with all her tenacity and unshakeable optimism and the hope she brought.

Nothing less would allow Cistine to step into her destiny.

"I thought I might find you here."

Thorne leaned against the fence, arms folded and eyes on her. He'd loosened the collar of his filigreed dark shirt, unbuttoned halfway down his chest to find some relief while dancing.

He'd left the celebration behind for her.

Cistine sat back on her heels, surveying her handiwork. The soil was tossed madly like windswept hair and the baskets were full of weeds, but she'd discovered some of the old growth had survived. Life would come again to Hellidom, to the Den—and to her garden. The first but by no means the final gift Thorne had ever given her.

Today was the greatest gift of all.

"Wildheart," he said. "Join me?"

Leaving the baskets, she swung over the fence and landed lightly beside him in her dirt-caked dress. He wrapped his arms around her and caressed her spine with his knuckles while she melted against him. Each stroke fizzled like lightning through her body.

"You were a vision of Cenowyn today," he murmured in her ear, and she flushed, burying her face in his shoulder. "But I thought you'd stay a little longer. The others noticed your absence."

How could she tell him *why* she'd fled on her own wedding day to till soil that had once been her responsibility? How could she tell her *husband* how much she feared she might leave him as quickly as she'd become his?

She shuddered, and Thorne took her face in one hand, brushing her damp cheek with the other. "What is it?"

"It's just unfair. The war. Time. *Everything.*" She raised her chin at the garden. "This place was so full of hope once, and now look at it. It's like a fire burned through our home."

Thorne was quiet for a moment, no longer merely brushing her tears away, but caressing the curve of her cheek. "A very wise woman told me once that no matter how badly a fire burns, whatever survives is often stronger than what came before."

Cistine smiled sheepishly. "I said that, didn't I?"

"You did." He gathered her face gently in both hands. "Wildheart, we are going to survive this."

She held his gaze and nodded, and found the strength to smile for his sake. "There's something else I want to do, now that you're here."

"Anything."

"I want more than just the Talheimic ceremony today," she said, and Thorne's eyes widened. "I want to forge the *valenar* bond."

CHAPTER
FORTY-ONE

THE KITCHEN WAS dim, only a promise of moonlight tumbling down the hall while Cistine faced Thorne across the table where they'd argued and laughed so many times—where they'd first discussed courtship rituals in their kingdoms. A candle, a chalice, and a knife lay between them, and an obscene wildness strummed within Cistine's heart. As monumental as this moment was for her, it meant so much more to Thorne, his eyes dancing like flame across from her.

He uncorked a flagon from his pouch, poured a kernel of fire into his palm, and offered it to her. She took half the power, a soft, intricate whorl of muted light, and watched Thorne graze his hand over the candle's first wick. "With this fire, I claim you as my closest star. My guiding light. My Cenowyn."

"With this fire, I claim you as my blended heart." Brushing the second wick, she recited the words he'd taught her while they'd gathered the items for this ritual from around the Den. "The light that burns nearest to me and leads me home when I lose my way. My Cenowyn."

They sent the fire out from their inkings so that only candlelight painted their faces. Thorne took up the chalice next, water lapping its rim like quiet music, and brought it to his mouth. "With this water, I claim you as my equal in this life. The bearer of my name and heirs. My world." He drank and handed the cup to her.

"With this water, I claim you as my equal in this life," Cistine echoed. "The father of our legacy. My world." She hadn't thought anything could feel more daringly intimate than her Naming in the House of Visions, but today proved a flurry of contradictions.

When she placed the chalice aside, Thorne handed her the knife and offered his palm with the same trust as when they'd first struck hands in a ruler's truce in this Den; enough trust to add just one more to the scars he wore. But of all the marks on his torso and back, the new one across his middle from Braggos, even, this one alone would be made with love.

Cistine drew the tip lightly over his skin and tried not to think of Kalt Hasa. When the blood ran between his fingers, she gave him the hilt, and her hand, with a faith to echo his.

But when Thorne took the blade to her palm and set the blood flowing, his breaths struggled, his eyes glinting with mist. The dagger clattered from his hand, thudding on the table. When their gazes met, his fear reached out to hers, threading together like this bond braided their lives into one another.

She rested her uncut hand on his jaw and smiled. "I claim you..."

Thorne drew in a shuddering breath and let it out slowly. "I claim you, Cistine Novacek, as my partner in war. The one I will fight for, and beside, to keep the faith beyond death. The only one I trust to guard my back on any battlefield. The only one I would walk through Nimmus beside."

"And I claim you, Thorne Starchaser, as *my* partner in war," Cistine whispered. "The one who I will fight for, and beside, to keep the faith beyond death. The only one I would walk through Nimmus beside. And the one I *will* come back for."

Unshed tears brightened his eyes as he extended his hand to her. "Forge the bond."

Laughing under her breath, she held onto him, torn palm against torn palm, and added, "With my whole heart. For my whole my life."

Thorne's smile broadened, the fear fading from his eyes.

"I claim you, blended blood, *valenar*. One heart. One blood. One life," they said in unison. "In Cenowyn, in this world, and in Nimmus. Nothing will take me from your side."

They stayed that way, hands clasped, until the candle guttered.

"Now what?" Cistine asked.

With his hand still in hers, Thorne rounded the table. "Now, whatever you wish, Wildheart."

She threaded her fingers into his hair and drew him into a kiss so deep, it didn't break even when she lurched up to wrap her legs around his waist. His stride was sure as he carried down the dark, empty hall to the bed where she'd first woken in his world nearly a year ago.

They had one night, awkward and clumsy in some ways; but in the dark, Thorne told her she was beautiful, and queenly, and fierce—and that he loved her. Over and over, that she was loved and safe. And she whispered it back as she traced the patterns of his scars, kissing each of the six gashes on his chest and the inkings on his clavicles, then finding his mouth again. She drank in every inch of him that she'd held at arm's length until she was certain he was devoted to all of her...not only to the princess she had been, but to the queen, the warrior, and the survivor she had become.

The music of the mill wheels, the river, the world outside these beloved walls danced through the balcony doors, enveloping and soothing their bodies from passion, to peace, to slumber. Outside, the moonlight limned their garden in silver branches and painted the gentle green buds of plants that had begun to sprout again through the wild, uncut patches of the world, these sacred places forgotten when the cabal had moved on.

And in that quiet light, the promises of a future began to grow.

CHAPTER
FORTY-TWO

B ANDS OF AMBER daylight soaked the walls, half-blinding Cistine when she finally pried her eyes open in the morning. Squinting and scrunching her face, she breathed in her familiar bed, its scratchy linens not quite uncomfortable, her hair tacky with drool and stuck to her cheek—and Thorne's arm looped around her bare back, pressing her into the mattress.

He drowsed beside her, dark-stained hair falling forward to cover his brow, breath stirring the sheets. Cistine ran shy fingers through his forelock; it felt stranger now than before, knowing she could touch him however she wanted, grazing his abdomen and face, his limbs, and anywhere else she pleased. She nestled her chin in the crook of his neck and breathed against his ear: "Thorne Novacek."

He buried his face deeper in the pillow, groaning quietly.

"*Starchaser.*"

A low growl fractured his steady breathing. His arm tightened over the dip of her back. "Say it again."

Cistine bit her lip, stifling a giggle. "Thorne Novacek. Star—"

He flipped them in one fluid motion, rolling on top of her and bracing his weight on one hand so he didn't crush her. His eyes sparkled with desire, shifting at once from drowsy to alert, and Cistine hid her face with both hands. Thorne tapped her wrist. "What's that all about, Wildheart?"

Her nerves sizzled at the Name, but she didn't drop her hands. "Stop looking at me."

"I'm afraid that's never going to happen." He kissed her knuckles. "Look at *me*, Cistine."

She peeked between her fingers and his smile greeted her, amused, crooked, heart-clenching. He pried one of her hands down and bent his head to kiss her, and Cistine mashed her palm over his mouth. "As much as I'd like to, I think we've already overslept."

Thorne's eyes flicked to the tawny light along the walls, and he cursed. "Stars, you're right."

In the ensuing flurry of sheets and limbs, Cistine went to root through her old chest for armor. Her eyes trailed back to her dazzling, dirt-smudged dress cast haphazardly over the back of a nearby chair where it had landed in a fit of passion the night before. Somehow it felt like a relic already, a sparkling memory of an unforgettable night. She hung it more delicately over the bedframe and prayed she would someday have the chance to give it the proper attention it deserved.

Thorne was rummaging under the bed when Cistine finished dressing, and he said without turning, "Are you ready?"

"I think I have to be."

He faced her, holding something made of dark straps. "May I?"

She shrugged, then stiffened when he crouched before her, his face level with her navel. He snaked her scabbard loop around her hips, drawing it comfortably into place, and Nail's familiar, heavy weight bumped her hip. She worked her restless fingers through the sweaty knots in Thorne's hair while he threaded the belt a second time, then rested his hands on her hips and his head against her stomach.

She went on stroking his hair, throat tight, saying nothing.

Finally, Thorne stood and took her hand again. They walked through the Den together, the empty kitchen, the dark hall, and Thorne's fingers tightened between hers. "I wish we had more time."

Cistine breathed deeply of the Den's familiar smells. "We will when this is over."

They stepped out onto the porch and met the entire cabal. Maleck, Ashe, Kristoff, and Aden leaned against the railing, sipping steaming mugs of tea. Tatiana perched on the rail between them, knocking her feet against the lower slats. Quill tossed chunks of cheese into his mouth, and Ariadne pared her nails with a knife.

The silence was profound, almost awkwardly intense. Cistine shifted her weight, flushing.

"Oh, God's bones. As if we're not all adults here." Ashe shoved a mug of tea into each of their hands. "Time to wake up, you two."

"I'm sorry we're late," Thorne said. "It won't happen again."

"Yes, it will." Tatiana grinned. "Trust me. Quill and I would know."

Quill nodded fervently. "We thought you'd need a little more time, so we cobbled everything together."

"Everything?" Cistine asked anxiously. "Even the armor?"

"As many sets as Tariq could spare." He jerked his chin at his smirking *valenar*. "And Tati found a...well, why don't you tell them, Saddlebags?"

Her eyes gleamed. "Just a little extra something for presentation...an invention I've had stashed in my armoire for years. Quill can teach you how to use it, he helped me dream it up."

Ariadne sheathed her knife and dusted off her hands. "It's time to go."

Cistine bit her lips together, peering through the skeins of steam from her mug and out over Hellidom. "But I haven't told everyone goodbye."

Quill and Tatiana exchanged a glance. Kristoff said gently, "It isn't farewell forever."

"You will see them again." Aden's firm tone allowed for no other possibility.

Their faith lifted Cistine's spirits from a sharp dip, and she shook out her shoulders. "Of course. You're right. Well, we *should* go, then. Bres must be waiting."

They made it only a half-mile up the path before they were accosted. Cassaida's family awaited them on the Nior's banks—Svetlana, Greta, and Hugo skimming rocks into the water, Aleida yawning in Oskar's arms. And with them, Pippet, crestfallen and shifting her weight moodily from foot to foot.

Cistine halted, pricked with guilt. Until now, she hadn't thought to ask what would happen to Pippet while they laid siege to Stornhaz.

"We appreciate you putting up one more mouth." Quill stepped forward to shake Cassaida's hand. "My sister can put away a lot."

Pippet pulled a face, and Cassaida laughed, tugging up the scars marring half her face. "We'll manage. Besides, it's only for a bit, isn't it?"

God willing, Cistine thought.

Cassaida's eyes leaped to her, softening like she'd heard that thought. She beckoned her nearer, and when Cistine joined her, the matriarch unlashed a satchel from across her own hips and offered it out. "A gift from the people of Hellidom."

Cistine's pulse stuttered; there were more than a dozen augments in that satchel, their power cavorting inside flagons she could feel without seeing: fire and ice, lightning and earth, darkness and light. "Cassaida, gods almighty, how did you—*where* did you—?"

"We know you're going back to the war. And we know how desperately low the flagon rations are. So we pulled together everything we had."

"I...we can't take this. What if the *mirothadt* come, what if *you* need them?"

"Our people are warriors, thanks to this cabal's training." Cassaida nodded to Thorne. "We're better fighters than we are augurs. Now take them."

Cistine accepted the pouch and lashed it above her hips, with her own satchel and Nail's sheath. "Cassaida. I don't know what to say."

"Then say nothing." Cassaida pressed a kiss to her cheek. "Just come back and visit with tales of your victory."

Cistine set her jaw and nodded. "I will."

"Good. And we'll see you soon." With a last dip of her head to them all, Cassaida led Oskar and Aleida down the path.

Quill hitched his own rations satchel high, tossing a smile his sister's way. "Pip?"

She avoided his gaze, angling away and trudging down the path. Quill's shoulders buckled and his grin fell, but he didn't go after her. Svetlana rested a hand on Quill's elbow. "She's just mad you're leaving her behind."

"Well, she shouldn't be. We need her here. She's going to help us shore up our defenses." Hugo crossed his arms, scowling up at Thorne. "You kill as many of those *bandayos* as you can. And if they break through the front, we'll hold the line right here, Chancellor."

Thorne mussed Hugo's hair. "If the front lines held half your courage, this war would already be won."

Cistine kissed both girls on their cheeks. "Remember, you never saw us this week."

Svetlana smiled innocently. "Never saw who?"

Cistine laughed as the siblings scurried away. Fingering the augment pouch, new hope—and new schemes—roiling in her mind, she turned away up the path.

Then a shout from behind them, and the pound of flying feet. Pippet skidded back into view on the trail, running with all her might, tears streaming down her cheeks, straight to her brother. She leaped into his arms so hard he crashed to his seat on the path, and she clung to him, wrapping her whole body around his torso, sobbing into the side of his neck.

"Please, Quill, *please*, I'll do anything, *anything you want me to*, just don't go! Don't fight them again!"

"*Pippet.*" Quill's voice broke at her anguish, but he steadied himself, sitting up straight with one hand braced behind him, the other circling his sister's heaving back. "Pip, I have to."

"Please, you don't, you *don't...*"

Quill pulled her head up from his shoulder and framed her face with his hands. "Listen to me, Hatchling. It's going to take more than a few *bandayos* in animal masks to bring down your brother."

She gripped his wrists and gazed into his eyes. "No, it won't. I saw you in Hvallatar."

Cistine's blood chilled, but Quill stared right back at her with a confident smile. "Beg to differ. How are they going to break me when I have someone this important to fight for?"

Pippet broke into fresh sobs, and Quill brought her near and pressed a kiss to the crown of her head, eyes squeezed shut. His tears disappeared into her hair. "I'm going to make this world safe for you," he said. "And then you can come home."

No one hinted that time was waning, or that they should go. They all waited in silence until Pippet's sobs ebbed into shuddering breaths and Quill whistled to Faer, bringing him down from the clefts by the falls to perch on Quill's arm. "I'm leaving this bag of feathers with you. Teach him some new words while I'm gone. Just nothing filthy, all right?"

Pippet sniffled deeply and withdrew to pass a shaky hand over Faer's head. "All right. I will."

Quill lifted them both to their feet, steadying his sister while she wiped her wet face on her sleeve. One last time, he kissed her head. "We're almost home, Pip. Just wait for me."

She lingered on the trail behind them, watching them walk away. A last, lonely croak from Faer traveled the winds on their heels when they turned a bend in the path, leaving the pair behind.

Thorne cleared his throat after several minutes of walking, the sound nearly indistinguishable over the rush of the falls. "Those augments are going to be useful."

"Yes, they are." Cistine's churning mind had begun to quiet, the plan settling into place. "Ariadne, Tati, I want you to take some of these wind augments and go meet the others. You know what to do."

"I've got Bres," Ashe said. "We'll catch their scent and rally until we see your signal."

"And us, *Logandir*?" Aden asked.

Cistine glanced at Thorne and found the quiet acceptance in his gaze—knowing what part he would play in this scheme. "We're going to the Dreadline."

CHAPTER FORTY-THREE

THE DREADLINE HADN'T abated since Cistine had returned to Valgard. Bound by power beyond reckoning, the augmented storm roiled near the border, its miasmic force billowing with such intensity Cistine, Thorne, Aden, Quill, Maleck, and Kristoff could hardly stand in its face. Even with a half-mile of sundered trees and barren Wildwood between them and the lashing clouds at its edge, the cold and mighty tempest whipped their faces, forcing them to anchor their heels and brace.

Quill cursed around the cinnamon stick wedged in his teeth. "You're sure you can do this, Stranger?"

"I have to." Though her voice wavered, Cistine's steps did not, drawing her nearer to the boundary that parted their kingdoms. Every pace deeper into the gloom reminded her this was unnatural; it was her prison, meant to keep her inside where the Bloodwights could hunt her at their leisure.

But they didn't know she could cross it. She'd torn back into this kingdom to save what was most precious to her...and now she would break out again.

Close enough to taste the Dreadline's power skimming along her molars, Cistine wedged her bootheels into the ravaged earth and sank her weight deep, anchoring by her calves, her abdomen, her shoulders. She could not seize the power; it danced just out of reach, unmoored to anything but the Bloodwights' will, without form to grip and reel from.

But if she couldn't steal it, she would break it.

The light augment shattered in her fist, and she raised her eyes to the Dreadline.

A hand grazed the back of her shoulder, that touch now so intimately familiar it sent delicious shivers curling down her spine. She looked to Thorne, who stepped up at her side and trailed his fingertips down to her wrist. "Let me help."

"*Us*," Quill added from her left. "We can take it, Stranger."

"They're right." Gray eyes glowing in light and lightning, Aden halted beside his cousin. "It may be less power to go around, but it's less power *you* spend. And we need you strong."

Cistine's gaze flicked to Kristoff, standing beside Quill, his smile grim but full of determination; then she looked back at Maleck, who stood behind their line, Starfall and Stormfury drawn, guarding the ranks.

Hope pounding in her chest, she took Thorne's hand on one side, Quill's on the other. The power sang through her body in one brilliant surge, passing through her fingertips to them, and through them to Aden and Kristoff. Five warriors lighting up the darkness at the edge of a war-torn kingdom, bodies singing with light, they faced the storm.

"Ready?" Cistine asked.

"Always," Quill replied.

She dropped their hands, and they dropped each other's. As one, they lifted their arms; and as one, they cast out the light.

The power of the gods cracked against the Bloodwights' darkness with head-throbbing force. At once Cistine reached past the edge of the augment she carried and into the depth of her own might, letting it feed off her strength, her very essence as the Key. On and on she poured into it, letting the light throb brighter and reach farther, lashing into the Dreadline. Wounding it. Breaking it.

But there was so *much* darkness to tear through.

Minutes passed like pulses of blood from an open wound. Power pummeled through Cistine, wave after wave, and though her jaw parted to scream at its sheer violence, only a wisp of air escaped. To her left and right, Thorne, Aden, Kristoff, and Quill burned like stars, inkings and armor laced with light, the augment cleaving from them in an endless golden torrent. She couldn't summon breath to warn them she was breaking with every scrap of strength she gave.

Then hands circled her shoulders, gnarled and broad and familiar, and Maleck pulled her against his chest. "Lean into me, *Logandir*."

The moment she did, too weak to pull away, her heartbeat steadied. A narrow pinpoint of purpose snaked through her; she couldn't let this augment touch Maleck, no matter what it cost her.

Her voice burst back into her, a shout brutal and nearly insane, and with all her weight braced into Maleck's grip, she flashed her palms at the Dreadline and *shoved*.

What came out of her was a memory of snowy stone peaks and light and laughter, of those first days after Salvotor's arrest when she'd showed her cabal what her power could do. That mountain-cleaving might roared from her now, hurtling toward the Dreadline, and it did not go alone.

Bellowing in anger, determination, and desperate hope, Thorne did the same; then Quill, panting open-mouthed; then Kristoff and Aden in perfect unison. The light strengthened, ice-white sickles locking together, screaming toward the storm with the force of every hand that had taught her to punch, to cut, to wield bone and steel and augmentation itself in defense of her people.

With a violent crack like the world shearing apart, the Dreadline sundered. The clouds fragmented, burned away by the light of Cistine and her husband, her brothers; and that light spidered out in a thousand seams and more, spilling down the line, shredding the storm for unseen miles in both directions.

Quill fell to one knee, cursing, and Aden wove where he stood. Cistine would've buckled with them if not for Maleck's hands on her arms. Thorne dropped beside Quill and stared through the storm-lashed horizon, then back at her, a silent question in his exhausted eyes.

"Go," she panted, sliding off her pack and flinging it into his hands.

"You know where I'll be."

His jaw firmed, and with a curt nod he lashed on the pack, gathered himself, and dashed through the deadlands wiped bare by the storm raging over them for nearly half a year. He vanished into the wilds between their kingdoms.

Cistine watched until he was gone; then, with the ecstasy of power still humming in her bones, she pushed up from Maleck's grip. Unsteady as a last autumn leaf clinging valiantly to its branch, she faced the others. "Kristoff, Aden, will you stay for him? I don't think the Dreadline can heal itself, but if the Bloodwights or *mirothadt* come to seal it off again..."

"We'll be waiting." Aden nodded.

Cistine turned. "Quill, Maleck..."

"We're with you, Stranger." Quill stuck out his hand, and Maleck clasped his forearm, hauling him upright. "We've got your back."

There was no one else she wanted there now but the death gods from the Vingete Vey, the men who'd protected and trained and loved her from her first days in Valgard. Shoulder-to-shoulder with them, Cistine turned north toward distant Lake Erani and whatever fate awaited them there.

With her brothers beside her, she unleashed the wind and stepped forward to meet it.

CHAPTER FORTY-FOUR

CISTINE, QUILL, AND Maleck lingered in the dark woods around the lakeshore until sunset—as much time as they could spare for Ariadne, Tatiana, Ashe, and Thorne. Yet as much as Cistine hated waiting, she still wished she could slow the sun's descent toward dusk.

"It never gets easier, does it?" she asked, and both Maleck and Quill looked up where they sat back-to-back to keep watch through the trees. "Running into danger, knowing it could be your death."

Quill thumbed his nose and shrugged. "Not really."

"You learn in time to fear other things more," Maleck added. "What you stand to lose by not moving at all."

"But it's not going to be your death." Quill's tone was fierce with a belief so true, Cistine almost trusted it. "We win the Courts over, we storm Stornhaz, we take back augmentation for ourselves. Then we slaughter these Bloodwight *bandayos* and have a long nap."

A giggle escaped her, perishing with the last light of the sun. She dropped her arms and flexed her tingling fingers when Quill and Maleck rose, twin shadows seething in the dark.

"I know you're worried, but I'm not," Quill added. "You were born for this, Wildheart. You're ready."

With her Name sparking in the air between them and Quill's steady eyes fixed on her, she knew without a glint of doubt she would not cower like a child before the Courts tonight; she would rise like a queen.

She stuck her hand out. "It's time."

Quill passed her a small, fragile globe—Tatiana's invention. The moment it was in her fist, the calm clarity of battlefields and negotiations settled into her bones.

She could shake and be nauseated later. Now was the time for action.

Maleck backed away, cupping his palms, and with a running leap Cistine vaulted into his hands and he boosted her up into the craggy branches of the nearest tree. She clung to the swaying limbs for a moment, looking down at them in the gloom.

"Remember," Quill said, "a mile and a half due west."

Cistine nodded. "I'll meet you there."

With a deft nod, both men dragged up their armored scarves, turned their hoods, and melted into the darkness. And Cistine began her journey through the treetops.

She'd practiced this sort of travel with Tatiana on their journey to find Maleck, when using augments was too dangerous in Pippet's presence. Climbing the falls was one thing, traveling through trees another entirely, and Tatiana had insisted on teaching her in case they ever needed to move above their enemies or avoid leaving a trail.

Though Cistine still didn't trust the branches beneath her like her friends did, there was no time to wonder whether the limbs would hold her weight; it was all intrinsic movement, spearing forward while the darkness deepened around her—shadows her friends moved through in a flanking position, hastening to her aid.

But the darkness was never complete; just when the very last of the daylight faded, low campfires smoldered to life in the far distance, turning the horizon to a ribbon of flame.

The Valgardan army. Or what remained of it.

Perched on a branch high above the broadest swath of cleared undergrowth, Cistine spied the Chancellors and Sander below, gathered at one fire, deep in discussion. Every face was harrowed, every eye heavy.

Adeima stooped, Bravis kneaded his temples, Benedikt and Valdemar peered dully into the flames. Sander alone still held a spark in his eye, but the frown grooved between his brows was beginning to look permanent. He hadn't seemed so tired when she'd fought him in the mountains.

Compassion burned through Cistine, tightening her hand around Tatiana's invention.

She was doing this for them. For *all* of them.

She dragged up her own armored scarf, tilted her hood, and with a last half-whispered prayer, cast the invention down to the ground and lunged after it.

A spew of black fumes engulfed her when she plunged into the soil, leaving her barely enough time or direction to tumble forward like Quill had taught her. She rolled to her feet, brushed aside the dark cloud with both arms like peeling back a veil, and stepped out into the Valgardan war camp to face the Chancellors, on their feet already, braced to attack.

Sander was the first to recognize her, his hand coming off his sword with a start. The other Chancellors were a heartbeat slower; then that gods-forsaken greed took hold of the men's faces, the lust Cistine hated and feared. She let her hand drift to Nail, the less-vicious of her two weapons and still the one she trusted more, but she didn't draw. "Talheim has come to bargain."

Benedikt snapped a hand in her direction like a falling guillotine, beckoning to warriors at the fires all around. "Seize the Key!"

Steel sang, and Sander's saber touched the Chancellor's throat. "I suggest not."

Benedikt's eyes cut to him, full of malice. "I *knew* it, you stars-forsaken traitor."

Cistine spread her arms. "I didn't come to shed blood."

"Then I hope you came to surrender." Bravis's tone was guttural with exhaustion. "Because this only ends one way."

Cistine shoved down the flutter of nerves at those familiar words. "I came to offer a compromise that gives us all what we want."

"Doubtful," Valdemar sneered. "What we want can only be achieved with your blood on a Door."

"Exactly." Cistine stepped forward. "You've always been right about the need for augments to win this war. Whether your methods were noble or not, the dilemma is true: the Bloodwights outmatch us in flagons."

Bravis bore forward on the balls of his feet. "What trick is this?"

"It isn't a trick. I've come to give you what you want: my blood on a Door, the augments returned to your hands. On one condition: March into Stornhaz with us, and I'll give you the largest Door in Valgard and every augment inside."

Stunned silence descended. Sander's sword dipped at last, his wide eyes fixed on her. Benedikt barked with dry laughter, cracking that cruel pause. "Madness."

"Then what was *your* plan?" Cistine demanded. "To spill my blood on the smallest Door? That seems like a waste."

Scowling, he gave no rebuttal.

"Yes, this will involve a fight," Cistine went on. "But to succeed greatly, you have to *dare* greatly. If you want enough power to defeat the Bloodwights, then you'll have to attack the largest well—right below them."

Bravis scoffed. "And what is your plan: lead our people on a death-mission into Stornhaz, and find all of us slaughtered and the Bloodwights possessing not only the Key, but also the greatest well? You won't save us, you'll hand the blade to this stars-forsaken *Aeoprast* and that will be the end of it!"

"And if you capture me and spill my blood on a different Door, you'll just prolong the inevitable!" Cistine argued. "I've been searching for a way to help you win this war, and this is it. This is all there is: all that we are, against all that they are, with Stornhaz as the prize."

"And the Key," Benedikt said. "The Key is *the* prize."

"The Key is not a prize," Cistine snarled. "She fights for herself. And she will fight for Valgard, if Valgard will fight beside her."

"Die beside her, you mean," Valdemar muttered.

"Of course people will die. They've been dying this entire war! But we *have* to do this. The only hope we have is to reform the lines and march on *them* before we fall back any farther."

"I see no reason why we should risk so much when we could have any well we wanted," Benedikt said. "Enough talk. The Key is ours now."

He stepped forward, and Adeima and Sander raised their weapons; Cistine gripped Nail, stepping back a pace, heart lunging into her throat.

"Do not lay a *hand* on her."

Maleck's bass growl heralded his arrival, shadow parting from shadow as he moved to her side, laying back his hood. Across the lines, gasps and curses rose—but not in rage. They were shock. And awe. And *wonder*.

And then, at one of the nearby fires, someone breathed, "*Navalo.*"

Cistine blinked, taken off guard at the Old Valgardan word—*wolf.*

"I know that man!" Another took up the cry. "That is *Navalo* of Blaykrone, the one who guards the villages!"

Maleck froze at Cistine's side, mouth tumbling open as all across the fires, warriors whispered. Hands fell from swords. The Chancellors cursed in shock as men and women bowed their heads to Maleck in reverent gratitude.

"*Him?*" Bravis gestured sharply. "This is the man who freed the villages? The one in the wolf mask?"

Cistine's mind reeled too much to reply.

"Of course it was him." Quill's rough drawl came from Cistine's left; he strolled casually into the firelight, sabers drawn and crossed along his shoulders, grinning. "Who else would go right into the heart of enemy ranks, save our children, steal the augments we need to open the Doors, and fight for our territories in an enemy disguise?"

Bulging eyes settled on Maleck from every side, and he flushed at their attention.

"I think there are more than a few in your army who would fight beside *Navalo* of Blaykrone." Breathlessness touched Cistine's voice, and Maleck swung his face toward her. Tears dampened his eyes.

"Not enough to win this fight if the rest of us don't agree to your madness," Bravis growled, "and Benedikt and I will certainly not go."

Despair laid Cistine's hackles flat. He was being just as cowardly as that day in the mountains. "Fine. Don't go with us, then. I'm not asking your permission."

"And if we refuse, how would you take the City?" Valdemar scoffed. "With what *army*?"

A gust of wind ruffled the trees—no natural breeze. Cistine smiled. "*My* army."

A drakonian roar set the earth itself quaking, and with a snap like enemy bones shattering, trees spewed into splinters under the weight of dragon bodies descending around them. Six, eight, a dozen and more dragons shot down like tumbling gemstones through the Sotefold's canopy, surrounding the army. At their head, eyes flickering with skeins of gold, Ashe lunged from Bresnyar's neck and landed at Maleck's side, drawing the new sword she'd acquired in Hellidom.

"The Wing Legions of Oadmark at your call, Princess," she drawled. "And we've brought friends."

From dragon backs all around, people descended in mismatched armor, some fine and some careworn, some reinforced with strange fabrics and materials, and all carrying unconventional weapons: strange spheres, retractable knives, refitted blades and cuffs and spears.

"*Heimli Nyfadengar*, at your call, Princess." From the lead, Tatiana flashed Cistine a wicked grin. "Chancellors, I think you might remember Kadlin and my papa, Morten?"

"A pleasure." Kadlin's clever eyes flashed. "For now."

"This," Bravis stammered, "you—"

A torrent of augmented wind from the east stole his words, bending the trees and sending more than a few warriors staggering, and from its roaring maw Ariadne emerged with Iri and Saychelle at her sides. Behind them, line after line of *visnprests* and *prestas* marched through the trees; so many augments hummed on their bodies, Cistine's heart nearly stopped.

"The *visnprest* Order, at your call, Princess." Ariadne winked.

"Holy *stars*," Benedikt began. "What—?"

Cistine knew what was coming next, a thread of warning in the shifting breeze—a strum across her spirit, the scent of dirt and grass and the sea. Of *home.*

A wind augment's rift tore open to the south, and from its violent folds, Thorne emerged, the last of the dark dye blown from his silver hair, blue eyes a scorching flame. Behind him, Rozalie, Aden, and Kristoff—and ranks of Wardens in cobbled-together Valgardan armor, stepping with wide-eyed wonder into the army of their treaty-bound allies.

The wind banked in their wake, and Thorne dipped his head. "The Wardens of Talheim at your call, Princess Cistine."

When he and Aden and Kristoff joined her, Cistine spread her arms and faced the Chancellors. "*We're* going to take Stornhaz, whether you stand with us or not. But we have a better chance together than apart."

"Then you don't fear the Bloodwights?" Benedikt asked.

"I have no need to fear the army before me if I trust the one behind me. And I *do* trust them. I know we can reach the Door. But we need help holding the Bloodwights at bay so they don't claim the augments when I free them."

No one spoke.

Thorne brushed forward. "It's time Valgard chose where it will make its stand. Kanslar has already decided." He met Sander's gaze, and at his High Tribune's nod, added sharply, "Thorne Novacek, *valenar* and prince-consort to the heir of Talheim, will lead his Tribunes and his cabal into the City. Stand with us as warriors or flee as cowards, but those who won't fight won't share in the spoils. That's always been Valgard's way."

"*Valenar?*" Bravis choked.

"What in the *stars* is a prince-consort?" Valdemar demanded.

"The husband to the future queen of Talheim," Cistine said, and startled murmurs spread among her own people. Bravis and Benedikt exchanged a simmering glance. "Whether Valgard prefers it this way or not, you need us. You need my power and you need our plan. You've handled things your way for months now, and all you've done is lost ground, lost territories...and lost lives."

Adeima sucked in a sharp breath, gaze cutting aside.

"Fight with us," Cistine pleaded. "I could have gone back home after the war camp fell, but I didn't. I'm standing before you now to give back what the North should never have lost: the gift the gods gave you. Talheim fights for Valgard. Will Valgard fight for itself?"

Silence held the camp in rigor, the Chancellors all looking around at one another. At last, Adeima said, "She's right. What do we have to lose? This battle is coming whether we want it or not. We might as well strike first."

"If she's willing to lay down her life on the Door," Valdemar muttered, "better we fight beside the Key than hunt for her with what little remains of our army."

Benedikt tossed up his hands. "First we accept Chancelloresses ushered in under suspect laws, now *prince-stars-damned-consorts* and Talheimic royalty choosing our battles for us?" When no one else raised a protest, he cursed under his breath. "Fine, have it your way! Die here or die in the City. As long as someone bleeds her out on a Door."

Cistine's heart crashed against her sternum like it was trying to slip a lifetime's worth of beats into what little time she had left.

"We will fight." Adeima's voice climbed through the dull roar in her ears. "Yager stands beside its oaths, beside its allies. And beside Talheim's future queen."

"Well, I suppose that settles it, then," Bravis grumbled.

"And my title?" Thorne asked.

Another round of weighted glances.

"Well," Bravis grunted, "as Benedikt so tactfully pointed out, we've already accepted a legal Chancelloress. And quite frankly, I'm sick to death of your insufferable High Tribune. Having you back would be a welcome reprieve, shocking as that might sound."

He and Thorne stepped forward first, clasping forearms with wary smiles and steel-bright eyes. Adeima was close on his heels, and with the tension fracturing, piece by piece, Cistine's gathered army closed in. Someone shouted her name, and she turned straight into Rozalie's arms. "I knew it, I *knew* you would manage it, Princess!"

"As if I didn't have help." Cistine peeled back to smile at her. "You won me my army, Roz!"

"My pleasure." The Warden dipped into a graceful bow, then startled upright when Ashe slung an arm around her neck.

"I've never been so glad to see you."

"And you!" Rozalie cuffed Ashe on the collar, grinning past her at the converging cabal. "Maleck! You, too! You're looking...tall."

"Still the astute observer," Aden deadpanned.

"Oh, spare me. You Valgardans aren't especially well-known for *your* skills of perception, either." Rozalie hiked a thumb at Maleck. "He didn't even realize Ashe was in love with him until *after* she came running back from the wilds to save his life."

"I didn't *run!*" Ashe scoffed.

"I didn't..." Maleck's cheeks colored. "Back then, she was not—"

"Hopeless," Rozalie and Aden chorused, and grinned at each other.

It was a moment Cistine wished she could freeze in time, the two armies blending together with back-slaps and hugs; Morten and Kristoff embracing in delighted reunion, Sander and Thorne bumping brows and gripping shoulders, Kanslar's Tribunes slinking forward to join the Wardens with curious handshakes. And the Oadmarkaic Wing Legions, led by a dark-haired woman strapped in weapons, fielding awestruck questions about their dragons from all sides—first scowling, then slowly smiling at the reverent admiration of their new allies.

Cistine hoped she would survive for a thousand more moments just like these.

The hour was nearly late enough to be early when the cabal at last broke free of their duties, with all their allies settled and the Chancellors and Tribunes spreading the plan among the people. They sat around their own fire at the fringe of the camp, Bresnyar lurking just outside the reddish glow, keeping watch for any double-mindedness from the Courts. Cistine sat between Tatiana and Maleck, and Tatiana pulled Cistine over to rest against her shoulder while Maleck's hand made comforting circles on her back.

"Do you think we gave them enough time?" Cistine fretted. "Half a week to prepare for a siege..."

Ashe flashed her a sympathetic smile across the fire. "We can't wait any longer with an army this large. And not so close to the City, either."

"Time, as always, works against us," Sander said. "But at least with Rakel's confession, we can move a large portion of the army into the City unseen. That should give us an advantage, however slim."

Thorne and Kristoff looked at him as one. "Kel is here?" Kristoff asked.

"I'm afraid not. Sent off to Felstrond in eastern Lataus...it's become a prison city for those who will stand trial after the war. It was too dangerous to keep her nearby."

"Good," Thorne said. "I have no interest in seeing her."

They were quiet for some time, and Cistine looked around at all their faces: Ashe, Aden, Sander and Maleck, Tatiana and Quill and Ariadne, Thorne and Kristoff.

Her precious ones. Her family.

She cleared her throat. "If something goes wrong in the City..."

"Don't start," Quill warned. "Not tonight, Stranger."

"There won't be time after this. We'll be too busy planning." When she sat up, Maleck and Tatiana released her. "This cabal has done more for me than I ever thought possible. I may not feel ready for what's coming, but...I *am* ready, because I had the greatest teachers in all the kingdoms."

"Please don't do this," Ashe muttered.

"I have to," Cistine whispered. "Because whatever happens to me, I want all of you to know I love you, and I'm so gods-forsaken *grateful* I had the privilege to know you. I just wish we had more time."

Thorne shut his eyes and held his head in his hands. No one spoke, and none of them would meet her gaze.

The fire popped, collapsed, and slowly died. None of them moved to revive it.

THE PRINCESS, THE QUEEN, THE KEY

CHAPTER
FORTY-FIVE

THE CITY OF a Thousand Stars looked how Tatiana imagined a Talheimic tomb would: empty, eerie, and cold as the Sable Gates.

There was little visible from the cabal's perch atop the wall; just the slopes of a few rooftops, the cold chimneys, the sluggish Channel. Even the artist's pallet of streets lay dull in the mist churned off the Ismalete and over the wall by the skilled hands of augment-wielding *visnprests* and *prestas*.

The cabal owed their ascent to *Heimli Nyfadengar,* the guild's adamant grappling hooks and winches tied to their belts, their armor inlaid with the same mirrors the Bloodwights had used to slip their siege towers up to Stornhaz unnoticed. Kadlin had come through for them beyond anything Tatiana had expected when she'd written to her after Landamot.

You said you wanted to make it right to me, that you were really my friend. Now prove it. Stand with the Princess of Talheim, and you'll have my gratitude and respect.

When she'd arrived in Blaykrone and hunted down *Heimli Nyfadengar's* encampment, Kadlin had been waiting with the entire guild, everyone above schooling age, armed and ready to fight—and with a vow to help Tatiana take back the City no matter what.

It was time to find out just what taking it would cost.

"There's a new chain across the inside of the gate." Thorne's murmur broke into Tatiana's thoughts, and he skimmed his thumb thoughtfully along his lower lip. "*Svarkyst* steel, by the look of it."

"It's conducting a wind augment," Cistine said. "Just like this wall."

"I would surmise no one imprisoned in this city has a scrap of armor to spare," Maleck said. "Even if they reached the gate and possessed a weapon that could dent *Svarkyst* steel..."

"The augment would kill them," Ashe concluded. "Bastards."

"There's a Bloodwight in the gatehouse," Cistine said. "Someone else will have to remove the augment from the chain while I deal with it."

"Quill, Tatiana, and Cistine, take the gatehouse," Thorne said. "Ariadne and Ashe, we'll rappel you down to the chain. If Ariadne absorbs the augment, Ashe can use my blades to hack through the steel."

"Then we open the gate." Quill pounded his fist into his other palm.

"And pray the Wing Legions are ready." Maleck drew Starfall and Stormfury. "When the Bloodwights sense Cistine, they will come."

Tatiana nudged the shivering princess. "Ready, *Yani?*"

Cistine nodded. Quill thumbed his nose. "We'll see the rest of you on the other side."

"Be careful," Thorne warned.

Tatiana grabbed the edge of the wall and swung herself over. With Cistine and Quill on either side of her, she descended toward the gatehouse.

The building itself wouldn't be difficult to enter; the problem was the platform it perched on. From the steps below, it was impossible to clamber up without being seen. A full panel of windows made approaching from the sides a waste, and the rooftop was slick as ice and so steeply sloped, to descend on it was a guarantee of rolling off the edge. But the plunge was a risk they had to take; once they landed, they would have seconds to enter the gatehouse and distract the Bloodwight before it lit the beacon along the edge of the Channel, which hung dark without need to communicate with the barges.

No sound filled the haze of augmented fog and the encroaching night but their steady breaths as they descended the wall. With several feet to go, Cistine froze, one leg extended below, body twisted awkwardly. Quill stopped, too. "What is it, Stranger?"

"Ariadne just absorbed the wind augment. I can feel it."

"Then so can the Bloodwight. Move!"

A blinding arc of firelight pierced the mist, burning it away, and Cistine cried out in shock. Her fingers unlocked from the stone, and Tatiana lunged away from the wall herself, catching the princess by the arm. But Cistine's weight yanked her down, and together they plunged toward the rooftop.

Ariadne's wind augment rushed to meet them, slowing their fall just enough that when they slammed into the sloped roof in a tangle of limbs, it didn't kill them. They toppled down onto the platform, and Tatiana's shoulder snapped out of place on impact. She roared in agony just as the gatehouse door blew open and ravaging darkness poured out from it, blanketing them in shadow.

Tatiana's lungs filled with oily, inky night, and she gagged, retching, grabbing her shoulder and struggling to her feet. By the time she did, the wind augment was under Cistine's control and cutting back the shadows. With a narrow path cleared, she flung herself toward the Bloodwight.

Quill dropped down next to Tatiana, grabbed her dislocated shoulder, and jammed it back into place. Eyes watering viciously, she piled into the gatehouse where Cistine had the Bloodwight backed into a corner, pinning it in place with torrents of wind. When Tatiana and Quill stepped inside, she dropped the augment and lunged, letting the creature catch her by the throat. In turn, she seized its wrists with both hands.

The currents of power shifted like a violent storm, scattering maps and parchment from the desk in the corner. Tatiana dropped low, cutting out the Bloodwight's legs, and Quill kicked off from the wall and swung onto its shoulders, grabbing its mask with both hands and wrenching its head back by the upper mandible of its wildcat skull.

Cistine gasped and spat a curse, her face paling. "*Now.*"

Tatiana rolled to her feet and brought her blade in from the left just as Quill brought his down from the right. The Bloodwight's unguarded neck popped wetly, the head separating; Cistine kicked free, sprawling on her back, and with one mighty thrust she sent the ravaging darkness out, blowing out the windows and masking the beacon in darkness.

Quill crawled to her side and propped her up, but she waved him off weakly, blood running from her nostrils. "The gate."

Tatiana and Quill darted outside to the complex pulley system framing the wall. High above, Ashe and Ariadne still hacked at the chain while Thorne, Maleck, and Aden faced a line of *mirothadt* approaching down the wall.

Tatiana hit Quill's ribs. "Hurry, Featherbrain!"

They both grabbed the lever, Quill's arms around her body and his hands over hers. His panting breath filled her ears and chased chills down her back as she leaned her entire weight into the winch and yanked down with all her might. It was like drawing boulders down from a mountain with her bare fingertips; her limbs strained and ached and sweat broke across her whole body, her hurt shoulder jabbing dizzy spasms into her head. All she could hear was the thunderous rush of her own pulse and Quill's voice urging her not to give up, they were so stars-damned close—

Then a third set of hands joined theirs, Cistine flinging herself at the winch from the other side. With her added strength, even taxed by the fight against the Bloodwight, the cogs and chains whose beautiful make Tatiana had admired from afar as a child gave up their resistance, and the doors began to slide apart. With a tremendous clatter, the *Svarkyst* barricade gave way, and the dark outlines of Ashe and Ariadne's bodies swung with them, drawn up toward the top of the wall by Thorne and Maleck, leaving Aden to face the *mirothadt* alone.

Cistine sagged against the platform railing. "That's one step."

The distant crack of shattering stone ripped through the city streets, bringing Tatiana's head swinging around. She cursed. "No, no, no..."

"Balmond. Someone saw that fire." Quill wrapped an arm around Cistine's waist and yanked her back from the railing. "Get to the steps!"

Tatiana could barely see where she placed her feet as she led Quill and Cistine in a blind sprint down the switchback steps from the gatehouse. Death bore toward them in the form of ink-dark, winged abominations flooding toward the doors, almost fully open now—and toward the gatehouse struts.

Tatiana dropped onto one of the landings and whirled toward Quill and Cistine. "Grab onto something!"

Quill pushed Cistine down against the railing and hurled himself toward Tatiana, bowling her over against the edge of the landing as the first creature slammed into the pillars below. The seams cracked where it struck once, twice, again—

Half the gatehouse foundation gave way, tipping precariously to the left, dangling them breathlessly over the docks. Then the supports snapped, and they crumbled toward the water, Quill's arms locked to the railing around Tatiana's body and Cistine clinging to the steps above them, screaming.

Something cold and clawed closed around Tatiana and Quill from behind, yanking them back. The docks shrank away so rapidly, Tatiana almost vomited; she twisted in Quill's embrace to look up, catching sight of scarlet-black scales flashing in the waning daylight.

The whole world lit up as an emerald-bodied dragon swooped after the Balmond, unleashing a banner of flame that set the maddened creatures alight. Screams rent the thick air as Meriwa's Legion descended from the clouds like strokes of multicolored lightning. A silver dragon flew abreast of them, holding Cistine in its fist, depositing all three of them on the wall with their cabal. *Mirothadt* littered the stone, and blood dripped from Maleck's cheek and Aden's scalp.

Tatiana struggled to her feet, body fizzing with adrenaline. Ashe peered up at the scarlet dragon who dwarfed even Bresnyar, and at Meriwa on his back, the frenzy of battle in her eyes.

"The children choke this city," the Legion Head hissed. "A dozen or more at the mouth of every street. What now?"

"Leave the children to us. Have the Legion guard these doors until all the barges sail through," Ashe said.

Meriwa yipped, sending her dragon blasting backward and dropping toward the channel to intercept a pair of Balmond diving toward the first barge full of Valgardan and Talheimic warriors.

"Divide," Thorne ordered. "Maleck, Ashe, meet Sander and Rozalie at the sewers and rally a force to capture the children. Aden, find your father and free whoever you find scattered in the city. Ariadne, Quill, and Tati, with us."

Ashe put two fingers in her mouth and whistled; she and Maleck took a running leap from the edge of the wall, and Bresnyar swooped in to catch them on his back, arrowing away into the city on the hunt for Sander's scent. Aden cast a curt nod to Thorne, a fleeting smile to Cistine, and then he was gone as well.

For a sickening instant, Tatiana wondered if she was seeing them all for the last time.

CHAPTER FORTY-SIX

Pockets of combat broke open across the city, echoing off damaged buildings never repaired from the first siege. The sickening sensation of *Nazvaldolya* spread through the glistering avenues as the Bloodwights descended, and dragonfire spread far beyond the Channel gates. Entire districts burned. To Cistine's horror, the place where Morten had lived looked like one of them.

They commandeered a gondola bobbing against a dock near one of the schools, skimming beneath the sulfurous plumes of smoke and ash. Cistine's eyes stung, and her lungs felt strangely cold. She could no longer tell her panic apart from the adrenaline of battle or the tremble of exertion after her fight with the Bloodwight in the gatehouse.

She'd hoped after what she did to Maleck, Pippet, and Vandred, it would be easier this time. But draining one creature had winded her almost to the point of collapse. Not enough training. Not enough time.

She prayed she had the stamina to reach the Door. And if not...

Slowly, her fingers drifted to her augment pouch.

"How are things ahead, Cistine?" Quill's voice jolted her from her thoughts.

"I can't tell anymore," she wheezed. "They're everywhere."

And so was the battle. Some of the Oadmarkaic Legion had carried warriors ahead, and now they clashed with *mirothadt* on both sides of the Channel, charging over the high augwain bridges above. For a moment she had to squeeze her eyes shut against the memory of a childhood nightmare, a story of a city aflame, madmen laughing while they stood over headless corpses...

"*Cistine!*" Fingers locked around her shoulders, shaking her. "Don't close your eyes."

She jolted upright, realizing they'd docked somewhere unfamiliar amidst the maze of streets. Thorne bent over her, still grasping her arms, worry sketching his brow.

Shaking her head wildly, she struggled out onto the dock. "We have to keep moving."

Some of her strength revived as they ran, her body clinging to the familiarity of exercise. The smoke was thinner here, the night somewhat calmer when they pulled away from the thickest of the fighting. The streets turned familiar; they passed the library, the House of Visions, a tavern, a cluster of shops, and finally broke out onto the bridge before the courthouse.

They skidded to a halt, five in a line, hands on their weapons.

Layer upon layer of children stood guard between them and the wall around the courthouse, wearing animal masks too large for their heads, hands going to their own weapons—their flagons.

"Well," Tatiana muttered, "this was never really going to be easy."

"Thorne, Ari, get Cistine into the courthouse," Quill growled. "We'll clear you a path."

"Quill..." Cistine began.

"You know the rules, Stranger. Just like training. Do what I say and don't ask why."

He and Tatiana lunged toward the children with a shriek of *Svarkyst* steel and the rip of augments unleashed. It seemed that time slowed between the swings of their weapons when they whirled between the children, fighting to distract without harming them. If they were hurt themselves, they made no sound. Cistine forced herself not to hunt for them while she watched for that precious seam.

When it finally opened, she nudged Thorne and Ariadne, and pointed. Together, they took it.

The peristyle, spacious and familiar, was deserted when they bolted across its broad hoop and into the courtyard full of rubble. The statues of the five Courts were broken at the bases, littering the yard with chunks of stone in the shapes of shadows and faces. Cistine wanted to stop and stare, but she forced herself to continue moving across the yard, up the steps, and into the market instead.

The moment her boots crossed the threshold, she nearly broke down again, an icy spear of pain whizzing through her head. The Door sang beneath her feet, insatiable and violent, filling her with a sense of imminent, unbearable dread. Burning agony reared and clawed at her hip—the augment from Kosai Talis adding its heated, vicious cry to the chant.

COME AND SEE COME AND SEE AND TAKE AND USE AND BREAK AND—

Thorne caught her arm when she staggered. "Keep moving, Wildheart, you can do this!"

Her Name jolted her back to focus, dimming the shriek in her ears. She sucked in a breath, drew her sword for the relief of her shaking hands, and led the way to the unguarded door down to the well.

The way was dark, and the air chilled sharply as they went, the call crescendoing beat by beat with her heart until Cistine feared she would vomit. Her head was splitting apart down the middle and tears and bile forced themselves up into her sinuses, but she kept going. She had no choice but to move on, step by step, down into shadow. Down toward her fate.

Thorne and Ariadne slowed suddenly. They'd reached the bottom of the stairs. They'd reached the Door.

She put her hands to their shoulders and shoved between them to behold the lid, the runes, her destiny.

Fire erupted through the room, blinding and wicked, painting the unnaturally tall figure of the *Aeoprast* before them—standing guard over the Door.

CHAPTER
FORTY-SEVEN

CISTINE JERKED BACKWARD as Thorne and Ariadne stepped forward, sabers shrieking, blocking the way to her. With a low groan, a wall of stone sealed off the steps behind them.

For a moment, Cistine was in Kalt Hasa again, buried inside black rock, facing her greatest nightmare. Not Salvotor—not anymore.

The leader of the Bloodwights regarded them with arms outstretched, skeletal fingers ticking, bringing the ring of fire closer and closer. "I see Maleck's not the only one easily lured to his fate."

Cistine drew her sword and Nail, bracing the dagger backhanded to her arm and holding the sword across her front the way Maleck had taught her. The *Aeoprast* dipped his head, and the smirk of his skull seemed to grow.

"Can you take his augments?" Ariadne murmured.

Cistine tugged her lower lip between her teeth, gathering her grit. "I can try."

Thorne and Ariadne lunged as one, a banner of flame rising to cut off their path. Cistine reached for the embers, but they scattered, congealing between her and Thorne. She skipped sideways, trying to gather a lasso of power around the leg of her armor and jerk the Bloodwight off-balance. But he recovered control in less than a heartbeat, and it was Cistine who reeled, slamming to one knee. The impact against the Door rang like a gong into her very essence.

Thorne lunged from the right, Ariadne from the left, swords wheeling, forcing the Bloodwight aside long enough for Cistine to climb to her feet. The cartilage felt like powder beneath her kneecap; but she forced herself forward, pushing off with her good foot and reaching out for the fire augment again.

A spray of wind set her skidding backward. Her head lashed the wall, and for a moment her vision spun with starlight. She plunged down, caught herself on one knee and both hands, and staggered up again.

The wind had snared Thorne and Ariadne, too. Thorne was just now clawing himself up against the opposite wall, blood streaming from above his eye, and Ariadne was on her feet already, palms skinned, gaze flashing. Between them, the *Aeoprast* turned with hungry, predatory intensity toward Cistine as she stooped to lift her blades again, hands quaking.

"This struggle is pointless," the *Aeoprast* said. "You were born to be unmade."

"Not by you."

His hoarse chuckle sounded eerily like Maleck's. "Yet here we are." He raised both hands, and a strange prickling began on the contours of Cistine's body, tugging and pulling, as if the skin was separating from her bones.

Ariadne lunged, slamming into the Bloodwight from behind and unbalancing him with a kick to the legs. They fell to the Door in a wild tussle, Thorne pouncing on top of them, and the tugging in Cistine's chest released. She staggered back and raked up her sleeve, staring in horror at the rippling blue lines of her veins. Bruises dappled her flesh.

He'd tried to dissolve her into blood mist, just as he'd done to Salvotor.

Cistine hurtled toward the Bloodwight and Thorne and Ariadne where they rolled across the Door, blades shrieking uselessly against the creature's armor. They weren't trying to kill it, only to purchase a moment for her to come close enough to rip the power from its bones.

The *Aeoprast* rolled onto his side and cast his head back, quick as a dagger's jab, and a soft, agonized hiccup moored Cistine's feet to the Door.

The Bloodwight's antler had plunged straight through Ariadne's armor, into her sternum.

Cistine's blades dropped from her numb hands. She stared in horror as the *Aeoprast* hurled Thorne away with a kick and straightened, Ariadne skewered on the rack of its mask. Thorne rolled back to his elbow, clutching his wounded middle and staring up at the creature impaling his friend.

"No," he choked. "*Ari!*"

Cistine's world went piercing white, blinding her for a moment. Then it flooded red with rage.

A sound shook the walls of the well, shook the Door itself, and she realized only when the *Aeoprast* whirled around to face her that *she*'d made it, that howl of rage and devastation. A quake shook the foundations of the courthouse as the augments under her feet leaped and tossed in reply, throwing the *Aeoprast* to his knees; Ariadne slid from the impaling antler and rolled in a heap, swords just beyond her grasp. Thorne struggled up and ran to her, skidding on his knees at her side, taking her face in his hands.

The *Aeoprast* rose and swayed toward Cistine, and with a surge of wild instinct, she drew the dark, locked flagon from her satchel. She still didn't know what it was, nor did she need to; she had a weapon of destruction that came with a price. And with her husband and her friend dancing with death across this Door, Cistine was willing to pay it.

The *Aeoprast* froze, catching sight of what she held. He took one step back from her, then another, the fire coalescing into a dim ring around him. "Do you know what that is?"

"A gift from the gods *you* want to cast down," Cistine seethed. "And if you take one more step, I'll send you to meet them."

"You're not prepared to pay the price."

She clenched her fist tighter around the flagon, and the *Aeoprast* flinched back from her. "Don't you *dare* tempt me."

A veil of darkness cascaded from the Bloodwight's cloak and blew through the chamber. Cistine ducked to one side, capturing a fistful of the shadows and yanking; though the motion nearly unbalanced her, the *Aeoprast* put up no fight. The augment spooled loose from his body, and she brought it into herself, fists up to fight. But in the vanishing of the shadows that melded into her armor, she saw the stone doorway turn to a gravel heap.

The *Aeoprast* had fled from the Door itself—from *her.*

She stared down at the *Stor Sedam,* hands rattling. There was something mighty beyond measure, terrifying beyond common reason about this flagon. So she would not use it; and she would not waste it.

Plunging it away, she staggered to Thorne's side and dropped next to him and Ariadne, shoving the hair from her friend's brow. Ariadne's eyes were open, but dim. Her stomach lurched, two quick flutters of pain tightening her abdomen for every breath she took; and already, those breaths grew shallow. Blood gushed from her chest, her diaphragm struggling to pull in air.

"I'm sorry," Thorne rasped, cradling her head against his knees. "I'm sorry, Lightfall, I—"

Ariadne shook her head, a rogue tear escaping the corner of her eye, and she laid her hand on his cheek—a silent farewell.

Panic froze Cistine's fingers on Ariadne's bloodied chest; then it made them fly. She reached into her augment pouch again and withdrew the healing and blood augments. Their strange, differing music rang louder than ever, almost deafening this close to the Door.

"Cistine," Ariadne wheezed, "don't. If you use that...there may not be enough to bring you back."

"I know." Tears scoured Cistine's cheeks. "But I can't let you die."

She uncorked the augments, poured a generous thread of power into each hand, and pressed her palms over Ariadne's chest.

She counted the seconds by the beats of that precious heart under her hands, thready at first, then slowly strengthening as organ, bone, muscle and skin begin to knit. Ariadne gasped and gagged, shuddering in Thorne's grip, and after several seconds she twisted, knocking Cistine's hands away.

"Stop. *Stop,* that's enough." Shaking violently, she propped herself up, grunting when Thorne wrapped his arms around her from one side, and Cistine from the other, pinning her between them. Her arms looped around their backs in turn, and another shiver rushed through her. "You should not have done that, *Logandir.*"

"Lecture me later," Cistine laughed unsteadily. "Right now, we have a job to do."

Ariadne slithered free, pushed on Thorne's shoulder to stumble to her feet, and snatched up her sabers. "I'll guard the way above."

She turned, and for a fleeting instant Cistine thought that would be it—that the regret and fury in Ariadne's eyes would be the last thing they shared before she bled.

Then her friend's brawny grip engulfed her, sabers hanging limp at Cistine's spine, and her fierce kiss pressed against Cistine's forehead. "Thank you, *Malatanda*."

And then she was gone, staggering up the steps as the violent shudder of an earth augment cracked the courthouse foundations somewhere nearby. Cistine trembled with it, rising to meet Thorne's anguished gaze. "I had to do it. I couldn't lose her."

Thorne drew her close and kissed her with all his might, the smell of fresh, hot blood on his clothes, on his hands. Its reek turned Cistine's body to sand pouring through an hourglass.

It was coming. The inevitable, her destiny, the end...

It was here.

Her knees contacted the cold stone again, and she twisted her fingers in Thorne's sleeves as he came back down with her. Her eyes budded with tears, terror choking her resolve. She almost begged him not to do it, to walk off this Door with her, to catch up with Ariadne and find another way.

But they needed this moment. This Door. The augments that would make it possible to protect not just themselves, but all the kingdoms.

Talheim had been blind, selfish, vain to believe the choice was ever theirs to make; that Valgard's weapons were another man's right to give or take away. It was her kingdom's mistake, and it was hers to make right.

She grabbed Thorne's *Svarkyst* saber and laid it in his hand. "It's time."

He stared at the sword, his hand trembling violently.

"Thorne, do it." Cistine wrapped her fingers around his wrist. "Do it and then bring me back."

He caught the back of her neck with his free hand and brought her up into another kiss, their breaths mingling. His mouth tasted of blood and tears, the touch of his lips both an apology and promise to make this right, to save her from the brink of death as she had just saved their friend.

Cistine trusted him to do it. But she had never been more terrified in her life.

Thorne released her and brought the blade to rest against the inside of her thigh, a sacred place his hands had so recently begun to explore.

Cistine wanted a lifetime of those touches. She wanted a future with him. She wanted hope.

But she couldn't keep any for herself. Not today.

"Do it," she sobbed, "please just do it, Thorne, I can't wait anymore, I can't..."

He steadied her with his hand to her jaw. "Look at me, Wildheart. Look at me," he said, and she did. "I love you."

He dragged the blade across her leg.

CHAPTER
FORTY-EIGHT

THERE WAS SO much stars-forsaken blood on Thorne's hands.

He was doing this. He was killing her, slowly and of their joint volition. He had never imagined the *valenar* bond could bring agony like this.

He gathered her into his arms, cradling her hip in one hand and her head to his chest with the other. The shakes had already begun, her body fighting against the flow of blood. She clung to his wrists, nails biting into his armor so harshly he felt it even through the plating, but he made no protest. He would let her claw the flesh from his bones if it would bring her a modicum of relief.

"Distract me," she gasped, her voice wet and raw with agony. "Tell me...tell me the story of Sillakove."

Thorne pressed his lips to her hair and spoke against her head, his voice shaking nearly beyond his control. "In ancient times when gods and men walked the world together, there was one they named Sillakove, who was called to herd all the stars in the sky..."

A distant boom shook the courthouse. Cistine startled and cried out, and Thorne gripped her tighter, leaning them both back against the wall. He forced himself to talk louder than the sounds of battle overhead, tears dripping from his jaw, his eyes tracing a steady stream of blood flowing into the Old Valgardan runes chiseled on the lid—words so ancient Thorne hardly knew them, only that they spoke of the profound power leaching the blood from his *valenar's* body.

When he fell silent, the story finished, Cistine tapped his wrist. "Thorne. One...one last lesson?"

"Anything," he croaked.

"If I...if I see the Sable Gates...what do I do?"

He gripped her chin, turning her head toward him. Her eyes flickered as she fought the losing battle for consciousness. "You take power," he growled. "Become the Mad Kingdom's Queen. And then wait for me, Wildheart. I'll be there soon."

"Not too soon." Her eyes drifted shut. "Save them, Thorne."

Her body went limp.

A simultaneous, violent jolt moved through the Door.

Thorne lunged for the blood and healing flagons, smashing the latter against Cistine's body, close to her thigh. As the white wisps of power began to stitch the arterial seam, he swung her up into his arms and staggered toward the steps, the lid bucking beneath him. He fixed his eyes on the dark maw of the staircase and pushed himself forward, step by step, heat building at his back and boots sticking to the lid.

A heart-rending *crack* climbed the walls, and with one last vicious lurch, the Door blew apart, flinging Thorne to his knees on the threshold of the stairs, shielding Cistine with his body. Cursing, he broke the blood augment against her armor, freeing the scarlet skeins to do their work. Then he rolled onto his back, holding her body down the length of his and watching the impossible unfold below them.

It was like being trapped in the heart of a falling star. Opaline lights sailed through the room, washing the walls in sweeps of silver and vermillion, coal and jade, peach and salmon. Sunsets and sunrises, blood and wine, life and death, daydreaming blue skies and cold gray reality clashed in a prism of everything that Valgard was, and had been, and would ever be. The might of purpose, of power, of necessity rolled through him, and for a moment he knew exactly who he was, and what he was, and why the gods had given this gift to his people.

Heat stabbed his eyes. Valgard had been so lost, so aimless—but slowly they were healing from that, and now, because of their choices, their alliances, their faith, the gods had given them back their power from the most unexpected of places: the woman who was Key and princess and future queen, Talheimic by birth and Valgardan by union.

"Cistine, open your eyes," Thorne breathed, shaking her gently. "This is glorious, it—Cistine?"

She didn't stir.

Thorne tore his gaze from the glory of the well and looked down at her. She was still limp in his arms, as colorless as sunbleached rocks. Her limbs draped bonelessly over his. Her head lolled.

Thorne laid her against the bow of the steps, cradling her neck carefully. He gave her another shake. "Cistine. *Logandir*. Can you hear me?"

She was unresisting to his summons when he touched her cold face, kissed her clammy brow, pressed his lips over her pale, unmoving ones.

"Wildheart." Thorne's arms seized tight around her in panic, lifting her up from the steps again. "*Wildheart!*"

The sheer amount of blood she'd spilled...the sacrifice she'd made, the augments she'd spent on Ariadne...

Not enough. Not enough.

"Cistine!" he roared. "*No!* Do not do this to me again!"

The song of the augments in the well turned from joyous to mourning. When Thorne looked back again, all he could see were the colors of death climbing the walls, reaching for his *valenar*.

CHAPTER
FORTY-NINE

MALECK COULD HARDLY believe that as hasty as their plan was, when he raised his head above the tide of battle for a moment to breathe, he saw more *mirothadt* fallen than Valgardan warriors. Above, the smoke of augmentation and dragonfire eddied with the bodies of the Oadmarkaic Legion themselves, diving toward and pulling back from the Bloodwights, keeping them distracted. Below, the warriors clustered and rallied, stabbing against the enemy ranks, driving them back again and again.

With three lands united, perhaps they were truly winning.

A gust of power arrested his focus. Maleck spun on the flat rooftop where he'd struck down an archer aiming into the pockets of Valgardan warriors, and faced the creature that ruled the City.

His blood turned to ice when the *Aeoprast* straightened, leering at him through that mask. "Breaking into our city once was a mistake, *Allet*. Breaking in again is a death wish."

"You've always been better at stealing into other people's homes than guarding your own," Maleck rasped, though fear corroded his throat.

The *Aeoprast* paced before him, all but trembling with pleasure at the chaos below. "A week back in their ranks, and you're already playing as if the last month was merely a nightmare. Don't tell me you don't miss the power. The augments. Tell me you didn't long for the excuse to *take, take,*

take—"

"I had every excuse, every day, for twenty years!" Maleck roared. "I *chose* not to use the augments, and then you sent me to Nimmus and reaped back this specter screaming in my head!"

"One nearly three decades in the making." A faint wind stirred the hem of the *Aeoprast's* cloak. "I don't know why you let her take the augments from you. You were finally free to be as you are. As we made you to be."

The wind slammed into Maleck's chest, tossing him to the edge of the rooftop. With a shout, he plunged his blades down, slowing his descent along the stone. With his heels draping over the Channel, he had no time to gather his wits before the *Aeoprast* was there, hand encircling his throat.

"If you truly love that woman who stole your power from you," the *Aeoprast* mocked, "you would take that dark flagon she holds. You don't want to see what becomes of her if she uses it. Some would call it greed if you chose to carry that burden yourself, but I call it mercy."

Maleck struggled to suck down air that didn't taste of rot and old dirt. "You know *nothing* of mercy. You only want me to take it because you can manipulate me, and you know you cannot manipulate Cistine."

"You think I fear her? The small, untrained princess of a foreign kingdom?" The *Aeoprast* tightened his grip, and Maleck let go of his sabers, latching onto his brother's fingers to pry them from his throat. "She is but a passing point in time. We are eternal. *You* could be eternal, if not for petty sentiment. There is too little of Father and Mother in you."

"A compliment of the highest order," Maleck gasped.

The *Aeoprast's* grip contracted, closing Maleck's throat completely.

A whistle of moving steel. The glint of a blade. A throwing dagger hacked toward them, and by instinct, perhaps remembering a time when he was vulnerable, the *Aeoprast* flinched. Maleck ripped free, staggering sideways out of reach and staring in wide-eyed horror at the nimble figure who flipped herself onto the rooftop, already drawing a second knife. "Stay *away* from him, *bandayo!*"

Her name left both their mouths at once. "*Pippet.*"

The *Aeoprast* stepped forward, hand extended. "Drop that blade. You know mortal weapons can't wound me."

"I'm not here to kill you," she spat. "I'm here to stop you from tricking my friends!"

"I've done nothing of the sort, you know that. They only deceive themselves."

Pippet's gaze flicked past him, landing desperately on Maleck. "Mal, *where is Cistine?*"

He shook his head, unwilling to speak it with his brother between him and Pippet, monolithic body coiled to strike at any moment.

"*I* know where she is, and that's the beauty of desperation," the *Aeoprast* purred, stepping nearer to Pippet. "It overlooks so much."

Pippet shook her head, gaze still riveted on Maleck. "I heard Cassaida and Oskar talking...Mal, tell me she's not at the Door!"

The *Aeoprast* moved so quickly, Maleck didn't have time to choke a warning. One moment, he was between them; the next, he blurred forward, fire bursting from his outstretched hand.

It didn't land on Pippet's unarmored body. Instead, it struck against a shrieking knot of inky feathers that dove between them—always between Pippet and danger.

Maleck swore and Pippet screamed in heartbreak as Faer plowed into the rooftop, augmented flames consuming his small, fragile body. His dying squawks blended into Pippet's sobs.

"No—*no, not him! Faer!*" She dove for the floundering raven, and Maleck surged after her, but not quickly enough.

The *Aeoprast* shoved Pippet back from Faer's flaming carcass, twisted her arm, and drove her own blade into her body.

Time turned sluggish as she fell to her knees, blood gushing from her side, screaming like when she'd fallen from a horse and broken her arm at six years old. But this was not a fall. It was worse. And *Maleck* would become worse, even become death itself to save her—

He took barely a step to intercept his brother when he felt it. Around him. *Within* him.

Something broke into the world, bright and blinding, stealing the air from his chest. A gusting wind screamed out from the courthouse, shoving past him and the *Aeoprast* and Pippet, swamping over the city and stealing across the world.

His brother whipped back to face the courthouse, tossing Pippet aside. "She's done it. At long last...."

Then the Bloodwight shrieked—truly *shrieked* in terror—as something bowled over Maleck, knocking him to his shoulder. Great scarlet jaws clamped around the *Aeoprast*, and with a toss of its head, Meriwa's dragon flung him high and slapped him with a whip of the tail, sending him soaring over Stornhaz's wall.

Shaking off a moment's paralyzing shock at his brother's sudden absence, Maleck staggered up just as the Legion Head leaped down. Together they ran to Pippet, writhing and weeping near the roof's edge, fingers spasming over her wound. "Maleck, Maleck, is Faer—is he—?"

A glance over his shoulder as he crouched beside her only confirmed what the reek of charred flesh, singed feathers, and Faer's silence foretold. His throat shuttered with grief.

"I'm sorry," he murmured, turning back to her. "Lie still." He laid a hand on Pippet's tearstained face, the other touching the knife handle buried deep in the meat of her side. One graze of the blood, the hot skin around it, and he knew it was beyond his triage skills.

"She needs a healing augment," he panted, meeting Meriwa's stricken gaze. "Will you help her?"

She stared down at Pippet—perhaps seeing a different dark-haired girl, the one Ashe had told him about, the sister she could not save. Then her face hardened. "I'll find your *Innuin*. Aeosotu can track the scent of herbs."

"Maleck," Pippet cried as Meriwa swept her up, "Maleck, wait—!"

"There's no time." He squeezed her hand and stepped back, nodding to the Legion Head. "Take her."

Ignoring Pippet's pained, pitiful sobs, he retrieved his sabers while Meriwa and Aeosotu took to the skies again. Then he knelt, scarred palms hovering over Faer's charred remains, and tears stamped his eyes. If he so much as touched him, the raven's body would crumble to cinders.

"I'm sorry, my friend." Maleck's scrubbed his damp eyes on his sleeve, looking across the city—seeking the bloodiest wound to stanch, the place he was needed most. But all he could see was Pippet's face, terrified and desperate, and unease swelled in his throat.

To reach them, she must've ridden for days without stopping, straight to the city while they'd plotted near Lake Erani. But *why* had she come—why had she feared Cistine being on the Door?

"Maleck!"

Relief nearly swept his legs from under him at the sound of Ashe's smoke-choked voice. Bresnyar descended from the gritty haze with a mighty boom of wings, and Ashe stared down at Maleck, horror and relief at war in her eyes.

"We saw the *Aeoprast*. Did you fight him?"

"Not alone." Maleck rubbed a hand over his throat. "He's gone."

"As are the other Bloodwights. They tucked their tails and fled." Bresnyar's gaze slashed across the City. "Do you two find it alarming they haven't gone for the courthouse instead?"

Before they could answer, the dragon snorted sharply, head jerking. His brow rippled with concern.

"What is it?" Ashe laid a hand on his neck.

"Thorne," Bresnyar said. "Something is wrong."

Fear banded Maleck's throat tighter than any Bloodwight's grip. He grabbed Ashe's hand and swung onto the dragon's spine behind her. "Take us to him."

Bresnyar skimmed over the clusters of ruins that now marked each corner of Stornhaz. No district was without scorch and decay; the dead littered every street, and Maleck could scarcely believe the carnage. Long before his brothers had become Bloodwights, they were ruthless criminals dominating the city's worst taverns and darkest streets, commanding its most violent aggressors. But to see the destruction they'd forced today was nearly incomprehensible.

They'd shed Pippet's blood. Killed Faer. Slaughtered countless more.

They coasted over the peristyle, and Maleck spotted familiar figures in the wreckage below: Quill's pale hair soiled with blood, Tatiana's curls bouncing loose of their tie. Kristoff, Aden, and Ariadne had rallied with them, dashing toward the courthouse doors. Ashe shouted their names, and they drew to a halt as Bresnyar crashed down, cracking the stones with his talons. One glance at Ariadne's armor, and Maleck's stomach ripped itself to tatters.

"Are you hurt?" He leaped down to take her shoulder.

Ariadne's eyes gleamed with anguish. "I was. Cistine…"

A ragged shout from near the courtyard doors silenced her reply. "*Help us!*"

Thorne stumbled into the peristyle, clutching Cistine to his chest, her limbs splayed and head draped over the crook of his arm; at the sight of them, Maleck's strength gave way. He stumbled forward a step, gaze fixed on their princess, a soft huff of breath falling from his lips—the beginning of her name, a whispered prayer given up halfway through.

She looked dead. No living person could be so limp and pale.

Ashe cursed, and they all ran, catching up to Thorne where he buckled to his knees, laying Cistine's body on the ground. His eyes, raw and red-rimmed, darted up to Kristoff, boyish terror in his face. "Do something."

Kristoff stripped off his gloves and pressed two fingers under Cistine's jaw. Aden knelt, resting a hand over Thorne's chest, caked with blood. "What happened?"

"The *Aeoprast* was waiting for us."

Sallow-faced, Ariadne sank down beside him. "I warned Cistine not to heal me, that it wouldn't leave enough power for her, but she didn't listen. She never does."

Ashe collapsed, gripping Cistine's hand in both of hers. "Kristoff, tell me she's alive."

"She is." A tremor moved through his voice. "Barely."

Thorne swore with relief, resting his hand on Cistine's thigh.

"Then why in God's name isn't she awake?" Ashe demanded.

"I don't know. This is beyond me."

Weary footsteps clinked along the stones behind them. The

Chancellors approached in various states of disarray; Bravis wore a slice of fabric bound around the side of his head, but judging by the amount of blood pouring down his cheek, he'd lost an eye. Limping Benedikt, Valdemar with his skull crusted in blood, and Adeima's ripped armor and torn lips suggested none of them had fared much better. But here they all were, drawn by the same sensation he'd felt up on that rooftop when the well tore open. They'd come for the power, to drink of the gift that felt like a curse.

Thorne rose with a grunt, lifting Cistine into his arms. Slowly the others followed him, holding onto various hurts all over their bodies, facing the approaching Chancellors.

"The well?" Bravis asked when they came within earshot.

"Sander led a group of warriors into the courthouse," Thorne said flatly. "They guard the well from above and below the steps."

Valdemar sagged. "Good."

"Then it's enough for you?" Maleck recognized the brittleness of Thorne's tone a moment before he started shouting: "Are you stars-damned *satisfied* now? She kept her word, she gave to the last drop of blood for you! She is twice the ruler any of you will ever be!"

"Thorne," Kristoff cautioned.

"No. I don't want to hear it," Thorne snarled. "Valgard didn't win this war. Talheim won it for us, with Talheimic blood spilled by its own choice. And if it costs them their sole heir, then stars damn every single one of you *Chancellors* for letting it go this far."

Tatiana winced, and Aden braced his hands on his weapons as if to leap to his cousin's defense, but none of the Chancellors rebuked Thorne. In fact, there was regret in Adeima's gaze, fixed on Cistine's body. "I thought there was a contingency."

"There was. But she destroyed that, too, saving *our* people." Thorne turned toward Kanslar's wing. "Take your flagons and collect the harvest of Cistine's blood. But remember why the gods gave us that power in the first place, and try not to squander it."

Without a backward glance, Talheim's prince-consort carried his bride away.

∽∼∾

Maleck was grateful to sink down on the sofa when they found a suitable chamber at last—Cistine's old room, the box garden wilted and floral arrangements musty. Aden tossed him a damp rag soaked in the stale washbasin, and he held it to his bruised neck, the cool water soothing his wounds.

"The Bloodwights are gone," Ashe offered the one bit of good news brought by this stars-forsaken night. "Fled the city or driven out. Our ranks outnumber theirs now."

"So, just like that?" Tatiana asked hoarsely. "Stornhaz is ours again?"

"So it seems." Kristoff's tired eyes followed Ashe as she went to join Thorne on the bed, Cistine lying between them. "But at what cost?"

"Too high," Thorne rasped. "I failed her."

Tatiana opened her mouth, but Quill laid a hand on her shoulder, shaking his head.

"At least she can rest now," Ariadne said. "And perhaps she'll recover, in time."

Maleck lacked the heart to tell them time was a commodity. The *Aeoprast* still lived, and his *mirothadt* would rally soon. They did not have forever to wait for their princess to wake.

Groaning, he peeled himself up from the sofa. "Quill. Tatiana. I need to speak with you."

They swapped uneasy glances and followed him out into the hall. Shutting the door gently, he faced the intimidating unified front they made; now, just as most days since Hvallatar, Tatiana would not look at him. But there was only weary trust in Quill's eyes. "What do you need, *Storfir*?"

He curled his blood-crusted fists at his sides. "Pippet came to the City."

A still, unbreathing moment. Then Tatiana's back struck the wall, hand covering her mouth, and Quill's fingers wrapped Maleck's collar, shaking him slightly. "*Tell me she's alive.*"

"She is," he said firmly, though he had no proof yet. "Meriwa's taken

303

her to the medicos."

"*Medicos?*"

"Did she fight a stars-damned *Bloodwight?*" Tatiana demanded.

Quill whirled on her. "You knew something about this?"

"I knew she was angry, she said she wanted them dead, but I didn't think..." Tatiana trailed off, shaking her head. "Where is she?"

"At one of the houses of healing, I imagine. It would be the easiest smell to track. Quill," Maleck added when his friend spun away up the hall, "there's something else."

Quill slowed, laying a hand to the sculpted doorframe. His back buckled, the ridges of his knuckles rising sharply against his skin. "Faer...Faer's gone, isn't he?"

The silence clapped tight around them, and Maleck's eyes sagged shut. "I'm truly sorry."

"I knew it. If she was hurt, it would be because they took him down first." A pitchy breath of half-amused grief surged under Quill's voice. "Stars damn it, I'll miss that bag of feathers."

Without another word, he staggered from the hall, and Tatiana said quietly, "It's good it came from you."

Then she was gone as well, leaving Maleck utterly alone, hands bloodstained and empty but enough grief in his chest to drown a kingdom.

The apartment door opened, and Ashe slipped out behind him, her arms winding around his waist and her face pressed to his shoulders. They came down to their knees in the hall, arms wrapped around each other, and did not move while the smoke thickened outside the gritty windows and the night gave way to a cruel, uncertain dawn.

CHAPTER FIFTY

T HEY FOUND PIPPET in the house of healing where Tatiana's mother and Aden's had once served together, before bloodcough took them both the year after the war against Talheim.

The medicos lacked enough healing augments to spare for her full wound; what few they had, they'd kept hidden all this time, risking the Bloodwights' wrath to heal whoever they could.

Quill didn't dare raise his voice at their haunted faces, the dark circles under their eyes. For months, these medicos had been imprisoned inside the City, forced to heal *mirothadt* and sacrifice their flagons for Bloodwight experiments. They did what they could.

Pippet would live, the woman reassured them. They had enough augments to stop the hemorrhaging. But it would be days before she woke, weeks before she could even think of lifting a dagger again.

It was almost absurd how alike her wound and Tatiana's were. Had the Bloodwight stabbed her there in mockery?

She felt like the enemy's plaything, her heart a target riddled with arrow after arrow. First the baby, then Quill and Maleck, now Pippet and Faer. And *Cistine*.

Half-numb, she wandered the halls until she found someone offering food to the wounded and their families, and mumbled her gratitude at the cloth-wrapped cheese and bread they gave her. She couldn't imagine ever feeling hungry again, but they needed their strength. *Quill* needed to eat.

She found her way back to Pippet's room by memory alone, though she was no longer the only one in it; they'd brought in a few Wardens, desperately in need of stitching as well. Pippet's cot was tucked behind a thin cloth curtain now, and Tatiana ducked behind it, feet stalling on the far side.

Quill sat cross-legged on the floor, facing the bed, shirtless. Someone had come along and bandaged his ribs in her absence, both sides bruised plum-purple from the fight in the peristyle. Tatiana had practically carried him the last half-mile to the house of healing.

But he'd been glorious tonight, beautifully savage in the fight. Her *valenar*, her Nightwing, the warrior she'd sworn herself to in life, death, and beyond. But now his sister was hurt again, and Faer...

Swallowing, she rattled the curtain lightly. Quill didn't turn, but he sighed in a way that loosened his body and bent his head.

Tatiana dragged her dark curls over one shoulder and sat behind him. She stretched out her legs on either side of his, straddling his hips and dragging her nails lightly down his bare back. "I brought food."

"I appreciate it," Quill said. "But save it for someone who really needs it. I'm all right."

She knew that wasn't true. She also knew he hurt in ways even a good meal couldn't help. She settled her hands on his hips and buried her face in the back of his neck. "We always knew this plan couldn't come without a cost. It was too risky."

"I know." Quill's voice held no emotion. "Faer was one of us. This cabal always accepted the danger. But...Nimmus' teeth, what am I going to say to her when she wakes up?"

Tatiana swallowed. "What you'd say to any of us. She's grown enough to take it. We'll have to tell her about Cistine, too."

Quill swallowed audibly. "What was she even doing here? She knows better." His back heaved in a violent shudder. "You don't think she...?"

"She wasn't here for augments. No." Tatiana linked her arms around

Quill's waist and squeezed tightly. "If she was, she would've gone straight to the courthouse. She must've sensed or seen the *Aeoprast* and hunted him down."

"Why? She knows she can't kill him."

"I don't know, Quill. We'll just have to ask her when she wakes."

At the weary dip she could no longer keep from her tone, Quill twisted slightly, wrapping his arm around her shoulders and hauling her into the shelter of his side. "Are you hurt?"

"Just a few scrapes." Tatiana shifted to sit sideways, casting her legs across his lap. He turned his head wearily toward her, his eyes and mouth drawn with deep lines of grief, and Tatiana brushed his hair gently behind his ear. "Whatever you need, Quill, I'm here."

He nodded, dropping his brow against hers. "Just hold me right now, all right? I feel like I'm falling apart."

She felt it, too. So she held him, sitting with the reek of herbs and blood on the air, vigilant over their sister while the weight of the day's battle bore down like a tide, changing everything in its wake.

CHAPTER
FIFTY-ONE

THE BLOODWIGHTS HAD taken advantage of the Chancellors' study. Mounds of books about the wells, ancient temples, and *Gammalkraft* covered the broad table where the negotiations between Talheim and Valgard had taken place. Restless warriors still carried empty flagons and debris from the room when Thorne answered the summons from Chancelloress Adeima the day after the siege.

He stood on the balcony for a moment, gazing down at his fellow Chancellors: Bravis fiddling with his newly-acquired eyepatch and scowling, Valdemar's smile missing teeth, Benedikt wielding a cane; Adeima alone sat tall, utterly in command. Thorne's chest ached that she stood in the light at this table where she'd always belonged without her *valenar* at her side.

A pain they shared now.

He dragged his palm along the railing as he descended. The other Chancellors looked up when he leaned his hands on the back of his usual seat. "If you called me here to reprimand me for what I said to you yesterday, you can save your breath. I meant every word."

"We know," Adeima said. "How is Cistine?"

"There's been no change. So I'd like to keep this meeting as brief as possible."

"Naturally." Bravis motioned to the seat, and Thorne slowly settled into it. "But there are matters we must discuss. The state of Stornhaz is...not good."

"We've corralled the acolytes your High Tribune rescued in some of the schools," Valdemar said. "But they cry out for augments day and night."

"They're withdrawing," Thorne said tiredly.

"We know," Bravis said. "I spoke to your man Quill this morning. He said you were able to save his sister from it, but he didn't say how."

"Cistine pulled the augments from Pippet beyond the shock of withdrawal. But now..." he broke off, too choked for words.

"Well," Benedikt said carefully, "I suppose we'll have to return to the old regimen from the fronts now that the Key is...indisposed, and the well is open here. Wean them slowly from the augments. Not all will survive, but those that do..."

Thorne shook his head, too weary and grief-stricken to entertain the notion of dead children. "What else?"

"We've lost whole districts," Adeima said bleakly, "and entire storehouses were emptied to feed the slaves and acolytes while the Bloodwights were in command. Between that and the prey that's been driven out by the Balmond and by battle..."

"Difficult to feed everyone in the city," Thorne said. "I'll have Ariadne and my Tribunes begin an allotment. There's someone in Hellidom who has experience with rationing. Between them, they should be able to help see us through to the planting season."

"Assuming the Bloodwights don't show their faces before then," Bravis muttered. "I doubt this is over."

Thorne doubted it, too. But with Pippet and Cistine both wounded and unconscious, Faer dead and his cabal grieving, he couldn't think past tomorrow.

"We'll begin repairs in both the common and elite districts," Benedikt said. "There's no sense leaving one to molder while the other thrives. We'd like to have the High Tribunes oversee that, if you can spare yours, Thorne."

"Sander is on a personal assignment to Holmlond," Thorne said. "Once he returns, he's yours. Is that all?"

"One last thing." Bravis flicked a glance at Thorne's left hand. "This business with your choice of *valenar*..."

"I don't regret it," Thorne said. "And I couldn't nullify a blood oath even if I wanted to. Whether you all approve or not, Cistine is my *valenar*, and she always will be."

"Was this done as an act of defiance?" Valdemar asked. "To spit in our faces?"

"Defying you means nothing to me." Thorne curled his fist on the tabletop. "I did it because I love her."

"Talheim and Valgard joined by blood," Adeima said. "What does that mean for *you*, in the broad scheme of things?"

Thorne traced the marriage band around his finger, a weight he was slowly growing used to. "It means if she doesn't recover in time, your distrust and dislike of me as a Chancellor will cease to be a concern. And you will be dealing with Sander in my position again...while I fill Cistine's."

Leaving them speechless, he departed the room. The second his boots hit the threshold, he was running for his *valenar's* side.

He did not leave it again for many days.

CHAPTER
FIFTY-TWO

T HE SOUNDS OF cleaning and repairs wafted through the open apartment window despite the midnight hour when Ashe slipped inside, carrying a tray of tea. Every day for a week now, she'd hoped the smell of jasmine and citrus would coax Cistine up from her slumber. And every day, she was disappointed.

Cistine was growing thinner. Her skin was nearly translucent now, the blue in her veins waxing gray in the dim ghostlight from the table where Ashe set the tray. She poured the tea even knowing her princess wouldn't wake to drink it, just to give her own trembling hands something to do.

"Is that cup for me?"

Ashe banged her elbow on the table and whirled. Maleck sat behind the apartment door, half-masked in shadows, passing a piece of fruit from Cistine's untouched supper plate from hand to hand.

"I'm inclined to say no, since you just scared ten years off my life." Ashe blew out a rough breath. "What are you doing lurking in that corner?"

"Relieving Thorne of watch. He hasn't bathed in a week, the blood was still on his clothes. Kristoff finally wrestled him from the room when I swore to stand guard in his absence."

"After you already spent half the day helping with repairs?" Ashe handed one cup to him and kept the other, sinking down at his side. "When are *you* going to sleep?"

"When Pippet recovers. When Cistine wakes. When the noose lifts from our throats."

They glanced at the bed, both hoping their favorite gossip was feigning this deep sleep, quietly listening for a trace of her name on their lips. But even when they spoke it, she didn't stir.

"I can't believe there's *nothing* we can do," Ashe muttered. "With all those augments they're bottling day and night..."

"There is no augment that can heal this, the sleep is too deep. The wound is mended, but the body..." Maleck shook his head. "There's little telling what she truly endured while she bled. Only time and the gods will decide if she recovers." Grunting, Ashe leaned her head on his shoulder and let her eyes tumble shut. Maleck pressed a kiss to her hair. "How was your patrol with Bresnyar this evening?"

"Long. Dark." Ashe frowned at the memory. "Something doesn't feel right out there, but I can't put my finger on it. It's just...wrong. Like the world is sick. We came back as fast as we could."

"That makes two of us." That voice, not Maleck's, came from the doorway; Thorne had returned on quiet feet, toweling off his still-wet hair, his torso heaving as if he'd run all the way back. "Any change?"

"Nothing," Maleck said. "You ought to be asleep. If Kristoff finds you here, there will be Nimmus on your doorstep."

"Let him come. I won't sleep anywhere else." Thorne trudged to the bed and sank down, wrapping one arm around Cistine's body. He took her limp hand in his and kissed her knuckles, looking into her face. "Report."

"The Legion is standing guard around the wall," Ashe said. "Bres and I didn't find anything within ten miles of the city, and that's as far as we went before we felt like we were needed here."

"For all that they fought to possess Stornhaz," Maleck mused, "the Bloodwights surrendered it without the fury I anticipated."

"Because there was something else they wanted," Thorne said. "Something more important than a defensible city full of child acolytes and slaves."

Now they all stared at Cistine.

"Did we turn the tide of this war, or hand them the victory?" Ashe stood, squeezed Maleck's knee, and joined Thorne on the bed. She rubbed Cistine's feet, even tickled the arches the way her Princess hated—but that garnered no response, not even a flutter in the muscles. Ashe slid a hand around Cistine's leg and didn't breathe again until she felt the faint, stammering pulse behind her knee.

"I need your council, Ashe," Thorne said, and she glanced up warily. He chafed Cistine's knuckles with his thumb, slow and deliberate. "How long should we wait before sending her cipher to Talheim?"

Ashe stared at him. "You're *not* giving up on her."

Thorne's eyes flashed back to her, bright with anger. "Of course not. But as prince-consort, I have to think how she would want me to proceed with her kingdom's future, if this...doesn't rectify itself."

"She'll wake up."

"But the question is when. Talheim can't wait forever."

Ashe gritted her teeth. To even conceive of acting on Cistine's behalf felt too much like resignation.

Thorne's face softened, reading the resentment in her eyes. "*I* will wait a lifetime for her. But I can't demand her kingdom do the same."

Ashe rubbed her brow. He was right. *He* was thinking of Talheim, and she wasn't...an absurd turnaround from when they'd first met. "Just...wait another week. If it's still needed by then, Rozalie, Bres, and I can fly with you to Astoria to vouch for your claim."

Gratitude smoothed what remained of the tension in Thorne's face. "I would be honored to have your support."

She didn't bother telling him just how badly he'd need it. Or what it would do to Talheim's royal family if a disgraced Warden returned on dragonback to tell them their sole heir, their only daughter, had died undoing all her grandfather's war had done.

CHAPTER
FIFTY-THREE

WAITING FOR PIPPET to recover was one of the longest pauses in Tatiana's life. Nowhere felt right, safe, or entirely real; not the apartment she and Quill had once shared, not Pippet's chamber where they sat vigil whenever they weren't watching over Cistine; not the princess's somber rooms, either, or Morten's old home and shop, so burned and torn.

Yet that was where Tatiana found herself when the tension within the courthouse and among the cabal became too much: standing in the doorway of the house she'd grown up in, gazing around at the cratered walls, scorched roof, and shattered inventions. So much talent, so much passion, so many dreams wasted.

"I'm afraid my home looks no better."

Tatiana shot a glare over her shoulder as Kadlin picked her way across the ruined threshold to join her. "What are you doing here?"

"Hoping to find something to lift your father's spirits." Kadlin pocketed her hands in her fine wool coat, shrugging. "He says he can't bring himself to see what the Bloodwights and their warriors made of this place. I thought perhaps if I found even one invention not destroyed, it would convince him we still have hope."

"I didn't realize you were in the business of inspiring people now."

"I came when you called, didn't I?"

That was true, though it did not utterly soothe the fester of hurt in Tatiana's heart from the first betrayal from this woman she'd come to see as a part of her future. Even her family.

"Despite what you think, Tatiana, I *do* care about your father. About you," Kadlin added gently.

"I know," Tatiana muttered. "But I've had my fill of people I love hurting me because they didn't have any other choice." Kadlin, Pippet, and Maleck...what they'd done to her father, to her, to Quill was a wound that never stopped bleeding.

Kadlin sidled up to Tatiana's side. Somber and quiet, she gazed into Morten's ruined home. "I don't wish to be a weapon against the people I love any more than you can bear to be hurt again. When I told my family in Blaykrone what I did, they were disgusted with me. So I suppose I do what I do not only for your forgiveness, but theirs."

Tatiana frowned. "Why are you telling me this?"

"Because I want you to understand I have nothing left in my life that can be used to make me turn against you." Kadlin laughed wretchedly. "I've lost my family. *Heimli Nyfadengar* follows your father now, not me."

Tatiana's arms dropped from their cross, shock dragging her jaw down. "But—I sent *you* that letter, not him."

"Yes, and I showed it to him and begged him to help. It was the first time we'd spoken in months." Another rough, unhappy laugh. "Trying to save everyone cost me everyone."

"Maybe." Tatiana tucked her elbows tight to her body. "But you earned something by taking that letter to the guild: my gratitude."

A flicker of a surprised smile turned Kadlin's mouth. "That is *very* precious. Something I don't want to lose again."

"I know I said I'm tired of loving people who hurt me," Tatiana added. "But I can't forget I was that person once, too." She rested her temple on the doorframe, keeping her eyes on Kadlin. "So, maybe I don't have a standard to hold you to that I haven't fallen short of. But you're out here trying to bring my papa something to hope for. That's two reasons I'm grateful."

This time, it was she who smiled. And it felt good—healing.

"Why don't we see what we can dig up from this wreckage?" she offered. "Easier for two than one."

A tentative and genuine grin put to death some of the pain in Kadlin's eyes. "I'd like that very much, Tatiana."

It was nearly sunset when they returned to the courthouse, fingers full of splinters and carrying with them a small box, its latch lid engraved with Morten's name. Of all the things they could've saved, Tatiana was glad it was this. When she'd explained its purpose to Kadlin, she'd listened in eager-faced wonder and trembled with the same excitement as Tatiana.

They found Morten in Kanslar's dining room, clustered with several members of *Heimli Nyfadengar* and poring over plans and manuals, and he looked up at their arrival. The tired warmth of his smile wrapped around Tatiana better than any soft blanket or steaming mug of tea after these long, heartbroken days.

"Where have you two been?" He hopped up and hurried to embrace Tatiana against his side.

"Home," she said. "Seeing what could be salvaged."

Kadlin whipped the box from her pocket and held it out, eyes shining. "We found this for you, Morten."

"Actually," Tatiana added, "*Kadlin* found it. This was all her idea."

Morten's eyes softened when he took the box and laid it on the table. He flipped open the lid with trembling hands and stared inside, jaw quivering. "My inking tool."

"Tatiana's told me all about it." Kadlin stepped forward, hand outstretched as if to take his shoulder—then hesitated and let it fall. "Mort, if the guild could replicate this design, think of what we could do for this army. Even if it was just a few simple runes on each warrior's body, somewhere for the augments to go..."

"So many lives saved." Eyes shining, Morten looked up at her again.

"With enough Atrasat ink, it's possible."

Kadlin drew her shoulders back. "Then there's no time to waste. With your permission, I'll spread the word to the inventors."

He swallowed and shut the lid. "Why don't we tell them together?"

Kadlin sucked in her breath. "Of course. I'd be honored to."

The room blurred before Tatiana when her father took Kadlin's hand and squeezed it. "Thank you, Kadlin."

"It was the least I could do."

"Tatiana." Aden's voice from the dining room doorway drew her attention sharply. He'd arrived soundless, but he breathed hard, gray eyes silvering with relief. "Pippet's awake. She's asking for you."

Tatiana's heart lurched. "I have to go. Papa, could we talk after supper? There's something I want to tell you."

"Of course. Anything for you, *Tatiyani*." Morten grinned. "Go see her."

She hated to know she'd be the death of that smile. But it was time to tell him about the child she'd lost—his grandchild.

Sucking in a deep breath, she slipped out past Aden, bumping knuckles with him in passing.

It was good to see these familiar corridors livelier, almost approaching bustle again. For the first few days back in the city, everyone had been too afraid to leave their apartments, keeping odd hours and stealing out whenever they thought no one else was around. For once, she was happy to elbow through crowded hallways and bump shoulders with elites. The division of rank and wealth was a forgotten thing, all of them made equal by war. A few familiar voices even greeted her on her way to Pippet's room.

And that, thank the stars, was no longer quiet either.

"Look who's awake," she breathed out a gust of relief in the doorway, and Pippet and Quill both looked up at her from the bed—her tucked under his arm, his cheek resting on her hair. Tears ran down Pippet's cheeks, and at the crooked tilt of Quill's mouth, Tatiana knew he'd just confirmed Faer's death.

Heart aching, she landed on the bed, wrapping her arms around Pippet. "Thank the stars you're awake. How do you feel?"

"Sore," she mumbled. "Where's Cistine? Quill won't tell me."

Tatiana glanced at him over his sister's head. His helpless grimace told her he was no surer how to answer than Tatiana was.

"Cistine is...recovering," she said carefully.

"I need to see her."

"Is that why you left Hellidom?" Quill's tone was mild, but his eyes flinty. "You came straight into the middle of a battle to find Cistine?"

"*Yes.*" A vein of impatience seamed Pippet's voice. "I came to find her and I have to talk to her right *now.*"

"You can't." Quill's jaw worked for a moment, pain flashing in his gaze. "She's asleep, Pip. Been asleep for a week."

Pippet's hands dropped. She stilled so absolutely, Tatiana's hackles bristled; the motionless intent reminded her far too much of the girl in the bird mask inside *Selv Torfjel.* "What did she do? Did she...Quill, tell me she didn't open the Door!" When he didn't speak, Pippet's head snapped toward her. "*Tati!*"

"It's all right, Pippet," she soothed. "She chose this. The Bloodwights didn't do this to her."

"Yes, they did! This was their plan!"

"No, it wasn't. It was Cistine's."

"Then why didn't you *stop* her?"

"We needed the augments." Quill laid a hand on Pippet's head. "It was the only way to turn this fight in our favor."

"You didn't turn it—you handed it to the Bloodwights!" Pippet swiped away his hand. "I heard them before, I heard them saying if they couldn't *take* Cistine, they'd make her so desperate she'd open one of the Doors!"

"We know." Quill's voice strained for patience. "But we have control of the well. Everything's all right."

"It. Is. Not." She whipped her head toward her brother, eyes wide with dread. "You just have the city, and that's not enough, Quill! Don't you understand?" She seized him by the collar. "If the Key opens one Door, it opens them *all.*"

CHAPTER
FIFTY-FOUR

THORNE'S MIND AND body had succumbed to an impenetrable fog ever since his meeting with the Chancellors. He drifted through the haze, short strokes of clarity occasionally moving him with blistering intensity toward one goal or another: assigning his Tribunes around the city, placing the cabal on rotation to guard the Door, having his wounds seen to whenever Aden and Ariadne reminded him. And when he stood beneath the spray of the ancient faucet that hadn't spat water since the last war, watching days of crusted blood and grime run off his battered chest, he'd had the sudden notion to ask Ashe about when and how to move on Cistine's behalf with the cipher.

Now he was here, standing inside a courtroom with Vaclav, Tadeas, Njal, Enar, Gunther, Hafgrim, and Aden, swimming up through a suffocating torrent of fog and breaking into choking waves of shock instead.

All the wells were open.

All of them.

Ashe, newly returned from a scouting mission to confirm the report from Pippet, stood between him and Aden. Her voice dragged Thorne back from the spinning vortex of disbelief as she addressed the Chancellors.

"At least three wells were open in Lataus," Ashe said. "So I think it's safe to assume that's true of the others as well."

"How is this possible?" Valdemar demanded. "How did we not know?"

"Consider that the Bloodwights are the ones who sealed the wells in the first place," Aden said. "They were not the ones who agreed to it, that was the Chancellors' doing. It's no surprise they plotted a long strategy to reopen all the wells at once."

"Build an army of Valgard's criminals and children," Adeima murmured, "take control, find the Key, then unleash its blood on the nearest Door, claiming them all at once."

Thorne dragged a hand through his hair. "Then we laid siege to this city for *nothing*. We could have gone to any accessible well." And Ariadne would not have fallen at the *Aeoprast's* hands, and Cistine would not have needed to deplete the augments to save her. She would be standing with them now.

Aden clapped him on the back. "We didn't know."

"How could we?" Benedikt scowled. "Those stars-forsaken Bloodwights played us all for fools."

"More than we realize, perhaps," Adeima agreed. "Why should they sacrifice their armies holding Stornhaz when there are countless wells open across Valgard now? It's no wonder they fled the city at our siege."

"We gave them augments," Bravis grunted. "We gave them everything we took for ourselves."

"Where are they now?" High Tribune Taj of Yager stepped up beside her Chancelloress. Her *valenar*, Dayo, rested his hand on her back, his dark eyes narrowed on Ashe.

"Bresnyar and I spotted Balmond near Jovadalsa. Wherever they've been until now, they're not hiding anymore."

"It's an invitation," Thorne said. "To end this, one way or another."

"I say we march out and meet them on our own timing. Our terms," Hallvard of Traisende growled.

"I agree. If they don't know that we know of the wells already, they soon will," Adeima said. "They won't hesitate to draw us to them by any means necessary, including strikes on our villages again."

"And this time, you don't have someone as powerful as a Bloodwight fighting to defend them," Ashe pointed out.

"We must force a confrontation, then," Valdemar said. "We have the augments now."

"But we lack the Key." Bravis glanced at Thorne.

"If we devastate their forces, we can render the Bloodwights themselves all but useless, even if we cannot kill them," Adeima said. "They will retreat for another twenty years to rebuild their army, and perhaps by then, the Key will return to us."

"Or we travel to Talheim," Benedikt offered. "If the keying is in the blood, then Cyril Novacek—"

"*No*," Thorne snarled, digging the heel of his hand into his opposite shoulder, pressing on a wound from the siege until clarity tunneled back out from the panic of the possibility that in twenty years, Cistine still might not come back to him. "Talheim's King is untrained in augmentation, and he may be all they have left to lead them. We are not compromising our allies for this. It's our fight."

Adeima nodded. "I agree. Crippling Talheim's monarchy does us no good if their King isn't trained...if he would even come."

"Then you would have us fight?" Bravis directed the question, and his heavy stare, at Thorne.

"I don't see that we have a choice. Retaking Stornhaz was never going to end this war, we knew that. We've reformed the lines and replenished our supplies. Now we drive the Bloodwights out."

"A last confrontation to decide the fate of Valgard," Bravis agreed.

It was Aden whose eyes Thorne met this time, finding the same unease that had sparked in him the moment the words left his mouth.

He truly didn't see how they had a choice. And if Kristoff had taught them anything, it was how forced decisions often led to the bitterest ends.

CHAPTER
FIFTY-FIVE

Aden HATED WHAT he had to bring back to the others...news to worsen the sour mood around Cistine's bed. When they entered, Quill, Tatiana, Maleck, Ariadne, and Kristoff had all gathered. Aden met his father's eyes across the room; one look held for too long, and Kristoff crumbled forward on the edge of the bed, mouth cupped in his hands. Tatiana sat up tall beside him, weight balanced on her palms, frowning. "What's the word?"

"It's true. The wells are open," Thorne said. "All of them."

Quill turned his hair across his head. "Stars-damned opportunists."

"Not opportunists. Strategists," Maleck murmured from his seat against the pillow, reclining beside Cistine. "The Bloodwights have orchestrated this from the start."

"And what is *our* strategy?" Ariadne demanded. "There are hundreds of wells across Valgard. We have *one*. They've likely spent the last week harvesting night and day."

"Both sides are topfull with augments for the first time in two decades," Thorne said. "Both will be reckless using them."

"Is that supposed to scare us?" Quill folded his arms behind his head, leaning back against the pillows on Cistine's other side. For the first time since Pippet's injury and Faer's death, eagerness edged his voice. "I've been tired of running for months. It's long past time we had the kind of fight our ancestors took for granted: face to face on a battlefield."

"I agree," Ariadne said, "but what about Cistine?"

The question plummeted through dead silence, and Aden watched Thorne's face, knowing it would be the first to betray any hint of an answer.

The pain in his eyes said it all.

"We're leaving her behind?" Ashe snapped.

"We have no choice." Thorne's gaze dragged reluctantly to her. "We'll leave her in the care of the medicos who stay behind. Pippet, too. She'll be safer than anyone else in this kingdom on the day of the battle."

"And what if she wakes up terrified or in pain without one of us here?"

"I hate to be the practical one," Tatiana said, "but we have no reason to believe she's any more likely to wake up in the next week than she did in the last one. And we can't postpone a war on her behalf."

"If she does wake up, she'll find Pip," Quill added. "They'll have each other."

"Asheila," Maleck said gently, "the battlefield is no place for an unconscious princess. She cannot come."

Ashe scowled. "I know that."

"Then there's no conversation to have." Ariadne pushed herself up from the wall. "One of us should see personally to who cares for her, Thorne."

"I'll do it," he said. "Ashe, rally the Wing Legions and meet me in the courtyard, I have a mission for you. Tati, see if there's anything the Guild can do for us. Ari, the *visnprests*. And the rest of you..."

"Pray," Ariadne murmured. "With all your might."

A drum of footsteps sounded in the hall, their weight and bearing familiar, and Sander burst into the room with robes askew and hair disheveled, the crackle of a wind augment still hanging in the folds of his robes. "Thorne! What in the stars is happening? I heard that the wells—*all* of them are—"

"Aden, you tell him." Thorne's gaze was fixed on the bed, on his unconscious *valenar*.

Aden rose and slung an arm around the High Tribune's shoulders, steering him out into the deserted hall. They walked some distance in silence, passing frantic elites moving through color-glazed sunlight falling from the mosaic windows, and at last they found an empty hall on the lowest level of the wing.

"Welcome back," Aden said at last. "How is Mira?"

"Fine, hale, and whole." Sander shrugged him off. "This is not about her. Tell me what you know."

They halted, facing one another, and Aden back his hair. "It's true. The wells are open. At week's end, we move our forces to Eben and finish this."

Sander fell back against the wall, a trembling hand passing over his mouth. "I just...I can't—stars damn it *all*, Aden. Mira is with child."

Aden stared at him, struggling to make sense of those words. "Your child?"

"Well, it's certainly not yours, *baesj*-for-brains!" Sander snapped. "Yes, *mine*. I...after Braggos, I could hardly think, much less eat or sleep. It was a difficult night and I...had a wind augment..."

"You stole a wind augment to go tumble with your *valenar*?"

"Oh, spare me. We both know Mira is more than worth breaking a few laws for."

"Be that as it may...no, nevermind, your idiocy isn't worth my breath." Aden pinched the bridge of his nose, praying for patience. "How is she?"

"The sickness just started a few weeks ago, and she's become much more moody. Did you notice when you visited Holmlond?"

"I've always thought she was moody."

Sander struck him upside the head. "That's my *valenar* you're speaking of."

"I know." Aden rubbed his head. "I know. And I'm sorry you have to do this, Sander. But we have no choice, we're Tribunes. Our Chancellor and our Court need us."

"Do you think I'm unaware?" Sander's eyes flashed with anger and frustration, sorrow and fear. "If there's anything this war has taught me, it's that love in times of peace is a gift. Love in times of war is a death sentence."

"I don't believe that. Love, any love, keeps us alive."

"You didn't see Mira's face when I left. What my absence does to her, what this war does to *us*...it's tearing me apart, Aden. But I can't afford to put her wants before the kingdom's needs, can I? Even if it destroys us both."

He'd never heard such pain in Sander's voice, as if he carried a weight suddenly too great to comprehend. As if leaving Mira behind had cost him everything.

"You do not break," Aden growled, and Sander's tawny eyes cut sharply to him. "For her sake. For your child's sake. For Thorne's. For *mine*. You are our High Tribune, and you *do not break*. We stand together, we win this battle, we end the war and come home, and you raise that child knowing their father is a hero. Victory is only possible if we hold fast to who and what we are. And what we fight for."

Sander held his stare for a long moment. "A better Chancellor."

"A better future." Aden gripped his shoulder. "I still believe in that."

Sander nodded. "So do I. Moreso now than ever."

"I can't imagine," Aden snorted quietly. "Congratulations to the both of you. It's high time we had some good news."

Sander surged forward, trapping Aden in an embrace so fierce he did not push back from it at once; and Sander, with a tinge of humor his voice, murmured, "This is from Mira."

They stepped back awkwardly, dusting off their clothes, and Aden grumbled, "Don't you have patrols to assemble? Things to do?"

"Apparently, yes. The first of which is to call a meeting of Kanslar's Tribunes to assure our Chancellor has everything he needs." Sander winked. "I'll see you in the dining room in half an hour."

CHAPTER
FIFTY-SIX

I T WAS TOO little time, and somehow endless as well. Ashe hardly slept during her mission from Thorne, which took all of the two days they had to spare; when she returned, it was a wild reunion with Maleck, a welcoming back and a farewell she tried not to think of too deeply. She woke from a short, deep slumber to him already awake, sitting on the edge of the bed and yanking on his clothes. Sweat streaked his back, another nightmare rattling his body and the mattress beneath him.

Frowning, Ashe laid a hand on his back. "Mal?"

"It's time," he said gruffly.

He was right; there was a hum within the city's heart, the movements of thousands of warriors traveling on barges and dragonback beyond the curtain wall where wind augments would carry them to Eben's plains. Some had already begun to call the place of their meeting the Deathmarch, from an ancient Valgardan story...a place where gods clashed with their enemies, where battles decided fates of whole kingdoms.

Fitting...and terrifying.

The tremors found Ashe too when she rolled from the bed and pulled on her armor, fumbling with the familiar clasps and buttons, cursing when her rattling fingers failed to tie her armored scarf. She'd been in plenty of battles, this one shouldn't frighten her so much. But with everything they had to lose, and everything they were leaving behind...

She felt Maleck behind her even before he spoke, his warmth folding around her. His fingers brushed hers, stilling her uncoordinated movements. "Let me."

He drew the knot loosely at her nape, fingers grazing her neck when he tucked the scarf into her collar. Then his hands slid down her shoulders, down her back, and rested on her hips. She shut her eyes when he banded his arms around her waist from behind, draping his chin over her shoulder.

"We will survive this," he murmured against her ear.

Her heart kicked out of beat, stepping into a familiar dance with reckless, senseless hope. "You don't know that. None of us do."

"*I* do. We've always found our way back to each other."

She reached back for him, wove her fingers into his warrior braids and held his cheek against her head, breathing in the cedar and charcoal scent of him. And she hated every gods-forsaken second she'd wasted over the past year, waiting to love him with her entire heart.

She should have known better. She should have stolen thousands more minutes with him.

Down the hall, someone shouted for them. Another shudder spiraled through Ashe's body, tightening her fingers in Maleck's hair, and a secret slipped over her lips. "I'm so gods-damned terrified we're going to lose this battle." The mission Thorne had sent her on was pure desperation. It had made it clear just how dire their circumstances were.

Maleck pressed his lips to the hollow behind her ear. "*Mereszar.* Remember what you are." He rested his face in her hair for a moment, then took her hand and tugged her around to face the door. For perhaps the last time, they went to meet their cabal.

They'd agreed already where they would convene before Kanslar's departure, and there was a funeral stillness inside Cistine's room when they entered. No one looked as if they'd slept well; dark circles stamped under every eye, faces harrowed, mouths downturned. For Thorne, her heart broke the most. He leaned against the edge of the dining table, head bowed into one hand as if he lacked the strength to raise his eyes to the bed and see

Cistine lying there, so gaunt and *lifeless*, knowing he would leave her behind.

"Well," Tatiana said after a beat, "it's time."

"Pip will be here the moment she wakes up this morning, and she won't leave until we come back," Quill added.

Ashe swallowed at the memory of saying farewell to Pippet the night before so she wouldn't have to rise and watch them go; how tightly they'd clung to each other, how Pippet had made her vow to come back. She prayed the girl would sleep straight through the morning, through the battle, and wake to a world free of Bloodwight shadows.

One by one, the cabal stepped forward to pay their farewells to Cistine in lingering touches and whispers on a deaf ear. Ashe was sharply aware that every goodbye could be their last; some of them might not return from this fight. And even if by some intercession of the gods they did, Cistine might not be alive when they came home.

She couldn't move to the bed even when Maleck did, squeezing Cistine's shoulder and murmuring in her ear. It was only when Thorne gestured her forward that Ashe realized he was waiting for her to give them a moment's privacy; she finally forced herself to sit on the bed, chafing her necklace chain against her throat. "A year ago, I would've been relieved to have some excuse to keep you safe from a fight. Now there's nowhere I'd rather have you than guarding my back. I just can't believe you'd sleep through the end of the gods-forsaken world." She stripped the starstone from her neck and tucked it into Cistine's limp fist. "So this is for you, just in case you want to come and join us on the Deathmarch. Eben's plains, Princess. Where they took Julian from us. I'll be waiting."

She kissed Cistine's knuckles and strode to the door, pausing to clap Thorne on the shoulder in passing. "I'll keep everyone moving in the right direction. Take as much time as you need."

When Ashe glanced back from the doorway, he'd already lowered himself onto the bed, bent with his brow pressed to Cistine's. His words were too low to hear, but judging by the unsteady rise and fall of his back, he was weeping.

Quietly, Ashe shut the door.

CHAPTER
FIFTY-SEVEN

T HE SPRING RAINS came sudden and hard, soaking the army and leaving Tatiana sour in mood while she waited with the cabal outside the city to travel to the Deathmarch. Packs of augurs moved the army in batches, ripping across the plains in a matter of moments, gobbling the rain in swirling vortices along their wake.

She hoped they weren't all being dropped into the middle of a massacre, but who knew? Maybe they were all going to die on the same ground where Julian had given up his life.

Shaking the rain from her curls, she glared up at the heavy sky. If she'd been superstitious, she might've wondered if the gods mourned the end of Valgard at the dawn of the Bloodwights' ascension to absolute power.

Quill paced at her back, raking a hand through his hair. "Does it make me a terrible person if I wish Cistine were here?"

"Knowing her, she'd wish the same thing," Ariadne sighed.

A horn blew from the wall, signaling them to make the journey to the plains. As one, the cabal broke the wind augments against their armor—all but Maleck and Ashe, sliding onto Bresnyar's back. At last, their Chancellor looked away from the horizon, eyes skipping to each of them in turn, full of sorrow and resignation.

"I hope you all know how much I love you," he murmured. "With everything I am. It's been an honor greater than any Judgement Seat to have fought and lived with you. And it will be a privilege to die beside you if that is our fate today."

There was no fear in their faces, only solemn acceptance and the quiet surety that wherever they went today, to Nimmus or Cenowyn or beyond, they'd go together.

"The honor has been ours, Thorne," Sander said.

"And the privilege," Kristoff added. "To see you all become the warriors you were born to be."

"To Sillakove," Aden said. "To a better tomorrow."

"To a future," Quill finished. "No matter the cost."

Tatiana laid a hand on her empty womb. *To* your *future.*

With eyes shut tight, she let the wind carry her off to war.

The sky was pitch-black fringed in scarlet, the echo of every thunderclap like bone drums resounding above Valgard's army on the Deathmarch.

Before them, the enemy lines arrayed beneath the coming storm.

Blood Hive criminals. Corrupted children. Blinded prisoners of the Lightless Pit who felt their way ahead by skeins of augments. Balmond leashed by *Svarkyst* chains that would be loosed in an instant. And somewhere behind those ranks, the Bloodwights, saddled with more power than they had any right to possess—the greedy theft of Cistine's sacrifice.

Disgusted, fearful murmurs rippled down the Valgardan lines, punctuated by the sharp draw of steel. On Tatiana's left, Maleck grimaced, wiping his knuckles across his brow. "This wetland burns with augmentation."

"Is this going to be a problem for you?" Quill asked.

Maleck hesitated for a moment, and Tatiana gripped her blades tighter, nerves rattling.

"Stay with me, and I'll endure," Maleck said at last.

"Whatever comes," Aden swore.

"Even that?" Sander gestured forward, and Tatiana shaded her eyes against the rainfall. Her pulse kicked when she spotted a dark shape gliding ahead of the ranks, toward the middle of the Deathmarch.

"Bloodwight," Ariadne said softly.

"The *Aeoprast*," Maleck murmured.

As one, the Chancellors stepped forward, each flanked by a pair of guards. When Tatiana glanced at Thorne, he flicked his head to her, then beckoned to Aden.

Her stomach fluttered with fear when she crossed the field at his side.

"Chancellors," the *Aeoprast* greeted when they halted before him. "I see you know of the wells."

"What do you want?" Bravis growled.

"To offer you an opportunity to surrender. Benevolent gods require no unnecessary sacrifices."

"You aren't gods yet," Adeima spat. "Nor will you ever be."

The *Aeoprast* swung its skulled head toward her. "I would be careful if I were you. You've seen what we do to your kind."

At Adeima's flanks, two of her spies, Astrid and Liv, fingered their weapons. Adeima fixed the creature with an icy glare. "You will pay blood for blood today."

"A Chancelloress should not make promises she can't keep. It discourages confidence. And you need them confident and compliant, because if they do not follow your orders to stand down now, they will be slaughtered without mercy."

"And if Valgard surrenders, what then?" Valdemar demanded.

"Then you may join us in bringing the other kingdoms into subjection as willing warriors in our army."

"You already have an army," Bravis said.

"We will need more when Talheim and Mahasar oppose us."

Thorne slid a step closer to the Bloodwight. Aden unleashed his sabers, and Tatiana tensed to strike. Quill's gaze branded her back; if she raised her weapon an inch higher, he'd be at her side in a heartbeat, and the battle would begin.

"Let me make this very clear to you." Thorne's voice was dark, deathly soft. "Talheim is mine to protect. You and anyone else who dreams of breaking their borders will have to break through my guard first."

The *Aeoprast* canted his head. "Such a loyal sentiment. Where, I wonder, is the one who was *born* to protect Talheim with her very blood? Didn't she come with you?"

Tatiana gripped her sword so tightly, her knuckles ached. Aden's arm brushed hers, a steadying motion commanding calm.

"You may have killed my father," Thorne said, his countenance unbreaking, "but I am not him. You shouldn't underestimate me."

The Bloodwight dipped his head just slightly. "Does this arrogant boy speak for all of you?"

Fleeting glances exchanged down the line. Then Adeima said, "Valgard does not surrender to threats."

"Your pride will be your undoing."

"And your arrogance will be yours." Thorne drew his own blade, gesturing toward the creature with it. "At my hand."

"Doubtful."

A skin-crawling flash moved across Tatiana's body like icy fingertips trailing along her essence, and Maleck shouted from the ranks. A roar blistered the sky in answer, and a stream of dragonfire set the grass alight between the Chancellors and the Bloodwight. The *Aeoprast* jerked back, and the clammy fingers of a blood augment released from Tatiana's body, letting her fall back on her heels.

The sky opened up in bursts of gemstone scales as the Oadmarkaic Legion dropped from cover, streaking toward the enemy flanks with Ashe at the head. Tatiana grabbed Thorne's arm and shoved Aden with her shoulder. "*Go!*"

They sprinted back to the ranks as the Legions circled overhead. Thousands of swords, maces, axes, and polearms glinted in the last of the light rapidly vanishing under the cloudbank. Flickers and pops of color moved between dark-armored bodies as flagons broke and augments unleashed on both sides.

Tatiana skidded to a halt beside Quill, and he raked a hand through her curls, pulling her head back until their eyes met. "Are you all right?"

"For now." She turned to face the enemy army. The *Aeoprast* had melted back into the ranks, and when he reached the back where the rest of the Bloodwights lingered like cowards, the fight would begin.

Quill rested his swords on his shoulders, tonguing a cinnamon stick across his lips as they watched the *mirothadt* lurking across the wetland. "I almost wish someone would give a grand speech."

"There isn't time for one," Thorne said. "You all know what to do. Bring down the criminals. Spare the children. Don't die yourselves."

The notion had seemed so much saner when they'd discussed it in Stornhaz.

"Any last words, Saddlebags?" Quill asked.

"Yes." She leaned her shoulder briefly into his. "I shouldn't have waited so stars-damned long to kiss you that first time."

"Didn't I do the kissing?"

"Not from where I was laying."

"Then maybe you should have been on top of me and not the other way around."

The riving screech of a maddened animal cut off her reply. The first Balmond took flight, bulky wings spread, cumbersome body shooting up toward the dragons.

"This is it." Quill spun his swords. "I'll see you all at the Sable Gates."

"First one there is the last one inside," Tatiana said, and Quill glanced down at her.

His face stopped her breath.

A thousand lifetimes of love in that stare, full of winter storms and summer kisses and battles fought side by side. Uncountable nights tangled up in the sheets together. Calm breakfasts and slow kisses and grappling sessions that turned to lovemaking in their Blaykrone home. Every day of the hundred years they should have had together, captured in his eyes.

Then the front line of *mirothadt* started forward, fire and water and lightning storming the air. The Balmond launched skyward with piercing screams, and the Legions swooped to intercept them.

Tatiana looked down the lines at the faces of her friends one last time. Then she gripped her weapons and did what no daughter of medicos and tinkers should ever have to do—but she'd chosen it for herself. For the memory of her child. For all those who might come after this day.

She went to war.

CHAPTER
FIFTY-EIGHT

*T*HE WELLS ARE *open…all of them.*

Both sides are topfull with augments for the first time in two decades.

It's long past time we had the kind of fight our ancestors took for granted:
face to face on a battlefield.

The battlefield is no place for an unconscious princess. She cannot come…

So long, Stranger. No use being careful this time.

Thank you for never giving up on me, Yani.

You are truly my sister in spirit. I will carry you with me always.

We owe this chance to you, Logandir. *We will not squander it.*

Whatever happens to us, you do not break.

I just can't believe you'd sleep through the end of the gods-forsaken world…so
this is for you. Eben's plains, Princess. Where they took Julian from us. I'll be
waiting.

I love you. With my whole heart, for my whole life. I fight for my kingdom
and for yours. And if I perish in that fight, then gods take me. But as much as it's
in my power, I will come back. I'm still not ready to say goodbye to you…I will
never be ready to say goodbye.

Wait for me, Wildheart.

Just wait for me.

∽⌒∾

It was one of her terrible nightmares, with King Jad standing over her bed, laughing while he smothered her.

She couldn't call out, couldn't beg for help from the ones who tickled her feet, clasped her hands, teased her hair from her brow, or stroked her cheeks. She couldn't answer the desperate need for the lips that pressed against hers, staining her senses with the briny taste of tears.

Jad held her paralyzed, his hand clapped to her face, stifling her pitiful cries as he pressed her deeper into silence after that faraway kiss, broken only by the stirring of distant motion, like wind through newly-budded leaves.

She wandered through one of the citrus orchards to the south of Astoria, bathed in sunlight. The pickers had gone into their station houses to escape the midday heat, ladders leaning against the thick trunks like casual drunkards against tavern walls. Countless healthy oranges littered the ground, and she scooped one up and peeled it.

"Such a waste, isn't it, when something precious and perfect is left to rot?"

She turned, teeth sunk into the orange, facing the old woman who ambled toward her between the gnarled trunks. Slowly, she pried her jaws apart. "Did I die? Is this Cenowyn?"

Baba Kallah pierced the dirt with her cane, peering up at the leaves. "Not quite. You stand with a foot on the pyre."

She had expected that. After so long lying prone under King Jad's heavy hand, listening to the conversations swirl around her... "Where are they? Where's Thorne?"

Sadness lurked under the heavy folds of Baba Kallah's face. "Come. I will show you."

They walked side by side through the orchard, while clouds stormed across the face of the sun, blotting out every trace of light. The wind turned sharply cold, sending her dress flapping against her knees, its silver dapples dancing on the edge of her vision.

Baba Kallah parted the hedges around the orchard. "Look."

She knew what waited even before she saw it.

She heard the cries, the screams, the hack of blades through flesh, and remembered the clench of Julian's hand around hers in a dark vision as she struggled through the brambles and tumbled out on the crown of a hill, staring at the massacre below.

Nazvaldolya.

"They went without me!" she cried.

"They had no choice. The time has come."

"Are they losing? Are they *dying*?"

The pause labored with the distant sounds of battle, the birthing pains of the Bloodwights' heinous vision struggling to make its way into their world.

"Yes," Baba Kallah said softly. "Yes, they are."

The orange thudded from her fingers. She covered her mouth with both hands and sank to her knees, the wind ripping mercilessly through her hair. Lightning augments plucked dragons from the sky, hurling them down to crush their own ranks. Warriors fell, ripped apart, the hope of the kingdoms winking out like stars—one life at a time.

"I have to do something," she whimpered. "Without the Key..."

"The Key cannot save them."

Shock evaporated her tears. "You don't mean that."

"You must hear me, *Yani*. The Key *alone* cannot save them. The Key opened the wells. But would the Princess have bled on that Door without knowing the havoc it would cause?"

"Fine! If I have to go after them as the Princess, then I'll do it!"

Baba Kallah shook her head. "The Princess lacks the strength for war."

"Then as a future queen, I'll—"

"The Queen has the strength, but lacks the Key's determination to do *all* that must be done."

"Then *what do you want from me*?" she sobbed. "When Thorne Named me, *you* said I could do this! How do I save them if *everything* I am is *wrong*?"

Baba Kallah slowly knelt beside her, leaning heavily on the cane. At the touch of the old woman's hand, she forced herself to look at the battle again.

Though she searched the ranks for a glimmer of silver hair, she saw none.

"How do I save them?" she repeated. "Tell me how to save them!"

Baba Kallah picked up the discarded orange and rolled it in her palm. "Such a versatile fruit, oranges. You can bake with them, cook with them, or eat them raw. Yet they look so simple, only skin and flesh and seeds. What is the thing if not the sum of its parts?"

The sounds of the fight below grew suddenly dim. She twisted to stare at Baba Kallah in the strange quiet.

"A book is pages and binding and ink," Baba Kallah added. "Take any one of those things away, and it ceases to be a book."

"A garden is soil and seed and water," she murmured. "Without all of those pieces, nothing grows."

"Then what are you, *Yani*? Princess, Queen, or Key?"

Every word brought a different lash of vigor to her body—a tide of hope, a blaze of power, an eternity of purpose. Her past, her present, her future. All that she had been since birth; all that she was now, by choice; all that she would become when she took the throne.

For so long, she had seen them as separate entities: the Princess of books and beauty. The Queen of ice and stone. The Key of life and power. The people's hope. Talheim's savior. The wells' defender.

But that was the lesson she'd failed to learn all this time.

"I'm all of them at once," she said. "Princess, Queen, *and* Key. And those things by themselves...none of them can save our kingdoms. But I can. When I'm all of them together, *I can!*"

"Then tell me, *Yani*, not *what* you are," Baba Kallah said. "Tell me *who* you are."

Her eyes flashed open again. "I am Cistine Novacek of Talheim. And that's who can save the kingdoms."

Baba Kallah smiled. "When the three are one."

"Cistine Novacek," she shouted to the battlefield, to the world, to the enemies below. "The Wild Heart of Flame. *Wildheart!*"

Light pierced her vision for the first time in so many days, Cistine screamed at its glare. Someone else screamed, too, and a tray smashed to the floor with the distinct crack of a shattering teapot. Cistine swiped her arm across her eyes and struggled upright, her body hollow, her bones aching.

Someone grabbed her shoulders. "Princess Cistine, don't move. I'll fetch a medico!" The voice was unfamiliar, but the blur of attire looked faintly like a servant's uniform. Footsteps retreated, and Cistine rubbed her bleary eyes and took deep, calming breaths as panic surged and sank through her. There was something heavy and smooth in her fist, the cord wrapping her wrist; she squinted, bringing it into vague shape.

Ashe's starstone.

She tossed off the blankets and struggled to her feet, barely registering that she was in her old room, her garden box rote at the bedside, the rafters empty of their old decorations.

Her cabal needed her. *Valgard* needed Cistine Novacek.

She staggered to the window. The sky was gray, throttled with pregnant stormclouds. There was no way of telling how long she'd slept...if she was already too late. But she brought the starstone to her lips anyway. "Bres, if you can hear me, come back to Stornhaz. *Now!*"

Then she threw the starstone around her neck, lashed Nail and her augment pouch to her waist, and grabbed her sword. Every movement was a new source of weakness and frustration; she was so gods-forsaken *thirsty*, like she'd been crawling across a desert for weeks. She snatched a wooden cup of water from her bedside table and guzzled it, then slid into her armor. She needed more preparation, but there wasn't time; every moment, the call toward Eben's plains strengthened.

She almost reached the door before she threw up the water all at once. Her empty stomach churned, and she clung to the table, shivering.

The door burst open; the servant was back, a medico in tow. They converged on her, hands fluttering, urging her down into a chair.

"I can't—I have to go!" Cistine shouted. "They need me!"

"You're going nowhere in this state," the medico snapped. "I've sent for thin broth from the kitchens. You will eat while I examine you, and then *I* will decide if you're fit to move about."

Cistine gritted her molars, glancing at the window.

No streak of gold to signify Bresnyar's arrival yet.

She could spare a moment to recover her strength for the battle ahead.

CHAPTER FIFTY-NINE

BRESNYAR'S ROAR CUT through the slam of weapons and shrieks of augmentation, and with a gasp Maleck staggered backward from the latest in a long string of *mirothadt* he'd beheaded. Cleaning the blood from his face with his sleeve, he squinted up at a sky choked with dragonfire.

Ashe's mount, riderless, pulled back from the fray in a mighty sweep of golden wings. With a stab of fear, Maleck wondered where his *valenar* was; he'd last seen her flying with the Legions toward the Bloodwights, only to be blown from the sky by a wind augment.

How many minutes had passed since then? All was blood and death and chaos, and the air crackled with godlike energy. Weapons sang and sailed. Blood ran from his sweat-soaked face and stained his teeth—his own blood, an enemy's, he no longer could tell.

Something crashed into him from behind, and he whirled, sword encountering flesh as a *mirothadt* tumbled past him, already decapitated.

"Don't stop moving, *Afiyam!*" Kristoff shouted, and sprinted away to rescue a Warden from the relentless strikes of a former Siralek fighter wielding a massive cudgel.

Bresnyar's second roar jerked Maleck around again—not a sound of triumph, but of agony this time. Lightning split the smoke, a deadly arc that pierced the dragon's haunches when he shot toward the north. He careened overhead, tines of lavender digging into the chinks of his armored scales near the tail-tip, and plowed shoulder-first into the dirt with a snarl of agony. He did not rise when enemies converged on him.

Starfall and Stormfury wheeling, Maleck sprang to Bresnyar's defense. His steel gobbled blood and spattered gore, and the *mirothadt* struggled to turn as he cleaved through their midst and vaulted onto Bresnyar's heaving flank. He stood above them, searching for a point of attack; but they were far too many, swarming like termites to the taste of rotten wood.

An ear-splitting bellow whirled the thick smoke to vortices around them, full of screams from the Oadmarkaic Legion. They descended on the *mirothadt* in a banner of fire and soot-dulled metal, lifting some into the sky, burying others in the dirt in passing. Spurred by their aid, Maleck raised his weapons and charged the few fighters who dared brave Bresnyar's hide.

"Maleck," the dragon wheezed as he plucked a *mirothadt* from his neck, "I need a healing augment, I must fly to Stornhaz—"

"I carry no augments." Maleck kicked aside a corpse that slumped on the dragon's flank and skidded down to the ground. "I'll find you someone who does."

But when he surveyed the visible slice of the plains, it was a black eddy of friend and foe locked together. He had lost sight of Kristoff again. He had lost everyone. Despair stabbed into his body—

No. Not despair. That was a *Svarkyst* blade, rammed through his shoulder and coming out his front.

His shout was of shock, not pain—the pain did not register yet—and he thrust himself forward, sliding clear of the weapon and whirling to face his attacker. Armored in a dark robe, his simian mask leering with overlarge mandibles, his presence evoked a name like a glimpse through vapors.

Navan. One of his brothers.

"Hello, Mal," the creature leered. "I've come to thank you."

Maleck held his ground, gripped his weeping shoulder, and glared at this enemy who shared his blood but held no place in his heart.

"You're not going to ask me why?"

"I don't need your lies twisting my mind," Maleck spat. "I know what I am, *who* I am. I've done nothing for you."

"I'm sure you'd like to believe that." Navan skimmed his hand along the flat of the blade, shedding Maleck's blood to the grass. "But you carried our mission out to perfection. You gave the blood and healing augments to the Key. You opened the wells by her hand. You set all of this in motion."

Maleck's heart faltered. "I didn't...none of it was for *you*."

"Are you certain?" Navan was close enough that Maleck could smell him now: the blood on his robes, the decay, and that clean white strike of power...sizzling cold, like the aftermath of close lightning. "You were so eager to believe she tore the creature out of you. But didn't you take your revenge on her? The wells are open. We are here and she is not. Through you, our vengeance against the Key is complete."

"I am not your *acolyte*! I obey no one's will but my own!"

"*Allet*, you will never be anything but the perfect culmination of our plans. You are our vessel at the gates of the Chancellors. You have the ear of the Courts. As long as you live, our work continues on."

Maleck bellowed in rage and unleashed Stormfury, swiping madly. Navan dodged to the side, and Maleck staggered, one arm useless and throbbing, the other wielding the blade before him.

"*I didn't mean for this to happen to her!*" His shout ripped the blood-thick air. "She's my princess. I would lay down my life for her!"

"If you weren't a coward, perhaps. But what have you ever had to offer her—or any of them? A blade at command and little else. What do you have to offer *Asheila*?"

"Don't you dare speak her name."

"You should've run before you made her believe there was something to see in you." Navan's masked face tipped. "You stayed, and your presence has sealed her death. Your precious, pretty *valenar*."

Smoke stung Maleck's eyes. He scuffed his face on his sleeve. "How— what did you—?"

"We know what she's hiding under those fine gloves." Navan flexed his own, a smirk leering in his voice. "Did you really think you could escape it?

They'll all die here today. And once they're gone, you'll have nothing left but the flagons. Nothing left but *us*."

Rage poured into Maleck's empty center. "*I will not be a Bloodwight!*"

"You already are. You always will be."

When Navan lifted a hand, fire licking along his palm, for an instant Maleck was back on the rooftop in Stornhaz—watching Faer fall, hearing Pippet scream.

Bellowing with hate, he lunged, smashing into his brother's arm and swinging him away from Bresnyar and the fighting Legion just as the fire erupted from his body.

Maleck had never been more relieved that he wore the Atrasat markings beneath his armor; though the fire winnowed into the cut in his back and front, the inkings absorbed it, and he unleashed it again, one brutal shove to keep its taste from teasing that need buried deep in his head.

The brothers landed hard, splashing and rolling in puddles of blood, and Navan rose first. Maleck was slower, gripping his shoulder, swaying in place. "Where *is* she?"

"Your *valenar*? She's being dealt with." Navan beckoned again, fire flirting with his fingertips. "Our brother has given the order. If you won't take the augments and join us, then you're too dangerous to be left alive."

Maleck let his sword tip scrape the soil. "I've chosen my place: standing between you and my cabal."

An unnatural current warped the grass at their feet, and Navan's hackles rose. "We should have smothered you in your sleep in that symphony hall as a boy. You always were the worst of us."

Wind whipped out, catching Maleck across the chest and knocking him backward. He was slow to recover and dodge, to brace his blade one-handed and lunge. The Bloodwight dropped his augment, letting Maleck press in; too late, he caught the gleam of steel, the *Svarkyst* blade that had impaled him moments ago aiming for his middle now.

It rang to a halt an inch from his gut. Blocked, but not by him.

Tatiana's sabers tossed glinting ripples across her face as she slipped into Maleck's path, Navan's weapon caught between hers. "I can't say I understand why you're wearing that mask, *bandayo*. What's underneath it can't be much uglier than the skull."

The Bloodwight ripped his blade free and fell back a step, spitting. "I will peel the flesh from your bones."

"I'm shaking in my enviably-expensive, insulated wildcat-leather boots," Tatiana deadpanned. "I hope your brothers are thinking up better threats while they're all cowering behind their army."

She slammed her shoulder into the Bloodwight's mask, snapping his head back with it. Her enviably-expensive boot connected with his chest at the same time, sending him skidding, then tumbling, before he recovered and rolled up to his feet. Tatiana spun her sabers, falling back at Maleck's side. Gratitude swelled in him so sharply, he almost choked. But he had no time to even glance at her.

Bellowing with hate, the Bloodwight attacked.

CHAPTER
SIXTY

EVEN WITH THE fires of Nimmus raging on every side, a new blade in her hands, smoke in her lungs, and hurt freckling her body, Ashe had never felt more powerful.

She'd descended from the sky long ago, freeing Bresnyar to race to the aid of his brothers and sisters while she and Meriwa dueled back-to-back, cleaving down *mirothadt* augurs in Aeosotu's shadow. There was something exhilarating in fighting with someone who understood the dragonfire in her spirit, the blaze of fury in her heart. Though she'd lost sight of Bresnyar, she wasn't afraid; he had his Legion watching out for him.

Spinning in tandem, she and Meriwa sliced the heads off a pair of augurs and watched the rest flee, the ground trembling beneath them as Aeosotu gave chase.

"The Three Kingdoms certainly know how to have a good war!" Meriwa chortled. "What now?"

Ashe cast her head back, gulping a current of clean air that cut through the smoke. Dragons pummeled the battlefield on every side, driving off *mirothadt*, clustering here and there to bring them down in packs. "Muster the Legion and have them surround the battlefield. Sooner or later, these bastards are going to turn tail even if their leaders won't. Let's cut them off with dragonfire at every side."

"My pleasure." Meriwa whistled for Aeosotu, swung onto his back, and took to the skies.

That was where Ashe wanted to be, too—keeping watch over her cabal from above, ripping up the storm with steel and fire against the Balmond. She needed to find Rozalie and Maleck, get airborne, and find the weakest places to shore up.

She shut her eyes and reached out to Bresnyar, cleaving—

A prick.

A cut.

Something slid into her. *Through* her. It knocked the breath from her body with a dull hitch.

A hand closed around her throat from behind, and a voice from her nightmares breathed against her ear: "This is for Andras."

Ashe's world erupted in blinding agony.

CHAPTER SIXTY-ONE

THIS WAS THE melee. This was Braggos. This was a war to decide the fate of all the kingdoms, and Aden could not break beneath it no matter how badly his body ached to. So much blood and gore, such chaos on every side, and whenever he stopped to catch his breath the stench and pain pounded into him from his wounds. Those would become trouble in time if the battle did not stop raging.

And there were no signs it ever would.

A surge of wind barreled into him from behind, slamming him off-balance, skidding sideways through mud slurred up by sweat and bodily fluids. Reeling, Aden fell to a knee, the world tipping around him.

A blade touched his throat, but did not bite.

"The Hive Lord is a coward after all." A woman's voice reeked in his ears from behind. "You really fled into dragon lands to escape me?"

"*Nimea.*" Her name stole from him as a curse.

She clicked her tongue. "What a wasted effort. You should've known I would find you, Aden. I always do."

"Then finish it!"

"*Not yet.*" Her voice dug in with the blade, opening a thin seam above his collar. "I'm not done taking you apart."

The blade skipped back. She wrenched him around with a hand in his hair and shoved him facedown in the mud.

"Come find me when you see my handiwork," she purred. "You'll know where I am."

Her grip and her weight vanished, and by the time Aden palmed the slick grass and lurched back up to his knees, spitting mud and the taste of old meat from his mouth, she was gone—carried off by her wind.

Fear clawing his insides, Aden spun in the midst of battle, searching the horizon desperately. Through the carnage, back the way Nimea had turned him and pushed him down, his eyes finally made sense of the macabre gift she'd left him amidst the carnage: a familiar shape slumped among the corpses, newest to fall among them at the top of the heap, dark curls loosed from their tie and armor too fine for these battlefields, too pretty. Like a peacock.

"Sander," Aden rasped, staggering toward him. He cut down two *mirothadt* on his way, heedless of their faces, whether they were men or deranged children. Roaring Sander's name again, he fell to his knees beside the heap of bodies and yanked the High Tribune onto his back, sliding him down the pile into an awkward sprawl in his grip.

Sander's eyes were open. But so was his chest, blood everywhere, bone and sinew and organ peeping through. Aden could number ribs, could've slipped his hand inside Sander's chest cavity.

Vomit flooded his mouth. He choked it back. "Stars damn it."

"Nimea," Sander wheezed. "It was—"

"I know. This is Blood Hive vengeance."

"Suppose it was coming," Sander panted. "That place was always going to catch up to me."

"Don't be a fool! We've never let her win, I'm not about to start now." He heaved Sander up by his collar, but the High Tribune's bark of agony, the wrench and coil of his body, stilled Aden's frantic movements.

It brought the grim truth too close to bear.

Sheltered by the gruesome wall of corpses, he laid Sander out on the weeping earth and braced a hand beside his head. "Sander. Stay with us."

"I c—I can't," he retched, blood flooding down his chin. "Stop fighting the war...you can't win. Fight the one you *can*."

With a trembling hand, Sander jerked the armored glove from his palm, bearing skin crisscrossed with scars; numerous blood oaths sworn over a treacherous life. Somewhere among them, the vow he'd sealed with Ashe in Siralek; and freshest of all, the one he'd sworn with Thorne in Jovadalsa, sealing his way to becoming High Tribune.

"Make me an oath," Sander gasped. "For Mira, for our child...for *me*. Swear you will make this world safe. Protect them. Protect what we've built."

Aden shook his head. "You're going to help me build the rest of it, *Allet*. That was *your* promise."

But they both knew.

"Swear it." Sander's voice was no more than a breath, blood misting from his lips. "One last time, Aden."

So he took the knife to his own palm, gripped his brother-in-arms by the hand, and pressed his brow against their knuckles. "To a better Chancellor. And a better future."

A smile wobbled across Sander's face. "Tell Mira—tell her I—"

The breath left him on a sigh, his last request unspoken, his final oath sworn into the blood pooling between his hand and Aden's.

For uncountable seconds, Aden crouched, brow-to-brow with the once-enemy who'd understood his specters better than any friend. Then the calm overtook him—brutal, life-taking calm.

Nimea had wanted him to see this. Had made Sander's death slow and painful enough that he could.

He'd show her Nimmus in return.

He stripped the augment pouch and weapons from Sander's body and lashed them onto his own, chose a wind augment and shattered it on his flank. With one step, he was flying across the battlefield, borne on wings of fury and vengeance, straight in the direction Nimea had disappeared.

She was right...he knew where she was.

He found her on a knoll, dueling with Quill—her next chosen victim. The next cut she intended to kill Aden by. Even in the wind's fist, he marked the leisure of her swings, waiting for his arrival like an arena fight. Like this was all for them, a great and glorious confrontation between Hive Lord and Hive Lady.

That much, at least, he would give her.

Aden cast out the wind with a boom like thunder and dropped, sabers aimed at Nimea from above. Her head snapped up along with her sword arm, and she caught his strike, steel shrieking on steel. He pirouetted above her and landed in a crouch on the edge of the hill between her and Quill, refusing to surrender the high ground.

"Go, Quill!" he snarled, and without question his friend took flight back into the battle. Before Nimea could muster a single taunt, Aden hurtled toward her.

They clashed in a blur of metal, the dark sky crackling with the sparks spat from their blades, and in those flickering flashes there was nothing but wild triumph in Nimea's eyes. He'd given her exactly what she wanted. She'd *taken* from him everything she needed to force this battle, to bring him to her, just as she'd promised at Kosai Talis—hands covered in blood not his own, loss and pain screaming in his chest. All his sins, all his failures gathered into one face full of hate, laughing at him over their locked swords.

"Couldn't you save him, Aden? Ashe's sponsor?"

Sweat fanned into the wound on Aden's palm as he shifted his weight to break Nimea's guard with a kick, but she anticipated it; her boot drove in quicker than his, shoving him back, unlocking their blades. Aden cast his aside and shattered a fire augment, rearing back to strike—

"He wasn't the first."

Aden's hesitated. Cold malice twisted Nimea's once-lovely features into something inhuman—something Aden ached to destroy. "*Who?*"

A flicker of a smile on Nimea's face. "You should've kept one eye on your rain-dancer, *Hive Lord.*"

The augment guttered, and Aden's breaths with it. "What have you done?"

Her cruel smile winked black in the slithering glow of the flames. "What I should have done in that stars-damned pit before I let you distract me. You should have heard how she *squealed* when I sliced her open."

Aden couldn't breathe, couldn't think, the battlefield washed in red before him.

Ashe.

She was out there somewhere on the wargrounds, gutted, dying like she'd nearly died in the Blood Hive the day of the chariot race, when he'd been there with Sander. But he was not there now.

Sander was dead. Ashe was dying. And Aden was panicking, his mouth tasting of bile and iron, every breath leaving in jagged rips as he saw her again in his mind, holding her guts in, afraid, alone, slit open, spending her last breaths wondering why no one had come for her. Why *he* hadn't come.

Cursing at the top of his lungs, Aden attacked. Nimea cast up a wall of her own fire, but he punched through it, pummeled against it, unstoppable in his armor, his inkings, cloaked in his own fury.

The fire winked out, and Aden saw how he'd erred. It was not an augment, but steel soaring toward him now. *Svarkyst* steel.

Too late, his mind screamed even as his hand whipped to Sander's sword belted across his back. *Too late—*

But he had to try.

Nimea was a specter, beautiful and ruthless as she struck, Aden's fire dropping along the bend of her steel as he reached for his weapon to parry.

Too stars-damned late.

A heavy weight bore into him, thrusting him out of the way, flinging him to his knees out of the path of that sure and unstoppable death.

And Nimea brought her blade down into Kristoff's unprotected back.

CHAPTER SIXTY-TWO

THE BATTLEFIELD VANISHED. Color leeched from earth, from sky, from bloodspattered corpses. Aden could see nothing but the way his father's spine arched inward, his shoulderblades peeled together, his arms twisted and head flung back in a soundless cry as Nimea's blade pierced into him. He fell to his chest and did not rise—but he crawled toward Aden, who stared at him from the mud with the eyes of a boy at fifteen, screaming for his father to get up.

He *was* screaming—no, roaring, a wordless howl of fury, as Nimea wiped her blade off and watched Kristoff drag himself across the hill. Blood plopped from his lips as they struggled to form words, mere hisses of breath, but Aden *heard* him: *Not for me, not for me, not for me.*

Nimea twisted her blade once in hand, and thrust down.

A sword slid into place under hers—not a Valgardan saber, but a Talheimic broadsword. A flash of dark armor and pale hair, a vicious snarl, and Rozalie spun on heel and jammed her boot into Nimea's chest, knocking her backward on the knoll. Stance spread, both hands locked around her weapon, Rozalie stood over Kristoff. "Get *away* from them."

Nimea's eyes danced from Aden to Rozalie, alight with cruelty. "You make this too easy with all your new friends, Aden."

She snapped forward, blade flashing, but this time Aden was ready, rising. He and Rozalie swung their blades up in a cross to catch Nimea's; then they dueled her in tandem, Rozalie catching her blade, Aden battling the augment strikes behind it. Talheim and Valgard moved as one, whipping and cutting around each other; Aden did not think, he simply *moved*, feeling Rozalie's stance at every turn and bobbing around her, watching her back and flanks, rage and hate guiding his every blow against Nimea.

But his father still lay in the grass, facedown, unmoving. They had to end this *now*.

"Rozalie!" he barked, and she twirled out from under Nimea's next strike, gaze meeting his for a heartbeat.

Then she dropped her sword and fled, sprinting and falling at Kristoff's side, shielding his body with hers. Aden unleashed his fire augment and sent it out in a billowing falcate, angling it high so it would not burn them. It blasted Nimea off-balance instead, and that was all Aden needed; he charged in the wake of the flames and hurtled his foot into her gut with all his might, flipping her over the hill's edge. She slammed down, blade flying from her hand, and he was already on her, driving a knee into her chest so hard he slid them both backward on the bloodsoaked grass.

Every scrap of compassion burned out of him when he looked down into her face, every lingering glint of shame for what he'd done to this woman and her friends carved from him by the blade that had pierced his father's back.

For Ashe and Sander, for Kristoff and himself, Aden ended the last of the Tumult with a clean slice of his sword.

Before Nimea's head had stopped rolling through the grass, Aden was back up the hill, jamming his saber point-first into the dirt and slamming down beside Kristoff and Rozalie. She scrambled back, hair singed but body unharmed thanks to her ill-fitting Valgardan threads, and Aden gripped his father's shoulder and rolled him over, cradling his cheek.

Blood frothed at the corner of Kristoff's mouth. Pain clouded his gaze. "Did she...hurt you?"

Vicious laughter yanked from Aden's throat. "You think I give one *stars-damned* care what she might've done to me?" The battle-craze harshened his panic to pure focus. "We're going to the medicos. Get on your feet."

But when he tried to sit his father up, Kristoff coughed and cringed, violent wracks of pain doubling him over until he slid from Aden's grasp. It was all Aden could do to lower his head gently to the grass.

"It's all right, it's all right, *Afiyam*, there's no need," Kristoff breathed. "I can rest. I've seen enough. Done enough."

"*You haven't.*"

"Yes, I have. I lived to see the man you've become." Kristoff's knuckles brushed Aden's blood-soaked beard. "That...is more than I deserve. More than I could've ever asked the gods for."

"No, no, no," Aden chanted through gritted teeth. "In the Isetfells, you swore you'd stay. I don't release you from that oath. You aren't finished— *I'm* not finished with you yet!"

But Kristoff merely gripped Aden by the back of the head, setting their brows together. "Keep fighting. Never stop."

No. He wouldn't stop.

He would *not stop.*

Aden whipped back, gripping Kristoff by the collar, towing him up from the ground and shaking him when his eyes fluttered shut and his heavy breaths began to ease. "Father, look at me—*look at me*! Lionsbane!"

But even at his Name, Kristoff hardly stirred. First Sander, and Ashe, and now—

"*Athar!*" Aden roared, voice cracking beyond his control, and at the Old Valgardan word, the plea from a boy to his father, Kristoff's eyes flickered open. "I need you to *get up!*"

Kristoff's tearstained gaze met his, life sparking and struggling in its depths. Rozalie laid a hand on Aden's back. "I'll clear you a path. Get him out of here."

He held her eyes for an instant—all he could spare for this woman of a once-enemy kingdom who'd already saved his father's life and aimed to do it again.

Then he forsook sword and shield, the battlefield, his friends. He dragged Kristoff's arm across his shoulders and pulled him up, bearing his father's weight against his side as he looked across the marred battleground.

Enemies were converging, *mirothadt* stalking them on every side. Augurs. Children. Balmond. To cut through them all, to clear a path to the triage tents so far away, he would have to go deep into himself, to open the gates Mira and Tatiana and Sander had helped him shut, and force the Hive Lord's ruthless strength out one last time.

Or else they would die. His *father* would die.

Aden gritted his teeth, Sander's blood, Nimea's blood, Kristoff's blood running from his lips. He freed his last wind augment and tossed it to Rozalie. "Do you know how to use this?"

She shook her head wildly.

"I'll tell you." He hefted Kristoff against him when he sagged. "It's no different from any other weapon. It's all about control. Give me your dagger and break it. We move as one."

She complied without argument, tossing him her offhanded blade. Aden gripped it in one hand, steadied Kristoff with the other, and drew his breath down deep.

And with Rozalie at his side, he punched back into the battle.

CHAPTER SIXTY-THREE

MALECK HAD NEVER been gladder to have Tatiana at his side; with adrenaline numbing the pain in his arm and her watching his back, he felt no fear. It was a dance, a familiar choreography, their steps weaving perfectly together after hundreds of swordfights and training sessions together. Some portion of Maleck knew the struggle itself was in vain; they couldn't kill this Bloodwight, not without Cistine. The most they could do was keep it distracted so no one else was harmed by it. But perhaps that was enough.

Perhaps that was his penance.

He ducked back from the fight a moment, flexing his aching fingers around his sabers, gasping for breath. It was difficult to see through the blood, the sweat, the heat shimmering on the air—

Something jammed through him, a sensation half-aberrant, barely there, like a brush of power had jolted into his ribs and broken them, one-by-one, on its way through. He cried out, and heat rushed against his left side; when he whirled back toward Navan, a wall of fire met his face—then transferred, caught in Tatiana's fist when she struck out her hand, interrupting its trajectory. She shoved Maleck out of the way just as Navan reclaimed control of the augment, jerking Tatiana back to him bound in ropes of fire. Maleck surged after her, but the Bloodwight threw her to the ground, knocking the wind audibly from her. She grabbed her chest and retched, doubling up.

Another burst of fire stopped Maleck from running to her. He changed course and leaped with blades leading, and the Bloodwight met him augment-for-swords. The dance quickened, an intense swirl of spark-spitting steel and godlike might. Maleck's fingers made Starfall and Stormfury whirl, and he spun and crossed again and again, keeping the Bloodwight turning, keeping its focus on him and away from Tatiana.

Navan tired of the game all at once. He caught Starfall and Stormfury's lethal cross in one augment-wrapped fist, thrusting the blades up so high, Maleck's shoulders wrenched in their sockets. In one deft pirouette, the creature swiveled and plunged the swords backhanded; but Tatiana was there once more, shooting forward and intercepting the strike with her dagger, shoving the creature back—straight into a blast of dragonfire from Bresnyar's mouth.

Navan screamed, and Maleck lunged, slamming both feet into the Bloodwight's chest and hurling him toward Bresnyar's hindquarters. With a snap of his tail, the dragon sent Navan soaring, just as Aeosotu had done to the *Aeoprast*, launching him away through the thicket of warring bodies.

Maleck rolled to his feet and faced Tatiana. "Find a healing augment for Bresnyar."

Tatiana nodded, still rubbing her chest, face twisted with pain. "Wait here, I'll be right back."

She was gone in an instant, breaking an augment now that there was no fear of Navan taking it. Wheezing as well, Maleck staggered backward a step, clutching his ribs and surveying the pockets of nearby fighting for any familiar faces, for anyone he could help while he waited.

"Mal."

Bresnyar's quiet rumble stopped him short. The dragon had never called him that before. *Never.*

He swiveled slowly back to find the pain was gone from Bresnyar's gaze. It was detached. Unfocused. Fixed on him.

Maleck slowly approached, swords lowered, heart thudding in his chest. "Asheila?"

Smoke plumed from the dragon's nostrils. "Hello, you beautiful, braided bastard."

His heart lurched into a gallop. "Why are you cleaving? What is it?"

"Just making sure you're all right."

It was more than that. Bresnyar's lip curled, fighting a hold stronger than his, fighting to say something Ashe didn't want him to. Warning rocked Maleck's middle as he stepped forward again. "Where are you?"

The answer came slower this time. "It's hard to say. It all looks the same. Like the tundra...like that battle before Talheim marched into Stornhaz. Were you even there when that happened? Gods, no, you must've gone home by then...you said Kristoff found you when you were still in the Wildwood..."

Bresnyar's eyes flickered, gold and red and *desperate*, and it was more difficult by far for Maleck to maintain his composure. "Tell me where you are, Ashe."

Another pause. Longer. Heavier. "I never apologized for how I behaved...when you were saving my leg. I wish I hadn't treated you like an enemy back then. You were one of the few people who ever thought I was worth saving just the way I was."

Cursing, Maleck plunged his sabers into the soil and knelt, gripping the dragon's cheeks in his hands and looking deep into his eyes, trying to see the warrior cleaving behind them. *"Asheila, where are you?"*

"Don't come, Mal. I don't want you to see this. No more nightmares...not for me."

Panic ripped his heart into shards. He bent until his brow nearly touched the dragon's. "Where is she? Bresnyar, *tell me where she is!*"

The dragon wrenched his head back and roared, talons tearing into the soil, neck thrashing as he fought to turn the tide, to see where his Wingmaiden had fallen. "At the edge of the marshes, beneath a shelf of green rock—there is another dragon near her, fallen. Go, Maleck, *go,* I can feel her life waning! *Go now!*"

He had never run faster in his life. Splashing through blood, feeling the battlefield rise and fall beneath him as earth augments rocked it, the sky painted in tongues of fire, but he didn't care. The pockets of fighting he burst through, the augur bellies he slit, the friends and foes eddying around him were merely a blur.

All that mattered was reaching her.

He cried out in relief when he spotted the jagged slice of green stone and the umber dragon sprawled halfway in the water nearby, scales torn off, blood leaking from its chest. The only enemies here were the dead, throats and chests rived by precise strokes, a mound of enemies struck down by Ashe—slumped under the stone's shadow, one pallid hand pressed to her middle as blood pumped around her fingers.

Another shout tore from him, this one of rage and grief as he slid on his knees in the mud and blood, *her blood*, pressing his fingers below the corner of her jaw. There was a pulse fluttering under her skin, thready but there, and she was still *breathing*, thank the stars—

Maleck sobbed her name, drawing her head up, but it hung limply in his grip. Beneath his fingertips, her pulse stumbled, stopped, then started again.

He pulled her into the crook of his arm and swung her up from the bloodsoaked soil, and she spasmed, eyes leaping open, wet with agony. "No, Mal—gods damn it, I *told* you—"

"And I told *you*, you are my choice." His voice tore as he staggered from under the stone shelter. "I will always come for you. *Always.* You are worth every nightmare in this kingdom."

A pitiful rasp escaped her, her chest jerking, fingers gripping the hinge of his shoulder. "Put me down, Maleck, I can't, just—just stay until I—"

"No, you *do not leave me.* Asheila! Do you hear me?"

But her eyes were fluttering shut, her grip weakening against his shoulder, and he was powerless to stop this. All he had were two hands covered in blood and a broken heart that loved her with every unsteady beat, and a spirit that would lie down on this battlefield and die with her if she went. If she tried to leave him behind.

So he spoke to her, words of terror and promise and love twining on his tongue while he stumbled across the battlefield, and with every step the mud sucked his boots and the war raged around him and he was fourteen years old again, fleeing the fight with Kristoff shouting after him, *Go, run to the lights, Afiyam, go home!*

But home was in his arms, home was dying as Maleck ran faster and harder than his body could bear, his lungs wrapped in white fire, his shoulder throbbing, every muscle aching, toward the faraway places where medicos waited. He forced words around the stitch in his chest, the pain clutching his lungs in iron hands: "You made me stay. When I wanted to leave this all behind, you made me stay, Asheila. Now you stay. For *me*."

Her breath wheezed against his neck.

"If you stay with me, I will go anywhere you ask me to. Back to Hellidom, back to Talheim if you wish...listen to me, we will sit on bridges and rooftops and drink wine until the stars go dark. Asheila, if you stay, I swear by all the gods I will never leave your side. Whatever you ask of me, for as long as you ask. I will do *anything*, just *stay*."

No answer. Just her breaths growing slower, shallower.

He ran faster, cursing, weeping, until his rambles became her name over and over, calling her back to him every step she took toward the Sable Gates.

Every step she took away from him.

CHAPTER SIXTY-FOUR

TATIANA COULDN'T SEE Quill among the pockets of fighting. She prayed to the gods that he was still alive...or if he wasn't, that he'd met his end so quickly there'd been no pain.

She managed to find Ariadne in the hunt for a healing augment for Bresnyar, but that was the farthest she got. Now their backs were pressed together, and on both sides of them, the *mirothadt* closed in. Balmond wheeled above, screeching for blood.

"*Abominations,*" Ariadne seethed, spinning her swords. "It wasn't supposed to be like this. Where are the gods?"

"If I were them, I wouldn't want to be down here, either," Tatiana panted, shaking blood from her eyes. "But at least I have you."

Ariadne's shoulders pressed tightly to hers. "If I'm to die here, it's my honor to fall at your side, *Malatanda.*"

Heat strangled Tatiana's throat. "Well, if we're making our last confessions to each other, I should probably tell you I used to steal your swords to cut vegetables."

Ariadne jammed an elbow into her ribs. "You are such a child."

The enemy lunged toward them, a forest of blood-spattered weapons closing around them, the reek of death and blood suffocating the air.

And then, heat. Harsh, glorious, *fresh* air poured across their faces, blowing the stench from Tatiana's nostrils, and a figure in gold-plated armor slammed down beside them, her augment blasting the enemies so far back they rolled and tossed like dolls and did not rise again.

Tatiana squinted against the gleam of a fire augment crackling within Kadlin's armor when she unleashed it, rising to her full height beside them. "Are you two all right?"

"Still breathing." Ariadne smiled. "Something we owe to you now."

The words nudged Tatiana's spirit, awakening something she had not felt since the battle first began. Something that tried very desperately to feel like hope.

"Shall we?" Kadlin directed the words at Tatiana.

With a curt nod—all she could manage, throat too tight to speak—she led the charge into the thickest of the fighting, Ariadne and Kadlin at her sides.

CHAPTER
SIXTY-FIVE

RAIN SOBBED AGAINST the windowpanes while Cistine sat at the dining table, sipping down her third helping of broth. Even though she was ravenous, her stomach writhed with nauseous nerves as she watched the sky for the flicker of gold scales.

She'd spoken twice more into the starstone while the medico was busy doling out orders to the servants, sending for more broth and water and blankets, but the dragon hadn't come. The possibilities for his absence were too grim to bear, but that was all she could think about.

That, and the augments' call.

Not from the well, though she sensed that, too; this one came from her pouch. Not a roar, not as demanding as she'd once heard, but a soft, gentle invitation, resigned and steady.

Come, Key. Come and see.

A gentle knock at the door yanked at her attention, and she swallowed the last spoonful of broth with an undignified, startled slurp. "Come in."

The door creaked open. "Cistine?"

She swiveled away from the window, shock bringing her halfway up from her chair. "Pippet? What are you doing here?"

Quill's sister was as wan as Cistine felt, her pallor accentuated by the dark twists of hair spilling around her cheeks. Her eyes, too large for her still-sunken face, glistened with some unnamable emotion as she and Cistine stared at one another.

"I felt you," Pippet whispered. "I felt you all the way across the wing when I woke up."

"What are you *doing* here?" Cistine repeated.

"I got stabbed." Pippet padded into the room. "Faer...Faer is gone."

Cistine fell back in her seat, tears burning her eyes. "Oh, Pippet. Oh, *no.*"

Pippet rubbed her arms. "Quill said he'd be back before I woke up this morning but he's *not* and I thought you were gone too and I was alone..."

Cistine opened her arms, and Pippet clambered into her lap, a gangly knot of long limbs and endless, frightened shudders. Cistine smoothed her hair and tucked her chin over Pippet's head, and for a moment they clung to one another, the sea of terror quieting between them.

"I'm so sorry about Faer." Cistine kissed Pippet's hair. "He loved you. Never forget that."

"I loved him, too. So much, even when I said mean things to him. I said mean things to *all* of you."

"You weren't yourself," Cistine soothed. "I know that. I never believed you really felt that way about me."

"I never said thank you for helping me, either," Pippet mumbled. "I missed you. And I'm sorry I hurt you."

"It's all right, Pip. That's behind us now."

The door opened again, and the medico returned, clearing her throat. Pippet sat up in Cistine's grip, looking shyly away from the woman. "Do I have to go?"

"I'd rather you stayed," Cistine said. "I could use the company while I get ready."

Pippet's eyes flashed back to her with some of their old sharpness. "Are you going to join the others?"

The medico scoffed quietly. "Not if she knows what's good for her."

Cistine nudged Pippet from her lap, clutched her thin blanket around her shoulders, and went to the window. With one hand on the sill, she peered out at the overcast, empty sky. Still no sign of Bresnyar.

"Princess," the medico urged, "you shouldn't be standing yet. In fact, I'd like you to accompany me to the house of healing. You ought to be watched for the next few days in case there's some sort of relapse."

"I've slept enough," Cistine said. "Besides, if I shouldn't be standing, I doubt I should walk all the way to your house of healing, either."

"Well," the woman said, "we would use a wind augment, of course..."

A wind augment.

The well.

Cistine's fingers corkscrewed the knot of blanket under her chin. "Is the well empty?"

In the reflection of the glass, she caught the medico's patronizing smile. "Of course not. The well will never be empty, I don't think."

Cistine let her own face slide into focus, searching for the conviction and clarity in the pale green eyes blinking back at her. Then she let the blanket tumble to the floor and snatched up her augment pouch, fingers shaking at the hum of the *Stor Sedam*. "I need to go."

"Princess..."

"That's right, she's a *princess*." Pippet perched her hands on her hips. "You have to do what she says."

The medico flicked an irritated glance between them. "I won't be part of this madness."

"Fine." Pippet took Cistine's arm. "Then we'll go ourselves."

Though Cistine felt stronger after the three bowls of bone broth she'd put away, she still wobbled every so often while they hurried through Kanslar's wing. She was grateful for Pippet's hand on her arm; there was a new steadiness in the girl, a maturity that came from experience rather than years. They would have many conversations if she survived this day—plenty to learn from one another.

Together she and Pippet jogged up the steps from the courtyard to the courthouse proper. The moment Cistine's feet crossed the threshold, the call seared through her, knocking a gasp from her open mouth. Where it had so often beckoned her like sweet, firm whispers with the occasional shout, this cry was hair-raising and discordant.

She led the way to the door at the top of the stairs where a pair of Vassora stood guard, polearms crossed. "Let me through." She flashed her scarred palm. "I am the *valenar* of the Chancellor of Kanslar Court. I need to get to the well."

"Chancellors' orders," one of the guards muttered. "Only the *visnprests* go below until the army returns."

"If you don't let her through, there won't be a Chancellor left to punish you for disobeying," Pippet snapped. "Unless you want to face the Bloodwights yourselves when they come back, you'll let her go down to that well! *Now!*"

When the guards still hesitated, Cistine lost her patience. She swept one man's legs with all her might and grabbed the shaft of his polearm when she kicked him against the wall. The weapon separated from his stunned fingers, and she swung it, cracking his companion on the side of the head, shoving him away from the open door. But even that small effort left her winded, and she had to lean on the polearm for a moment before she stepped into the stairwell.

Pippet backed away, hands upraised. "I can't go down there. I promised Quill I wouldn't go near any augments for a long time."

A spear of guilt jabbed Cistine's chest. "I know I shouldn't leave you by yourself—"

"Yes, you should. You have to fight. That's what princesses do." Pippet's smile wobbled. "You taught me that. The crown is heavy, but you can wear it. Just promise me you'll bring them home."

Cistine nodded. "I give you my word."

Pippet stepped back again, glancing over her shoulder. "I can hear more guards coming. You should go. I'll distract them...I'm going to start crying as loud as I can. I've gotten lots of practice lately."

Cistine tossed the polearm back to Pippet and bolted down the steps.

She had to pause several times to gather her strength and master the waves of agony slamming into her skull. The scream of augmented energy grew in intensity and volume until it became a shrill wail. She stumbled at the base of the steps and gripped the narrow walls, gazing ahead at what her blood had unleashed back into the world.

Someone had used an earth augment to form a ledge above the well. *Visnprests* moved along it, an assortment of flagons in wooden containers at their feet, and before and below them...

Augments, everywhere, dancing and swirling like mist. Their distinctive patterns played around one another: fire and wind, darkness and light, lightning and water.

This time, Cistine not reach out to the augments. She called them to her. *Come. Come and see* me.

The shrieking in her head dropped away to silence. Time slowed in the moment between action and reaction. The *visnprests* froze as the augments whispered into stillness, the power suspended in vapors all around the room.

Then it heeded her call.

Cistine shut her eyes as the power rushed toward her, slamming through her body in waves. With each one, she cast the door wider, reaching deeper for the well of her *own* power, for the might that belonged to her alone. It was the same depth she'd plunged into for the strength to endure training with the cabal, to endure Kalt Hasa, to survive this war; the Princess's fierce will, the Key's power, and the Queen's stamina.

She gathered the energy around her, heavier and warmer than the blanket she'd shed in her apartment, but she stopped long before she felt the farthest fathoms of her strength, calling the wind at last. It wrapped around her and almost pulled away again, but she clung to it by the tips of her fingers, melding it to her will.

She didn't know how much power she held now. It seemed limitless, an unending shroud of augments on top of augments. Her head vibrated with all the power that had heeded her call.

With one last glance at the *visnprests*, Cistine dispatched the wind and let it carry her away to the battlefield.

CHAPTER
SIXTY-SIX

DEATHMARCH. THE NAME was certainly fitting. Death did march on this battlefield.

Even when Thorne gave over to the same killing rage that had helped him survive the first few months of this war, to leave Braggos alive despite all the odds, it was not enough. For every warrior he leaped to save, there were two more who fell. He wrapped an arm around a Wingmaiden and spun her away from a cleaving battle-axe, only to watch two Yager archers fall with maces buried in their skulls. He beheaded a pair of augment-drunk Blood Hive fighters, one with each saber, but when he turned from their crumbling corpses, he watched a Balmond make quick work of four Kanslar warriors, rending out their throats. He chased the beast away with a fire augment, and then he had to halt and catch his breath. He'd used so many augments already trying to keep the other Chancellors alive, and his strength felt like a scorched wick. There was little left to burn down.

A wild shout rent the damp air—not one voice, but many, raised in bloodthirsty elation. Thorne wiped his eyes on his sleeve, looking east and then west, his heart climbing into his throat as the Legion high above yipped and hollered in glee.

The fruition of Ashe's secret mission had come to bear at last.

Warriors from the villages and cities across Valgard fanned the horizon on every side: lumber workers from Hvallatar, warriors of Landamot, the people of Blaykrone and from Hellidom—even Magnus and his archers, men Thorne had shed blood with so many times—all poured onto the battlefield, screaming the names of their stolen children, their beloved dead, their fallen homes and sundered families.

Valgard's people smashed against the enemy ranks and drove them back, their bodies sheathed in firelight, augments from the widespread wells leaping against their armor. Under the wild barrage, the Blood Hive fighters and criminals fell back. The remaining Balmond wheeled away from their mindless charge, the dragons shooting after them like arrows, bellows shaking the dark clouds. With a wild whoop of triumph, Benedikt led his remaining Tribunes in pursuit. The rest of the Chancellors rallied Valgard's army with shouts, and streamed on the enemy's heels.

Thorne held his place for a moment, torn between their elation and his own dark doubt. The Bloodwights were gaining more ground with every hack of power, yet now their ranks fell back. Were they truly intimidated by the reinforcements from the territories, or had they waited for this moment?

There was no time to stand and wonder. The tide carried him relentlessly now, and there was nothing he could do but run, side-by-side with his fellow blood-spattered Valgardans, toward the Bloodwights' distant hill where they watched the battlefield from afar.

That distance was the most important part of their strategy. If Thorne could just close it—

Someone shouted in shock and horror, a sound taken up by many voices. Before Thorne's horror-struck eyes, the foremost line froze, Benedikt at their head, and began to quiver in place, screaming as if they were burning from within.

"Fall back!" Thorne bellowed, plunging through the ranks, shoving chests and grabbing shoulders, hurling his people away. "*FALL BACK!*"

But there were those on the front line who couldn't heed him. They could do nothing as the Bloodwights turned them all to blood mist, spraying their remains across the battlefield.

Horrified screams littered the air as another slash of power turned a swath of their ranks to blood. The puddles were mid-calf deep now. Snarling with rage, Thorne waded in and snatched hold of Adeima and Bravis, shoving them to safety.

That was where it caught him, a blood augment seizing him instead of them, latching him in place while they bolted away. It burrowed into his body, setting his organs and blood boiling. He was dying just like his father, his pulse racing faster and faster, climaxing on the verge of giving up altogether—

Wind and lightning and *thunder.*

A tremendous roar fractured the air, and a jettison of light speared down on the battlefield to the left of the Bloodwights' hill. Scythes of fire and lightning ripped through the smoke, and the augment's wicked claws released Thorne. He buckled in agony, retreating step by stumbling step out of reach, eyes fixed on the edge of the warground.

It couldn't be—it wasn't possible—

But he knew the taste of that power.

The ranks parted before the cyclone of sheer augmented might, and an armor-wrapped figure stepped from its chaotic strands, hickory hair torn by the wind tamed to her grasp.

"You wanted the Key?" The wind amplified her voice, blasting it across the battlefield. "Come and claim her, you gods-damned Bloodwight *bastards!*"

Half the *mirothadt* ranks whirled back to the hill where their leaders perched. And Thorne watched in open-mouthed awe as his *valenar* spooled a lightning augment between her hands, sprouted a shield of fire at her back, and lunged to meet them.

CHAPTER
SIXTY-SEVEN

THE FIRST MOMENT she looked across the battlefield at the sheer enormity of the carnage, the dead bodies everywhere, the dragons torn from flight and hurled down to their end on the plain, Cistine couldn't breathe.

It was her worst nightmare played out before her. Ever since her Naming, the gods had warned her of this.

Nazvaldolya. The end of all life as it was known.

Instinct. Let everything come into focus. Maleck's lesson cut through the haze of panic. She couldn't afford to freeze.

She called up a lightning augment from the separate storms raging across her body. It answered at once, and the fire slipped into her hold as well, blooming in a flaming brace across her shoulders as she surged forward, the *mirothadt* wheeling away from the fight below to intercept her.

Brace! Don't tense!

Cistine pulled up short in her charge at the last moment, dropping her breath through her body and channeling the augments, not toward the Bloodwights, but toward the *mirothadt.* It had taken her one glimpse of the battlefield to see the back ranks were overwhelmed despite the fresh wave of reinforcements pouring in from the far plains.

If she could do something about that, if she could draw their ire—

Long, bony fingers closed over her wrist. Cistine dug in her heels and twisted her arm, latching onto the Bloodwight's sleeve in turn. She grappled with him for a moment over the current of his power, found purchase as if on water-slick stones, and *yanked*.

It came easier this time. Maybe because of the Door, maybe because of all the power she carried...or perhaps because this Bloodwight felt younger, fresher, not quite as strong. She ripped the power from him in a few sharp pulls and spent it against the *mirothadt* as well, cutting down the enclosing flank. With a wild burst of glee, she watched the Valgardan warriors break through the rest of them.

But now all the Bloodwights were surging toward her—all except the *Aeoprast*, who leered from behind, trusting his brothers to dispense with her. As if she wasn't worth his time.

She would have to make it clear how wrong he was.

Cistine focused all her strength on the Bloodwights that leaped toward her; she envisioned the augments they unleashed as chains, binding them to her. Several spurts of power impacted her armor before she could dodge, sending her staggering as points of pain budded on her ribs and chest and stomach. But then she found the rhythm of it; if she never stopped moving, like when she faced Quill, it slowed them. Especially those ones in the front, the ones who felt weaker, less accustomed to holding so many augments at once.

They were inexperienced like her. And she knew *exactly* how to bring them down.

After that, it was just a matter of coiling and striking, coiling and striking, dodging their augments and then grabbing those threads of power and unraveling them. She disarmed three Bloodwights and smashed them backward into the ranks before she tasted a speckle of blood, and the warriors below ripped into them, beheading and dismembering them in swift strokes.

Three Bloodwights dead. But there were so many still alive.

Cistine swiveled to face them again, wiping blood from her lip, and saw that several had retreated—wary of what she could do. Though the *Aeoprast* hadn't shifted in the slightest, she sensed that he was no longer leering.

She spread her feet, braced, and curled both hands.

He shivered out of sight. Before Cistine could even catch her breath, he was right in front of her, his fingers enclosing her throat.

She grabbed his wrist, but he snapped her grip with his free hand; so she seized that one instead, locking fingers with him, her stomach contorting at its grisly boniness. His other hand constricted, piercing the column of her neck, and Cistine clutched wildly at the current of augments transposed across his body.

He carried as many as she did. More, even. It was like scooping handfuls of maggots out of a festering corpse.

"You've served your purpose," he seethed. "The call brought the Key. The war forced its hand. Its hand opened the Doors. Your survival was an insignificant issue I intend to rectify *now*."

Red-hot rage seared through Cistine, forcing a gasp from her gritted teeth. "The call didn't bring the Key to Valgard, she came to save her kingdom. And you're standing in her way!"

She grabbed the *Aeoprast*'s arm with both hands, planted her boots in his ribs, and kicked with all her might. He grunted, and as he buckled, Cistine shut her eyes, shut out the battlefield, shut out everything. She latched onto the paths of power in his body and sprang down them.

Ever since she'd watched this creature dissolve Salvotor with a flick of power, she'd known he led the Bloodwights; but now, for the first time, she truly understood *why*. His fanaticism was stamped into the very essence of his being. Whatever Maleck had done in the Azkai cult, whatever augments he'd ingested, he still felt like himself inside; still a man in all the ways that mattered.

But not the *Aeoprast*. He'd taken whatever the Order had learned from their cruel experiments and exploited it beyond reason. He was a tapestry of godlike power, his organs, muscles, and bones all knit together by augmentation. That ethereal energy was the sinew that braided him together.

But Cistine was other, too. She was made differently, too. And what was made differently could unmake differently.

As the *Aeoprast's* body struck the blood-dampened soil, Cistine reached the middle of who he was, a flashing, furious clamor at his center where all the augments overlapped. Purple smoke and flashes of lightning, fire dancing with darkness, a microcosm of the wells and the world. He was a burning star, his essence the core of all that augmentation had ever been, and could be, and shouldn't be.

This was not why the gods had given this gift. And as the Key, Cistine felt the terrible burden to end this madness and misuse. To end *him*.

She plunged her own strength, all of it to the last drop, into that horrific tangle of overlapping augments. And she started to unravel him.

Distantly, she heard the *Aeoprast* scream. She was on top of him now, pinning his limbs, but that reality clashed with this one, where she could see all the blazing threads of power churning through his body. The augments struggled between the *Aeoprast's* command and hers, writhing in a wild dance like grass flattened between opposing winds.

Not winds—*wills*. Hers and his, battling in the pocket of reality where only the power of the gods existed.

Cistine slammed into her own limit again. The taste of hot, thick blood filled her mouth, breaking her concentration, and with an inexorable push the *Aeoprast* gained ground, peeling her fingers away from the center of his strength, forcing her out.

She'd gone too far, made herself too much of a threat. Either he walked away from this battle vulnerable, or she and her cabal would never walk away from it at all.

She reached for her threshold. One arm to his augments, one to her own will, which met its end in fear and weakness and discord. She reached, and when she finally laid hands on that hollow end of her power as the Key, she let the rest of her power rise.

Like new beginnings, like daybreak, the strength of the Queen and the determination of the Princess blew through the restraints on the Key's power. New vigor washed through Cistine, a burning white energy, and the *Aeoprast* cursed and snarled as she seized hold of that augment knot in the middle of him again. She no longer tried to untangle it; she pictured it like low-hanging fruit, grabbed for the stem, and with one last deft cut of her own power, she severed it.

The stem broke. The sinew shattered. The augments exploded out of the *Aeoprast* so violently Cistine toppled back, landing hard on the grass. Flat on her back, blood flooding her throat, running from her nostrils and eyes, she watched the augments fume across the sky toward the army. Valgardan warriors leaped to catch them, not even questioning where they came from.

The *Aeoprast* panted as he struggled upright. Cistine pushed herself up on her hands and saw that the other Bloodwights had retreated to the base of the hill. Their masks hid their shocked faces, but their posture was flighty, on the verge of fleeing.

And then, while she struggled to muster the strength to attack them, praying for a second wind, the *Aeoprast* started to laugh.

That gloating, dark sound hurled shivers through Cistine's body. Before her disbelieving eyes, the *Aeoprast* stood, and ravaging darkness began to rise from his body once again.

He shook out his hand, and the shards of a flagon sifted down at his feet. "Steal as many augments as you like, Key. We will just break open new ones. Steal those, and there will be more after that. You will tire long before we deplete our stores, this wonderful gift you gave us."

Panting in open-mouthed horror, she realized he was right. They'd harvested countless augments from the wells, and she was still only herself. She would never be able to weaken them all if she couldn't even stop *him*.

But maybe...

Maybe she didn't have to.

Cistine hurled down her last wind augment and let it carry her out of reach. Then she slid her hand into her pouch and drew out the sealed flask.

The *Stor Sedam*.

The *Aeoprast* feared it. It was perhaps the only thing he had ever feared, and the cost must be equal to the power it unleashed if it had made him flee from her while standing above the largest of all the Doors. It had to be a key itself—the key to destroying him and his brothers and their army.

She didn't know what that meant. She only knew that this was the moment to decide if that cost was worth paying.

The cabal would never forgive her. But she would never forgive *herself* if she let the kingdoms fall when she could save them.

Whatever the cost. She'd promised that to save Talheim long ago. Now it was time to save them *all*.

She pressed her fingers to her bloodstained lips, then to the bloodlock.

Her breath caught when it gave way. So frighteningly simple, as if she'd been born for that lock, too, and it for her—this rune seal crafted long, long before her time.

Gammalkraft, augmentation, and Cistine Novacek. Soil, water, and seed.

The flagon within the armored flask was so lightless, it made her stomach twinge. Not like ravaging darkness with its sensual swirls of purple and blue; this was core shadow, a night without moon or stars. Even when she shook it, nothing stirred or shifted inside. It was black sand in an hourglass already run out.

Cistine blinked the blood from her lashes and looked through the army for a glimpse of Thorne, but she found none. He was buried in the battle, far beyond her reach. If he even still lived.

Just the memory of his touch, his face, his eyes, would have to do.

The *Aeoprast* appeared before her suddenly, wind stirring his robes, darkness curling around him—and stumbled back when he saw what she held. His shout had no words; only violence, only hate, and he coiled up and lunged for her, fire and shadows shooting from his outstretched hands.

And Cistine broke the black flagon against her armor.

CHAPTER
SIXTY-EIGHT

BETWEEN ONE BREATH and the next, the atmosphere above the Deathmarch changed. An unnatural chill and harsh stillness took hold, as if they'd all floated off suddenly into the arms of the gods in some distant, breathless place.

Thorne halted, yet another *mirothadt* warrior tumbling at his feet, and swiveled back toward the hill. Every living head within sight pivoted the same way, to the place where Cistine had charged the *Aeoprast*, the last glimpse Thorne had caught before the fight had buried him, drawing him away from her.

Now he saw her again, but he didn't know what he was truly seeing.

Cistine and the *Aeoprast* were framed against the low bank of black clouds and the pale strip of sky not quite swallowed by smoke. He was frozen, arm outstretched, lean fingers an inch from her face. And from Cistine herself, a black, clawed, brutal thing broke free, riving slowly from her body like the legs of a Skurkopp spider from the Sotefold. Talons of power extended toward the *Aeoprast*, still frozen perhaps by her malignant force, his own lust, or even terror.

The wind stirred Cistine's hair, and for a moment, that was all Thorne could see. Because the roots, visible by that last shaft of white daylight, were turning silver.

Everything hung suspended in the space between heartbeats, and Thorne stopped breathing, every hair on his body standing at attention for his princess.

Then the power snapped loose, a talon spearing straight through the *Aeoprast*.

He crumbled dead at Cistine's feet. No blood. No wound.

He was simply *dead*.

Horrified screams sundered the sky, and all the Bloodwights broke rank. Some retreated down the hillside, running mad and horrified onto the battlefield; most didn't make it that far. Cistine's dark augment lashed across their backs, a cruel whipping Thorne felt in every muscle of his body, and they all dropped dead. Heaps and heaps of robes, masks tumbling off, exposing warped faces beneath.

Cistine strolled to the edge of the hill, hands outturned at her sides. Only the flick of her eyes told the augment where to go, and it pierced the Bloodwights still scattering. It pierced the Balmond, too, ripping them from the sky, but Thorne didn't watch them fall. It was those eyes he couldn't look away from.

Those were not Cistine's eyes. Some sort of madness possessed them, a deep, internal rage, and Thorne realized at last what he was seeing.

She'd broken the *Stor Sedam*. This was the augment they'd feared.

It was Death and Slaughter, a fate from which there was no deliverance, no mercy. Even the armored Bloodwights were powerless against it; the augment passed through them as if they had no substance at all. And in Cistine's eyes, there was no pity, no compassion. There was no thought or reason. The princess, the queen, the Key...they were gone. The power of the augment had possessed her as entirely as the might of many had once twisted Maleck and Pippet.

Someone shouted his name, cutting into his horrified daze. Thorne looked up sharply as Quill darted toward him, bloodied and wide-eyed and spraying damp sod when he skidded to a halt. "What do you need?"

"Pull the ranks back and tell the Chancellors to bring down the Bloodwights Cistine disarmed."

"Where are *you* going?"

"To stop her before that augment breaks free and kills us all."

"Thorne, wait." Quill snagged him by the shoulder. "Wait."

"I can't. I have to help her. She can't do this alone."

Either you stand alone...

"Thorne, look at her!" Quill shouted. "That's not our princess. She'll kill you, too."

Thorne watched his *valenar* carve through the Balmond as if they were nothing, his heart cracking with every painful beat in his chest. If he didn't reach her—and even if he did—

You fall together.

He shook the memory of that nightmare away. "Find the rest of the cabal and get them to safety. Don't come after me."

He ripped free and sprinted toward the hill, sabers drawn, pushing against the fleeing Valgardan army and vaulting over the dead, his stomach rebelling at the stink of death that was already beginning to rise when he approached the bottom of the hill. He spotted two Wardens there, unhurt by all appearances, but facedown and dead in the dirt. Cistine was killing in broad, indiscriminate strokes—even her own people. If she lashed out again before he drew her from that mania, it would mean *his* death. He wouldn't even have time to feel it.

He couldn't define, not even to himself, how much it was worth it. She was worth every risk. Even when she turned toward the retreating army and those jagged talons rose slowly, almost thoughtfully, as if she was deciding which Valgardans to carve down first.

"Cistine!" Thorne bellowed, leaping up the hillside. She froze, and the augment with her. "You have to stop this. *Now.*"

She stared at him, eyes half-lidded with boredom; one lazy limb spiraled out, piercing a Bloodwight who'd cleverly fallen and tried to crawl away through the dead. Thorne watched him slump and felt the harsh bite of his own mortality stalking closer with every second.

Cistine gazed at him with those blank eyes, daring him to interfere again.

Thorne gritted his teeth. He had just gotten her back from the jaws of Nimmus, and he would not allow a stars-damned *augment* to take her away again. "*Enough*, Cistine." He let the metal edge of a Chancellor's command slide into his voice. "The Bloodwights are gone. Let it *go*."

She tipped her head, silver hair draping over her shoulder, shocked threads falling across her eyes. She looked at him, but didn't really *see* him.

Then her eyes flicked to the army retreating at his back. Those molten limbs of shadow and death unfurled, rising up, coiling to dispatch again.

"Cistine, *stand down!*" Thorne lurched the last few steps to the hilltop, and her head flashed back. Her talons shot toward *him*.

Thorne planted his feet, cast down his swords, and held up both hands, though he knew there was no catching it, no bracing, no stopping this. "*Wildheart!*"

An inch from his fingertips, the death-augment halted.

Cistine's eyes widened and her brows slanted, a look of confusion and concern he'd always found devastating in its charm. But even with that familiar twist to her features, he didn't move closer to her. The slightest flicker of intent on his part might coax those blistering shadows to finish their task.

He was staring at his own death, and it wore the face of his *valenar*.

"Wildheart," he repeated, "the battle is over. You saved us. Now let go of the augment before it undoes everything you fought for."

The talons retreated slightly, just enough that Thorne could shift his weight forward, ready to spring aside if she lashed out again.

"Wildheart, look at me," he said, and the skeins of death recoiled even further. "*Let go.*"

Cistine blinked. Her eyes flickered. Then she dropped and swiveled in a broad arc on one knee, dispatching the augment in a cut on both sides of her body, turning the grass to rot. It cleaved Eben's plains worse than any fire, a brand of absolute and instant death pouring out into soil that might never give life to grass and shrubs again.

In moments, the venomous power spidered away into the grass. Cistine crouched in the center of the dark scorch, and Thorne watched clarity return to her eyes.

Still, he approached with caution, keeping his hands outstretched while he sidled toward her. "Cistine, do you see me?"

Her hands covered her cheeks. Her eyes darted from the dead Bloodwights and fallen Balmond up to his face. "I...I see you."

"And I see you." A relieved half-smile jerked at the side of his mouth. "I see that your hair matches mine now."

Cistine's chest jumped up and fell in a great, shuddering sob. "Thorne, what happened? What did I do?"

He opened his mouth, then shut it again, shaking his head. "You won the war, Wildheart."

She sobbed at the sound of her Name and leaped, wrapping her legs around his waist and her arms around his neck. Thorne staggered backward as he caught her thighs, clutching her to him, and her lips crashed down to cover his. He tasted blood on her breath and felt her shaking uncontrollably, but in seconds it no longer mattered. Nothing mattered but her hands in his hair and the feeling of her body beneath her armor pressed to his.

Stars, he'd missed her, had been terrified for her, and *of* her. But she was still Wildheart, still Cistine, still his.

His fingers fell away from her legs, and she dropped down in the soil before him, cradling his neck, her mouth still desperately scouring his. Thorne felt as if his head was coming apart from the rest of him under her touch, a warm, dark rush filling his body.

"I'm so sorry," Cistine whimpered, "I didn't know what it would do, I just knew he was afraid of it and I had to do *something*—"

"You were...magnificent." The words demanded all his strength.

"Thorne?" Cistine's hands framed his cheeks now, and he struggled to focus on her face. "Thorne, what's wrong?"

"Nothing." He chuckled, bending his head and seeking her mouth again, unsteady as a drunkard. "I love you."

Agony shot from his skull down through his shoulders. The breath rushed from his chest all at once.

Thorne Starchaser felt his own heart stop beating.

CHAPTER SIXTY-NINE

THORNE?" CISTINE CAUGHT her *valenar* around the chest as his weight sagged against her, dragging them both down. "Thorne, what's wrong, what is it—*Thorne!*"

He slumped onto his elbow when she lowered him, his head thudding onto the dirt. No breath lifted his ribs. She fumbled at the side of his neck, fingers shaking.

There was no pulse.

Panic choked her, turning her world white. She pushed Thorne onto his back, grabbing his collar, shaking him, screaming his name and screaming for help from anyone, *anyone* still alive who could hear her.

Footsteps pounded the soil. Quill was the first to reach them, armor scorched, hands soaked in blood. Cistine leaped backward as he slid to his knees beside his Chancellor, laying an ear to Thorne's chest, then stripping his armor open. "His heart isn't beating. Ariadne, help me!"

Ariadne tumbled down beside him just as Tatiana crested the hill. Ashe was not there. Nor were Maleck, Aden, or Kristoff.

Cistine wanted to vomit. She wanted to scream again.

They all stared at Thorne, whose voice had pierced the black nothing after Cistine broke the augment, the sound of her Name like a light tower cutting through the power and madness. He'd rescued her, redeemed her from the tide that consumed her the moment she'd shattered that flagon.

Now the Bloodwights were dead, the *Aeoprast* was *dead* behind her, and before her, Thorne, who was also limp, not moving, not *breathing...*

"What did I do?" She clapped a hand over her traitorous mouth that had kissed him, that had done this somehow. "*What did I do?*"

"No one said it was you, Cistine!" Tatiana hurried to her side. "Just let them help."

"Did I kill him?" Cistine shouted. "*Tell me I didn't kill him!*"

Quill started to compress Thorne's chest, urging his heart to beat again. Cistine's knees wavered, the blood fleeing from her face, and Tatiana's hands shot out to catch her.

"Tatiana, *do not* touch her!"

Cistine nearly broke down again at the sound of Maleck's voice. She wanted to run to him, to hide her face in his chest when he appeared at the crest of the hill behind Quill, gasping for breath, his face and front drenched in blood. Agony and grief clouded his gaze, fixed on her. "Death lingers with you, *Logandir*. I can feel it. That augment hasn't left your body."

She stared at him, horror squeezing her throat like a noose.

This *was* her fault—that Thorne wasn't breathing, that Ariadne was breathing *for* him while Quill worked over his chest, shouting at him to come back, to hold on, not to leave them.

She dropped to one knee and slammed the power out, turning the grass to pulse in a small sphere around her body. Tatiana skipped back, cursing as Cistine dealt out blow after blow of augmented energy; but with every stroke, there was more to spend. She yanked at the spool, and it continued to unravel. There was no limit to the death pouring from her body.

"Why won't it—why won't it *stop?*" she sobbed.

"Perhaps this is the price," Maleck murmured. "The price to wield the Undertaker's scythe is that death never leaves you."

"*Did I kill Thorne?*"

Maleck's eyes flashed damply. He offered no reply.

Cistine clung to the soil and killed it over and over as her world pitched like a ship on unsurvivable waves. "Quill please, please, bring him back to me...oh, gods, tell me I didn't, tell me I *didn't* kill him..."

Quill laid a hand on the side of Thorne's neck again, looked at Ariadne, and slowly shook his head. She laid her brow to her fallen Chancellor's, a litany of prayers rising from her lips. "Please, gods, if ever you loved me, if *ever* I served you well, I'm begging you, not this, not him...send him back to us, bring him home, please, *please...*"

Cistine didn't realize she'd slumped over until her head and shoulder impacted the dirt, and she lay there, tears leaking down to join the blood on her cheeks and lips. Shudders wracked her body as she stared at her fallen *selvenar*, stealing whatever strength remained in the limbs that had dispatched death over this battlefield, to the Bloodwights. Death to *Thorne*.

She couldn't feel the augment, but she knew it was still there. A taint on her body. A taint in her blood.

There was no coming back from this.

Warmth dusted over her after a moment, a hot flush pouring through her alongside the wracking grief, and for an instant her tears eased and the choking sobs quieted. Overhead, the augmented storm thinned, that faint light along the horizon prodding its fingers through, reaching out to paint Thorne's body in a pale glow like godly fire.

A whisper, soft and warm, brushed Cistine's ears. *Stornjor.*

Her heart stopped.

A breath of movement through the cabal's midst, a faint scent of cinnamon-and-orange on the wind. Through blurry eyes, Cistine watched the light anneal into a hint of form, of shape, of memory.

An old woman with a ruined leg and strong hands, crouched beside her beloved grandson.

"That...that's not possible," Quill rasped.

But it was the second time Cistine had seen that beloved face today. And after everything that had become of them, on this battlefield and beyond—how could they do anything at all but believe the impossible?

"The True God hears your prayers." Her familiar voice gathered them all close like loving arms. "He has sent a gift for you all."

Glittering eyes, stars-forged in a softly-lined face, turned toward

Ariadne. "For the daughter who remained faithful, even when the world turned its back on her."

Her focus angled toward Quill and Tatiana. "For the warriors who never stopped believing."

Maleck broke down on his knees when her gaze settled on him.

"For the wayward child who conquered his own darkness."

When Cistine met Baba Kallah's eyes, the tears flowed anew—tears of blind grief, and love, and hope so powerful it took her breath away.

"For the princess who laid down her life for all the kingdoms."

Baba Kallah bent, and her dry lips touched Thorne's bloodstained brow. "For my boy. Who has not even begun to chase his stars yet."

The light shattered, spraying across the battlefield in a blast as warm as summer heat, yanking the last few sobs from Cistine's chest and blinding her eyes; when she blinked the glittering green dapples away, there was only daylight and the faces of the cabal around her, every cheek tearstained, every eye wild with wonder.

Then Quill cursed in relief. "His heart's beating!"

Gasping, Cistine flipped over and crawled to the edge of the dead grass to see for herself how her *valenar's* chest rose in a thready, shallow breath...then another, and another. With a sob of joy, Ariadne gathered Thorne into her lap, propping him up so he could breathe.

Cistine fell back on her heels, her elation and relief guttering, a kernel of darkness nudging in.

Ariadne held him. Maleck and Quill and Tatiana circled them, arms around each other, brows pressed together.

All while she gripped the green grass and watched the blades turn black as char, wilting at the touch of her hand.

THE
AFTERMATH

CHAPTER SEVENTY

THORNE DRIFTED IN and out of a dream of starlight wreathed with the smell of orange and cinnamon. A familiar kiss on his brow, gnarled hands that reminded him of dancing and dreaming and screaming obscenities in an abandoned cabin until his lungs gave way—then a whisper that carried over from dreaming to awake.

For my boy. Who has not even begun to chase his stars yet.

He wanted to beg her not to go, but it was only a dream.

Slowly, he came aware. His chest ached as if he'd challenged Quill to a two-hundred-push-up match. Every limb felt like a metal cast clamped in a blacksmith's vise. Even when he was fully conscious of sounds and smells trickling past him, for a time he couldn't open his eyes or move his tongue to wet his lips. But he did know a crisp, clean, cold scent, and the artificial burble of a fountain; the voices of the cabal, murmuring nearby; and the sounds of city life, always coming and going, until he parsed out exactly where he was.

"House of healing."

These were the first words he managed after stars-knew how long. That dull rasp stopped the conversation around him with impressive finality.

Then Aden's voice, equally dry: "Yes, we're in Stornhaz."

Thorne grimaced. He still couldn't open his heavy eyes. "Cistine?"

This beat of silence was longer, deeper, as if they were all waiting for something. At last, Tatiana said, "She's not here. Not inside the city, either."

Frowning, he fought again, and this time finally won the battle to open his eyes. There was no mistaking the house of healing where his aunt Natalya once served, the familiar ivory walls with their fine gilding, the reek of death hidden by cloying herbs and potted vases.

Thorne was lying on the room's only bed, overstarched sheets sticking to his bare chest. Someone had removed his armor and redressed him in linen pants; he hoped for his own sake it was Cistine. The cabal gathered at the walls, their faces in varying states of sleepless worry; Aden nearest to the door, Quill and Tatiana in bedside chairs, Ariadne cross-legged at his feet.

No sign of Cistine or Maleck. Of Ashe, Kristoff, or Sander.

Thorne looked at Quill. "Report."

He cleared his throat, flipping his hair across his head. "Not enough healing augments to go around. The army was in poor shape, so the Chancellors brought everyone back. They..." he trailed off, eyes flicking toward the corner.

"They requested Cistine not show her face here," Ariadne growled. "At least not until they quiet rumors about what happened on the Deathmarch."

Thorne tucked away his anger and made a silent vow to speak with his fellow Chancellors at length in private. "Who did we lose?"

Tatiana stared down at her hands. "Sander."

"And as for Ashe and my father," Aden's voice shook, "we don't know yet. Maleck is with him, Pippet with her. They'll come for us if..."

"If *anything* changes," Ariadne supplied firmly.

Fear spiked in Thorne's chest, his stomach clenching with nausea, but there was nothing to give. "Who else?"

"Halfgrim and Vaclav," Ariadne said. "Half the Legion. Bresnyar nearly lost a wing; the medicos are keeping him unconscious while they try to save it."

"Benedikt is dead," Aden added. "Kyost will take power soon. For now, the Courts are leaning on one another. They've left some people behind to build pyres and burn the *mirothadt*. That will take several weeks, but they'll manage."

"And us?" Thorne asked.

"We're...alive," Tatiana said. "Not whole, but alive."

"We had to carry your ass all the way here from the wall." Quill's tone was mock-stern, but a tremble of emotion belied his annoyance. "You're really heavy, you know that?"

"So I've been told." Thorne pushed himself up against the pillow. "What happened on that battlefield?"

"Cistine was carrying the killing augment when she touched you," Ariadne said softly. "She still carries it."

Thorne grimaced. "How many days has it been?"

"Half a week," Tatiana said. "I've been with her every second I'm not here. The augment isn't going away."

A hum of disbelief filled his ears. "That's not possible. All augments run their course."

"Not this one."

Deafening silence gripped the room, and Thorne pushed himself all the way up, gritting his teeth against the throb in his head, his back, and his chest. "I have to see her."

"*Allet*, wait." Quill hopped to his feet, raising both hands in warning. "You *died* out there. You just woke up, you can't—"

"Watch me."

Ariadne rose when he did, putting a hand to his chest, halting him in place. Something in that touch, in her look, jolted him; a faint thread of memory that went deeper than his flesh and bone, straight to his heart, teasing loose that dream again.

A whispered voice. A prayer. An anchor for his spirit, grounding him when he was halfway to the Sable Gates.

Ariadne took his hand, turned it over, and pressed a wind augment into it. "Ten minutes. Then we come after you."

Thorne kissed her temple and limped from the room, out into the mercifully-empty hall, where he broke into a tilted, staggering run.

⁓⁓⁓

The wind augment could carry him no farther than the edge of the wall, and from there he followed his sense of Cistine up the broken stairs to the top, where she sat alone, cross-legged, staring at the plains beyond. The dragons healed there, stretching scorched wings and injured limbs, their Wingmaidens tending their wounds. Sunset painted the world in fuchsia and gold light, streaking his *valenar's* tearstained face and silver hair.

She was wearing a simple, sheer dress, and his old, armored leather coat over it—the one he'd sent her off with to Talheim. It nearly engulfed her whole frame, her knees drawn inside the bottom hem, the last two inches of the sleeves flopping limply against her ankles.

His body weak again from the climb and the augment, Thorne padded down the wall toward her. "Wildheart."

She flinched, head snapping toward him. "*Thorne?*"

A smile yanked at his mouth just to see her. But when he approached, she cast up a hand and scrambled backward on her knees.

"Don't!" she shouted. "*Don't* come any closer."

He halted. "Cistine—"

"I killed you once. I might do it again."

"I know you didn't mean to hurt me."

"But I *did*." Fresh tears traced down her cheeks, and everything in him longed to wipe them away, to press his lips to her brow.

But he *couldn't*, and that was just now beginning to sink in, erasing the flicker of joy at seeing her. It brought him so low he buckled to the top of the wall, folding his legs beneath him. "Tell me what you need."

Her stomach lifted with a long, trembling breath. "I don't know. I can't think, I can't plan...it's like that augment took my mind and shredded it, then stuffed it back in the wrong way."

"That was more power than any of us has wielded...than perhaps anyone ever has. You're stronger than any augur, but you aren't immune. Give yourself time to heal."

"But I can't just *sit* here, all I can think about is what happened on that hilltop, what I did to you..." She trailed off, pressing a hand to her mouth and shutting her eyes. Thorne's fingers flexed uselessly at his sides, aching to hold her.

"I think the only reason you were able to come back was because of your armor and inkings," Cistine added between her fingers, eyes still shut.

"You think they conducted the augment?"

She nodded. "But not enough that you could touch me again."

"Would you let me try?"

She slowly shook her head.

Thorne didn't know what else to say, his heart fracturing at the pain in her face. He stared across the fields for a moment, the dragons roosting and basking below, tending to their wounds. It seemed a lifetime ago when the creatures had littered the forest around Lake Erani, the night after he'd married Cistine, and now here they sat, at arm's length from one another, the promise of death hanging between them.

So much had changed in such a short time.

A thought struck him then, sizzling with another memory of that night. "The *visnprestas*."

Cistine's eyes swiveled to him. "What about them?"

"What if they know something about the *Stor Sedam*? How to end their effects?"

She blinked, hope darting like a flicker of lightning through her gaze. "Do you really think they might?"

"It's possible." Thorne knocked his fist on the stone, squinting down over the wall. "And if any *visnpresta* does, I know which one."

CHAPTER
SEVENTY-ONE

ASHE HAD NEARLY slipped through Maleck's fingers. He would've known it even if he hadn't seen the medicos' faces when he'd brought her to them on the battlefield's edge. The same way death had called him to his cabal on that hill, away from her side, it hung over her, too. It lingered still in her room in the house of healing where he and Aden had come as boys to pester Natalya, a place of buttermilk walls and cream drapes and quiet, soft misery. This gentle corner of Nimmus where Asheila Kovar lay wrapped in linens, face so pale her hair lit like fire around her sallow, jutting cheekbones.

At least she no longer thrashed and moaned. Those long hours where her agony was so visible he felt like a villain himself for clinging to her while the medicos measured the waves of her pain, seeking herbs and augments to cure it, had been among the worst of his life. Of Aden's, too, his voice cracking with every growl of *You do not break, you do not break*, while Maleck could not speak at all—could only weep at the agonized whimpers and pants and sobs she made, like nothing he'd ever heard from her before. They'd both gripped her hands and held fast through those rollicking seas, but now...

Now he was alone, and she was so still, he wasn't certain if that was better or worse. Better for her sake, perhaps; but in his mind, the screams went on and on.

Death lurked down every corridor here. Dead warriors, dead smiles on vacant faces robbed of joy. The weight rubbed against his back, bowing him low over Ashe's bedside, his folded arms hiding a face that ached from weeping.

It hurt to be with the cabal. It hurt to be alone. Ariadne had sat with him and prayed over Ashe for so many hours they both lost their voices. Tatiana and Quill had brought food and comfort with their arms around him and their heads pressed against his, passing the time in silence. Pippet had crawled into his lap and braided birch bracelets that hung limp from Ashe's wrists now, and Rozalie had stood watch at the door, shedding her own tears in silence for her friend.

Aden came most often. He divided his time constantly between his father's room and Ashe's, always with the same shadows stamped under his eyes and his fingertips digging into the new scar on his palm.

Not a battle-wound, he'd told Maleck over Ashe's bed one day. An oath he had yet to fulfill—Sander's dying wish.

Maleck could hardly keep his hands on all the pain everyone was feeling, all the different hurts within himself. His mind was a constant storm whether he woke or slept or *tried* to sleep.

Funeral or pyre, Talheimic or Valgardan sendoff, what do I give her, what does she need? Not to be returned to the Wardens, Talheim is her home, her life, but she's one of us now. Stars, how do I tell Bresnyar his Wingmaiden is—

My valenar *is—*

A dry heave rasped from his chest, and he tightened the cross of his arms. He'd been too slow, gotten her to the medicos too late, had taken too long to reach the house of healing, and now it was just a matter of time, they said. Time would give her strength, or take the last of it.

His *Mereszar*, his fearless one. She would either step back into his reach or walk away from him for the last time.

He couldn't bear it. Couldn't think beyond her passing. Stars, he couldn't *breathe*.

"I wish you wouldn't leave me." The words escaped him in the gentle quiet of the room, on a night as dark as all the others before it. "But if the pain is too great, then let go, Asheila. I'll..."

He couldn't force the lie to his lips. He would not be all right. But he would not force her into this shell, locked in agony, if her spirit stretched out for Cenowyn and eternal rest.

"On that battlefield," he said instead, "when the world seemed to be at its end...in that moment, my whole life passed before me. And you were the best part of it all." He gripped her limp hand in both of his and kissed her callused knuckles. "Nothing will change that. I will carry you with me always, even if you choose to go."

A quiet knock on the doorpost roused him. He swiveled his gaze to find Tatiana leaning against the frame, one arm crossing her middle. She tossed an orange to herself, then held it up for him. "Hungry?"

"I can't remember when I last was."

"That makes eight of us." She limped to the bedside and slumped in the chair next to him, peeling the fruit in two. "Thorne's awake."

"I know." Whispers had reached him already of his Chancellor tearing from the house of healing, no doubt on his way to find Cistine. "I should have been there."

"But you were afraid to leave her, I know." Tatiana gave a chin nod to Ashe. "Any change?"

"None. Whether or not that's good..."

"Time will tell." Her breath blew out in a rush. "I know what that's like. Stars, the times I've sat like this with Quill..."

Guilt snarled his insides like thorny vines, and he dropped his gaze to the bedclothes.

Half an orange appeared under his nose.

"I've decided I forgive you," Tatiana added. "Addiction can make you feel like you're an entirely different person who wants different things and takes different risks. And what happened in Hvallatar wasn't just you, either. *You* didn't pick that fight."

"I tried to stop it."

"I know you did, which is why I didn't beat *your* face in once you came back." She waved the orange, wafting sweet citrus notes into his nostrils, his stomach seizing with hunger. He took the fruit and tore into it while she tore into hers, and together they sat back and watched Ashe's inert face.

"If the worst happens," Tatiana said at length, "you know you won't be alone, don't you?"

Dry mouth stinging with sweetness, Maleck wiped his lips on his wrist and forced a nod. "I've never been."

She offered her fist to him. "You never will be."

Maleck bumped knuckles with her, and they went back to eating. But it was good not to be alone.

The door burst open again, and this time it was Rozalie, scowling. "Trouble at the wall, Mal. Ashe's dragon is awake and he's trying to climb it. They can't talk him down, but he can't fly. He's going to hurt someone or himself if he doesn't stop."

Maleck shot to his feet. "I'm on my way."

Without the wind augments most took to cross the city, it seemed an eternity before he reached the wall; but Bresnyar was not difficult to find on its edge, his bellows a beacon more animal than intelligent for once. Vassoran guards lined the top of the wall when Maleck ascended, polearms aimed fearfully at the dragon's golden snout jutting over the cracked stone.

Cursing, Maleck shoved between them, forcing down their weapons. "This is a Wingmaiden's mount who helped win the war, and you repay him with threats?"

"He'll crush the wall if he keeps flailing like that!" one man shouted. "Call him off!"

Maleck faced the falcate of guards, his back to Bresnyar, arms outflung. "Raise a weapon against him again, and you answer to me."

"What's going on here?"

Maleck's spine nearly bent in relief at the sound of Thorne's voice. For the first time in days, he laid eyes on his Chancellor, not bedridden, but awake, limping down the wall. Cistine trailed far behind him, Thorne's old armored leather coat tight around her shoulders, eyes wide.

"Bres, what is it?" she shouted.

His eyes, fiery-gold with pupils narrow as needles, revolved between them all. "Where is Asheila? Why can I not *cleave* with her? Why are these tiny, edible *bastards* keeping me from her?"

Maleck met Thorne's eyes, intent conveyed in a single glance. His Chancellor whistled, bringing the Vassora around, and Maleck turned and strode to Bresnyar's side, laying a hand on his snout.

"Come down off this wall with me, and I'll tell you," he rasped. "But not like this. She wouldn't want to see us this way."

Bresnyar's nostrils steamed, his pupils flaring wider. A hint of sense returned; then he scooped Maleck to his chest with one hand and fell backward from the wall.

It was a short, steep spiral, exhilarating until the moment Bresnyar tried to snap out his wings—and tilted sharply. Their shouts broke out in tandem when the dragon plowed into the soil, the pound of his impact overshadowed by sympathetic groans from his fellow dragons.

Maleck crawled from the cage of Bresnyar's grip, spitting sod, and staggered around to face him. Embarrassed shivers twitched the dragon's flanks like horsehide when he stumbled up as well, one wing hanging useless at his side. "I'd forgotten, this damaged thing..."

Maleck slipped under the wing, skimming his hands over fiber and joint. "Did Tatiana never find that healing augment?"

"*Navalo.*" Bresnyar tugged the wing painfully against his side, bringing Maleck back into the light. "Where is she?"

He let his hands fall at his sides, flexing uselessly, looking away from the dragon across the field where so pitifully-few Wingmaidens remained. "She was...injured. Badly."

Hot breath steamed his back. "But she *lives.*"

Maleck nodded, but fear bladed his chest. What if even now, while he was gone, she slipped away?

He pivoted sharply back to the wall, to return to the city, then froze.

Bresnyar had fallen silently on his haunches, legs folded, head bent and wings tucked like armor against him. His injured limb shuddered with pain.

"If she is gone," he rasped, "I do not know...what I am now. To have met and bonded with her, that is unheard of. Did she ever tell you that? Two Wingmaidens in one lifetime is beyond belief. I do not know what becomes of me without her."

Maleck swallowed his own grief and stepped forward, looping an arm around the base of the dragon's neck and smoothing a hand down his shoulder. "You will still be mine. Three as one, or two as one. I will not abandon you, whatever comes."

After a moment, Bresnyar's chin scraped his spine, his body loosening in a sigh that smelled of scorch and salt. They stood there for a long time, man and dragon united in their fear and grief for the woman they loved, dancing down the edge of life and death—beyond their power to save her.

CHAPTER
SEVENTY-TWO

*F*OR A BETTER *Chancellor. A better future.*

The words hummed in Aden's sluggish mind while he sat at his father's bedside, fingertips following the jagged, unhealed slash across his palm.

He'd developed a minor infection in it. One of the medicos had offered him a healing augment, a privilege for a Tribune, but he settled for a tincture instead. He wanted it to scar, to become gnarled and white and cratered, to sting during cold winters and rub hard and cumbersome against every weapon he wielded from this day to his last.

He wanted to carry that vow with him always, to remind him what was lost, what was nearly taken from him...and what he was fighting for.

He looked away from the scar, flipping his hand to grip his father's. Kristoff lay prone, as he had for days, eyes loosely shut, breathing shallowly. The healing augments had done their work, but he'd been so close to death, so stars-damned close to slipping away from Aden once again, that he was afraid of what would happen if he shut his eyes.

A knock on the doorframe, and Quill jutted his head into the room. "Thorne just snuck Cistine into his room."

Aden tensed, looking between Quill and his father. His feet felt rooted, but his heart knew his cousin needed him. With a last squeeze of his father's wrist, he dragged himself from the chair.

They were the last to arrive in Thorne's room; even Maleck was there, smelling faintly of char and churned earth. But it was strangest to see Cistine tucked into a corner, wearing a poached scarf like a cowl over her jacket and dress, while all of them gave her a wide berth.

He wasn't certain he'd ever grow used to this new way of being, or to the agony in his cousin's face while he stared at his *valenar*.

The moment the door shut, Cistine said, "I'm going to Holmlond."

Pain and dread cut through Aden so swiftly, he braced himself against the wall to keep his legs beneath him.

"Why there?" Tatiana asked.

"Because Iri and Saychelle went back to help look after the people there once we reclaimed Stornhaz," Cistine said. "I'm hoping they might know something about this augment. And if not them, Mira might've uncovered something more in the books."

Mira. The very reason Aden dreaded the mention of that place. But the scar across his palm twinged like a blade prodding his back, forcing the words from him: "I'll accompany you."

Her eyes shot to him, full of surprise at first—then quiet, sympathetic understanding.

Thorne stretched and stifled a groan. "So will I."

"No," Cistine argued. "You were *dead*, you're still recovering—"

"Then we'll go slowly." He held up a hand when she started to protest. "I'm your husband, Cistine. We do these things together. That was the vow we made."

Her jaw snapped shut. She glared at him.

"What about the rest of us?" Tatiana demanded. "We're not just going to sit around looking pretty while we wait for you to come back."

"If you're eager for a challenge, you can appeal to the Chancellors," Thorne said. "Make it clear that when I return, it will be *with* Cistine, and she will not be shut out. They will not throw her from a city that only stands free because of her sacrifice."

"It's not that simple," Cistine mumbled.

"For me, it could be no simpler."

"Thorne, I almost killed you. I *did* kill you." Her voice shook. "I killed *our* people, Wardens, augurs...they all saw what I can do."

"And the fear of power rather than the respect of it is what brings war. Do what you do best...show them that a princess will not be denied."

Cistine opened her mouth, then shut it, looking away from him. Ariadne shrugged up from the wall. "I'll speak to Adeima."

"I'm with you," Quill said.

"And the three of us had best find wind augments," Thorne said. "There's no need to make this trek by foot."

Aden bit back his argument. There really was no sense in delay, except that he did not want to have this conversation. Not now. Not ever.

But he had a promise to keep.

He turned to go, and Thorne said his name, quiet, level. A command.

One by one, the others slipped out, Cistine last to go with a glance back at Thorne, whose eyes Aden could feel branding the back of his skull. The moment they were alone, Aden swung back to him. "Don't say—"

His cousin's arms closed around him, an embrace so fierce it knocked the wind out of him.

"Thank you," Thorne said gruffly. "Ariadne told me you were there for Sander's pyre when I was still unconscious. Thank you, *Allet*."

Aden cleared his throat and clapped Thorne on the back. "It was the least I could do for both of you."

"It wasn't the least of anything. It was exactly what needed doing, what you always do. Which is why I'm going to name you High Tribune in his stead."

Cursing, Aden shoved Thorne out at arm's length, searching his face for a hint of humor—or madness. But he found none; just Thorne staring back at him, steady and fierce as ever.

"You want *me*," he growled, "to take Sander's place."

"There's no one else in the kingdoms I'd give the task to. Besides, you're already a Tribune. It's just one more step."

"It's more than that. It's the line of succession. If anything happens to you..."

He would become Chancellor. *Chancellor* Aden Bloodsinger.

"Luckily for us both, I have no intention of anything happening to me. Well, nothing that hasn't already happened," Thorne said with a touch of humor. "But Kanslar can't be without a High Tribune, and of those who still live, there's none I trust with my back or my Court more than you."

"I don't deserve this honor."

Thorne studied him frankly. "Do you trust me, Aden?"

"You know the answer to that."

"Then trust I know what you deserve better than you do." Thorne cuffed him on the shoulder. "You helped make me the man who could lead Kanslar. Now it's time for you to lead it with me."

Aden curled his hand into a fist, fingers digging into his palm; into the scar. Into the memory of that promise.

A better Chancellor. A better future.

"All right. I'm with you," he said quietly. "As far as you go, for as long as it takes."

CHAPTER SEVENTY-THREE

MALECK DID NOT return to Ashe's room alone that evening. Rozalie was already there, sitting at the bedside, speaking in hushed tones while she sharpened a blade; and on Maleck's heels, twice the shadow he'd ever been, Cistine slipped into the room as well.

Rozalie shifted to her feet at once, arm across her chest. "Princess." An exhausted twinkle sparkled in her eyes. "Mal."

"Rozalie." He inclined his head, then looked again at Cistine. She pressed herself to the wall, mouth faintly agape and eyes fixed on Ashe.

"She looks so *tired*."

Panic noosed Maleck's throat. She was right, his *Mereszar* looked exhausted—bruised eyes and puckered veins and a pallor that made him aware, for the very first time, of a spray of freckles across her brow and shoulders. How had he never noticed these things before? And now he feared he collected them to remember her by when she was gone.

Cistine crossed to the bedside and stood over it, not touching even the hem of the blanket. She pulled the starstone from around her neck and coiled it on the pillow beside Ashe's head.

"I love you, Ashe." The words fell with the tears rolling down her cheeks. "And I still need you. I'm sorry I didn't come sooner, but I'm here now, and you *have* to listen to me. You have to come back."

Hope plucked Maleck's spirit like wobbling piano chords, but there was no change; only a quiet, disappointed sigh through Rozalie's barely-parted lips when Ashe did not stir.

Cistine stepped back after a moment, cleaning her face on her sleeve. "I should go. The wind augments."

"Be careful," Maleck cautioned. "And be quick. The sooner you're healed, the sooner we can all return to the Den and continue our lives."

A foolish offer, he knew. Things would never be the same, and he had sworn a promise to Ashe that might take him away from them still. But he saw how much the notion meant to Cistine in the brightening of her eyes, her fleeting smile before she scurried out the door.

Rozalie dropped back into the bedside chair, grasping Ashe's wrist. "You know, I never thought I'd say this, but I miss petty criminals and Mahasari threats. Dragons and Deathmarches and killing augments might just be beyond a Warden's purview."

Reluctant laughter shook out of Maleck as he lowered himself to the chair beside her. "If it's any consolation, Aden tells me you fought magnificently. And what will you do now that you know of these things?"

"I'm not sure." Her eyes cut to him, wearied yet warm. "Try to be better than what I was. Remember there's a whole world I know nothing about, and take my time to learn what I can, when I can." She stood and squeezed his shoulder, her gaze lingering on Ashe. "I'd better check in with the rest of the Wardens. Send word if—"

"I will."

With Rozalie gone, Maleck watched the shadows lower and elongate across the walls, and his brief spurt of raised spirits faded into them. Somehow sleep found him in the darkness with his arms folded on Ashe's bedside once again; but in the shadows of dreams his brothers found him, too. Terror added feet to their height, murky-edged beasts filling his whole world. Skulls leered and hands grasped and his throat burned with every drop of a blood augment forced down his throat, pooling in his middle, twisting and reshaping him into something heinous and bloodthirsty again.

From a distance, he watched the unfettered cold of the death augment blasting across the battlefield, cleaving down warrior after warrior, and at the heart of it, *Wildheart,* burning like a fallen star.

In his nightmares he relived that moment in the medico tents, pacing at Ashe's bedside while the medicos worked feverishly over her, when the wind had banked and turned frigid and he knew, deep in his spirit, that something worse had come than even his brothers. Darker than anything ever faced before.

But though he ran to Cistine in his dreams, roaring her Name, his brothers' bony hands clattered shut in steel-tipped cages around his arms and his legs, towing him back and dragging him down.

You let this happen you gave her the blood augment you carved the path from there to here and now she is broken she is set apart she is destroyed because you made the way you did this to her YOU DID THIS YOU—

Mal.

The battlefield burned, Bresnyar bellowed, Thorne cried out for Cistine, his pained voice shattering the sky.

Maleck.

Ashe bled, the cabal crumbled, the Bloodwights chanted with victory as the world fell at their feet.

Darkwind.

Maleck sucked in a sharp breath through his nostrils, eyes flying wide, head jerking up from his arms at the summons of his Name. Sleep released its aching hold on his temples and he was back, the room guttering in late-night shadows, a ghostlamp winking soft shades of fire-orange against the walls.

A scarred, strong hand rested over his.

His gaze flew to Ashe's face and found the slits of her blue-and-green eyes watching him through dark lashes.

"Hello, you beautiful, braided bastard." A smirk hung in her voice, heavy though it was with sleep. Tears sprang to his eyes at the sight of hers.

She was *awake.*

"Mal. Say something. Am I really that hurt?"

He choked on something—a laugh, an answer, her name—then

wrapped both hands around hers and kissed her knuckles, letting out all the breath he'd been holding so quickly it dizzied him. He slid onto the bed, took her face carefully in both hands, and kissed her with all his might, letting the unspoken words dance between his tongue and hers until she jabbed her knuckles into his ribs and forced him to let go.

They were both panting, but some of the color returned to her face, to her eyes—wider now, fixed on him. "That bad?"

Maleck set his brow against hers. "I thought you were gone, Asheila. Truly gone. There was so much blood, and it took me so long to reach you..."

"The gods must love me," Ashe grunted. "Or maybe not. This hurts worse than anything I...what did I miss? Did we win? I thought I heard Cistine."

Maleck hesitated, a chill raking up his spine.

Ashe's eyes narrowed. "*Mal.*"

"There were...many losses. Sander is gone."

Ashe's chest stopped rising. She stared at him for uncountable seconds, not blinking, not moving, and he watched her rise and fall along an incomprehensible swell of pain like the agony of being birthed into a new world, emptier and quieter with the High Tribune ripped from it.

"Nimea?" she said at last.

Maleck cocked his head. "How did you—?"

"I remember. I was trying to cleave, and she cut past my guard." Her hand drifted to her abdomen. "She said the blow was for Andras, but I figured it was more than that. She wouldn't die until she took everything and everyone Aden cared about."

"She nearly succeeded. You, then Sander, then Kristoff..."

Ashe's hand dropped to his again, seizing tight. "*Tell me he's not dead.*"

"Not dead, but unconscious still."

"God's bones," Ashe hissed, pressing her free hand to her wounded middle. "If I had just brought her down with me—"

"You would not have survived a fight in that state."

"Then I should've ended it with my sword in her skull. I could've lived with that." She winced again. "In a manner of speaking."

"I couldn't. Nor could Aden, I think."

Her gaze focused on his face. "How is he?"

"Hurting. He doesn't like to speak of this...any of it. Not even Sander. I suspect he's holding his words for Mira."

"She doesn't know yet?"

"If she does, it isn't by our mouths."

Ashe cursed softly, head falling back among the pillows. "What about the others?"

"Alive. Healing. But Cistine is...unwell."

Ashe's hand scraped up his arm, birch bracelet rasping on his armor, and her fingers closed around his elbow. "Tell me."

"Not yet. You need to rest, to recover your strength."

Her eyes narrowed, but she didn't argue. "Bresnyar's wing?"

"Salvaged, but barely. He and the rest of the Legion are recovering outside the walls. I've been to see him every day, and today he was awake." He brushed his thumb over her knuckles. "He fears for you, for what he'd become without you. It's a concern we share."

"You can tell him I'll be fine. I'll cleave with him once this damned dizziness passes." Ashe blew out her breath and shut her eyes.

Fear rocked through him, and he rested one hand on the pillow and cupped her neck with the other. "Asheila."

"I'm not dying, Maleck. Just...you're right. I need more sleep."

"Don't go."

Pitiful, selfish, but the words slid through his teeth all the same. If this war had taught him nothing else, it was that he was not strong enough to let the girl from the tundra, the woman from the Vingete Vey, the warrior from every prayer and every hope for his future, leave him for the last time.

He would *never* be ready.

Ashe's eyes flickered back open. Her hand slid down his arm again, and her fingers laced between his. "Lie down."

Heat stormed his face. "That isn't allowed here."

"Since when have we ever cared what's allowed? Lie *down*, Maleck."

Slowly, he stretched out, Ashe's body lying along the curve of his, his head on the pillow next to hers. She shut her eyes again and dragged his hand to rest over her bandaged middle where he could feel it rise and fall with every breath.

"*You* stay," she mumbled, "right here. Like you promised."

Then she slept. But it was a gentler sleep, lighter than before, and that gave him enough peace to close his eyes as well.

He was drifting, just on the edge of dreams, when he heard the quiet press of a boot on the floor. A breath sucked in with a shallow, wobbly curse—Aden's voice. "No, no, *no...*"

The rasp of his palm on Ashe's neck, feeling for a pulse. And then Ashe's unsteady hiss: "*Rargh.*"

Aden's knee banged into the bedside and he cursed again, sharp and full of shock, and it took all Maleck's strength not to chuckle—to keep his eyes shut and feign sleep for both their sakes while Ashe's quiet laughter shook the bed.

"I'm sorry. It was too perfect."

"You're still the biggest thorn in my side."

"Oh, really? Is that why Maleck says you've been weeping at my bedside day and night?"

"No, that...that was because I was terrified to lose you."

The silence stretched on, an ache building steadily in Maleck's gut at the anguish in his brother's voice.

A brush of hands together. A squeeze of bone and muscle. "I'm sorry about Sander. We owe him our lives...I'll never stop being grateful for that."

"Nor will I. For that, or for yours."

Aden's breaths stuttered nearer to Maleck's face when he pressed a kiss to Ashe's brow.

"I'm sorry I wasn't there."

"You were right where you needed to be." A beat. "Now you need to stop stalling and go tell Mira. She has to hear it from you."

If there were any other words exchanged between them, Maleck did not hear them; sleep claimed him, dragging him deep and quick into the shadows. It was daylight again when he stirred, warm and drowsy and content; someone had tossed a blanket over him and Ashe. A quick glance over the room showed him they were not alone: in the corner, Quill and Pippet slept, backs against the wall, her head on his shoulder and his arm wrapped around her. And Ashe was in Maleck's arms, pressed to his chest, blended hearts beating next to each other, steady and in rhythm. Perfectly one.

Love rose up in him, choking and blinding and healing.

Perhaps it was all a gift. Perhaps he didn't deserve any of this, but he whispered a silent prayer to the gods all the same, for every piece of it. Every moment they were alive.

CHAPTER
SEVENTY-FOUR

THE MOMENT THEIR wind augments deposited them on the black basalt span outside Holmlond, Aden wanted to flee. He'd never considered himself a coward—not when facing undefeatable Balmond, *mirothadt* hordes, Siralek fighters, or his own mortality. But telling Mira her *valenar* was dead at the hands of Aden's own nemesis threatened to turn his courage to embers. It was only Cistine and Thorne's resolute presence that dragged him up the long path to that distant door, palms sweating and jaw gritted.

He reached the threshold well behind his Chancellor and the Princess, and they did not wait for him, focused ahead on hope in the hands of the *visnprestas*.

Aden held no such hope. Only a task that must be done.

He entered the foyer, warm and deserted, and stood for a moment in its center to gather his strength. This was not like telling Siralek fighters who among their ranks had perished in matches; there was grief in him, and gratitude, and sorrow beyond measure. Like a piece of him had been carved away, and he now had to carve that piece out of someone else.

Someone who did not deserve to bleed.

Footsteps thudded in the hall above, and before Aden had fully gathered himself or chosen the words to deliver the blow, Mira hurried into the tower—and froze halfway down the staircase, catching sight of him.

For a long moment, they stared at one another, and for the first time in his life Aden deeply and truly felt his heart break.

"Aden?" Mira took another uncertain step down.

He dipped his head, sparing himself the confusion in her eyes. "Hello, Mirassah."

"I don't understand." She descended to the foyer floor, banding her cardigan around her body like armor. "The Vassora said...they said Chancellor Thorne and his High Tribune were here."

Aden was going to dismember whoever had delivered the news that way. "Mira..."

When he stepped toward her, she retreated an equal step, brow creasing. "No. No, Sander? *Sander* is High Tribune."

Aden halted, hand curling into a fist, pressing into the scar. "He was...among the greatest to ever serve the Courts. I don't know how I'll measure up to what he did for Kanslar. For all of us."

She shook her head. "Is. He *is* among the greatest."

"He *was*, Mira."

Her hand slapped to her mouth, but it was not enough to muffle the sob of, "*No, stars, please, no...*" that broke from her lips. Her legs buckled, and Aden moved without thinking, catching her and bringing them both down to the floor in a heap. Tears wracked out of her, loud and mighty, full of agony beyond reason, and her nails dug into his forearm, scraping bloody crescents with a grip so strong she would have anchored Sander to life had she been the one holding him on that battlefield.

It was some time before either of them spoke. When the sobs quieted at last, Aden offered to send for Hana and Kendar, but Mira refused. She stood, quiet, icily calm all at once, and walked from the tower. Aden followed when she left the door open, a silent invitation.

They walked some distance to the west, to the verge of sky and sea where the waves drank the setting sun. Mira sat down on the cliff, and Aden shed his armored jacket and spread it over her shoulders. Pulling it tight around herself, chin high and gaze fixed, she stared across the waves. "Was he alone?"

"I was with him," Aden said. "For all the good it did."

"It meant everything. His greatest fear was dying alone the way his father did. He used to have one of our warriors sleep in the room with him wherever he went...even when he traveled to Siralek."

Aden linked his arms loosely around his knees, gazing down at the black sand between his boots. Blood still crusted their tips—some of it Sander's. "I didn't know."

"Few did. He never wanted to seem weak, particularly in front of men like you with so much skill and reputation." Mira tipped her face back and shut her eyes against the briny wind. "He wanted so badly to be worthy of his place in Kanslar. Worthy to serve under Thorne."

"He was beyond worthy. He led the Court while the cabal scattered. He found us a way into Stornhaz. We owe victory to him."

Fresh tears spilled down Mira's cheeks, and Aden cursed himself for ever opening his mouth.

For a time, they were silent again, watching the sun settle lower and lower on the horizon. Then Aden ventured another painful truth: "Sander has named you the full inheritor of his family's lands and heritage, both in Stornhaz and Nordbran. You will want for nothing."

Her smile was small and sad, drifting at the edges of her lips. "*Nothing*. Nothing but for the man I love to go on living. I will want that for the rest of my days, Aden."

He raked a hand through his hair and stifled a curse. "Forgive me. That was insensitive."

"In my trade I've learned most attempts at comfort are." Mira turned her cheek against her shoulder, watching him through tear-spangled lashes. "Have you ever been in love?"

Notions of desert sand, sun-bronzed skin and wicked two-colored eyes danced through his mind. He shrugged. "Perhaps once. Briefly. But that was not to be."

"You would know if you had been, especially if it left you. I've...I have *never* felt a pain like this." Surprise lilted her tone at the measure of her grief, the burden of such an unexpected blow. "I never told him how much

I feared being alone, too." She sniffled deeply, and smiled in earnest now—bravery offered in the face of agony. "I'm glad you were there, of all people, at the end. And I'm glad you're here now."

"I'll be here as often as you need me. However you'll have me. I gave him my word."

Mira covered his hand with hers and squeezed. Silent once more, they watched the sunset wreath the Agerios Sea with the memory of blood spilled across the land.

Blood that was precious to them both.

CHAPTER
SEVENTY-FIVE

IRI AND SAYCHELLE'S shared chamber was bright and warm, the dark rock braided over with sashes and streamers, and Saychelle was tending to a superficial burn on a woman's hand when Thorne and Cistine arrived. She finished knotting off the bandage before she looked up at them, and her eyes flashed in surprise.

Thorne smoothed a calming hand through the air and settled himself against the wall to wait, Cistine taking the opposite side of the door. Iri looked up from the book in her hand, seated at the small dining table, and opened her mouth to greet them—then broke off with a frown.

Saychelle sent the burned woman on her way, and the moment the door shut, Iri rose. "They say the war is finally over...that you marched out to Eben's plains to face the Bloodwights and won. Is that true?"

"It is," Thorne said.

Saychelle's eyes dazzled with the sort of joy that had first awakened love in him so long ago. She cast her arms around him in a quick, tight embrace, then turned to Cistine. "*Thank you—*"

"Don't," Cistine warned, and Saychelle froze. "You can't touch me. No one can."

Iri's frown deepened. "Why not?"

Cistine glanced at Thorne, and he nodded, though he wasn't certain what encouragement she needed. She smoothed her hand down her armor, fingers lingering a moment at her empty augment pouch. "When I faced the Bloodwights, I didn't have the strength to weaken them all. So I had to use an augment we stole from Kosai Talis."

Saychelle's eyes narrowed. "One of the ancient temples Mira's been studying?"

"*Stor Sedam*," Iri breathed, and Cistine nodded. "What did it do?"

She looked at Thorne again, and this time he recognized the silent plea in her gaze. He rubbed the side of his neck. "When she unleashed it, it was like nothing we'd ever seen. Something sprouted from her back, some talons of shadow—"

Saychelle raised a hand, face sallow. "*Haval.*"

"Death itself," Iri breathed. "Oh, stars, Mira was right about *everything*."

"You could wield it?" Saychelle demanded of Cistine. "One of the *Stor Sedam*?"

"I did, but the cost..." Her voice trembled, and she circled her arms around her middle. "Everything I touch dies. Even though it's been a week since I shattered the flagon."

"You *have* dispatched the augment, haven't you?" Iri asked.

Cistine nodded. "And removed my armor. I've tried everything I can think of. I can't even feel the power in my skin, but if I touch a plant, or...or a person..."

Her eyes slid to Thorne, and the knot in his stomach matched the blaze of fear in her eyes.

"Is the death instantaneous?" Saychelle asked.

"For the plants, yes," Cistine said. "If a person is armored, then they have longer. Even with the plants, it happens more slowly than when I attacked the Bloodwights."

"Then its power is diminished," Iri said, "but very much still present."

"How do I get rid of what's left? Is there some ritual, *Gammalkraft*, a cleansing of some kind that I...?"

And here she trailed off. Because to Thorne's horror, Saychelle was shaking her head.

"I know of none," she said softly. "As with any augment, its effects are its effects. You can't train or rest or eat away the strain of a fire flagon. The body simply takes time to recover."

"Then, with time..." Cistine said breathlessly.

Thorne despised the pity in Iri's eyes. "The *Stor Sedam* are like nothing else in this world, Cistine. Nothing else the gods ever gave us. There are some wounds that time cannot heal, and some augments take a greater toll than others. Your situation is unique, because this is not merely an effect created by the power, but the power *itself* still dwells within you. It may be that this augment would have killed anyone else who unleashed it...anyone who was not a Key."

"But I lived," Cistine's voice turned brittle, "and I can't touch any living thing."

Suddenly, the warm air was stifling, too humid to breathe. Thorne shoved himself up from the wall. "Is there anyone else we can ask?"

"No one that I know of," Iri said. "I'm sorry."

Cistine offered a slight, unhappy smile and ducked from the room, leaving Thorne to say, "Thank you for offering what you could. We won't stop searching."

He turned to go, but halted when Saychelle murmured his name. "This was not your fault." She laid a hand on his arm. "I know you're blaming yourself, but you shouldn't."

"I'm not," Thorne began, but she shot him such a dry look of disbelief, he fell silent.

"You have a habit of loving strong women who face impossible choices. But my choice to break with you was mine alone to make, and not your burden to carry. Cistine's choice to use that flagon was not your doing, either. Remember that."

Thorne braced his hand on the doorframe and navigated through three deep, calming breaths, the tension in his calves loosening. "She's my *valenar*. And I can do nothing for her."

Saychelle's hand slid from his arm. "You can be there, Thorne. And for now, that is what she'll need most."

He met Saychelle's eyes and found no bitterness or longing or regret there. Only grief on his behalf—and on Cistine's. "Thank you for your council."

She stretched up and kissed his cheek. "You always have me for that, Chancellor."

Cistine was already halfway down the long staircase when Thorne finally caught up to her. He kept distance between them, letting her lead the way through the towers and down the steep road outside—not waiting for Aden. He finally caught up to her at the base of the trail where she stopped and covered her face with both hands. Her legs shook.

"Cistine." Thorne moved around her side to face her, but she didn't drop her hands. "We'll find some other way. Saychelle and Iri are brilliant, but they don't know everything."

"Thorne, there is no other way." The words were monotone, and his heart clenched at the surrender in them. "The gods said there would be a price if I decided to use that augment. This *is* the price. I can't...I'll never..."

She slammed down in a heap on the sand and curled forward over herself, face to her legs, hugging her middle while sobs slashed from her throat. They built on top of one another so quickly they turned to hyperventilating, ripping Thorne's spirit into tatters as he crouched before her, almost knee-to-knee, but not touching her. His hands rested on his thighs, palms up, a helpless, anguished emptiness filling the gaps of his fingers that wanted so badly to hold hers.

She was right stars-damned *there*, falling to pieces before his eyes, and he couldn't do anything.

"Wildheart, I'm here," he said softly. "I'm right here."

She squeezed into a smaller huddle, and tears streaked Thorne's cheeks, itching his stubble, dripping from his chin.

She was right there. But they might as well have been kingdoms apart, for all he could do for her now.

CHAPTER
SEVENTY-SIX

AT LONG LAST the room was quiet—not just the medicos leaving her in peace, not just Maleck and Rozalie taking Pippet for the afternoon to weave flower crowns for the wounded. But inside her, the pain finally ebbed enough that Ashe could think past it. She lay in silence, shut her eyes, and reached past the boundaries of her own agony and across the bridge in her spirit.

Traces of gold flickered behind her eyes. A spectral pain carved along her side from a limb that wasn't there. And then a growl of guttural relief in her mind: *ASHEILA.*

A smile twisted her mouth. *There you are, Scales.*

GREAT FATHER ABOVE, YOU DON'T KNOW HOW I FEARED FOR YOU. ARE YOU ALL RIGHT?

I will be. I owe you and Maleck for that.

A beat of silence. *DO NOT EVER, EVER CLEAVE WITH ME THAT WAY AND EXPECT ME NOT TO COME FOR YOU OR SEND SOMEONE WHO CAN. YOU DON'T KNOW WHAT I SAW, WHAT I REMEMBERED WHEN I FELT THAT.*

Ashe swallowed. *Ileria?*

LIKE BEING IN THOSE MOUNTAINS WITH HER AGAIN. I THOUGHT MY HEARTS WOULD FAIL.

Guilt scratched at Ashe's spirit. *I'm sorry, Bres.*

I DON'T WANT APOLOGIES. I WANT YOUR VOW YOU WILL NEVER AGAIN FORCE ME TO FEEL YOU DYING AND TRY TO SHUT ME AWAY FROM HELPING.

I give you my word. And she meant it. She'd never come so close to dying before, not even in Siralek when she was stabbed. And she'd never had so much to live for.

GOOD. YOU'LL COME TO SEE ME SOON?

As soon as they let me leave the city. How's your wing?

MENDING. I'M FORTUNATE...NOT ALL MY KIN LEFT THAT BATTLEFIELD. WE ALL LOST LOVED ONES THAT DAY.

Ashe's mind filled with her last memory of Sander's face when they'd parted on the plains, how he'd promised a drink with her and Maleck afterward to share some impossible news; and now he was gone, his body sent up in fire, no goodbyes or last words of gratitude between them for all he'd done for her. And she thought of Cistine, so far from reach, a portion of her spirit perished on that battlefield as surely as if the Bloodwights had cut her down.

Grimacing, Ashe shoved herself upright. A dull ache twinged in her middle, but she knew the feeling of a healing augment's handiwork even if it had nearly come too late this time.

ILYANAK, WHAT ARE YOU DOING?

I'm going to find my cabal. Ashe gripped an arm around her middle and raised her eyes to the open doorway. *The people I love who are still alive. And I'm going to make the most of every moment people like Sander don't have.*

And after that...she didn't know. Once the pain annealed into its own metal, she didn't know how she'd wield it. All she was certain of was that she couldn't stay in this bed and dwell on loss anymore. She was tired of these sights and smells, too much like Talheim's infirmaries.

She wanted to be with her people, her tribe. Her family.

And that thought, more than any other, gave her the strength to stand.

CHAPTER SEVENTY-SEVEN

TATIANA WAS SO engrossed in her needlework at the dining table that when Quill floundered awake on their bed, cursing, she almost stabbed herself in shock.

They stared at one another. He'd drawn the knife from under his pillow, but hadn't swung it; it reflected stripes of the pale buttermilk light by which Tatiana sewed together her latest invention. Heart pounding, she waited for him to lower the blade before she even took another breath. "Good dreams?"

"My favorite kind. The ones where I'm running from a hoard of Balmond." Quill swung up from the bed, running a hand through his hair. Sweat beaded down his bare chest and abdomen as he glanced at the cot in the corner where Pippet slept, undisturbed by his violent awakening. Then he padded barefoot to the table. "You?"

Tatiana smirked, but it felt hollow. "The usual. Nightmares about Cistine on the battlefield with that stars-forsaken augment, killing us all."

Quill hooked out the other chair with his foot and sank down in a sprawl. "How long do you think it takes for the dreams to fade?"

She shrugged. "Ask Maleck and Ashe, they're the ones who've gone through a war before."

"Well, then there's no hope for any of us."

With a sigh, she boosted herself from her seat and plopped down on his lap, bringing her invention with her. "Was there ever?"

"I had my moments of raging doubt during that battle on the Deathmarch." Quill rested his face against her back and linked his arms around her waist. "What are you making?"

"Well," she drew the word out with the thread, finishing another loop in the stitching, "I was thinking about the dilemmas Cistine might face if Saychelle and Iri can't fix this, and I realized she's not going to want to train with you anymore. Even those quick hits..."

Quill cursed softly. "Nimmus' teeth, I hadn't thought of that."

"I'm sure there are plenty of things we haven't considered. But for this one, I had a solution: Papa made this durable mesh, and some of it survived in the shed, even though the shop and the house burned down."

She paused, the ache of loss moving through her in a softer, subtler wave than before, and Quill nuzzled her curls aside and pressed a kiss to the back of her neck. "Tell me about the mesh."

Tatiana shook off her melancholy. "Well, I know your proportions better than anyone's, so I'm building a beating effigy to your size and shape and filling it with sand."

His chin hooked over her shoulder. "Hard, but pliable if she hits strong enough."

"Assuming I use the right measures. It's fighting me at every turn...you could help me with that if you want."

"I'd be happy to." He gripped her hips and lifted her off him, sliding to his feet behind her. "But maybe it's not my help you need. Maybe you need an inventor."

Tatiana pushed the mesh aside and craned her head back to look up at him. "Did you have someone in mind?"

"Mmhmm." He pressed his lips over hers. "And it's not Mort."

She stabbed her elbow backward into his ribs, and he laughed, pulling back and swaggering off to their closet to retrieve a shirt, leaving Tatiana surveying her handiwork.

She knew what she was really doing here, what they were all trying for, what Quill wanted for her: picking up the pieces. It felt like bandaging broken bones without setting them first, like grasping at something, anything, to feel normal and whole and sane again. But none of them knew what else to do. Lines had been crossed and broken during the war. She couldn't remember the last time she'd felt like a simple tinker's daughter with a home waiting for her in Blaykrone, a future with the Guild.

Still. The war was over. And maybe it wasn't terrible—despite the emptiness in her womb, the gaping gash of that death augment, and Cistine's pain shared among them—to want those things again. To fight for them. To claim the future they'd fought so hard for.

She stood, snatched up her cloak, and tossed the mesh bag over her shoulder. "I'm going out."

"Figured you would."

Tatiana stuck her tongue out at his back. "I love you, Featherbrain."

"Figured that, too."

Somehow her smile managed to stay in place all the way out into the streets, through the stretches still being repaired, the elite districts and the poorer avenues no longer easily distinguished by rank or ruin. The walls had come down, the boundaries muddled or erased altogether.

It was time to settle the last of her own.

It only took two knocks on the familiar, smoke-scarred door to bring an answer. A face with fresh wounds greeted her from inside the pillaged home, furniture dented and walls smashed in. But it still reminded Tatiana of better days, brighter ones. Almost like home.

"Tati." Surprise lilted Kadlin's voice. "What brings you here so early?"

She shrugged. "I'm trying to make something for Cistine's training, and I'm not sure I have the dimensions right. I thought you could help me."

Kadlin's eyes softened—the face of that woman Tatiana had seen on the battlefield sweeping in to defend her and Ariadne. When she swung the door wide, something cold around Tatiana's heart fractured and fell away. "It would be my honor."

Though Tatiana couldn't bring herself to say it, in some ways it felt like it was really hers.

CHAPTER
SEVENTY-EIGHT

IT WAS LATE, but Maleck couldn't sleep again.

Thorne, Cistine, and Aden had been gone for days. He prayed that was a good sign, but how could any of them know? Meanwhile Ashe healed and Kristoff remained unconscious, and he felt suspended between all these things, waiting for the next nightmare to come true.

He wandered Kanslar's wing at night after another long day helping the Tribunes and his cabal mend the damaged walls and scorched corridors. He allowed his feet to take him where they willed, aberrant from thought or reason, simply outpacing the loss and grief that hung in the halls.

A room opened up ahead of him, puffs of laughter spilling out like dust blown from a shelf—Quill, Tatiana, and Pippet's room. Pippet ducked into the hall first, framed by ghostlight, grinning; and to Maleck's shock, Ashe followed her out, limping heavily, one arm curled around her middle. Panic ripped through him, shooting him forward to join them. "Asheila, what are you doing here? You should be in the house of healing still!"

"If one more person tells me that, *they're* going to need my old sickbed," she groaned, scowling playfully. "I already heard it from Quill before I threw him out so Pippet and I could catch up." She swung an arm around the girl's shoulders, and Pippet beamed up at her. "You of all people should know walking is part of healing, Mal. I'm not going to run any footraces, I just needed to get out of that place. I can recover better here than in a room by myself."

Maleck opened his mouth, then shut it again. It was useless arguing with her when she had that look in her eye. And besides that, he was tired of waiting for her to join him in their bed again. The floor was just as hard and void without her.

He took her hand and kissed her knuckles. "Welcome home, Dragonfire."

Pippet grabbed his other hand and tugged. "We're going for a walk out to the peristyle. Do you want to come with?"

"I believe it's past your bedtime," Maleck said mildly.

"That's what I told her, after the fifth lullaby," Ashe snorted.

"Well...I couldn't sleep." Pippet peered up at Maleck, the joy in her face shifting to something darker—a pain they shared.

Ashe's eyes flicked between them, then settled on Maleck. "Are you coming, or not?"

He nodded, and kept hold of both their hands when they set off down the hall.

"How are you?" Maleck asked Pippet while they passed through the dark of Kanslar's wing together.

"Better than everyone who went to fight," Pippet sighed. "I hate seeing everyone hurt. I hate how Quill and Tati *never* sleep anymore. And I miss Faer. I miss Thorne and Cistine and *Aden*. When are they coming back?"

Ashe glanced at Maleck. "Soon, we hope."

"Will they be all right?"

"We all will be," Maleck said. "It just takes time."

"How much time? Did you know they're already rebuilding the school?" Pippet demanded. "What am I going to do when it starts again? What if the other children don't want me in their classes because I'm— because I was—?"

"Then they're blind and prejudiced," Ashe said, "like Viktor. You remember him? He wasn't worth our attention, and neither are they."

Maleck squeezed Pippet's hand until she raised her glassy eyes to him.

"There are some people who will never believe in you again, and that is their choice. Don't waste your heart on them. Spend it on the people who will not let you go at any cost."

Pippet's fingers were wrapped so tight around his, the calluses ached. "Like *you*, *Navalo?*"

Heat climbed Maleck's neck. "Where did you hear that?"

Ashe blinked innocently. "She needed a story to help her sleep."

"Then I can see why it eludes her. Really, Asheila? A tale of Bloodwights and augmentation—"

"A story about a hero who helped save Blaykrone." She dug her thumb into the back of his hand. "It's the perfect bedtime story."

"I like it," Pippet said. "It makes me feel like we weren't all terrible. Like we deserved to be saved."

Ashe smirked smugly, and Maleck shot her a half-smile, letting go of Pippet's hand to wrap his arm around her shoulders and kiss the top of her head.

They wandered into the courtyard, so bare without the effigies of the Courts standing on their pedestals; but there was a clearer view to the door of every wing now, and perhaps that preceded a shift among the Courts as a whole. In battle, they had all become one Court—not as Salvotor had envisioned it, united under one ruler, but sharing rule equally among many, shedding blood together.

He hoped that sense of unity was their future.

Pippet gazed at the empty patches of bare, clean stone, too, and new resolve overtook her weary features. "I think I should still become a Tribune."

Ashe's brows leaped. "Really?"

Pippet nodded. "I'll craft laws to help people like us, Maleck. Something that makes it illegal to hate us."

"You can't legislate people's thoughts," Maleck said. "You cannot outlaw hate...they will think what they wish, regardless of law. But you can make it easier for those who are suffering to receive the care they need."

Pippet chewed her lip thoughtfully as they crossed the courtyard and entered the peristyle. "You're right. Maybe if there had been someone to help people like Svan and Olaf and Gisli, they wouldn't have gone back to Zoran when he offered them augments."

Maleck's feet snagged on the cobblestones at the sound of that name. Images of blood and fire blew through him, the heat of an augment trickling down his throat, his limbs locked in sheer terror—

He hadn't realized the *Aeoprast* had told her his true name.

They both stopped and looked back when he halted. Ashe's brow tightened with concern. "Mal?"

He forced an unsteady smile for Pippet's sake and shuffled forward to join them again. "You're right, Pippet. People who have suffered these things deserve help, not more punishment."

Her shoulders loosened with relief when he didn't pursue the matter; nor would he ever, unless she came to him. Like the wound augments had left behind, the *Aeoprast's* manipulation would take time to heal.

They were halfway across the peristyle when he sensed something, like a smell but not quite, coming from the gates to the outer yard. Skin crawling, Maleck halted and looked straight to the three figures standing an arm's length apart below the archway into the outer yard. From one of them, latent power fumed. From the other two, palpable despair.

Pippet burst forward with a gleeful shout, streaking across the peristyle, only slowing when Cistine flashed up a hand and recoiled, bringing her skidding to a halt. Maleck and Ashe hurried forward, and Cistine peeled off around the circle of the peristyle—deliberately avoiding them.

Maleck halted before Thorne, who stared after Cistine with haunted features. Pippet watched her go as well, eyes wet, and Aden took her shoulders from behind and bundled her backward into his chest, broad arms enfolding her narrow shoulders.

"What happened?" Ashe demanded. "What did Iri and Saychelle say?"

Thorne's chest rose and fell in a long and deliberate breath, and then he spoke the words that destroyed the last flicker of hope. "There is no way to remove the augment. There's no cure."

CHAPTER
SEVENTY-NINE

IT WAS A full day after his return to Stornhaz when Aden finally visited his father's room. Pain still hung over him, a heavy shroud slowing his stride, yet he knew it was nothing compared to the burden Mira now carried—a weight he'd helped foist on her with his report. They'd stretched out their visit to Holmlond three days, for his sake more than anyone's. In the end, Mira had pushed him out the door with a promise to write soon, particularly about Sander's vacant seat as Tribune over Nordbran.

The schemes in her clever, determined gaze were for another day.

He came into the room after a wearying afternoon of High Tribune duties and his brief, casual swearing-in to find it silent and dim, Ariadne stretched out in the bedside chair, head pillowed on her arm, fast asleep. Her foot pressed the edge of the bed, ready to be woken at the first hint of movement.

For a time, Aden lingered in the doorway, watching her and his father sleep, throat tight and face warm. Then he snatched up the blanket he'd used for a bedroll before his trip to Holmlond and fluffed it over Ariadne's shoulders. She stirred only faintly, and Aden laid a hand on her hair. "Go back to sleep. I'll keep watch."

No protest; seconds later, she was snoring again. Aden settled into the other seat, thumb brushing his scar.

"I think I've been better guarded in this sickbed than I ever was as a Tribune."

Aden jolted, cursed, and swung back to his feet at the dull rasp of his father's voice. Kristoff's eyes were open to faint slits, a smile tracing the grooves beside his mouth. "Where have you been?"

"You knew I was gone?"

"Dimly. I guessed when only Maleck and the others came to visit. You're all right?"

"*Me?*" Aden yanked his hands through his hair. "*You* were nearly gone. You nearly left me again."

"I'm sorry."

"Don't apologize. Tell me how you feel."

"Tired. Sore." Kristoff craned his neck slightly, frowning. "From my hips up, anyway."

Aden stared at him, the words struggling through the haze of relief, souring into panic. Then he jolted toward the door. "I'll find the medicos."

"Aden." Kristoff's voice halted him mid-pivot. "It's all right."

"No, it isn't. You took that blow for me, because I was reckless—"

"I would do it again in a heartbeat. I would make the same choice even if you had everything perfectly in hand."

Scarred palm resting on the door, Aden shut his eyes and let the tears escape. "If you don't walk out of this place..."

"Then I'll wheel myself. Or I'll crawl. What matters is I'm here. *We* are here." Kristoff patted the sheets. "The medicos can wait. Come tell me how the others are. Tell me where you went."

Aden swung back to face him. "How can you be *calm* about this? You can't feel your stars-damned *legs.*"

"I'm calm because I'm looking at my son, alive and whole. That is all the victory I ever needed."

Aden's nails bit into his scar until it throbbed. Then he returned to the bed, sank down at its edge, and elbowed his father's legs aside until Kristoff chuckled. "Not all of it is good, *Athar.*"

"It doesn't have to be. Tell me what's broken, and we'll find a way to heal it together."

That was what Thorne saw in him, Aden realized; the blood he came from, that found hurts and made them right. That stepped into the flood and stopped the pain from gushing out.

That was what it was to be High Tribune. What he had sworn to become today, for his cousin, for his people. His kingdom.

In the quiet dark of the house of healing where his mother had labored for so many years to save so many lives, he told his father everything—about Sander and Mira, and Thorne and Cistine. About what they'd won and what they'd lost.

And in many ways, it felt like finally coming home.

CHAPTER
EIGHTY

D IMINISHED, BUT NOT gone. Lessened, but still present. Trapped in flesh from which it could not escape.

That was the death augment. That was precisely how Cistine felt.

She barely knew how she came to be in this familiar place, these walls that had held so much promise and joy, rebuilt in the weeks leading up to their small Darlaska celebration. But with the gaping abyss of the future stretching out before her in the absence of any hope from Saychelle and Iri, her feet took her straight to Aden's home.

Fitting, somehow, that this place still stood when so much of the city had burned...a relic and a taunt, a reminder of the life she'd hoped to lead. A life gone up in smoke, but this house of wishes and promises remained.

She found a bed wedged in one of the upper rooms and stayed in it for days, judging by the patterns of light and darkness dripping along the walls, locked in a cycle of sleeping and crying and raging and crying and sleeping again.

She felt sick, but not. Alive, but not. It was impossible to fit her hands into the gaps that were still bleeding, so she let them run scarlet and bitter and furious, weeping until the pillow smelled of salt. Every morning and afternoon and evening when she woke from bouts of agitated slumber, she thought of something new that plagued her, a long list of *nevers* filling up the empty space in the room.

She would never touch her friends again. Never garden, never ride a horse, never be kissed or held or made love to. Intimacy was little more than a fleeting dream of amber-flecked wood and warm bedclothes, her hands over her face, Thorne's weight pressing against her body.

She would never carry a child in her womb or hold it in her arms. She would never embrace her parents again, train with Quill again, twine fingers with Thorne again. She could never plunge her hands into soil without killing everything that grew in it.

She was already forgetting what it felt like to kiss her *valenar*.

Now and then she stumbled from the chamber to pour old, stale water from the pitcher in the washroom and wet her mouth, but her stomach rebelled even against that. Dehydrated, dizzy, exhausted, she chased the litany of *nevers* from dawn until dusk or whenever sleep claimed her again.

And then she woke to the sound and scent of sizzling meat from downstairs.

She lay prone, splayed out on the bed, unsure if she was dreaming. No one knew she was here...or if they did, why come for her now? It had been days, weeks for all she knew. What had changed?

After a few more minutes of listening and waiting, the smell of meat intensifying, she peeled herself from the sweat-and-tear-tacky sheets, pulled Thorne's leather jacket around her shoulders, and padded slowly down to investigate.

It was her first time out of the room in far too long—long enough that someone else had moved in. A thick throw blanket and pillow took up the foot of one sofa, a stack of books homed beside the chair. And in the kitchen, adjacent to the dining room, someone was frying bacon.

She slammed to a halt in the doorway, mouth watering but stomach curdling. "Kristoff?"

He looked up at her, not down for once—because he was sitting in a chair with wheels, rolling himself between the counter and the squat stove where a skillet and pot and kettle all sang their tempting songs.

Her throat clenched. "What happened? What are you *doing* here?"

His raised-brow look was eerily like his son's. "Strictly speaking, this is still my house, you know."

A flush swept across her cheekbones. "Of course, I know that, but...why are you *here*? Do the others know? Are they coming?" Panic sharpened her voice like a blade on a whetstone at the thought of any of them seeing her like this, ratty and haggard and no better adjusted to her new killing power than when she'd abandoned Thorne and Aden at the wall after Holmlond.

Kristoff held up a hand, stalling her questions. "Aden knows I'm here, yes. He also knows I need to adjust to things privately."

He rolled himself to the table, a platter of bacon and a bowl of broth balanced awkwardly in his lap. Cistine watched him, heart grinding painfully at every turn of the wheels. "I'm sorry I didn't come see you."

"I'm too old for that kind of sentiment." He set down the platters and gestured her to sit; while she did, he retrieved two cups and brought the kettle, filling both with the floral notes of jasmine tea. "I was busy being unconscious, and you had better things to do than pine at my bedside."

"I'm so sorry." It felt utterly inadequate, but she couldn't seem to stop saying it.

"I'm not the only one adjusting to wounds that won't heal." Kristoff leveled his gaze into her across the table.

She pulled her arms inside the jacket's too-long sleeves, pressing the empty cuffs together. "You don't seem surprised I'm in your house."

"You forget who was with you in Kalt Hasa. I've seen how grief takes you. I had a feeling you'd need solitude...and that you'd find it somewhere safe where the others wouldn't look. When Aden said he rebuilt the house, I guessed."

"Did you come here for me?"

"That. And I meant what I said, about adjusting to things." He glanced down at himself. "It's difficult to be this way when you're used to being a warrior and a politician."

"You still could be. Just run over people's toes when they argue with you in meetings."

"Now, there's the woman I knew in that mountain hall." Kristoff nodded to the table. "Eat?" She reached tentatively for the bacon, and his hand shot out quick as a lightning cut, fork smacking the back of her knuckles. "You'll make yourself ill. The soup's for you."

She recoiled, watching him with breath snagged in her chest; but the killing power didn't seem to extend through utensils. Still, she waited a full minute before she dared drop her gaze and pull the soup bowl closer to herself.

"How are the others?" she mumbled. "Have you seen Thorne?"

"I won't lie to you, I haven't seen a cheerful face since I woke." Kristoff snapped a bacon spear in half. "They love you. They're worried for you. And they want to see you, but they also want to respect the space you need to heal."

A tear slid down the side of her nose, dripping into the soup. "I wish I could give them what they need, but I don't know how to."

"Give it time. No one is demanding that from you yet. All you need to be concerned with today is eating."

She did eat, in silence and tiny sips, the plain broth soothing a throat torn from sobs. Kristoff didn't press her for conversation, simply ate his bacon, then his soup. When their bowls were empty, Cistine curled on the chair, cradling her cooled tea in both hands.

"What about tomorrow?" she asked at last. "What do I need to be concerned with tomorrow?"

She almost expected Kristoff to laugh, but his face was solemn as he studied her over his own rim. "You eat again. You get out of bed...or don't. I won't tell you how to grieve, none of us can do that for each other. But I'll be here if you need someone to speak with. Or cry with. I've done my share of that when Aden and Maleck aren't visiting."

She dropped her gaze, studying the wheeled chair. It was of such fine make, she was certain someone in *Heimli Nyfadengar* must've made it...perhaps even a special, rushed commission for the beloved former Tribune. "The medicos really can't do anything?"

"They can't. Healing, such as it is, is up to me now."

It was such a vast burden, such a difficult, fathomless thing to navigate, it almost choked her. "I wish I could do something."

He didn't answer for a moment. "You could come speak to me, if you notice I've gotten too quiet."

She took a careful sip of tea and found that it was the first thing in weeks that truly tasted good. "I think I can do that."

Silence descended again, gentler this time, beckoning less to grief.

"Kristoff," she added after a moment, "could you send a letter to the courthouse?"

It was the hardest thing she'd ever written, because it hardly counted for a letter at all. One line was all she could manage before the tears turned the parchment crusty.

I need more time.

The answering note was waiting for her when she woke at sunrise, gutted by more dreams, in a fine envelope left at the base of the stairs to greet her, steps masked by Kristoff's snores from the sofa.

You have it. You are still a princess worth waiting for.

CHAPTER EIGHTY-ONE

SENSE TOLD ASHE it was bright daylight, but the world still felt masked in shadow when she finally mustered enough strength to visit Bresnyar face-to-face. It coaxed a blanket of melancholy over her spirit when she rode a barge from the city and spotted the dragons frolicking in the grass and taking to the sky, keeping their muscles warm. Aeosotu sunned himself on the riverbank not far from the barge docks, Meriwa leaning against his chest. Bresnyar lay nearby, sprawled on his side, his wings stretched out to welcome the sunlight.

"Glad to see you survived," Meriwa called when Ashe disembarked and limped toward them. She flashed her a rude gesture and walked straight to Bresnyar; he raised his head, nostrils distending at her approach, eyes ablaze and smoke fuming from his craw like he couldn't quite believe it was her he smelled.

Ashe raised a hand. "Don't get up on my account. You look so comfortable."

He surged to his feet and winnowed toward her, wrapping his whole body around hers like an embrace. "Forgive me, *Ilyanak*. I failed you in battle."

Ashe laid her branded hand to his ribs, the only part of him she could reach. "You survived. I survived. I call that success, unless you have a deathwish."

"But I was not at your side. Nor was I able to heed Cistine's call."

"I'd rather be apart from you and survive it than have us ripped out of the sky and fall to our deaths together."

"A poor Wingmaiden you make with talk like that," Meriwa snorted.

"Good." Ashe made her way between Bresnyar's forelegs and flopped down, scratching his jaw. "How's the wing?"

"Better now. I will fly again."

"A relief indeed." Meriwa sauntered over to join them. "I've seen the pair of you fly. You would be an asset to the Legions."

Ashe snorted. "I really must've come close to dying if you're paying me compliments now."

"It's more than a compliment. Call it an offer."

Ashe blinked as the Legion Head sprawled beside her. "What?"

Meriwa bent forward, tugging up threads of long grass and rolling them between her fingerless gloves, squinting at the horizon. "I had no cause to tell you before, but now we are battle-kin." Her gaze slid sideways to Ashe. "The Legions have been in turmoil ever since Ileria died." Bresnyar raised his head, tensing at her name. "Not because of her death, so to say, but...you saw how old Killik is. When Ileria died, Asiaq threw himself wholeheartedly into his family's legacy. He's finally becoming ambitious, as Novuam has always been. And she does not appreciate that."

Ashe studied her by the sun's harsh glare. "That's why she was so desperate to outwit him...why she suggested the *Apiriak* for me. To gain her father's approval."

"And she succeeded." The bitterness in Meriwa's tone made it all too clear which side she stood on. "It will all come to a head in time. The whispers say there may be a revolt when Allfather dies, and the Legions will have to choose sides. We will need all the dragonfire we can muster if Novuam does not go quietly."

Ashe shook her head. "It's not my fight."

"And this wasn't ours. But we came, because what affects one kingdom affects others. If Oadmark falls to infighting, it will not leave Valgard untouched when we share a border."

"What does Novuam have in mind?" Bresnyar growled.

"I'm not certain. Yet."

"So it's Asiaq's side you come down on?" Ashe asked.

Meriwa looked away. "In most things."

That crooked glance, the way her neck reddened— "You're in love with him? Your sister's—"

"*Quiet,*" Meriwa seethed, snapping her head back toward Ashe. "What I am is invested in my kingdom's future. Asiaq believes Oadmark would benefit from being named among the kingdoms—becoming one of four, not three. I see the merit to it after these battles. But if we fight for that, will you stand with us, Ashe? As we stood with you?"

Ashe glanced up at Bresnyar, his fiery gaze meeting hers. And she did not need to cleave to know his thoughts this time. "We'll think about it."

Meriwa was quiet for a moment, then got to her feet. "I suppose that's the best we can hope for." She offered her hand. "I'm glad you live. There are precious few Wingmaidens in this world, and fewer still who love their dragons the way you do. Ileria would be proud to have you succeed her as Bresnyar's wing."

Ashe dipped her head. "The honor is mine."

Meriwa opened her mouth, then snapped it shut again and looked away. "We'd best return to our land, then."

Ashe realized by that awkward refrain that the Wing Legion had only stayed this long because Meriwa waited to speak to her, to see if she would aid them the way they'd aided her.

And perhaps even to ensure she survived.

"What would you have done for Bresnyar if I hadn't pulled through?" she asked.

Meriwa's gaze cut back to her, narrowing slightly—weighing those words. "Nothing. Your braided man made it quite clear who holds his future, if not you."

She turned and strode away, and Bresnyar let out a low, deep snort. His muzzle bumped Ashe's back, and she sighed, pushing up to her feet. "Meriwa! If trouble comes, send a message. If we're in a position, we'll see what we can do to help. No one needs another war."

Meriwa blinked, looking back at her. "Thank you."

"Don't thank me. Consider it a gesture of good will...and good luck."

"Oh, Ashe," Meriwa chuckled, "if you believed luck could win, you wouldn't have come to us for help."

She strolled away, whistling the Wingmaidens up from the grass all around. Ashe settled back against Bresnyar's chest and watched them go, plucked up like jewels from the grass, soaring into the sky—back to report their victory to the Grand Council, and to fight their own battles within.

"Are you glad you're staying, or wish you were going?" Ashe asked Bresnyar as they watched the Legion take wing.

"Oadmark really does have terrifically cold winters and filthy politics," Bresnyar said. "And besides, my place is at your side now, for better or worse. I belong wherever you and Maleck are."

Ashe smirked. "What exactly did he tell Meriwa while I was asleep?"

"It was less what he said and more how he is." Bresnyar's nostrils crinkled. "A man of his word. One who makes others belong."

Belonging. The word washed her with warmth. That was what she felt now—with him. With Maleck. Three as one, until the stars burned out.

But it went beyond them, too; to sandy arenas and tavern meals, to oaths sworn over daggers in dark chambers and a shared love of dragons. To strategies and sparring and a kingdom held close in their hearts.

She belonged with Aden and Kristoff, too. Even with Thorne, Quill, Tatiana, and Ariadne. And always with Cistine.

And if that was all she gained from this war—nightmares and freedom and belonging with them—it was all worth it. Even the scars.

CHAPTER EIGHTY-TWO

SHE NEVER KNEW if the days would be good or bad—but they did pass, one after the other, slow and staggering. Bit by bit, Cistine forced herself to linger longer after every dinner, helping Kristoff with the dishes but keeping healthy space between them. While he washed and she dried, he told her of the repairs in the city, the slowly-reforming Courts, the houses of healing gradually emptying.

She was glad to hear Ashe had given up her bed weeks ago, taking refuge in the courthouse with Maleck again. Aden was easing into his position as High Tribune, though it seemed he and Kristoff met frequently away from the house for sessions of counseling and complaint. Ariadne filled her hours answering questions from uneasy elites desperate to know more about augments and the Order and what would change now that the wells were open. Quill and Tatiana were preparing Pippet to visit Mira in Holmlond, when both were ready...a visit Cistine suspected she could benefit from herself. She hadn't even spoken to her friend on her mission to interrogate Saychelle and Iri.

Kristoff was right. Absolute healing was impossible now; learning to move forward was in her hands.

Still, the thought crushed her, the path forward dark and unsure. It found her again the moment she woke sweating and shaking from a dream of the battlefield, hands fisted in her sheets where they'd twisted in Thorne's shirt in her memory, trying to keep him up while he'd died from her kiss. It was several long minutes of hopelessness, lying prone under memories and aberrant thoughts and despair, before she realized what had rescued her from her dreams.

A quiet piano melody floated through the floorboards.

Cuffing tears from her cheeks, she hurried from the room and down the stairs, halting in the entrance to the main parlor. Kristoff had pushed the piano bench aside and rolled right up to the ivory keys, his fingers coaxing out a sweet, sorrowful tune. Judging by the skew of his hair and the slant of his half-undone shirt, he was fleeing his specters just as his song called her from hers.

She leaned against the doorframe, eyes shut and head turned into the sleek wood. The music called her heart to follow its rhythm, sinking from a gallop to a gentler cadence, tempting her panic away with it. The placid lash of seasonal spring rain on the windowpanes and roof played in harmony as Kristoff finished the song, then began it again, segueing flawlessly from end to beginning once more.

A loop, like grief. But he played it a touch faster this time, arriving at the climax and the ending and beginning again. Then again. It came faster every time, his fingers pounding the keys, punishing them with anger better meant for the things that kept him awake—both of them awake, battling shadows together.

Cistine barely told her feet to move, but she came to the slanted bench and sat in it, watching him play. Under her gaze, his fingers slowed. "Would you like me to teach you the accompaniment?"

She snatched her fingers deep into her sleeves. "I can't. I might…"

Stumble. Touch you. Kill you.

A frustrated sob hacked at her throat. "How did you do it, when you lost Natalya? How do you come back from something like *this*? I feel like I can't even breathe, and it doesn't *stop*, every single day!"

He finished playing, turning his chair to face her. She tucked her feet on the bench so there was no risk of grazing his legs. "I know."

"I keep thinking I'll wake up from this nightmare, but I never do. Tell me how I'm supposed to *heal* from this!"

"You eat," he said, and spoke over her when she scoffed. "You do the dishes. Then you remember the people who are still looking to you for something. The sons who need raising. The people who need leading." He braced his hands on the edges of the bench on either side of her feet. "You do it for them. At first, that makes it no easier, but it does make it make sense. And then no matter where you find yourself, whether it's in an empty bed meant for two or in a mountain prison or a strange village or a chair with wheels, you remember why you started. And that becomes the reason you go on."

She clenched her hand around his old compass, hot at the base of her throat. "What if I can't do it?"

"Only you can decide that."

A familiar challenge hung in his words. She met his gaze, kind but stern, and a thread of the knot in her chest loosened. She bore a shaky breath deep into her lungs, and when that came easier than the last, she took another. Then another.

"Will you keep playing?" she asked. "Until I fall asleep?"

She went to the other sofa, across from his things, and curled up, facing toward the back. Eyes squeezed shut and hand tight around the compass, she brought to mind the faces of her cabal, one by one. She mouthed their Names silently. *Darkwind. Dawnstar. Nightwing. Lightfall. Bloodsinger. Dragonfire. Starchaser.*

Just like Kalt Hasa, her last prison. And though she couldn't walk away from this one, she could bring their light inside with her.

She was only as alone as she made herself.

She didn't realize she fell asleep, and she didn't dream; but she woke dry-eyed and stayed that way, lying on her back on her sofa while Kristoff slept on his. Watching the light slowly climb from the sliver of dawn to the full glory of a cloudless spring morning across the ceiling, the mellow citrus tones painting the walls and molding and wainscoting, she found herself thinking of Baba Kallah, the day Cistine and Thorne had returned to

Hellidom after Ashe's capture.

Fall a princess, Baba Kallah had told her that day. *Rise a queen.*

Cistine waited for the tears to come with that memory, but they didn't. Her rage and anguish had spent themselves. She would think of other things to cry about in time, but for now she was blissfully numb, keeping her gaze fixed even when Kristoff swung himself by his strong arms into the chair, left the house, then returned and began to fix a meal of bread, meat, and something that smelled deliciously sugary.

The light reached its pinnacle and slowly began to lower again, and when it did, Cistine rose. Weak and trembling, she went to the kitchen and helped him cook, not speaking, but fostering the small ember that had stirred in her chest the night before. She breathed on it in the quiet, coaxing it from a tiny spark to a full flame.

When they sat to eat, she blurted out, "I'm ready to see them."

Kristoff's mouth slid into a smile. "They'll be relieved to hear it. All of them?"

Swallowing, she nodded. "But...tomorrow. I should clean myself first."

"I was hoping you would. I didn't want to say anything—"

Gasping in mock-offense, she hurled one of the sweet dinner rolls at him. "How did someone like you raise a man as well-mannered as Maleck?"

"That was all Natalya."

She paused with the next roll halfway to her mouth. "Do you think you could tell me about her?"

A new glint ignited in Kristoff's gaze, one she'd never seen before. And while she ate, he did tell her—in a way that brought her some hope. Because if he could speak of his lost *valenar* with dry eyes and a warm smile full of memory, then perhaps someday she could do the same for the life she once knew, now turned to ashes.

Perhaps she could still rise a queen.

CHAPTER EIGHTY-THREE

TREMBLING BUT DETERMINED, Cistine entered the bathing room as soon as Kristoff left to fetch the cabal. Shedding her filthy dress and Thorne's jacket on the tiled floor, she stared at the water flagon, towels, and citrus soap on a shelf beside the claw-footed bath; Kristoff's, no doubt. Or perhaps he'd left it for her, in hopes of coaxing her to clean off.

The inkings on her skin glowed faintly when she broke the flagon and let the water cascade from her grasp, filling the stone basin. She dipped into the bath with a moan of relief, her itchy skin soothed by the warm water. She hadn't bathed since her wedding day...maybe that was another mercy, that the cabal hadn't come before now and endured her stench.

Laughter burst from her, an unamused, hysterical cackling that could only be the next stage of grief. But she threw her head back and leaned into it, laughing until her sides cramped and her voice was hoarse.

It felt good to do *something* other than cry.

She floated in the water until she pruned and turned cold, then scrubbed vigorously from head to toe and dragged herself out, shivering, wrapping in the towel. The dim echo of voices downstairs halted her, dripping on the tiles, her heart crashing against her ribs.

She couldn't do this. Could she do this?

"Don't be a coward," she hissed. "You have to face them someday. You have to face *this*."

Dimly galvanized, she scooped up the dress and jacket, opened the door, and nearly tripped over a folded pile of clothes left outside: a pair of silk pajamas from her apartment in the courthouse.

Throat tight, she changed into her first clean set of clothes since Holmlond, surprised by how much more herself she felt that way. Then she tossed the putrid jacket and dress into her room to deal with later, steeled herself with a last heavy breath, and padded down the stairs.

The voices swelled in the parlor when she reached the bottom step, and she stopped, eyes shut, simply listening.

Maleck saying something to Aden. Aden giving a biting retort, chastened hastily by his father. Ashe interjecting, then Quill and Tatiana talking over each other. Ariadne chiming in with a steady rebuke. Only Thorne's voice was absent; and it was that silence that urged her into the adjacent room.

The parlor was bathed in ghostlight and the last dregs of the drowsy sun. The cabal took up the couches and armchairs, and they all stopped talking when she entered—all except Thorne, who wasn't even there.

Cistine swallowed, then joked weakly, "Were you all talking about me?"

Everyone looked at her from the corners of their eyes, and she banded her arms around her body, then dropped them just as quickly, furious with herself. "Ashe, you look..."

"Not torn in half?" Ashe supplied wryly. Maleck paled, pinching the bridge of his nose. "Thank you, I do hear that a lot these days."

"I'm sorry I didn't—"

"Let's not start with apologies," Tatiana cut in. "How about *I'm so glad to see you all?*"

"We're glad to see *you*, Stranger." Quill's crinkle-eyed sincerity nearly put her on her knees.

"I'm sorry it took me so long to find my way back."

"It often does," Maleck rumbled. "But we would have waited far longer, if needed."

"A lifetime," Ariadne agreed, and Aden nodded. His gaze, haunted with specters of his own and the weight of new responsibility, held hers unerringly—reading the silent question and need there.

"On the terrace," he grunted.

With an apologetic smile, she slipped outside.

Seeing Thorne there, standing in the very place he'd proposed to her, arms crossed on the railing and head bowed, brought immeasurable grief and melancholy and an odd sense of belonging, none of which Cistine could put words to. She slid the door shut with an audible *click*, and his shoulders rose and fell; but he didn't turn, and he didn't speak.

"Thank you for the pajamas," she said, for lack of anything better to breach the silence between them.

"It was all I could do." His tone made it clear how much he despised that, and it wrenched something deep in her chest. She shuffled to the railing, keeping several feet between them, and leaned her folded arms on the cold iron, staring across the Channel.

"Well, it means everything to me," she murmured. "I haven't even bathed since we came back."

"I forget to do that, sometimes. Or to eat or sleep, if Aden doesn't remind me." He dragged a hand through his hair. "Strange, the things you forget to do when you're..."

Grieving. The word hung unspoken between them.

"I'm glad you've had Aden," Cistine offered.

"And you had Kristoff." Thorne leaned back, hands locked around the railing. "You were here all this time, and I never came for you." He blew out a breath. "I never knew how to."

"I don't know if I would've answered if you did," she admitted. "I didn't know what to do, and I've been so afraid of hurting you again."

"It's...been a different sort of pain, Cistine."

She winced. "I know, and I didn't think of it like that. I'm sorry. But I want to do better. I *want* to still be part of this cabal, even if it can't be the same as before. I just need you to be patient with me while I try."

"You have whatever you need from me."

She turned to face him, looping one arm around the railing this time and rocking on her feet. "I need you to tell me what *you* need."

He angled toward her as well, anguished hope blazing in his eyes. "Just you. Will you come back to the courthouse?"

She swallowed a spurt of unease and nodded. "After I go shopping for new armor."

"You should invite Tati. She's missed you."

"Not as much as I've missed *you*, Starchaser."

A glimmer of light pealed through his eyes like the trail of a shooting star. "And you, Wildheart."

She sniffled, wiping her nose on her sleeve. "So, now what do we do?"

"I think we go inside." He tilted his body toward the door. "We find some way to make sense of this together, all of us. And we have whatever Kristoff's promising to make for dinner."

She forced a wobbly smile. "I'd like that."

When she stepped toward the door, he moved back, quietly but pointedly, into her path. She slammed to a halt, and he didn't move; but they breathed the same air, sharing the same space, gazes locked together. Unmoving, for so long Cistine was dimly aware how absurd it would look to anyone but them.

But his gaze embraced her. Branded her. Promised she was still his, and he was still hers, as one as they had become that night in Hellidom— even if they couldn't join hands or bodies anymore.

"I love you." He said it like a promise, like a reassurance about everything that was to come. Then he reached back, opened the door, and ushered them both inside.

It wasn't the easiest meal she'd ever had with the cabal, stilted here and there by uncertainties and twists in the conversation that left Cistine bereft with talk of dragon-riding or training.

But she forced herself to listen more than she wallowed, to learn how they were healing more than she worried how she would do the same; and in time, Maleck's laughter and Thorne's crooked smiles, Tatiana's feral grins and Ashe's teasing, Quill's cackles and Ariadne's whip-quick remarks, and the way Aden kept the peace with biting comments and Kristoff shook his head at them, all began to feel like home again.

No. Better than home.

This was Sillakove Court, a group of wounded, fierce visionaries gathered around a familiar table, sharing meals and dreams within beloved walls with hears that echoed their ambitions.

Tonight, and always, this was where she belonged.

CHAPTER EIGHTY-FOUR

IT WAS SHEER luck Tatiana, Cistine, and Pippet found a shop not destroyed during the sieges in Stornhaz. No tailor could lay hands on Cistine for her measurements, so they had to piece together armor from an array of different premade pieces in the small establishment: a spider-silk shirt and trousers, feathered shoulderguards, leather vambraces and boots. Tatiana tried not to wrinkle her nose when she tossed a soft hide scarf to Cistine. "Go try all this on."

Cistine ducked into the changing booth and drew the curtain tight across its front. Cloth fluttered audibly to the floor, and Pippet settled against the wall, pulling a book from her satchel. Tatiana reclined beside her, arms folded, eyes scouting the shop. It was empty apart from them; few people ventured out for anything more than necessities in the market yet.

Reclaiming the city—and their kingdom—didn't mean they'd gotten their lives back yet.

When the curtain snapped back, Pippet looked up and Tatiana whistled. "That armor, *Yani*."

Cistine's eyes flicked to the gilded mirror leaning against the wall across from the booth, and she smoothed her hands down her torso and thighs, studying the angles of silver-inlaid-black. She brushed her fingers over the feathers that rose in a gentle collar against the sides of her neck and trailed halfway down the backs of her arms. "Well, it looks like how I feel. Like I'm put together from all different kinds of things now." She turned back to them and nodded. "Let's buy it."

"Only if you'll let me buy you a pastry, too," Tatiana said.

"Well, if she won't, I will!" Pippet hopped back to her feet. "Food may not solve everything, but it does solve *lots* of things."

"I'd love one," Cistine said with a small smile.

Tatiana tried not to give a foothold to sadness when Cistine paid and left the shop still clad in the armor, as if she was afraid to be without it. She moved through the world now like Maleck always had, deliberate and delicate and afraid of brushing into things, stirring the air around her when she breathed.

They would have to do something about that; but for now, they bought pastries and sat in the bakery's fenced-off courtyard. Pippet leaned her chair back on its hind feet and shut her eyes, face tilted up to the sky. Tatiana nudged her foot across the cobblestones, just shy of touching Cistine's, and left it there when the Princess didn't pull away.

They stayed quiet until Pippet blurted out suddenly, "Tea."

Cistine breathed out sharply, like she'd been dozing and the word had slapped her awake. "What?"

"Tea is something you can still have, even with the augment in your body! And books, of course. What else?"

"Clothes," Tatiana offered.

Cistine fiddled with the finger loops of her armor. "I can still write laws and legislate things."

"You can still clean a house," Tatiana said, and Cistine lobbed her empty pastry wrapper at her head. "And you can use Nail and that sword Thorne gave you."

"I love that sword!" Pippet grinned. "Does it have a name?"

"Kaisill." Cistine tossed Tatiana a mischievous grin. She draped her neck against the seatback and laughed until her sides hurt.

"I don't know what that means!" Pippet complained. "What is it?"

"Just an Old Valgardan word," Tatiana said with a sly wink. "A good name for a sword."

"I can't train anymore, though," Cistine said, stopping the laughter cold. "All that progress I made..."

"Actually," Tatiana said, "I have something that might help with that."

Cistine sat straight, eyes wide. "You do?"

Tatiana hopped up and grabbed Cistine's bag with her old clothes inside. "I'll show you. Let's go, Pip!"

And just as she'd known it would, that mystery goaded Cistine to her feet, leaving a slice of her sadness behind in that courtyard as they sprinted back to the courthouse.

∽∿

The cabal was waiting for them in the usual parlor, just as Tatiana had told them to that morning. And just as she'd asked him, Quill had brought her invention and strung it up for use.

Cistine halted just over the room's threshold, staring at the mesh bag hanging from a hook in the corner of the ceiling. Tatiana slipped around her and tossed her bag onto one of the sofas, winking at Quill, who smirked; Pippet sidled over to sit next to him, watching Cistine's dumbfounded look with a gleeful grin.

"What...what *is* that?" Cistine breathed.

Tatiana grinned. "A training sack. Outfitted to Quill's proportions, so it'll feel just like you're hitting him."

"Although it's for training, I like to think it could have other uses," Ariadne offered. "Such as on frustrating days when you want to take your anger out on someone and you'd prefer to imagine you're pummeling his ribs. Or strangling him."

"It's good to know how you all really feel about me," Quill deadpanned. "It's also the perfect proportion for *hugging* if you feel lonely."

Cistine made a full circle around the sack, introducing her fingers to its surface on all angles. "Tatiana, did you make this?"

"Kadlin helped," she admitted. "I think this about makes us even."

Cistine smiled, true and full for the first time in days. Then she cocked back her fist and punched the bag with all her might.

"*Yes!*" Quill crowed at the satisfying *thud* of knuckles to sand.

Cistine spun on heel and punished the mesh with a backward heel-kick, knocking it the other way. Aden lifted his mug of coffee in approval, and Ashe laughed as Cistine whipped around and jabbed her elbow into it, then drove her knee into the satchel at groin-height.

Tatiana lost count of how many blows she landed before the spectacle changed from amusing to unnerving. She just kept hitting the mesh, over and over—elbows, knees, feet, hands, again and again and again.

Tatiana glanced at Maleck, who reclined next to Ashe, one hand over his mouth. Ariadne's eyes were drawn with lines of concern rather than humor now.

The blows slowed, became rhythmic. Punch. Punch. Punch. Then she switched hands. Punch. Punch. Punch again. Each hit was punctuated with a sharp "*Hah!*" of breath, pushing the anger out through her teeth.

Aden stared at the ceiling, jaw tight. Tears glazed Tatiana's lashes no matter how many times she thumbed them away.

Cistine's augment-bleached hair straggled out of its tie, swinging in wild hanks around her face with every blow she landed into the bag at ribs-level now, elbows tucked close to her body, pummeling the mesh without mercy. And somewhere between the relentless blows, her growls of exertion blended into one long, unbreaking scream of fury and heartbreak.

Thorne crossed the parlor soundlessly, drawing to a halt behind her. "Wildheart."

She stopped hitting, wrapped one arm around the mesh satchel, and buried her face against it, back heaving. Her other arm hung limp at her side. Blood dripped from her knuckles onto the floor.

Thorne inclined his head until his brow almost grazed Cistine's hair. "Breathe. Just breathe, Cistine. Listen to me. You are not alone. This does not separate you from us. We're right here. All of us. Do you understand me? None of us will leave because of this."

She nodded raggedly against the mesh.

"You still touch our lives, even if you can't touch *us*," he added. "And you're still our princess, come what may. Nothing will ever change that."

She swung around to face him. "You didn't ask for this. You didn't ask to be shackled to someone you couldn't touch for the rest of your life."

"True. But you didn't ask for this either. What we both chose was to be bound in every way, to keep the faith beyond death. I still want you, in any way I can have you, for as long as I live."

Cistine's mouth twitched. "With your whole heart?"

"For my whole life."

The parlor door swung open, punctuating his words, the creak of turning wheels bringing all their heads snapping around.

Tatiana wasn't certain she'd ever get used to Kristoff, who had always seemed like a giant to her, sitting below eye level now; but it wasn't the sight of his wheeled chair that stopped her breath or raised her hair. It was that *look* in his eye.

Aden bolted to his feet. "What is it?"

Kristoff held up a sealed envelope between two fingers. "An urgent message from the southern forts. It arrived just as I did...I asked to deliver it myself."

Tatiana looked swiftly to Ariadne. "Do you think a Bloodwight managed to slip away from the battle?"

"Doubtful," Ariadne said, gaze fixed on the note in Kristoff's hand. "That envelope has Cistine's name on it."

Kristoff flicked it sideways to Cistine, and she caught it, ripping it open and spreading it with both hands to read.

And then Tatiana feared she might be sick.

Cistine went utterly white and grabbed for something to steady herself, clinging to the mesh satchel with one hand. The other rattled the letter so badly, it chattered like a leaf in a strong breeze.

"Cistine, what's wrong?" Ashe demanded, shooting to her feet.

"It's from my mother." Cistine's voice was strangely soft, heavy with disbelief. The letter fell from her hand, and she looked up at the cabal. "King Jad has declared war against Talheim."

CHAPTER
EIGHTY-FIVE

Tea and books, clothes and weapons, the cabal's unwavering support, and *time*. Those were the things Cistine had thought might help heal her heart and restore meaning to her life.

But in the end, it was a letter from her mother, fluttering from her hand and sliding to the floor, that did it. All of a sudden, the world popped around her again, resplendent with light and purpose, and the first thing that smashed against her reawakened senses was Ashe and Maleck roaring in unison, "*What?*"

"It was a ruse," Cistine rasped. "The way he withdrew...he *lied*. He's taken Middleton and now he's marching on Astoria."

Ashe slammed her fist into the wall. "Gods *damn* it!"

"What do you need from us?" Maleck demanded, rage of a personal, vicious nature blazing in his eyes.

"A meeting with the Chancellors," Cistine said.

Thorne was already halfway to the door. "Meet me in the sanctum in fifteen minutes."

Cistine spun on the cabal. "Aden, can you muster enough augurs to take Rozalie and the others home by wind augment? Whatever happens now, Talheim needs them. Get them home." He dipped his head and turned for the door, and with a spark of memory, she called him back. Dipping into her augment pouch, she tossed him a flagon. "Give this to Rozalie, too. Tell her to put the contingency in motion. She'll know what to do."

"What about the rest of us?" Tatiana demanded.

"Gather your weapons. If the Chancellors keep their word, we're leading an army out of this city today. If not..."

"Then you'll still have us," Quill said.

"We'll be ready. Just go." Ashe jerked her chin at the door.

Their faith and certainty, the lack of even a single uncertain glance among them, filled Cistine with violent affection that made her feel capable of anything. She stepped to the doorway, and Kristoff put out a hand, blocking her way.

"Whatever happens now," he said, "you're ready. You can do this."

She nodded, held his calm, urgent gaze for a moment, and wished fiercely for words to express everything she owed him—a mound of gratitude that choked her all at once. Instead, she squeezed the arm of his chair, then broke into a sprint all the way to the Chancellors' sanctum.

Thorne had left the door open for her, and she strode inside to the top of the balcony to find them already clustered below, hushing at the sight of her. They all pulled back when she descended except for Thorne. Ignoring their fear, she planted herself on one side of the table. "I've just received word from Talheim. They're under siege from King Jad."

"What *exactly* did the letter say?" Thorne asked.

"Word spread to the southern border about Valgard's war-state and the Dreadline," Cistine said. "After Jad learned our new allies were occupied, he wasted no time. His spies murdered Lord Dorminger and took the city of Middleton. By the time anyone escaped to send word to my father, Jad had already marched his Enforcers into the city."

"What is Middleton?" Valdemar demanded.

"A strategic stronghold, built like Stornhaz. Now Jad has a war camp for his people inside *my* kingdom, and they're marching toward Astoria from there." Cistine's voice cracked. "They have a week at most."

"Hardly any time," Adeima murmured.

"Which is why I'm here." Cistine paused to take in their faces, ravaged by time and trial, the empty space at Adeima's right hand one of a hundred reminders of what the war had taken, how much they'd all given and had still to lose. "I know...I know the burden each of us carries. I know the weight this war left behind, and I'm sorry to even ask this. But Talheim has sacrificed, too. And if you don't help us now..."

She couldn't bear to say it; everything she'd witnessed here in the north, everything her heart had shattered for, the very fate she'd given up her life to prevent, would visit Talheim now.

"Please," she breathed, "I *need* your help. For the treaty, for every favor we owe one another, I am begging you to stand with Talheim."

Bravis opened his mouth, but Adeima silenced him with a flick of the hand. She rounded the table and came nearer to Cistine—closer than anyone but the cabal had dared since the Deathmarch. So near Cistine recoiled, and winced at her own cowardice.

But Adeima did not recoil from *her*. Those intelligent, wise eyes searched her face without fear. "Princess." When Cistine dropped her gaze at the word, the Chancelloress added sternly, "*Logandir*. Look at me."

Heart hammering at her title spoken like a call to arms, Cistine did.

"You do not beg us for anything you have not earned." Adeima's tone gentled, but passion burned behind it. "You are enough. You have given enough. Now it is *our* turn to give. For all you have done, for all that you've sacrificed, and for the oaths between our kingdoms, Yager remembers. We will answer the call."

Bravis cleared his throat. "Traisende will answer the call."

"And Skyygan," Kyost said.

"And Tyve," Valdemar's tone was more solemn than she had ever heard, and the dip of his head held respect she had never fathomed from him.

Thorne smiled. "Kanslar is with you, *Logandir*. Always."

Cistine sucked in a breath that brought strength beyond measure—and hope beyond reckoning.

"Now," Adeima said, "walk with us, Princess. And let us see about saving your kingdom once and for all from this Mad King Jad."

EPILOGUE

ROZALIE DOHNAL WAS on a special mission from her princess.

Even a few weeks ago, this task might've seemed like a betrayal to the crown she served and the royal family she loved. But after that battle on the Deathmarch, seeing what men did with blades and flagons alike, what real *war* was...the nature of the power she carried felt far less important than what it would do for them now. For their people.

Particularly in the right hands.

She stole up one of the winding stairwells to the gap between the Citadel towers. Her fellow Wardens were already dispersing, augurs in their midst; not enough of a contingent to turn the tide, but enough to help hold this assault at bay and give reinforcements time to come.

If they were coming at all.

She could barely believe it when Aden had told her what was happening, the note Cistine had received; that Jad had sprung on Valgard's suffering and Talheim's vulnerability and sank in his claws without hesitation. She hadn't truly thought it was possible until the Wardens she passed on the northern bridge on the way into the Citadel had told her of the thirteen thousand Enforcers closing in from land, four hundred warships from the sea.

Mahasaris were nothing but vicious, gods-damned opportunists. She was truly looking forward to killing a few.

Shaking that thought away, she slowed her stride. Over the moan of wind along the stone walls and the distant throb of war drums shaking her beloved kingdom, she heard voices at the top of the steps and spotted two men through the cracked door: Cyril Novacek in gold-and-blue armor, Rion Bartos in black battle threads. King and Commander preparing to take the battlefield.

Scalp prickling, Rozalie pressed her back to the wall.

"*Don't* say it," Cyril muttered to his closest friend, squinting into the chilly breeze.

Rion raised both hands. "I wasn't going to say *anything*, Brother."

"Well, I wish you would."

"Make up your mind, you mad bastard."

"I can't." Cyril shrugged his shoulders. "I hoped I'd never have to wear this armor again. Had to have it let out, too. It's still snugger than it used to be."

"And that's why you're acting this way?"

"No, I'm *acting* this way because my city is under siege and all I can think about is that I'd still be in bed with Solene right now if I'd just chopped that sand-riddled son-of-a-harlot's head off when we met in Middleton."

Rozalie almost laughed. That was her king.

Rion did chuckle. "You kiss your wife with that mouth?"

"Better than you kiss yours."

The Commander shifted to press his shoulder hard against Cyril's. Together they watched the tiny, dark specks on the ocean that would soon coagulate into King Jad's naval fleet, the blow no one had expected—likely part of the reason he'd taken twenty years to exact his vengeance. Now he could besiege Astoria, his coveted prize, by land and sea. And with Astoria's most vulnerable gathered into the safety of the Citadel, the greatest prize of all, the palpable stench of fear filled Rozalie's nostrils.

Silently, she begged Rion to go. And to her relief, no sooner did she do so than the King cuffed him on the back. "It's time. Get to the streets and rally with Viktor."

Rion cast him a glance full of doubt. "You're sure you'll be all right up here? You're practically a beacon."

"Let them come. Leney and Eboni have the reinforcements in place, the doors shored up, and reserve weapons readied. Three layers of defense at each level. *If* the Enforcers reach the doors, each of those will hold for five to ten minutes."

Rozalie's heart clenched. Rion shook his head. "I should stay."

"No. We keep to the plan." Cyril glanced to the left of the balcony, where the long thread of a stone crosswalk joined it to a guardpost high on the frame of the south-facing bridge. "*Go.*"

Rion clasped his shoulder, bumped brows with him, then jogged away at last. The moment he was out of sight, Rozalie shoved open the door and stepped out. "Your Majesty—"

Cyril cursed, whirled with hand to blade, then loosened when he recognized her. "Dohnal! Gods damn it, what are you doing here? Didn't we dispatch you to the northern barracks months ago?"

"You did. Actually, I've been in Valgard. No time to explain," she added when the King's mouth leaped open. "I have a gift for you from Cistine."

He released his sword, hand to his mouth. "She's all right?"

"She's alive," Rozalie said awkwardly, then dipped into her pocket and held out the flagon Aden had given her. "She sent this for you."

Cyril's eyes widened, hand falling and fingers opening in an entranced, half-desperate plea. "What is this?"

Rozalie passed the flagon to him. "A contingency. If the Bloodwights ever breached our borders and came after you, she wanted me to bring you one of these. She said you would be ready to finish what was started."

Cyril rolled the flagon in his palm, eyes narrowing with stark realization. "A trench. I'm to use this to seal off the city."

Rozalie nodded. "I suspected as much."

"Where is she?" Cyril's voice pitched lower, a father's desperate yearning—the way Rozalie liked to imagine her own father had sounded if he'd ever searched for her after she was stolen away to that brothel.

"Still in Valgard, doing what she does best: negotiating. She sent us ahead to shore up the ranks."

A slight smile graced the King's mouth. "You're a good Warden, Dohnal. And an excellent friend."

They turned together toward the balcony's edge, the city deserted below. The people were as safe as possible, sheltering in their homes or in the Citadel; but still Rozalie's heart ached to reach out to every inch of Astoria, to gather it under the shelter of hers arms, to protect the people, their homes, their livelihoods, their own precious memories in the places they belonged.

She would do anything—*anything*—to protect her people, to protect the royal family. That was the oath she'd sworn as a wide-eyed girl of barely sixteen, and she would never let it falter.

The Deathmarch had been a battle for Valgard. This...this was *her* kingdom. *Her* war.

The sounds of marching feet echoed from the plains, swelling louder and louder, like thunder booming between the houses. Cyril walked swiftly to the edge of the balcony, laying one hand to the stone railing as he looked south. "Damn them. They have catapults."

He closed his fist around the flagon, shut his eyes and breathed deeply, then raised the augment high.

A wild roar split the air. The King jumped, cursing, as Ashe's golden dragon landed hard against the cap of one of the Citadel's domes, coiling his body around its arch. He bellowed again in defiance at the distant ships, wings spreading around him—one slightly crooked, the other strong and high.

Rozalie's chest heaved, and at a whistle behind them, she spun toward the balcony above. Eight warriors arrayed in black armor on its edge, their bodies limned in sunlight and weapons drawn, all but one festering with augmented energy. At their head, haloed in wind and golden light, Cistine gazed down at her father with a look of fierce love.

Her name escaped Cyril, a wild gasp of relief.

She vaulted lightly down onto the balcony, Thorne at her side, moving in perfect tandem. "I got Mama's letter," Cistine announced. "And I brought reinforcements."

"I can see that." Cyril cocked his head at Thorne, who watched him with slack-jawed disbelief. Maybe he just wasn't used to seeing kings. "Who are you?"

Cistine grinned, pride and adoration gleaming in her gaze. "This is Thorne."

Thorne clamped his mouth shut, swallowed, and spanned his arm, stepping aside. "Your army awaits, Your Majesty."

And suddenly Rozalie understood where that ceaseless wind came from: dozens of augments, bringing the Valgardan army to their backs, spread across the plains around Astoria and charged across the emerald grass to confront Jad's people on the far side of the city.

"Where do you need us most?" Thorne demanded.

"As you can see, we have a bit of a problem." Cyril gestured at the horizon. "The land army for one. The ships for another."

Cistine's eyes speared to those ships. Thorne followed her gaze, and a smirk twisted his mouth. "You want them, don't you?"

"I want to burn them." The fury in Cistine's voice nearly stopped Rozalie's heart, but Thorne simply nodded.

"Let's take them together."

Cyril nodded and gestured to Rozalie. "We'll guard the Citadel."

Cistine's eyes narrowed. "I don't think Jad will get that far."

Distant cannonfire rippled. Thorne tensed. "It's time."

Cistine jerked a flagon from her satchel and crushed it against her thigh. Wicked, wild flames coursed through her threads, and Rozalie hoped that on the plains, Jad's people saw her burn—and feared. She hoped that, in their homes and shops, in their stations of war, their own people saw—and believed.

The legacy of Talheim shone on this balcony; their princess had come to defend them. Valgard stood at their backs. The two kingdoms would take this battlefield together—and triumph.

Cistine broke a second augment, new wind whipping across the balcony, and Thorne's eyes flashed in the glow of her fire. "The hunt is yours, Wildheart."

Cistine threw a portion of the wind to him. "No. It's *ours.*"

And as the dragon burst from his perch on the rotunda, shooting toward the horizon in a golden blaze, as the cabal leaped down to land around Cyril and Rozalie, unleashing weapons of their own, her future Queen and King stepped off the ledge to meet the wind—falling together.

"Are you ready?" Ashe asked from Rozalie's side.

"Always, thanks to you."

They swapped smiles and dashed for the crosswalk to the bridge, Maleck and Cyril on their heels, just as the first volley of arrows rose from the plains around the city; as the catapults unleashed, hurling chunks of stone toward Astoria; as Aden and Ariadne, Quill and Tatiana, vanished in cuts of wind to meet the enemy forces and bring the strength that might save the capital—save them all.

And the war for Talheim began.

End

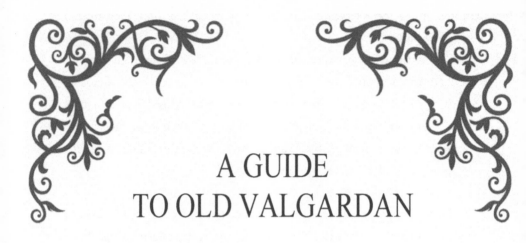

A GUIDE
TO OLD VALGARDAN

Words:

Allatok – Heathen

Bandayo – Bastard (roughly)

Tajall - Infant (roughly)

Storfir – Big One

Stornjor – Great Love

Izten Torkat – Throat of God

Muunvat – Spit

Yani – Sweet

Sillakove - Starchaser

Selvenar – Blended hearts

Valenar – Blended blood

ACKNOWLEDGEMENTS

SIX BOOKS IN. Originally, this was where the series ended—bittersweet and barely hopeful, which was how I was feeling when I wrote it. Luckily, that wasn't the end of Cistine's story...or mine.

First, as always, to God; for the inspiration that helped me power through the impossibility of drafting both the original version of this book, and its rewrite. For beautiful "Ah-ha!" moments and glimpses of eternity that came through telling the story You wanted me to tell. I will continue following those threads of inspiration You send for the rest of my life.

To my family: for not giving up on me when I wanted to give up on this book, my writing, and myself. You are my reason for getting up in the morning and persevering no matter how hard this gets.

To my soul-sisters, Miranda and Cassidy: for kicking my butt and hyping me up, for being my cheerleaders, editors, CPs, best friends. I love you both forever and always.

To Katie and Meaghan: for helping make this book what it needed to be. The best beta-reading team an author could ever ask for. I love you, my hybrid pirate starchasers.

To Maja: for another fantastic cover that perfectly brings together two of my favorite elements—Asheila Kovar and DRAGONS. So thankful for your inspired talent bringing the covers of this series to life!

To every reader, supporter, and fan: THANK YOU for your presence, your encouragement, your support. For your messages and reviews, your encouragement, and yes, for screaming at me for what I've done to these poor characters! I wish I could name you all by name, but the list would take up the whole book. I am blown away by your love and can never fully articulate just how much it means to me that you read my books, place them on your shelves, name them on your bookish lists, and make these characters a part of your lives. Thank you, thank you, forever and ever. <3

See you in the LAST one! <3

Read On For a Sneak Peek at

THE STARCHASER SAGA
BOOK VII

CHAPTER ONE

IN THE VIVID lavender glow of late autumn lightning, Princess Cistine Novacek of Talheim fled for her life, fifteen Mahasari Enforcers in pursuit.

The thick undergrowth snapped against her armor while she bent nearly double, scaling the slope of the lower Calalun Peaks. Everywhere her fingertips brushed the last valiant threads of autumn foliage, they crumbled away from her touch. She did not look back to watch them die or to spot her enemies in the gloom. Eyes trained forward, vision cut with snaking tendrils of augment-shocked silver hair spilling from the knot behind her ears, she ran with all her might.

Only a half-mile to go.

She burst over the crest of the hill and skidded down the far slope, arms windmilling to break her fall. Arrows peppered the vegetation around her, smooth-tipped and reeking of Mahasari paralytics, and panic closed her throat. If she'd misjudged the distance or the direction...

There was no time to question the plan. Popping to her feet at the base of the hill, she dodged another volley of arrows and tore forward, legs pumping, lungs heaving.

The half-mile blurred by in a wash of rain and crackling thunder, and with every bolt of lightning she fought not to think of augmented energy, diamond-hard skin, or midnight eyes. Heedless of the death fuming from her body, she punched through the last wall of living undergrowth, killing it in her wake, and skidded to a halt on rain-slick rock.

She'd reached a ledge looming into the deep valley between the Calaluns. Shadow-dipped hills rolled before her, limned in lightning flashes and soaked in rain. There was nowhere else to run.

She spun back, hand to her dagger Nail, as the sounds of pursuit slowed and the Mahasari patrol prowled into the open. Their leader's familiar, pale face reared up a memory of a late-night ambush, striking pain into an old scar on her side. Setting her teeth, she regarded his approach.

"*Faes alykar,* Princess." The musical Mahasari syllables rolled from his tongue, but he bit out her title in the common language of the Three Kingdoms. "We've been looking for you."

"You'd think I'd be used to that by now," Cistine muttered, half to herself.

"You are quite the prize. And now you have nowhere to go." He extended a hand.

"I don't think you want to do that, Vezzik." Cistine crept back from him, nearer to the ledge. "You've probably heard the stories."

"Of the princess who can kill with a single touch?" he scoffed. "Talheim has always been keen on tall tales. I'm willing to take my chances." On either side, his men fanned out—a fourteen-bowed falcate with their weapons primed. Training clamored in Cistine's mind, half a dozen voices warning her against sudden movements. "Come with us, and you can live in luxury until the game is over."

Her heels snagged the edge of rock and sky. "*Game?*"

Bowstrings twanged. Vezzik lunged for her. And she jerked back.

The ledge vanished. She plummeted.

A great roar cleaved the whistling wind; a blur of gold streaked past her, shooting up toward the ledge where the Enforcers' cries of shock turned to screams of terror. Fire lit the sky, burning the rain to steam.

For a heartbeat, Cistine closed her eyes and envisioned a river below her, a gorge above, and strong arms shielding her body.

Glass pinged and shattered, and wind wrapped around her. Power surged through her fingers like breath blown from the True God's nostrils, and then she was rising—a star falling in reverse, alighting with bent knees and hair ripped loose from its tie to find the stone aflame and a battle raging across it. Fifteen Enforcers dueled five warriors in a halo of dragonfire, bows traded for blades in close quarters. A summoning whistle cut through the clash of Valgardan steel and Mahasari metal, and with brilliance that seared Cistine's vision in bright mint dapples, a fire flagon exploded.

Tatiana, limbs striped in trembling heat, ducked and swiveled, hurling a globe of flame to Quill. He flipped over two opponents to catch it from the air, handspringing backward to clap hands with Ashe, who portioned the fire to Ariadne. All of this while Maleck, braided death-god and swordmaster, dueled ferociously against six Enforcers at once, drawing their ire; and in the sky above, Bresnyar slithered through the clouds, cutting off their escape with his own fire.

Cistine's chest swelled with fierce love for her cabal.

Before she could gather her wind and leap into the fray, it was already over; Maleck drove the Enforcers back toward the others, and in a cage of fire, one by one, they brought them to their knees. Quill discharged the fire augment and pounced on Vezzik, driving him face-first into the rock and perching on his back. Eyes battle-bright, he tossed a grin at Cistine. "You know, I'm not usually one for using our own as bait, but that went better than expected. Good strategy, Stranger."

She sketched a curtsy. "We aim to please."

"We succeed." Sending out her fire in a gust, Ashe sheathed her blade Starfall, kicked an Enforcer onto his back, and planted her knee on his chest. "Why are you hunting the princess?"

"Don't answer that," Vezzik mumbled against the rock.

"Do answer that." Maleck spun Stormfury into its harness. "If you value your lives."

When no Enforcer spoke, Ashe craned her head back. Flickers of gold speared through her eyes, and the man in her grip squirmed under the heavy press of her knee to his chest. "What—what is she doing?"

"Cleaving." Tatiana's smile was a feral glint. "If I had to guess, she's summoning her dragon for an evening feast of Mahasari flesh."

"It's for the game!" A younger Enforcer, barely Cistine's twenty-one years if that, broke first. Vezzik spat a curse Cistine ignored, passing him and Quill to crouch before the Enforcer—though not near enough to touch.

"What *game?*" she demanded.

Dark eyes, round with terror, fixed on her. "You really don't know?"

Ashe's ragged scream burst across the rock; in the clouds above, Bresnyar roared, and the cleaving severed so suddenly Ashe pitched from the Enforcer's chest, saved from crashing into the stone only by Maleck's arm swooping around her shoulders and spinning her back to her feet.

"They have *gods-damned dragons!*" Ashe bellowed.

In a flash of lightning, a small, dark streak shot through the clouds, colliding with Bresnyar's golden bulk; from the treeline, through the dragonfire still gulping the dead grass, a line of scaled bodies emerged, driving against the cabal like a scythe.

Sulfuric breath blasted Bresnyar's wall of flames to deadly whips. The cabal dove left and right with shouts of shock and rage, and the dragons bowled into their midst; not sharp-edged, horned creatures like Ashe's dragon, but snake-sleek with tapered muzzles agape, foul breath pluming the wet air. The rotten-egg stench sent Cistine gagging as she scrambled up and dodged the barbed whip of a tail aimed for her legs.

While the cabal evaded the dragons' vicious breath, the Enforcers rallied and struck again. Steel sang, and not for the first time in this war, Cistine heard the cruel slice of deadly Mahasari metal cleave through threads she'd once believed all but indestructible. With a bark of pain, Maleck fell to one knee, blood streaming from his upper arm; Ashe's answering cry was world-ending in fury, Starfall a glistening flame in her hand when she sprang over her *valenar's* bent form and kicked his attacker down, running him through.

Despair gripped Cistine's throat. The plan was crumbling. Above, blood mingled with rain as Bresnyar and the Mahasari dragon shredded one another, ripping the clouds with bass roars and owl-like shrieks; all around her, fighting raged, Ariadne dueling three Mahasaris, Ashe towing Maleck back to his feet, Tatiana and Quill guarding one another's backs but still overwhelmed when the dragons charged them.

Cistine knew what must be done. Even as her conscience rebelled, stomach cringing at the choice; even as she stripped off her gloves, flexing her cold fingers into the blood and rain—into the power lying dormant beneath her skin, girdling her bones. The augment that would never be fully spent, never dispatched like the fire dazzling in the lines of Ariadne and Tatiana's armor still.

This was her curse. But she would use it to defend her family.

She hurtled toward Vezzik, arm extended, death unspooling between her fingertips—

The rain stopped.

For a moment, the battle halted as well. Cistine stumbled to a standstill, hair prickling on her nape and gooseflesh pebbling her body.

Augmented power rode the wind's currents, and a sensation three months buried reared within her so violently her heart staggered its pace. She sucked in her breath, choking on a Name.

Starchaser.

The rain descended all at once, flooding the rock, driving Mahasaris and Valgardans alike to their knees; two warriors drove from the scorched treeline, crashing into the enemy flanks, sending the dragons into a spinning, spitting whirlwind. Arms slashing in tandem, the men smashed their water augments into the Enforcers once, twice, three times...buying Ashe a moment to break a healing augment against Maleck's arm, Ariadne to fall back with Quill and Tatiana, and all five of them and Cistine to rally and attack.

Overwhelmed, the Enforcers broke, lunging onto their mounts. Vezzik led the charge, swinging onto the back of a piebald dragon and drawing a whip from the saddle; hatred burned in his gaze when it found Cistine's across the ledge, promising theirs was not the last patrol who would hunt her personally. Just as it hadn't been the first.

In that moment he paused to convey his silent rage, Quill reached him.

When the whip reared back to snap against his mount's hide, Quill leaped, catching the lash against his armor and yanking with all his might. Vezzik hauled back, cursing and driving his heels into the dragon's flanks. With a pained screech, the creature lofted, dragging Quill up with him. Steel flashed as Quill drew his dagger Fjadar, driving toward the dragon's brow—then hesitated.

Heart in throat, Cistine watched him dangle. Then he let go.

The crack of boots on rock boomed in tandem with thunder and more than a dozen pairs of dragon wings slashing down all at once, and in a torrent of rainfall the beaten patrol vanished into the same peaks they'd haunted for nearly a year.

Tatiana was at Quill's side in a heartbeat, dragging him up from his landing crouch. "What was that? Why did you let him go?"

He brushed his hands off on his thighs, furious gaze scouting the clouds that shuttered to hide the Enforcers from their view. "Those scales felt like a red adder's. Didn't want to blunt my dagger if I couldn't break through."

Cistine blew out a long breath, spraying rain from the tip of her nose. Her body didn't know whether to slump with defeat or straighten with relief when she sheathed her weapons and swiveled to face the newcomers who'd turned the tide. Their leader shoved back his hair, dark marriage band snagging in strands far too silver for his age—barely thirty years old. "Honestly, that wasn't the worst scrape I expected to find you all in when we returned."

Cistine flashed a sheepish smile. "Hello, Thorne."

Soft blue eyes swung to her. "Hello, *Logandir*."

A rough sigh. "I'm here, also."

Laughing, Tatiana burst forward to fling her arms around the other man's neck. "*We* missed you, Aden."

"The new *valenar* glow just hasn't worn off for those two quite yet," Quill added wryly. "How's Pip?"

"Good. Missing you," Aden chuckled, squeezing Tatiana.

Thorne shaded his eyes as Bresnyar descended in a blur of gold, smashing into the ledge and staggering toward them. Ashe swore and hurtled to meet him, the last silver threads of the healing augment gliding from her fingers and running over his golden scales. "So, I wasn't seeing things. Those were *Iteilach Tayir* the Enforcers rode out on."

"Yes, my delightful southern cousins," Bresnyar spat. "Fireless, but full of venom."

Quill flung up his hands. "Here we go again. Shei, Thorne, and Bresnyar, our walking bestiaries."

Tatiana chucked a crumbled bit of stone at his head. "At least they bother with books every once in a while, Featherbrain."

Ashe's gaze swung from her dragon to Thorne. "So now Jad has dragons in his army?"

"Judging by the look of those spurs and whips, they were not drafted of their own volition." In Ariadne's tone hung a *visnpresta's* indignation for all abused creatures formed by the True God.

Aden scratched his thick golden beard. "For what purpose? Fireless dragons do little at long range, and less for stealth."

"And their poison wasn't even that potent," Quill pointed out. "Mostly putrid. Seems like all they're good for is a quick escape."

"Speaking of that." Thorne's gaze leaped back to Cistine. "Your father seems to think the cabal is on a reconnaissance mission to the east, not the south."

Cistine sopped her rain-soaked hair from her brow. "That's because I didn't want him to know what we were doing. He'd never agree with it."

He cocked a brow. "With his only heir making herself bait to his decades-long enemy?"

"Well, when you put it that way," Quill muttered under his breath. Tatiana jabbed him in the ribs.

"We know they've been targeting her," Ashe said grimly, laying a hand on Bresnyar's shoulder until he stood steady again. "Patrols have twice as much engagement when Cistine is with them. She can barely set foot outside Astoria without encountering a slew of Enforcers. We want to know why."

Concern drew a divot between Thorne's brows. "What did they give you?"

"Nothing," Maleck sighed. "And with the aid of their dragons, we have no one left to question."

"You'd think we'd be used to that by now," Ariadne said wryly, squeezing Thorne's shoulder on her way to embrace Aden.

"How did *you* know where we were?" Cistine demanded.

A half-smile crooked her husband's mouth. "By following the scent of danger and desperation." She jutted her tongue, and he snorted. "You know how, *Logandir*."

Of course; he'd sensed her power. Few but the cabal were so attuned to the way she could wield many augments when they only managed one at a time. He'd likely set off into the wilds the moment he'd returned to the Citadel and realized she was gone, then waited for the bond between their blended hearts to strum with the Key's power, showing him the way.

"I'm sorry I wasn't there to greet you." She sidled closer to him, still maintaining distance.

"I didn't fall in love with a princess who pined for the people she loved to come home. I married the warrior who took up her sword to save her Warden."

"Can we *please* let that go?" Ashe groaned, and Thorne laughed, leaning into a sideways embrace from Quill. One by one, the others surged forward to greet each other—first Ashe, then Maleck knocking foreheads with Aden, Tatiana joining Quill in embracing their Chancellor.

Left on the fringes, Cistine could do nothing but tug on her gloves, shielding her fingers once more from the rain. Thorne's gaze followed her, watching tan skin disappear beneath armored threads that could win a few precious seconds if she touched the wrong person. She hadn't slipped once since that first time on the Deathmarch...but once was enough.

Sadness and concern stamped his eyes when they flicked back to her face. She offered him a smile that felt braver than she truly was, and he knocked his fist against his armored shoulder three times.

Tears sprang to Cistine's eyes. She'd missed that silent cipher of beats—had missed *him* more than she'd thought possible during his furlough home to Valgard. She knocked her shoulder in return, three times, then burst into shaky laughter when Quill slung an arm around Thorne's neck. "So, how was it? I can't believe we had to miss your first cycle as Chancellor!"

"Later," Thorne chuckled, shaking him off. "Let's get all of you back to the Citadel."

"Someone journeyed back with us," Aden added with a nod to Cistine. "Someone who very much wants to see you."

She blinked at him. "Who?"

Kanslar's High Tribune flashed her a wild smile reminiscent of the Lord of the Blood Hive he'd once been. "I'll give you just one hint: your mother had to pull your old cradle out of hiding."

ABOUT THE AUTHOR

Renee Dugan is an Indiana-based author who grew up reading fantasy books, chasing stray cats, and writing stories full of dashing heroes and evil masterminds. Now with over a decade of professional editing, administrative work, and writing every spare second under her belt, she has authored *THE CHAOS CIRCUS,* a portal fantasy novel, and *THE STARCHASER SAGA,* an epic high fantasy series. Living with her husband, son, and not-so-stray cats in the magical Midwest, she continues to explore new worlds and spends her time in this one encouraging and helping other writers on their journey to fulfilling their dreams.

Find Renee Dugan online at:
Reneeduganwriting.com

And on social media: **@reneeduganwriting**